HEART AND SOUL

From This Day

and

Storm Warning

• *Portrait in Death* • *Imitation in Death* • *Divided in Death*
• *Visions in Death* • *Survivor in Death* • *Origin in Death*
• *Memory in Death* • *Born in Death* • *Innocent in Death*
• *Creation in Death* • *Strangers in Death* • *Salvation in Death*
• *Promises in Death* • *Kindred in Death* • *Fantasy in Death* •
Indulgence in Death • *Treachery in Death* • *New York to Dallas*
• *Celebrity in Death* • *Delusion in Death* • *Calculated in Death*
• *Thankless in Death* • *Concealed in Death* • *Festive in Death* •
Obsession in Death • *Devoted in Death* • *Brotherhood in Death*
• *Apprentice in Death* • *Echoes in Death* • *Secrets in Death* •
Dark in Death • *Leverage in Death* • *Connections in Death* •
Vendetta in Death • *Golden in Death* • *Shadows in Death*
• *Faithless in Death*

ANTHOLOGIES

From the Heart • *A Little Magic* • *A Little Fate*

Moon Shadows
(with Jill Gregory, Ruth Ryan Langan, and Marianne Willman)

The Once Upon Series
(with Jill Gregory, Ruth Ryan Langan, and Marianne Willman)
Once Upon a Castle • *Once Upon a Star* • *Once Upon a
Dream* • *Once Upon a Rose* • *Once Upon a Kiss* • *Once Upon
a Midnight*

Silent Night
(with Susan Plunkett, Dee Holmes, and Claire Cross)

Out of This World
(with Laurell K. Hamilton, Susan Krinard, and Maggie Shayne)

Bump in the Night
(with Mary Blayney, Ruth Ryan Langan, and Mary Kay McComas)

Dead of Night
(with Mary Blayney, Ruth Ryan Langan, and Mary Kay McComas)

Three in Death

HEART AND SOUL

From This Day

and

Storm Warning

TWO NOVELS IN ONE

NORA ROBERTS

St. Martin's Paperbacks

This is a work of fiction. All of the characters, organizations, and events portrayed in this book are either products of the author's imagination or are used fictitiously.

First published in the United States by St. Martin's Paperbacks, an imprint of St. Martin's Publishing Group

HEART AND SOUL: FROM THIS DAY copyright © 1983 by Nora Roberts and STORM WARNING copyright © 1984 by Nora Roberts.

All rights reserved.

For information, address St. Martin's Publishing Group, 120 Broadway, New York, NY 10271.

www.stmartins.com

ISBN: 978-1-250-79648-6

Our books may be purchased in bulk for promotional, educational, or business use. Please contact your local bookseller or the Macmillan Corporate and Premium Sales Department at 1-800-221-7945, ext. 5442, or by email at MacmillanSpecialMarkets@macmillan.com.

Printed in the United States of America

St. Martin's Paperbacks edition 2021

10 9 8 7 6 5 4 3 2 1

From This Day

CHAPTER 1

Spring comes late to New England. Snow lingers in isolated patches. Trees begin their greening hesitantly, tiny closed buds of leaves against naked branches. Early blooms of color burst from the earth's womb. The air is fresh with promise.

B.J. tossed open her window with a flourish and welcomed the early breeze into her room. *Saturday,* she thought with a grin, and began to braid her long, wheat-colored hair. The Lakeside Inn was half-full, the summer season three weeks away, and if all followed her well-ordered plans, her duties as manager would be light for the duration of the weekend.

Her staff was loyal, though somewhat temperamental. Like a large family, they squabbled, sulked, teased, and stuck together like mortar and brick when the need arose. And I, she mused with a rueful grin, am head counselor.

Pulling on faded jeans, B.J. did not pause to consider the incongruity of the title. A small, childlike woman reflected in her glass, curves disguised by casual attire, braids hanging impishly astride a heart-shaped, elfin face with huge smoky eyes dominant. Her only large feature, they swamped the tip-tilted nose and cupid's-bow mouth and were prone to smolder or sparkle with the fluctuations of her mood. After lacing dilapidated sneakers, she jogged from the room, intending to check on breakfast preparations before stealing an hour for a solitary walk.

The main staircase of the inn was wide and uncarpeted, connecting its four sprawling stories without curve or angle, as straight and sturdy as the building itself. She saw with satisfaction the lobby was both tidy and deserted. The curtains were drawn to welcome the sun, needlepoint pillows plumped, and a vase of fresh wildflowers adorned the high, well-polished registration desk. The clatter of cutlery carried from the dining room as she passed through the downstairs hall, and she heard, with a long suffering sigh, the running argument between her two waitresses.

"If you really like a man with small pig eyes, you should be very happy."

B.J. watched Dot shrug her thin shoulders with the words as she rolled a place setting in white linen.

"Wally does not have pig eyes," Maggie insisted. "They're very intelligent. You're just jealous," she added with grim relish as she filled the sugar dispensers.

"Jealous! Ha! The day I'm jealous of a squinty-eyed little runt . . . Oh, hello, B.J."

"Good morning, Dot, Maggie. You rolled two spoons and a knife at that setting, Dot. I think a fork might be a nice touch."

Accompanied by her companion's snickers, Dot unrolled the linen. "Wally's taking me to a double feature at the drive-in tonight." Maggie's smug statement followed B.J. into the kitchen, and she allowed the door to swing shut on the ensuing retort.

Unlike the casual, old-fashioned atmosphere of the remainder of the inn, the kitchen sparkled with twentieth century efficiency. Stainless steel glimmered everywhere in the oversized room, the huge stove attesting that the inn's main attraction was its menu. Cupboards and cabinets stood like veteran soldiers, walls and linoleum gleaming with fresh cleaning. B.J. smiled, pleased with the room's perfection and the drifting scent of coffee.

"Morning, Elsie." She received an absent mutter from the round woman working at a long, well-scrubbed counter. "If everything's under control, I'm going out for a couple of hours."

"Betty Jackson won't send any blackberry jelly."

"What? Well, for goodness' sake why not?" Annoyed by the complication, B.J. plucked a fresh muffin from a basket and began to devour it. "Mr. Conners always asks for her jelly, and we're down to the last jar."

"She said if you couldn't be bothered to pay a lonely old woman a visit, she couldn't be bothered to part with any jelly."

"Lonely old woman?" B.J.'s exclamation was hampered by a mouthful of muffin. "She runs more news items through that house of hers than the Associated Press. Blast it, Elsie, I really need that jelly. I was too busy last week to go listen to the latest special bulletins."

"The new owner coming Monday got you worried?"

"Who's worried? I'm not worried." Scowling, she confiscated another muffin. "It's simply that as manager of the inn, I want everything to be in order."

"Eddie said you were muttering and slamming around your office after you got the letter saying he was coming."

"I was not . . . muttering. . . ." Moving to the refrigerator, B.J. poured a glass of juice and spoke to Elsie's wide back. "Taylor Reynolds has a perfect right to inspect his property. It's just, blast it, Elsie, it was all those vague comments about modernizing. Mr. Taylor Reynolds better keep his hands off the Lakeside Inn and play with his other hotels. We don't need to be modernized," she continued, rapidly working herself up into a temper. "We're perfectly fine just the way we are. There's not a thing wrong with us, we don't need anything." She finished by folding her arms across her chest and glaring at the absent Taylor Reynolds.

"Except blackberry jelly," Elsie said mildly. B.J. blinked and brought herself back to the present.

"Oh, all right," she muttered and stalked toward the door. "I'll go get it. But if she tells me one more time that Howard Beall is a fine boy and good husband material, I'll scream. Right there in her living room with the doilies and chintz, I'll scream!"

Leaving this dire threat hanging in the air, B.J. stepped out into the soothing yellow sunlight.

"Blackberry jelly," she mumbled as she hopped on a battered red bike. "New owners with fancy notions. . . ." Lifting her face to the sky, she tossed a pigtail behind her shoulder.

Pedaling down the maple-lined drive, quicksilver temper ebbed, her resilient spirits were lifted with the beauty of the day. The valley was stirring with life. Small clusters of fragile violets and red clover dotted the rolling meadows. Lines of fresh laundry waved in the early breeze. The boundary of mountains was topped by a winter's coat, not yet the soft, lush green it would be in a month's time, but patched with stark black trees and the intermittent color of pines. Clouds scudded thin and white across the sky, chased by the teasing wind which whispered of spring and fresh blossoms.

Good humor restored, B.J. arrived in town with pink cheeks and a smile, waving to familiar faces along the route to Betty Jackson's jelly. It was a small town with tidy lawns, picket fences and old, well-kept homes. The dormers and gables were typical of New England. Nestled like a contented cat in the rolling valley, and the brilliant shimmer of Lake Champlain to the west, Lakeside remained serene and untouched by big city bustle. Having been raised on its outskirts had not dulled its magic for B.J.: she felt, as always when entering its limits, a gratitude that somewhere life remained simple.

Parking her bike in front of a small, green-shuttered house, B.J. swung through the gate and prepared to negotiate for her jelly supply.

"Well, B.J., what a surprise." Betty opened the door and patted her gray permanent. "I thought you'd gone back to New York."

"Things have been a bit hectic at the inn," she returned, striving for the proper humility.

"The new owner." Betty nodded with a fortune teller's wisdom and gestured B.J. inside. "I hear he wants to spruce things up."

Resigned that Betty Jackson's communications system was infallible, B.J. settled herself in the small living room.

"You know Tom Myers is adding another room to his house." Brushing off the seat of an overstuffed chair, Betty shifted her ample posterior and sat. "Seems Lois is in the

family way again." She clucked her tongue over the Myers'
profligacy. "Three babies in four years. But you like little
ones, don't you, B.J.?"

"I've always been fond of children, Miss Jackson," B.J.
acknowledged, wondering how to turn the conversation
toward preserves.

"My nephew, Howard, just loves children."

B.J. braced herself not to scream and met the bland smile,
calmly. "We've a couple at the inn now. Children do love to
eat." Pleased with the maneuver, she pressed on. "They've
simply devoured your jellies. I'm down to my last jar. No-
body has the touch you do with jellies, Miss Jackson; you'd
put the big manufacturers out of business if you opened your
own line."

"It's all in the timing," Betty preened under the praise, and
B.J. tasted the hint of victory.

"I'd just have to close down if you didn't keep me supplied." Gray eyes fluttered ingenuously. "Mr. Conners would
be crushed if I had to serve him store-bought goods. He
simply raves about your blackberry jelly. *Ambrosia,*" she
added, relishing the word. "He says it's *ambrosia.*"

"Ambrosia." Betty nodded in self-satisfied agreement.

Ten minutes later, B.J. placed a box of a dozen jars of jelly
in the basket of her bike and waved a cheerful goodbye.

"I came, I saw, I conquered," she told the sky with auda-
cious pride. "And I did not scream."

"Hey, B.J.!"

She twisted her head at the sound of her name, waving to
the group playing sand lot ball as she pedaled to the edge of
the field. "What's the score?" she asked the young boy who
ran to her bike.

"Five to four. Junior's team's winning."

She glanced over to where Junior stood, tall and gangly on the pitcher's mound, tossing a ball in his glove and grinning.

"Little squirt," she mumbled with reluctant affection. "Let me pinch hit once." Confiscating the boy's battered cap, she secured it over her pigtails and walked onto the field.

"You gonna play, B.J.?" Suddenly surrounded by young bodies and adolescent faces, B.J. lifted a bat and tested it.

"For a minute. I have to get back."

Junior approached, hands on hips, and grinned down from his advantage of three inches. "Wanna bet I strike you out?"

She spared him a brief glance and swung the bat to her shoulder. "I don't want to take your money."

"If I strike you out," he yanked a pigtail with fifteen-year-old audacity, "you gotta kiss me."

"Get on the mound, you apprentice lecher, and come back in ten years."

His grin remained unabashed as B.J. watched, stifling a smile as he sauntered into position. He squinted, nodded, wound up and pitched. B.J. swung a full circle.

"Strike one!"

She turned and scowled at Wilbur Hayes who stood as umpire. Stepping up to the plate again, the cheers and taunts grew in volume. She stuck out her tongue at Junior's wink.

"Strike two!" Wilbur announced as she watched the pitch sail by.

"Strike?" Turning, she placed her hands on her hips. "You're crazy, that was chin high. I'm going to tell your mother you need glasses."

"Strike two," Wilbur repeated and frowned with adolescent ferocity.

Muttering, B.J. stepped again into the batter's box.

"You might as well put the bat down," Junior shouted, cradling the ball in the mitt. "You're not even coming close to this one."

"Take a good look at the ball, Junior, 'cause it's the last time you'll see it." Shifting the hat lower on her head, B.J. clutched the bat. "It's going clear to New York."

She connected with a solid crack of bat and watched the ball begin its sail before she darted around the bases. Running full steam, head down, she heard the shouts and cheers to slide as she rounded third. Scott Temple crouched at the plate, mitt opened for reception, as she threw herself down, sliding into home in a cloud of dust and frenzied shouts.

"You're out!"

"Out!" Scrambling to her feet, she met Wilbur's bland blue stare, eye to eye and nose to nose. "Out, you little squirt, I was safe by a mile. I'm going to buy you some binoculars."

"Out," he repeated with great dignity, and folded his arms.

"What we need here is an umpire with two working eyes." She turned to her crowd of supporters and threw out her hands. "I demand a second opinion."

"You were out."

Spinning at the unfamiliar voice, B.J. frowned up at the stranger. He stood leaning on the backstop, a small lift to his well-formed mouth and amusement shining from his dark brown eyes. He pushed a lock of curling black hair from his brow and straightened a long, lean frame.

"You should have been content with a triple."

"I was safe," she retorted, rubbing more dirt on her nose. "Absolutely safe."

"Out," Wilbur repeated.

B.J. sent him a withering glance before turning back to the man who approached the heated debate between teams. She studied him with a mixture of resentment and curiosity.

His features were well-defined, sculptured with planes and angles, the skin bronzed and smooth, the faintest hint of red in his dark hair where the sun caught it. She saw that though his buff-colored suit was casual, it was obviously well tailored and expensive. His teasing smile widened at her critical survey, and her resentment deepened.

"I've got to get back," she announced, brushing at her jeans. "And don't think I'm not going to mention an eye exam to your mother," she added, giving Wilbur a final glare.

"Hey, kid." She straddled her bike and looked around idly, then smiled as she realized the man had grouped her with the teenagers. Restraining her smile, she looked up with what she hoped was the insolence of youth.

"Yeah?"

"How far is it to the Lakeside Inn?"

"Look, mister, my mother told me not to talk to strange men."

"Very commendable. I'm not offering you candy and a ride."

"Well." She frowned as if debating pros and cons. "O.K. It's about three miles up the road." Making her gesture vague, she finished with the obligatory codicil. "You can't miss it."

He gave a long stare into her wide gray eyes, then shook his head. "That's a big help. Thanks."

"Any time." She watched him wander toward a silver-blue Mercedes and, unable to prevent herself, called after him. "And I was safe. Absolutely safe." Tossing the borrowed hat back to its owner, B.J. cut across the meadow and headed toward the inn.

The four stories of red brick, with their gabled roof and neat shutters, loomed ahead of her. Pedaling up the wide, curving drive, she noted with satisfaction that the short cut had brought her ahead of the Mercedes.

I wonder if he's looking for a room, she thought. Parking her bike, she hauled out her treasure of jellies from the basket. Maybe he's a salesman. No, she contradicted her own thoughts, *that was no salesman*. Well, if he wants a room, we'll oblige him, even if he is an interfering busybody with bad eyes.

"Good morning." B.J. smiled at the newlyweds who strolled across the lawn.

"Oh, good morning, Miss Clark. We're going for a walk by the lake," the groom answered politely.

"It's a lovely day for it," B.J. acknowledged, parking her bike by the entrance. She entered the small lobby, and moving behind the front desk, set down the crate of jelly and reached for the morning mail. Seeing a personal letter from her grandmother, she opened it and began to read with pleasure.

"Get around, don't you?"

Her absorption was rudely broken. Dropping the letter, she lifted her elbows from the counter and stared into dark brown eyes. "I took a shortcut." Unwilling to be outmatched by his height or faultless attire, she straightened and lifted her chin. "May I help you?"

"I doubt it, unless you can tell me where to find the manager."

His dismissive tone fueled her annoyance. She struggled

to remember her job and remain pleasant. "Is there some problem? There's a room available if you require one."

"Be a good girl and run along." His tone was patronizing. "And fetch the manager for me while you're about it. I'd like to see him."

Drawing herself to her full height she crossed her arms over her chest. "You're looking at her."

His dark brows rose in speculation as his eyes swept over her incredulously. "Do you manage the inn before school and on Saturdays?" he asked sarcastically.

B.J. flushed with anger. "I have been managing the Lakeside Inn for nearly four years. If there's a problem, I shall be delighted to take it up with you here, or in my office. If you require a room," she gestured toward the open register, "we'll be more than happy to oblige you."

"B.J. Clark?" he asked with a deepening frown.

"That's correct."

With a nod, he lifted a pen and signed the register. "I'm sure you'll understand," he began, raising his eyes again in fresh study. "Your morning activity on the baseball diamond and your rather juvenile appearance are deceptive."

"I had the morning free," she said crisply, "and my appearance in no way reflects on the inn's quality. I'm sure you'll see that for yourself during your stay, Mr. . . ." Turning the register to face her, B.J.'s stomach lurched.

"Reynolds," he supplied, smiling at her astonished expression. "Taylor Reynolds."

Struggling for composure, B.J. lifted her face and assumed a businesslike veneer. "I'm afraid we weren't expecting you until Monday, Mr. Reynolds."

"I changed my plans," he countered, dropping the pen back in its holder.

"Yes, well . . . Welcome to Lakeside Inn," she said belatedly and flicked a pigtail behind her back.

"Thank you. I'll require an office during my stay. Can you arrange it?"

"Our office space is limited, Mr. Reynolds." Cursing Betty Jackson's blackberry jelly, she pulled down the key to the inn's best room and rounded the desk. "However, if you don't mind sharing mine, I'm sure you'll find it adequate."

"Let's take a look. I want to see the books and records anyway."

"Of course," she agreed, gritting her teeth at the stranger's hold over her inn. "If you'll just come with me."

"B.J., B.J." She watched with an inward shudder as Eddie hurtled down the stairs and into the lobby. His glasses were slipping down his nose, his brown hair was flopping around his ears.

"B.J.," he said again, breathless, "Mrs. Pierce-Lowell's T.V. went out right in the middle of her cartoons."

"Oh, blast. Take mine in to her and call Max for the repair."

"He's away for the weekend," Eddie reminded her.

"All right, I'll survive." Giving his shoulder an encouraging pat, she guided him to the door. "Leave me a memo to call him Monday and get mine in to her before she misses Bugs Bunny." Feeling the new owner's penetrating stare in the back of her head, B.J. explained apologetically. "I'm sorry, Eddie has a tendency toward the dramatic, and Mrs. Pierce-Lowell is addicted to Saturday morning cartoons. She's one of our regulars, and we make it a policy to provide our guests with what pleases them."

"I see," he replied, but she could find nothing in his expression to indicate that he did.

Moving quickly to the back of the first floor, B.J. opened the door to her office and gestured Taylor inside. "It's not very big," she began as he surveyed the small room with desk and file cabinets and bulletin board, "but I'm sure we can arrange it to suit your needs for the few days you will be here."

"Two weeks," he stated firmly. He strolled across the room, picking up a bronze paperweight of a grinning turtle.

"Two weeks?" she repeated, and the alarm in her voice caused him to turn toward her.

"That's right, Miss Clark. Is that a problem?"

"No, no, of course not." Finding his direct stare unnerving, she lowered her eyes to the clutter on her desk.

"Do you play ball every Saturday, Miss Clark?" He perched on the edge of the desk. Looking up, B.J. found her face only inches from his.

"No, certainly not," she answered with dignity. "I simply happened to be passing by, and—"

"A very courageous slide," he commented, shocking her by running a finger down her cheek. "And your face proves it."

Somewhat dazed, she glanced at the dust on his finger. "I was safe," she said in defense against a ridiculously speeding pulse. "Wilbur needs an optometrist."

"I wonder if you manage the inn with the same tenacity with which you play ball." He smiled, his eyes very intent on hers. "We'll have a look at the books this afternoon."

"I'm sure you'll find everything in order," she said stiffly.

The effect was somewhat spoiled as she backed into the file cabinet. "The inn runs very smoothly, and as you know, makes a nice profit." She continued struggling to maintain her dignity.

"With a few changes, it should make a great deal more."

"Changes?" she echoed, apprehension in her voice. "What sort of changes?"

"I need to look over the place before I make any concrete decisions, but the location is perfect for a resort." Absently, he brushed the dust off his fingers on the windowsill and gazed out. "Pool, tennis courts, health club, a face lift for the building itself."

"There's nothing wrong with this building. We don't cater to the resort set, Mr. Reynolds." Furious, B.J. approached the desk again. "This is an inn, with all the connotations that includes. Family-style meals, comfortable lodgings and a quiet atmosphere. That's why our guests come back."

"The clientele would increase with a few modern attractions," he countered coolly. "Particularly with the proximity to Lake Champlain."

"Keep your hot tubs and disco lounges for your other acquisitions." B.J. bypassed simmer and went straight to boil. "This is Lakeside, Vermont, not L.A. I don't want any plastic surgery on my inn."

Brows rose, and his mouth curved in a grim smile. "Your inn, Miss Clark?"

"That's right," she retorted. "You may hold the purse strings, Mr. Reynolds, but I know this place, and our guests come back year after year because of what we represent. There's no way you're going to change one brick."

"Miss Clark." Taylor stood menacingly over her. "If I

choose to tear down this inn brick by brick, that's precisely what I'll do. Whatever alterations I make or don't make remain my decision, and my decision alone. Your position as manager does not entitle you to a vote."

"And your position as owner doesn't entitle you to brains!" she was unable to choke back as she stomped from the office in a flurry of flying braids.

CHAPTER 2

With relish, B.J. slammed the door to her room. Arrogant, interfering, insufferable man. Why doesn't he go play Monopoly somewhere else? Doesn't he already have enough hotels to tinker with? There must be a hundred in the Reynolds chain in the states alone, plus all those elegant foreign resorts. Why doesn't he open one in Antarctica?

Abruptly, she caught sight of her reflection in the mirror and stared in disbelief. Her face was smudged. Dust clung to her sweatshirt and jeans. Her braids hung to her shoulders. All in all, she thought grimly, I look like a rather dim-witted ten-year-old. She suddenly noticed a line down her cheek, and lifting her hand, recalled Taylor's finger resting there.

"Oh, blast." Shaking her head, she began to quickly unbind her hair. "I made a mess of it," she muttered and stripped off her morning uniform. "Looking like a grimy teenager and then losing my temper on top of it. Well, he's not going to fire me," she vowed fiercely and stalked to the shower. "I'll quit first! I'm not staying around and watching my inn mutilated."

Thirty minutes later, B.J. pulled a brush through her hair and studied the new reflection with satisfaction. Soft clouds of wheat floated on her shoulders. She wore an ivory dress, nipped at the waist, belted in scarlet to match tiny blazing rubies at her ears. Heels gave her height a slight advantage. She felt confident she could no longer be mistaken for sixteen. Lifting a neatly written page from her dresser, she moved purposefully from the room, prepared to confront the bear in his den.

After a brief excuse for a knock, B.J. pushed open the office door and slowly and purposefully advanced toward the man sitting behind the desk. Shoving the paper under his nose, she waited for his brown eyes to meet hers.

"Ah, B.J. Clark, I presume. This is quite a transformation." Leaning back in his chair, Taylor allowed his eyes to travel over the length of her. "Amazing," he smiled into her resentful gray eyes, "what can be concealed under a sweatshirt and baggy pants. . . . What's this?" He waved the paper idly, his eyes still appraising her.

"My resignation." Placing her palms on the desk, she leaned forward and prepared to give vent to her emotions. "And now that I am no longer in your employ, Mr. Reynolds, it'll give me a great deal of pleasure to tell you what I think. You are," she began as his brow rose at her tone, "a dictatorial, capitalistic opportunist. You've bought an inn which has for generations maintained its reputation for quality and personal service, and in order to make a few more annual dollars, you plan to turn it into a live-in amusement park. In doing so, you will not only have to let the current staff go, some of whom have worked here for twenty years, but you'll succeed in destroying the integrity of the entire district. This is not your average tourist town, it's a quiet, settled community. People come here for fresh air and quiet, not for a brisk tennis match or to sweat in a sauna, and—"

"Are you finished, Miss Clark?" Taylor questioned. Instinctively she recognized the danger in his lowered tones.

"No." Mustering her last resources of courage, she set her shoulders and sent him a lethal glare. "Go soak in your Jacuzzi!"

On her heel, she spun around and made for the door only to find her back pressed into it as she was whirled back into the room.

"Miss Clark," Taylor began, effectively holding her prisoner by leaning over her, arms at either side of her head. "I permitted you to clear your system for two reasons. First, you're quite a fabulous sight when your temper's in full gear. I noticed that even when I took you for a rude teenager. A lot of it has to do with your eyes going from mist to smoke, it's very impressive. That, of course," he added as she stared up at him, unable to form a sound, "is strictly on a personal level. Now on a professional plane, I am receptive to your opinions, if not to your delivery."

Abruptly, the door swung open, dislodging B.J. and tumbling her into a hard chest. "We found Julius's lunch," Eddie announced cheerfully and disappeared.

"You have a very enthusiastic staff," Taylor commented dryly as his arms propped her up against him. "Who the devil is Julius?"

"He's Mrs. Frank's Great Dane. She doesn't . . . she won't go anywhere without him."

"Does he have his own room?" His tone was gently mocking.

"No, he has a small run in the back."

Taylor smiled suddenly, his face close to hers. Power shot through her system like a bolt of electricity down a lightning rod. With a jerk, she pulled away and pushed at her tumbled hair.

"Mr. Reynolds," she began, attempting to retrieve her all too elusive dignity. He claimed her hand and pulled her back toward the desk, then pushed her firmly down on the chair.

"Do be quiet, Miss Clark," he told her in easy tones, settling behind the desk. "It's my turn now." She stared with a melding of astonishment and indignation.

"What I ultimately do with this inn is my decision. However, I will consider your opinion as you are intimate with this establishment and with the area and I, as yet, am not." Lifting B.J.'s resignation, Taylor tore it in half and dropped the pieces on the desk.

"You can't do that," she sputtered.

"I have just done it." The mild tone vibrated with authority. B.J.'s eyes narrowed. "I can easily write another."

"Don't waste your paper," he advised, leaning back in his chair. "I have no intention of accepting your resignation at the moment. Later, I'll let you know. However," he added slowly, shrugging, "if you insist, I shall be forced to close down the inn for the next few months until I've found someone to replace you."

"It couldn't possibly take months to replace me," B.J. protested, but he was looking up at the ceiling as though lost in thought.

"Six months perhaps."

"Six months?" she frowned. "But you can't. We have

reservations, it's nearly the summer season. All those people can't be disappointed. And the staff—the staff would be out of work."

"Yes." With an agreeable smile, he nodded and folded his hands on the desk.

Her eyes widened. "But—that's blackmail!"

"I think that term is quite correct." His amusement increased. "You catch on very quickly, Miss Clark."

"You can't be serious. You," she sputtered. "You wouldn't actually close the inn just because I quit."

"You don't know me well enough to be sure, do you?" His eyes were unfathomable and steady. "Do you want to chance it?"

Silence hung for a long moment, each measuring the other. "No," B.J. finally murmured, then repeated with more strength, "No, blast it, I can't! You know that already. But I certainly don't understand why."

"You don't have to know why," he interrupted with an imperious gesture of his hand.

Sighing, B.J. struggled not to permit temper to rule her tongue again. "Mr. Reynolds," she began in what she hoped was a reasonable tone, "I don't know why you find it so important for me to remain as manager of the inn, but—"

"How old are you, Miss Clark?" He cut her off again. She stared in perplexed annoyance.

"I hardly see . . ."

"Twenty, twenty-one?"

"Twenty-four," B.J. corrected, inexplicably compelled to defend herself. "But I don't see what that has to do with anything."

"Twenty-four," he repeated, obviously concluding she had finished one sentence and that was sufficient. "Chronologically, I have eight years on you, and professionally quite a bit more. I opened my first hotel when you were still leading cheers at Lakeside High."

"I never led cheers at Lakeside High," she said coldly.

"Be that as it may—" he gently inclined his head "—the arithmetic remains the same. My reason for wanting you to remain in your current position at the inn is quite simple. You know the staff, the clientele, the suppliers and so forth . . . during this transition period I need your particular expertise."

"All right, Mr. Reynolds." B.J. relaxed slightly, feeling the conversation had leveled off to a more professional plane. "But you should be aware, I will give you absolutely no cooperation in changing any aspect which I feel affects the inn's personality. In point of fact, I will do my best to be uncooperative."

"I'm sure you're quite skillful at that," Taylor said easily. B.J. was unsure whether the smile in his eyes was real or in her imagination. "Now that we understand each other, Miss Clark, I'd like to see the place and get an idea of how you run things. I should be fairly well briefed in two weeks."

"You can't possibly understand all I've been trying to tell you in that amount of time."

"I make up my mind quickly," he told her. Smiling, he studied her face. "When something's mine, I know what to do with it." His smile widened at her frown, and he rose. "If you want the inn to remain as is, you'd best stick around and make your sales pitch." Taking her arm, he hauled her up from the chair. "Let's take a look around."

With all the warmth of a January sky, B.J. took Taylor on a tour of the first floor, describing storage closets in minute detail. Throughout, he kept a hand firmly on her arm as if to remind her of his authority. The continued contact made her vaguely uneasy. His scent was musky and essentially male and he moved with a casualness which she felt was deceptive. His voice rolled deep and smooth, and several times, she found herself listening more to its cadence than to his words. Annoyed, she added to the layers of frost coating her tone.

It would be easier, she decided, if he were short and balding with a generous middle, or, perhaps, if he had a sturdy mole on his left cheek and a pair of chins. It's absolutely unfair for a man to look the way he does and have to fight him, she thought resentfully.

"Have I lost you, Miss Clark?"

"What?" Looking up, she collected her wits, inwardly cursing him again for possessing such dark, magnetic eyes. "No, I was thinking perhaps you'd like lunch." A very good improvisation, she congratulated herself.

"Fine." Agreeably, he allowed her to lead the way to the dining room.

It was a basic, rustic room, large and rectangular with beamed ceilings and gently faded wallpaper. Its charm was old and lasting; amber globed lamps, graceful antiques and old silver. Local stone dominated one wall in which a fireplace was set. Brass andirons guarded the empty hearth. Tables had been set to encourage sociability, with a few more secluded for intimate interludes. The air was humming with easy conversation and clattering dishes. A smell of fresh baking drifted toward them. In silence, Taylor studied the room, his eyes roaming from corner to corner until B.J. was certain he had figured the precise square footage.

"Very nice," he said simply.

A large, round man approached, lifting his head with a subtle dramatic flourish.

"'If music be the food of love, play on.'"

"'Give me excess of it, that, surfeiting, the appetite may sicken, and so die.'"

Chuckling at B.J.'s response, he rolled with a regal, if over-sized, grace into the dining room.

"Shakespeare at lunch?" Taylor inquired. B.J. laughed; against her will her antagonism dissolved. "That was Mr. Leander. He's been coming to the inn twice a year for the past ten years. He used to tour with a low budget Shakespearean troupe, and he likes to toss lines at me for me to cap."

"And do you always have the correct response?"

"Luckily, I've always been fond of Shakespeare, and as insurance, I cram a bit when he makes his reservation."

"Just part of the service?" Taylor inquired, tilting his head to study her from a new angle.

"You could say that."

Prudently, B.J. scanned the room to see where the young Dobson twins were seated, then steered Taylor to a table as far distant as possible.

"B.J." Dot sidled to her side, eyes lighting on Taylor in pure feminine avarice. "Wilbur brought the eggs, and they're small again. Elsie's threatening to do permanent damage."

"All right, I'll take care of it." Ignoring Taylor's questioning stare, she turned to her waitress. "Dot, see to Mr. Reynold's lunch. Please excuse me, Mr. Reynolds, I'll have to tend to this. Just send for me if you have any questions or if something is not to your satisfaction. Enjoy your meal."

Seeing Wilbur's eggs as a lucky escape hatch, B.J. hurried to the kitchen.

"Wilbur," she said with wicked enjoyment as the door swung shut behind her. "This time, I'm umpire."

A myriad of small demands dominated B.J.'s afternoon. The art of diplomacy as well as the ability to delegate and make decisions was an intricate part of her job, and B.J. had honed her skills. She moved without breaking rhythm from a debate with the Dobson twins on the advisability of keeping a frog in their bathtub to a counseling service with one of the maids who was weeping into the fresh linen supply over the loss of a boyfriend. Through the hours of soothing and listening and laying down verdicts, she was still conscious of the presence of Taylor Reynolds. It was a simple matter to avoid him physically, but his presence seemed to follow her everywhere. He had made himself known, and she could not forget about him. Perversely, she found herself fretting to know where he was and what he was doing. Probably, she thought with a fresh flash of resentment, probably he's even now in my office poring over my books with a microscope, deciding where to put in his silly tennis courts or how to concrete the grove.

The dinner hour came and went. B.J. had decided to forego supervising the dining room to have a few hours of peace. When she came downstairs to the lounge, the lighting was muted, the hour late. The three-piece band hired for the benefit of the Saturday crowd had already packed their equipment. The music had been replaced by the murmurs and clinking glasses of the handful of people who remained. It was the quiet time of the evening, just before silence. B.J. allowed her thoughts to drift back to Taylor.

I've got two weeks to make him see reason, she reminded herself, exchanging goodnights as stragglers began to wander from the lounge. That should be plenty of time to make even the most insensitive businessman understand. I simply went about things in the wrong way. Tomorrow, I'll start my campaign with a brand new strategy. I'll keep my temper under control and use a great many smiles. I'm good at smiling when I put my mind to it.

Practicing her talent on the middle-aged occupant in room 224, B.J.'s confidence grew at his rapidly blinking appreciation. Yes, she concluded, smiles are much better than claws at this stage. A few smiles, a more sophisticated appearance, and a brisk, businesslike approach, and I'll defeat the enemy before the war's declared. Rejuvenated, she turned to the bartender who was lackadaisically wiping the counter. "Go on home, Don, I'll clear up the rest."

"Thanks, B.J." Needing no second urging, he dropped his rag and disappeared through the door.

"It's no trouble at all," she told the empty space with a magnanimous gesture of one hand. "I really insist."

Crossing the room, she began to gather half filled baskets of peanuts and empty glasses, switching on the small eye-level television for company. Around her, the inn settled for sleep, the groans and creaks so familiar, they went unnoticed. Now that the day was over, B.J. found the solitude for which she yearned.

Low, eerie music poured out of the television, drifting and floating through the darkened room. Glancing up, B.J. was soon mesmerized by a horror film. Kicking off her shoes, she slid onto a stool. The story was old and well-worn, but she was caught by a shot of clouds drifting over a full moon. She reached one hand absently for a basket of peanuts, settling them into her lap as the fog began to clear on the set to reveal the unknown terror, preceded by the rustle of leaves, and heavy breathing. With a small moan at the stalking monster's distorted face, B.J. covered her eyes and waited for doom to claim the heroine.

"You'd see more without your hand in front of your eyes."

As the voice came, disembodied in the darkness, B.J. shrieked, dislodging a shower of peanuts from her lap. "Don't ever do that again!" she commanded, glaring up at Taylor's grinning face.

"Sorry." The apology lacked conviction. Leaning on the bar, he nodded toward the set. "Why do you have it on if you don't want to watch?"

"I can't help myself, it's an obsession. But I always watch with my eyes closed. Now look, watch this part, I've seen it before." She grabbed his sleeve with one hand and pointed with the other. "She's going to walk right outside like an idiot. I ask you, would anyone with a working brain cell walk out into the pitch darkness when they hear something scraping at the window? Of course not," she answered for him. "A smart person would be huddled under the bed waiting for it to go away. Oh." She pulled him closer, burying her face against his chest as the monster's face loomed in a close-up. "It's horrible, I can't watch. Tell me when it's over."

Slowly, it dawned on her that she was burrowing into his chest, his heartbeat steady against her ear. His fingers tangled in her hair, smoothing and soothing her as though comforting a child. She stiffened and started to pull back, but the hand in her hair kept her still.

"No, wait a minute, he's still stalking about and leering. There." He patted her shoulder and loosened his grip. "Saved by commercial television."

Set free, B.J. fumbled off the stool and began gathering scattered peanuts and composure. "I'm afraid things got rather out of hand this afternoon, Mr. Reynolds." Her voice was not quite steady, but she hoped he would attribute the waver to cowardice. "I must apologize for not completing your tour of the inn."

He watched as she scrambled over the floor on her hands and knees, a curtain of pale hair concealing her face. "That's all right. I wandered a bit on my own. I finally met Eddie when not in motion. He's a very intense young man."

She shifted away from him to search for more far reaching nuts. "He'll be good at hotel management in a couple years. He just needs a little more experience." Keeping her face averted, B.J. waited for the heat to cool from her cheeks.

"I met quite a few of the inn's guests today. Everyone seems very fond of B.J." He closed the distance between them and pushed back the hair which lay across her cheek. "Tell me, what does it stand for?"

"What?" Diverted by the fingers on her skin, she found it hard to concentrate on the conversation.

"B.J." He smiled into bemused eyes. "What does it stand for?"

"Oh." She returned the smile, stepping strategically out of

reach. "I'm afraid that's a closely guarded secret. I've never even told my mother."

Behind her, the heroine gave a high-pitched, lilting scream. Scattering nuts again, B.J. threw herself into Taylor's arms.

"Oh, I'm sorry, that caught me off guard." Mortified, she lifted her face and attempted to pull away.

"No, this is the third time in one day you've been in this position." One hand lifted, and traveled down the length of her hair as he held her still. "This time, I'm going to see what you taste like."

Before she could protest, his mouth lowered to hers, at once firm and possessing. His arm around her waist brought her close to mold against him. His tongue found hers, and she was unaware whether he had parted her lips or if they had done so of their own volition. He lingered over her mouth, savoring its softness, deepening the kiss until she clung to him for balance. She told herself the sudden spiraling of her heartbeat was a reaction to the horror movie, the quick dizziness, the result of a missed dinner. Then she told herself nothing and only experienced.

"Very nice." Taylor's murmured approval trailed along her cheekbone, moving back to tease the corner of her mouth. "Why don't we try it again?"

In instinctive defense, she pressed her hand into his chest to ward him off. *Lightly* she told herself, praying for the earth to stop trembling, *treat it lightly*. "I'm afraid I don't come in thirty-two flavors, Mr. Reynolds, and . . ."

"Taylor," he interrupted, smiling down at the hand which represented no more of an obstacle than a blade of grass. "I decided this morning, when you stalked me in the office, that we're going to know each other very well."

"Mr. Reynolds . . ."

"Taylor," he repeated, his eyes close and compelling. "And my decisions are always final."

"Taylor," she agreed, not wanting to debate a minor point when the distance between them was lessening despite the pressure against his chest. "Do you engage in this sort of activity with all the managers of your hotels?" Hoping to wound him with a scathing remark, B.J. was immediately disappointed when he tossed back his head and laughed.

"B.J., this current activity has nothing whatever to do with your position at the inn. I am merely indulging my weakness for women who look good in pigtails."

"Don't you kiss me again!" she ordered, struggling with a sudden desperation which surprised him into loosening his hold.

"You'll have to choose between being demure or being provocative, B.J." His tone was mild, but she saw as she backed away, his eyes had darkened with temper. "Either way we play, I'm going to win, but it would make the game easier to follow."

"I don't play this sort of game," she retorted, "and I am neither demure nor provocative."

"You're a bit of both." His hands slipped into his pockets, and he rocked gently on his heels as he studied her furious face. "It's an intriguing combination." His brow lifted in speculation. An expression of amusement flitted over his features. "But I suppose you already know that or you wouldn't be so good at it."

Forgetting her fears, B.J. took a step toward him. "The only thing I know is that I have absolutely no desire to intrigue you in any way. All that I want you to do is to keep your resort builder's hands off this inn." Her hands balled into tight fists. "I wish you'd go back to New York and sit in your penthouse."

Before he could answer, B.J. turned and darted from the room. She hurried through the darkened lobby without even a backward glance.

CHAPTER 3

B.J. decided that making a fool of herself the previous evening had been entirely Taylor Reynolds's responsibility. Today, she resolved, slipping a gray blazer over a white silk shirt, *I will be astringently businesslike.* Nonetheless, she winced at the memory of her naive plea that he not kiss her again, the absurd way her voice had shaken with the words. *Why didn't I come up with some cool, sophisticated retort?* she asked herself. *Because I was too busy throwing peanuts around the room and making a fool of myself,* she answered the question to her frowning mirror image. *Why did a simple kiss cloak my brain with layers of cheesecloth?* The woman in the mirror stared back without answering.

He had caught her off guard, B.J. decided as she arranged her hair in a neat, businesslike roll at her neck's nape. It was so unexpected, she had overreacted. Despite herself, she relived the sensation of his mouth claiming hers, his breath warm on her cheek. The knee trembling, brain spinning feeling never before experienced, washed over her again, and briskly, she shook her head to dispel it. It was simply a matter of the unexpected creating a false intenseness, like pricking your thumb with a needle while sewing.

It was important, she knew, to refrain from thinking of Taylor Reynolds on a personal level, and to remember he held the fate of the Lakeside Inn in his hands.

Dirty pool, her mind muttered, recalling his easy threat to close the inn if she pressed her resignation. Emotional blackmail. He knew he held all the aces, and waited, with that damnably appealing smile, for her to fold or call. *Well*, she decided, and smoothed the charcoal material of her skirt, *I play a pretty mean game of poker myself, Taylor Reynolds*. After trying out several types of smiles in the mirror, polite, condescending, dispassionate, she left the room with brisk steps.

Sunday mornings were usually quiet. Most of the guests slept late, rising in dribbles to wander downstairs for breakfast. Traditionally, B.J. spent these quiet hours closeted in her office with whatever paperwork she felt merited attention. From experience, she had found this particular system worked well, being the least likely time for calamities, minor or major, to befall guests or staff.

She grabbed a quick coffee in the kitchen before plunging into the sea of invoices and account books.

"How providential." She jerked slightly as a hand captured her arm, and she found herself being led to the dining room. "Now, I won't have to have breakfast alone."

The dozens of flaming retorts which sprang to mind at Taylor's presumptuousness were dutifully banked down. B.J. answered with her seasoned polite smile. "How kind of you to ask. I hope you spent a pleasant night."

"As stated in your public relations campaign, the inn is conducive to restful nights."

Waving aside her hostess, B.J. moved through the empty tables to a corner booth. "I think you'll find all my publicity is based on fact, Mr. Reynolds." Sliding in, B.J. struggled to keep her voice light and marginally friendly. Remnants of their argument in her office and their more personal encounter in the lounge clung to her, and she attempted to erase both from her mind.

"So far I find no discrepancies."

Maggie hovered by the table, her smile dreamily absent. No doubt she was thinking of her date last night with Wally, B.J. thought. "Toast and coffee, Maggie," she said kindly, breaking the trance. The waitress scribbled on her pad, her cheeks flushed.

"You know," Taylor observed after giving his order, "you're very good at your job."

B.J. chided herself for her pleasure at the unexpected praise. "Why do you say that?"

"Not only are your books in perfect order, but you know your staff and handle them with unobtrusive deftness. You just managed to convey a five-minute lecture with one brief look."

"It makes it easier when you understand your staff and their habits." Her brows lifted in easy humor. "You see, I happen to know Maggie's mind is still focused on the double feature she and Wally didn't watch last night."

His grin flashed, boyish and quick.

"The staff is very much like a family." B.J. was careful to keep her tone casual, her hands busy pouring coffee. "The guests feel that. They enjoy the informality which is always accompanied by quality service. Our rules are flexible, and the staff is trained to adjust to the individual needs of the guests. The inn is a basic place, not for those who require formal entertainment or unlimited luxury. Fresh air, good food and a pleasant atmosphere are our enticements, and we deliver."

She paused as Maggie placed their breakfast order on the table.

"Do you have a moral objection to resorts, B.J.?"

The unexpectedness of Taylor's question put her off. Blinking in confusion at the long, lean fingers as they held a knife, spreading Betty Jackson's jelly on toast, she stammered, "No . . . why of course not." Those fingers, she recalled irrelevantly, had tangled in her hair. "No," she repeated more firmly, meeting his eyes. "Resorts are fine if they are run correctly, as yours are. But their function is entirely different from ours. In a proper resort there's an activity for every minute of the day. Here, the atmosphere is more relaxed, a little fishing or boating, skiing, and above all the menu. The Lakeside Inn is perfect exactly as it is," she concluded more fiercely than she had intended and watched one brow rise, nearly meeting the curling thickness of his hair.

"That's yet to be determined." He lifted his cup to his lips.

His tone was mild, but B.J. recognized traces of anger in the disconcertingly direct eyes. She dropped her eyes to her own cup as if enticed by the rich, black liquid.

"'The gray-eyed morn smiles on the frowning night.'"

The quote brought her head up sharply, and looking into Mr. Leander's smiling, expectant face, B.J. searched her brain. "'Chequering the eastern clouds with streaks of light.'"

Thank goodness I've read *Romeo and Juliet* a dozen times, she thought, watching his pleased saunter as he moved to his table.

"One day, he's going to catch you, and you're going to draw a blank."

"Life's a series of risks," she returned flippantly. "Better to accept its challenges."

Reaching over, he tucked a stray lock behind her ear, and she jerked away from his touch, unexpectedly shy.

"For the most part," he drew the words out with infuriating emphasis, "I believe you do. It should make things very interesting. More coffee?" His question was pleasant and easy as if they had shared the morning meal on a regular basis. B.J. shook her head in refusal. . . . She felt uneasily inept at parrying words with this domineering, sophisticated man. . . .

* * *

Sunlight poured through the many-paned windows, spilling in patchwork patterns on the floor, a lawn mower hummed along the outer edges of lawn, and somewhere close, a bird sang his enjoyment of a golden day. Closeted in the office with Taylor, B.J. tuned even these small pleasures out, keeping her mind firmly on the business at hand. Here, with the impersonal wedges of invoices and account books between them, she felt confident and assured. In discussing the inn's procedure, her feet were on solid ground.

Honesty forced her to admit that Taylor Reynolds knew his profession down to the finest detail. He skimmed through her books with the sharp eye of an accountant, shifted and sorted invoices with the ease of a business manager.

At least, B.J. told herself, he doesn't treat me like an empty-headed imbecile who can't tally monthly accounts. Rather, she found him listening to her explanations with attentive respect. Soothed by his obvious appreciation of her intelligence B.J. decided if he did not yet look on the Lakeside Inn as she did, perhaps that too would come.

"I see you deal with a great many small businesses and local farms."

"That's right." She searched the bottom drawer of her desk for an ashtray as he lit a cigarette. "It's advantageous on all sides. We get more personal service and fresher produce, and it boosts local economy." Finding a small ceramic ashtray under a pile of personal correspondence, B.J. placed it on the desk. "The Lakeside Inn is essential to this district. We provide employment and a market for local products and services."

"Umm."

Finding his response less than illuminating, B.J. opened her mouth to continue when the door burst open.

"B.J." Eddie stood, bottom lip trembling. "It's the Bodwins."

"I'll be right there." Suppressing a sigh, she made a mental note to tell Eddie to knock during Taylor's stay.

"Is that a natural disaster or a plague?" Taylor asked, watching Eddie's speedy exit.

"It's nothing, really." She edged toward the door. "Excuse me, I'll just be a minute."

Shutting the door behind her, B.J. hurried to the lobby.

"Hello, Miss Patience, Miss Hope." She greeted the elderly Bodwin sisters with a wary smile.

Tall and lean as two aged willows, the Bodwins were long-standing guests.

"It's so nice to see you both again."

"It's always a pleasure to come back, Miss Clark," Miss Patience announced, and Miss Hope murmured in agreement. Habitually Miss Patience announced, and Miss Hope murmured. It was one of the few things which separated them. Over the years they had melded into mirror images from their identical wire rimmed spectacles to their identical orthopedic shoes.

"Eddie, see that the luggage is taken up, please." Miss Patience flashed a knowing smile which B.J. tried not to notice. B.J. saw her sharp-eyed glance drift over her head. Turning, she spotted Taylor.

"Miss Patience, Miss Hope, this is Taylor Reynolds, the owner of the inn." Miss Patience shot her a meaningful look.

"A pleasure, ladies." Gallantly, he took each thin-boned hand in his. A blush, dormant for twenty-five years, rose to Miss Hope's wrinkled cheek.

"You're a very fortunate young man." Miss Patience gave Taylor a thorough survey, then nodded as if satisfied. "I'm sure you know what a treasure you have in Miss Clark. I hope you appreciate her."

B.J. resisted grinding her teeth for fear the sound would be audible. With a smile, Taylor laid a hand on her shoulder.

"I'm quite convinced Miss Clark is indispensable and my appreciation inadequate."

Satisfied, Miss Patience nodded.

B.J. shook the offending hand from her shoulder and assumed a coolly professional manner. "You have your regular table, number 2."

"Of course." Miss Patience moved her lips into a smile and patted B.J.'s cheek. "You're a good girl, Miss Clark." Smiling vaguely, the two ladies drifted away.

"Surely, B.J.," Taylor turned to B.J. with an infuriating smile, "you're not going to give those two dotty old girls the second table?"

"The Lakeside Inn," she said coldly, turning to precede him to the office, "makes it a habit to please its guests. I see no reason why the Bodwins shouldn't sit wherever they want. Mr. Campbell always seated them at number 2."

"Mr. Campbell," Taylor countered with infuriating calm, "no longer owns the inn. I do."

"I'm well aware of that." Her chin tilted higher in defiance. "Do you want me to turn out the Bodwin sisters and place them at the table near the kitchen? Don't they look fancy enough for you? Why don't you think of them as people rather than little black numbers in the bloody account book?"

Her tirade was sharply cut off as he gripped her shoulders. She found she had swallowed the remaining words before she could prevent herself.

"You have," he began in an ominously low voice, "a very unfortunate temper and some very odd ideas. No one tells me how to run my business. Absolutely no one. Advice is accepted upon request, but I only make the decisions, and I alone give the orders."

He moved toward her. She could only stare, fascinated and faintly terrified.

"Do we understand each other?"

B.J. nodded, wide-eyed, then gathered courage to answer audibly. "Yes, perfectly. What would you like me to do about the Bodwins?"

"You've already done it. When you do something which displeases me, B.J., I'll let you know." The underlying threat brought storm warnings to her eyes. "Of course you know," Taylor continued, his tone softening, "you're a very ingenious lady. You've managed to share my breakfast table and work with me throughout the morning without once using my name. You've skirted around it, jumped over it and crawled under it, fascinating me with the acrobatics."

"That's ridiculous." She attempted to shrug, but his hands were firm on her shoulders. "Your imagination needs re-oiling."

"Then perhaps . . ." His arms moved to capture her waist. She arched away only to be brought steadily closer. "You'd say it now." His mouth hovered above hers. She felt the unfamiliar sweet flow of weakness, the trembling warmth just under her skin.

"Taylor." She failed to bring her voice above a whisper.

"Very good, you'll use it more often." His mouth curved, but she saw the smile only in his eyes. "Do I frighten you, B.J.?"

"No." Her denial was faint. "No," she repeated with more firmness.

"Liar." His laugh was both amused and pleased as his mouth teased hers. It rubbed lightly, holding back the promise until with a moan she drew him closer and took it.

Her breasts crushed against his chest, her lips instinctively found his. She felt herself tumbling in helpless cartwheels down an endless shaft where lights whirled in speeding colors. His hands moved from her waist to her hips, his strong fingers discovering the secrets of subtle curves as his mouth took everything she offered. Craving more, she strained against him until her sharpened senses began to dim, and the world spun hazily around her and vanished.

Fear rose like a phoenix from the flames of passion, and she struggled away, stunned and confused. "I . . . I need to check how lunch is going." She fumbled behind for the doorknob.

His hands in his pockets, Taylor rocked back on his heels and held her gaze with steady assurance. "Of course. . . . Now run away to your duties. But you understand, B.J., that I intend to have you sooner or later. I can be patient up to a point."

Her hand connected with the knob. She found her voice. "Of all the appalling nerve! I'm not a piece of property you can have your agent pick up for you."

"No, I'm handling this strictly on my own." He smiled at her. "I know when something's going to be mine. Acquiring it is simply a matter of timing."

"I'm not an it." More outraged than she had thought possible, she took a step toward him. "I have no intention of being acquired and added to your trophies! And timing will get you nowhere!"

His smile was maddeningly confident. B.J. slammed the door full force behind her.

CHAPTER 4

Mondays always kept B.J. busy. She was convinced that if a major calamity were to fall, it would fall on a Monday simply because that would be the time she would be least able to cope with it. Taylor Reynolds's presence in her office was an additional Monday morning burden. His calm statement of the previous day was still fresh in her mind, and she was still seething with resentment. In an icy voice, she explained to him each phone call she made, each letter she wrote, each invoice she filed. He would not, she decided, accuse her of being uncooperative. Frigid perhaps, she thought with wicked pleasure, but not uncooperative.

Taylor's impeccable, businesslike attitude did nothing to endear him to her. She was well aware that her cold politeness bordered on the insulting.

Never had she met a man more in control or more annoying. Briefly, she considered pouring her coffee into his lap just to get a reaction. The thought was satisfying.

"Did I miss a joke?" Taylor asked as an involuntary smile flitted over B.J.'s face.

"What?" Realizing her lapse, B.J. struggled to compose her features. "No, I'm afraid my mind was wandering. You'll have to excuse me," she went on, "I have to make sure that all the rooms are made up by this time of day. Will you be wanting lunch in here or in the dining room?"

"I'll come to the dining room." Leaning back, Taylor studied her as he tapped his pencil against the corner of the desk. "Are you joining me?"

"Oh, I'm terribly sorry." B.J.'s tone was falsely saccharine. "I'm swamped today. I recommend the roast beef, though. I'm sure you'll find it satisfactory." Satisfied with her delivery, she closed the door quietly behind her.

With ingenuity and luck, B.J. managed to avoid Taylor throughout the afternoon. The inn was nearly empty as most of the guests were outdoors enjoying the mild spring weather. B.J. was able to slip down the quiet corridors without running into Taylor. She kept her antenna tuned for his presence, however. Though she knew it was childish, she found herself enjoying the one-way game of hide and seek. It became a self-imposed challenge that she keep out of his sight until nightfall.

* * *

In the pre-dinner lull, the inn was drowsy and silent. Humming to herself, B.J. carefully checked off linens in the third floor supply room. She was confident Taylor would not venture into that area of the inn, and relaxed her guard. Her mind traveled from her task, touching on pictures of boating on the lake, walks in the woods, and long summer evenings.

Though her daydreams were pleasant, they were underlined by a nagging dissatisfaction. She tried to shrug it off but found it stubborn. There was something missing from the images, or rather someone. Whom would she be boating with on the lake? Whom would she be walking with in the woods? Who would be there to make the long summer evenings special? A distressing image began to form in B.J.'s brain, and she squeezed her eyes tight until it faded.

"I don't need him," she muttered, giving a pile of freshly laundered sheets a pat. "Absolutely not." B.J. backed from the tiny room and quietly pulled the door shut. When she backed into a solid object, she shrieked and fell forward against the closed door.

"Jumpy, aren't you?" Taylor took her shoulders and turned her to face him. His expression was amused. "Muttering to yourself, too. Maybe you need a vacation."

"I . . . I . . ."

"A long vacation," he concluded, giving her cheek a fatherly pat.

Finding her tongue, B.J. responded with reasonable calm. "You startled me, sneaking around that way."

"I thought it was a rule of the house," he countered as his grin broke out. "You've been doing it all afternoon."

Furious that her cunning had fallen short of the mark, she spoke with frosty dignity. "I have no idea what you're talking about. Now, if you'll excuse me . . ."

"Did you know you get a half-inch vertical line between your eyebrows when you're annoyed?"

"I'm very busy." She kept her voice cool as she did her best to keep the space between her brows smooth. *Blast the man!*

she thought as his engaging smile began to have its effect on her. "Taylor, if there is something specific you want . . ." She stopped as she saw his grin widen until it nearly split his face. "If there's some business you want to discuss—" she amended.

"I took a message for you," he informed her, then lifted a finger to smooth away the crease between her brows. "A very intriguing message."

"Oh?" she said casually, wishing he would back up so that she did not feel so imprisoned between his body and the closed storeroom door.

"Yes, I wrote it down so there'd be no mistake." He took a slip of paper from his pocket and read. "It's from a Miss Peabody. She wanted you to know that Cassandra had her babies. Four girls and two boys. Sextuplets." Taylor lowered the paper and shook his head. "Quite an amazing feat."

"Not if you're a cat." B.J. felt the color lacing her cheeks. *Why would he have to be the one to take the message? Why couldn't Cassandra have waited?* "Miss Peabody is one of our oldest guests. She stays here twice a year."

"I see," said Taylor, his mouth twitching. "Well, now that I've done my duty, it's your turn to do yours." Taking her hand, Taylor began to lead her down the corridor. "This country air gives me quite an appetite. You know the menu, what do you recommend we have?"

"I can't possibly," she began.

"Of course you can," he interrupted mildly. "Just think of me as a guest. Inn policy is to give the guests what pleases them. It pleases me to have dinner with you."

Cornered by her own words, B.J. offered no argument.

Within minutes, she found herself seated across from the man she had so successfully avoided during the afternoon.

B.J. thought dinner a relatively painless affair. She felt too, as it neared an end, that she had done her duty and done it superbly. It was, however, difficult to resist the pull of Taylor's charm when he chose to put it to use. The charm itself was so natural and understated that she often found herself captivated before she realized what was happening. Whenever she felt her walls of indifference crumbling, she retreated a step and shored up the holes. *What a shame he isn't someone else,* she mused as he recounted an anecdote. *It would be so nice to enjoy a quiet dinner with him if there weren't any boundaries. But there are,* she reminded herself, quickly pulling out of the range of his charm. *Very definite, very important boundaries. This is war,* she reflected, thinking of their conversation the previous day. *I can't afford to get caught behind enemy lines.* As Taylor raised his glass and smiled at her, B.J. wondered if Mata Hari had ever been faced with a tougher assignment.

They had reached the coffee stage when Eddie approached their table. "Mr. Reynolds?" B.J. looked on with approval as Eddie neither fidgeted nor seemed ready to burst with the tidings he bore. "There's a phone call for you from New York."

"Thank you, Eddie. I'll take it in the office. I shouldn't be long," Taylor told her as he rose.

"Please, don't rush on my account." B.J. gave him a careful smile, resigning herself to the fact she was a coward. "I still have several things to see to this evening."

"I'll see you later," Taylor returned in a tone that brooked no argument. Their eyes met in a quick clash of wills. In a swift change of mood, Taylor laughed and bent down to kiss B.J. on the forehead before he strolled away.

Mouth agape, B.J. rubbed the spot with her fingertips, wondering why she suddenly felt lightheaded. Forcing herself back to earth, she drank her coffee and hurried off to the lounge.

Monday nights at the inn were an old tradition. The lounge was the center of activity for the weekly event. As B.J. paused in the doorway, she ran a critical eye over the room. The candles had been lit inside each of the coach lanterns which sat on the huddled tables. The lights flickered against the wood. Scents of polish, old wood and smoke melded. The dance floor was gently lit with amber spotlights. Satisfied that the mood was set, B.J. crossed the room and halted next to an ancient Victrola. The faithful mechanism was housed in a rich mahogany cabinet. With affection, B.J. trailed a finger over the smooth lid before opening it.

People began to wander in as she sorted through the collection of old 78s. The hum of conversation behind her was so familiar, it barely tickled her consciousness. Glasses chinked, ice rattled, and an occasional laugh echoed along the walls. With the absentminded skill of an expert, B.J. wound the Victrola into life and set a thick black record on the turntable. The music which drifted out was scratchy, tinny and charming. Before the record was half over, three couples were on the dance floor. Another Monday night was launched.

During the next half hour, B.J. played an unbroken stream of 1930s tunes. Over the years, she had noted that no matter what the mean age of the audience, the response to a trip through the past was positive. *Perhaps,* she mused, *it's because the simplicity of the music suits the simplicity of the inn.*

With a shrug, she abandoned her analysis and grinned at a couple fox-trotting over the dance floor to the strains of "Tea For Two."

"What the devil is going on in here?"

B.J. heard the demanding question close to her ear and whirled to find herself face to face with Taylor. "Oh, I see you're finished with your call. I hope there isn't any trouble?"

"Nothing important." He waited until she had switched records before he asked again, "B.J., I asked you what's going on in here?"

"Why, just what it looks like," she answered vaguely, hearing from the tone of the record that it was time to replace the needle. "Sit down, Taylor, I'll have Don mix you a drink. You know I'd swear there hasn't been time for this needle to wear out." Delving into her spares, B.J. began the task of changing needles.

"When you're finished, perhaps you'd take a look at my carburetor."

Engrossed in the intricacies of her job, B.J. remained untouched by Taylor's mockery. "We'll see," she murmured, then carefully placed the new needle on the record. "What would you like, Taylor?" As she straightened, she glanced toward the bar.

"Initially, an explanation."

"An explanation?" she repeated, finally giving him her full attention. "An explanation about what?"

"B.J." Impatience was beginning to thread through his tone. "Are you being deliberately dense?"

Liking neither his tone nor his question, B.J. stiffened. "Perhaps if you would be a bit more specific, I would be a bit less dense."

"I was under the impression that this lounge possessed a functional P.A. system."

"Well, of course it does." As she became more confused, B.J. pushed away the thought that perhaps she actually was dense. "What does that have to do with anything?"

"Why isn't it being used?" He glanced down at the Victrola. "And why are you using this archaic piece of equipment?"

"The P.A. system isn't being used," she explained in calm, reasonable tones, "because it's Monday."

"I see." Taylor glanced toward the dance floor where one couple was instructing another on the proper moves of a two step. "That, of course, explains everything."

His sarcasm caused indignation to flood through her. Clamping her teeth on a stream of unwise remarks, B.J. began to sift rapidly through records. "On Monday nights, we use the Victrola and play old records. And it is not an archaic piece of equipment," she added, unable to prevent herself. "It's an antique, a museum quality antique."

"B.J." Taylor spoke to the top of her head as she bent to change records. "Why?"

"Why what?" she snapped, furious with his ambiguity.

"Why do you use the Victrola and play old records on Monday nights?" He spoke very clearly, spacing his words as if speaking to someone whose brain was not fully operative.

"Because," B.J. began, her eyes flowing, her fists clenching.

Taylor held up a hand to halt the ensuing explanation. "Wait." After the one word command, he crossed the room and spoke to one of the guests. Seething, B.J. watched him use his most charming smile. It faded as he moved back to join her. "You're being relieved of Victrola duty for a bit.

Outside." With this, he took her arm and pulled her to the side door. The cool night air did nothing to lower B.J.'s temperature. "Now." Taylor closed the door behind him and leaned back against the side of the building. He made a small gesture with his hand. "Go right ahead."

"Oh, you make me so mad I could scream!" With this dire threat, B.J. began pacing up and down the porch. "Why do you have to be so . . . so . . ."

"Officious?" Taylor offered.

"Yes!" B.J. agreed, wishing passionately that she had thought of the word herself. "Everything's moving along just fine, and then you have to come in and look down your superior nose." For some moments, she paced in silence. The romance of the moonlight filtering through the trees seemed sadly out of place. "People are enjoying themselves in there." She swung her hand toward the open window. A Cole Porter number drifted back to her. "You don't have any right to criticize it. Just because we're not using a live band, or playing top forty numbers, doesn't mean we're not entertaining the guests. I really don't see why you have to . . ." She broke off abruptly as he grabbed her arm.

"O.K., time's up." As he spun her around, the hair fell over B.J.'s face, and she brushed it back impatiently. "Now, suppose we start this from the beginning."

"You know," she said between her teeth, "I really hate it when you're calm and patient."

"Stick around," he invited. It began to sink into her brain that his voice was dangerously low. "You might see the other end of the scale." Glaring at him did not seem to improve her situation, but B.J. continued to do so. "If you'll think back to the beginning of this remarkable conversation, you'll recall that I asked you a very simple question. And, I believe, a very reasonable one."

"And I told you," she tossed out, then faltered. "At least, I think I did." Frustrated, she threw both hands up in the air. "How am I supposed to remember what you said and what I said? It took you ten minutes to come to the point in the first place." She let out a deep breath as she realized she did not yet have control of her temper. "All right, what was your very simple, very reasonable question?"

"B.J., you would try the patience of a saint." She heard the amused exasperation in his voice and tried not to be charmed. "I would like to know why I stepped into nineteen-thirty-five when I came into the lounge."

"Every Monday night," she began in crisp, practical tones, "the inn offers this sort of entertainment. The Victrola was brought here more than fifty years ago, and it's been used every Monday night since. Guests who've been here before expect it. Of course," she went on, too involved in her story to realize she was being drawn closer into Taylor's arms, "the P.A. system was installed years ago. The other six nights of the week, we switch off between it and a live band, depending on the season. The Monday night gathering is almost as old as the inn itself and an important part of our tradition."

The low, bluesy tones of "Embraceable You" were floating through the open window. B.J. was swaying to its rhythm, as yet unaware that Taylor was leading her in a slow dance. "The guests look forward to it. I've found since I've worked here, that's true no matter how old or how young the clientele is." Her voice had lost its crispness. She found her trend of thought slipping away from her as their bodies swayed to the soft music.

"That was a very reasonable answer." Taylor drew her closer, and she tilted back her head, unwilling to break eye contact. "I'm beginning to see the advantages of the idea myself." Their faces were close, so close she could feel the touch of his breath on her lips. "Cold?" he asked, feeling her tremble. Though she shook her head, he gathered her closer until the warmth of his body crept into hers. Their cheeks brushed as they merged into one gently swaying form.

"I should go back in," she murmured, making no effort to move away. She closed her eyes and let his arms and the music guide her.

"Um-hum." His mouth was against her ear.

Small night sounds added to the lull of the music from the lounge; a whisper of leaves, the quiet call of a bird, the flutter of moth wings against window glass. The air was soft and cool on B.J.'s shoulders. It was touched with the light scent of hyacinth. Moonlight sprinkled through the maples, causing the shadows to tremble. She could feel Taylor's heartbeat, a sure, steady rhythm against her own breast. He trailed his mouth along her temple, brushing it through her hair as his hands roamed along her back.

B.J. felt her will dissolving as her senses grew more and more acute. She could hear the sound of his breathing over the music, feel the texture of his skin beneath his shirt, taste the male essence of him on her tongue. Her surroundings were fading like an old photograph with only Taylor remaining sharp and clear. Untapped desire swelled inside her.

Suddenly, she felt herself being swallowed by emotions she was not prepared for, by needs she could not understand.

"No, please." Her bid for freedom was so swift and unexpected that she broke from Taylor's arms without a struggle. "I don't want this." She clung to the porch rail and faced him.

Closing the distance between them in one easy motion, Taylor circled the back of her neck with his hand. "Yes, you do." His mouth lowered, claiming hers. B.J. felt the porch tilt under her feet.

Longing, painfully sweet, spread through her until she felt she would suffocate. His hands were bringing her closer and closer. With some unexplained instinct, she knew if she were wrapped in his arms again, she would never find the strength to resist him.

"No!" Lifting both hands, she pushed against his chest and freed herself. "I don't!" she cried in passionate denial. Turning, she streaked down the porch steps. "Don't tell me what I want," she flung back at him before she raced around the side of the building.

She paused before she entered the inn to catch her breath and to allow her pounding heart to slow down. Certainly not the usual Monday evening at Lakeside Inn, she thought, smiling wryly to herself. Unconsciously, she hummed a few bars of "Embraceable You," but caught herself with a self-reprimanding frown before she entered the kitchen to remind Dot about the bud vases on the breakfast tables.

CHAPTER 5

There are days when nothing goes right. The morning, blue and clear and breezy, looked deceptively promising. Clad in a simple green shirtdress and low heels, B.J. marched down the stairs running the word *businesslike* over and over in her mind. Today, she determined, she would be the manager of the inn conducting business with the owner of the inn. There was no moonlight, no music, and she would not forget her responsibilities again. She strolled into the dining room, prepared to greet Taylor casually, then use the need to oversee breakfast preparations as an excuse not to share the morning meal with him. Taylor, however, was already well into a fluffy mound of scrambled eggs and deep into a conversation with Mr. Leander. Taylor gave B.J. an absent wave as she entered, then returned his full attention to his breakfast companion.

Perversely, B.J. was annoyed that her well-planned excuse was unnecessary. She scowled at the back of Taylor's head before she flounced into the kitchen. Ten minutes later, she was told in no uncertain terms that she was in the way. Banished to her office, she sulked in private.

For the next thirty minutes, B.J. occupied herself with busy work, all the while keeping her ears pricked for Taylor's approach. As the minutes passed, she felt a throbbing tension build at the base of her neck. The stronger the ache became, the deeper became her resentment toward Taylor. She set the reason for her headache and her glum mood at his doorstep, though she could not have answered what he had done to cause either. *He was here,* she decided, then broke the point of her pencil. *That was enough.*

"B.J.!" Eddie swirled into the office as she stood grinding her teeth and sharpening her pencil. "There's trouble."

"You bet there is," she muttered.

"It's the dishwasher." Eddie lowered his eyes as if announcing a death in the family. "It broke down in the middle of breakfast."

B.J. let out her breath in a quick sound of annoyance. "All right, I'll call Max. With any luck it'll be going full swing before lunch."

Luck, B.J. was to find, was a mirage.

An hour later, she stood by as Max the repairman did an exploratory on the dishwasher. She found his continual mutters, tongue cluckings and sighs wearing on her nerves. Time was fleeting, and it seemed to her that Max was working at an impossibly slow pace. Impatient, she leaned over his shoulder and stared at tubes and wires. Bracing one hand on Max's back, she leaned in further and pointed.

"Couldn't you just . . ."

"B.J." Max sighed and removed another screw. "Go play with the inn and let me do my job."

Straightening, B.J. stuck out her tongue at the back of his head, then flushed scarlet as she spotted Taylor standing inside the doorway.

"Have a problem?" he asked. Though his voice and mouth were sober, his eyes laughed at her. She found his silent mockery infuriating.

"I can handle it," she snapped, wishing her cheeks were cool and her position dignified. "I'm sure you must be very busy." She cursed herself for hinting at his morning involvement. This time he did smile, and she cursed him as well.

"I'm never too busy for you, B.J." Taylor crossed the room, then took her hand and raised it to his lips before she realized his intent. Max cleared his throat.

"Cut that out." She tore her hand away and whipped it behind her back. "There's no need to concern yourself with this," she continued, struggling to assume the businesslike attitude she had vowed to take. "Max is fixing the dishwasher before the lunch rush."

"No, I'm not." Max sat back on his heels and shook his head. In his hand was a small-toothed wheel.

"What do you mean, no you're not?" B.J. demanded, forgetting Taylor in her amazement. "You've got to. I need . . ."

"What you need is one of these," Max interrupted, holding up the wheel.

"Well, all right." B.J. plucked the part from his hand and scowled at it. "Put one in. I don't see how a silly little thing like this could cause all this trouble."

"When the silly little thing has a broken tooth, it can cause a lot of trouble," Max explained patiently, and glanced at Taylor for masculine understanding. "B.J., I don't carry things like this in stock. You'll have to get it from Burlington."

"Burlington?" Realizing the situation was desperate B.J. used her most pleading look. "Oh, but, Max."

Though well past his fiftieth birthday, Max was not immune to huge gray eyes. He shifted from one foot to the other, sighed and took the part from B.J.'s palm. "All right, all right, I'll drive into Burlington myself. I'll have the machine fixed before dinner, but lunch is out. I'm not a magician."

"Thank you, Max." Rising on her toes, B.J. pecked his cheek. "What would I do without you?" Mumbling, he packed up his tools and started out of the room. "Bring your wife in for dinner tonight, on the house." Pleased with her success, B.J. smiled as the door swung shut. When she remembered Taylor, she cleared her throat and turned to him.

"You should have those eyes registered with the police department," he advised, tilting his head and studying her. "They're a lethal weapon."

"I don't know what you're talking about." She sniffed with pretended indifference while she wished she could have negotiated with Max in private.

"Of course you do." With a laugh, Taylor cupped her chin in his hand. "That look you aimed at him was beautifully timed."

"I'm sure you're mistaken," she replied, wishing his mere touch would not start her heart pounding. "I simply arranged things in the best interest of the inn. That's my job."

"So it is," he agreed, and leaned on the injured dishwasher. "Do you have any suggestions as to what's to be done until this is fixed?"

"Yes." She glanced at the double stainless steel sink. "Roll up your sleeves."

It did not occur to B.J. to be surprised that she and Taylor washed the dozens of breakfast dishes side by side until it was *fait accompli*. The interlude had been odd, B.J. felt, because of the unusual harmony which existed between them. They had enjoyed a companionable banter, an easy partnership without the tension which habitually entered their encounters. When Elsie returned to begin lunch preparations, they scarcely noticed her.

"Not one casualty," Taylor proclaimed as B.J. set the last plate on its shelf.

"That's only because I saved two of yours from crashing on the floor."

"Slander," Taylor stated and swung an arm over her shoulder as he led her from the room. "You'd better be nice to me. What'll you do if Max doesn't fix the dishwasher before dinner? Think of all those lunch dishes."

"I'd rather not. However, I've already given that possibility some consideration." B.J. found the handiest chair in her office and dropped into it. "I know a couple of kids in town that we could recruit in a pinch. But Max won't let me down."

"You have a lot of faith." Taylor sat behind the desk, then lifted his feet to rest on top of it.

"You don't know Max," B.J. countered. "If he said he'll have it fixed before dinner, he will. Otherwise, he'd have said I'll try, or maybe I can, or something of that sort. When Max says I will, he does. That," she added, seeing the opportunity to score a point, "is an advantage of knowing everyone you deal with personally."

Taylor inclined his head in acknowledgement as the phone

rang on the desk. Signaling for Taylor not to bother, B.J. rose and answered it.

"Lakeside Inn. Oh, hello, Marilyn. No, I've been tied up this morning." She eased a hip down on the edge of the desk and shuffled through her papers. "Yes, I have your message here. I'm sorry, I just got back into the office. No, you let me know when you have all your acceptances back, then we'll have a better idea of how to plan the food and so on. There's plenty of time. You've got well over a month before the wedding. Trust me; I've handled receptions before. Yes, I know you're nervous. It's all right, prospective brides are meant to be nervous. Call me when you have a definite number. You're welcome, Marilyn. Yes, yes, you're welcome. 'Bye."

B.J. hung up the phone and stretched her back before she realized Taylor was waiting for an explanation. "That was Marilyn," B.J. informed him. "She was grateful."

"Yes, I rather got that impression."

"She's getting married next month." B.J. lifted a hand to rub at the stiffness in the back of her neck. "If she makes it without a nervous breakdown, it'll be a minor miracle. People should elope and not put themselves through all this."

"I'm sure there are countless fathers-of-the-bride who would agree with you after paying the expenses of the wedding." He rose, moving around the desk until he stood in front of her. "Here, let me." Lifting his hands, he massaged her neck and shoulders. B.J.'s protest became a sigh of pleasure. The word *businesslike* floated quietly out of her mind. "Better?" Taylor asked, smiling at her closed eyes.

"Mmm. It might be in an hour or two." She stretched under his hands like a contented kitten. "Ever since Marilyn set the date, she's been on the phone three times a week to check on the reception. It's hard to believe someone could get that excited about getting married."

"Well, not everyone is as cool and collected as you," Taylor remarked as he ran his thumbs along her jawline, stroking his other fingers along the base of her neck. "And, by the way, I wouldn't spread that eloping idea of yours around if I were you. I imagine the inn makes a good profit doing wedding receptions."

"Profit?" B.J. opened her eyes and tried to concentrate on what they had been saying. It was difficult to think with his hands so warm and strong on her skin. "Profit?" she said again and swallowed as her brain cleared. "Oh well . . . yes." She scooted off the desk and out of his reach. "Yes, usually . . . that is . . . sometimes." She wandered the room wishing the interlude in the kitchen had not made her forget who he was. "It depends, you see, on . . . Oh boy." She ended on a note of disgust and blew out a long breath.

"Perhaps you'd translate all that into English?" Taylor suggested. With a twinge of uneasiness, B.J. watched him seat himself once more behind the desk. *Owner to manager* again, she thought bitterly.

"Well, you see," she began, striving for nonchalance. "There are occasions when we do wedding receptions or certain parties without charge. That is," she rushed on as his face remained inscrutable, "we charge for the food and supplies, but not for the use of the lounge . . ."

"Why?" The one word interruption was followed by several seconds of complete silence.

"Why?" B.J. repeated and glanced briefly at the ceiling for assistance. "It depends, of course, and it is the exception rather than the rule." *Why?* she demanded of herself. *Why don't I learn to keep my mouth shut?* "In this case, Marilyn is Dot's cousin. You met Dot, she's one of our waitresses," she continued as Taylor remained unhelpfully silent. "She also works here during the summer season. We decided, as we do on certain occasions, to give Marilyn the reception as a wedding present."

"We?"

"The staff," B.J. explained. "Marilyn is responsible for the food, entertainment, flowers, but we contribute the lounge and our time, and," she added, dropping her voice to a mumble, "the wedding cake."

"I see." Taylor leaned back in the chair and laced his fingers together. "So, the staff donates their time and talent and the inn."

"Just the lounge." B.J. met his accusatory glance with a glare. "It's something we do only a couple of times a year. And if I must justify it from a business standpoint, it's good public relations. Maybe it's even tax deductible. Ask your C.P.A." She began to storm around the office as her temper rose, but Taylor sat calmly. "I don't see why you have to be so picky. The staff works on their own time. We've been doing it for years. It's . . ."

"Inn policy," Taylor finished for her. "Perhaps I should have you list all the eccentricities of inn policy for me. But I should remind you, B.J., that the inn's policy is not carved in stone."

"You're not going to drop the axe on Marilyn's reception," B.J. stated, prepared for a fight to the finish.

"I've misplaced my black hood, B.J., so I can't play executioner. However," he continued before the look of satisfaction could be fully formed on her face, "you and I will have to have a more detailed discussion on the inn's public relations."

"Yes, sir," she replied in her most wintry voice, and was saved from further argument by the ringing of the phone.

Taylor motioned for her to answer it. "I'll get us some coffee."

B.J. watched him stroll from the room as she lifted the phone to her ear.

When Taylor returned a few moments later, she was seated behind the desk just replacing the receiver. With a sound of annoyance, she supported her chin on her elbows.

"The florist doesn't have my six dozen daffodils."

"I'm sorry to hear that." Taylor placed her coffee on the desk.

"Well, you should be. It's your inn, and they are actually your daffodils."

"It's kind of you to think of me, B.J.," Taylor said amiably. "But don't you think six dozen is a bit extreme?"

"Very funny," she muttered and picked up her coffee cup. "You won't think it's such a joke when there aren't any flowers on the tables."

"So, order something besides daffodils."

"Do I look like a simpleton?" B.J. demanded. "He won't have anything in that quantity until next week. Some trouble at the greenhouse or something. Blast it!" She swallowed her coffee and scowled at the far wall.

"For heaven's sake, B.J., there must be a dozen florists in Burlington. Have them delivered." Taylor dismissed the matter of daffodils with an airy wave.

B.J. gave him an opened mouth look of astonishment. "Delivered from Burlington? Do you have any idea how

much those daffodils would cost?" Rising, she paced the
room while she considered her options. "I simply can't tolerate artificial flowers," she muttered while Taylor sipped his
coffee and watched her. "They're worse than no flowers at
all. I hate to do it," she said with a sigh. "It's bad enough
having to beg for her jelly, now I'm going to have to beg for
her flowers. There's absolutely nothing else I can do. She's
got the only garden in town that can handle it." Making a
complete circle of the room, B.J. plopped down behind the
desk again.

"Are you finished?"

"No," B.J. answered, picking up the phone. "I still have
to talk her out of them." Grimly, she set her teeth. "Wish me
luck."

Deciding all would be explained in due time, Taylor sat
back to watch. "Luck," he said agreeably and finished off his
coffee.

When B.J. had completed her conversation, he shook his
head in frank admiration. "That," he said as he toasted her
with his empty cup, "was the most blatant con job I've ever
witnessed."

"Subtlety doesn't work with Betty Jackson." Smug, B.J.
answered his toast, then rose. "I'm going to go pick up those
flowers before she changes her mind."

"I'll drive you," Taylor offered, taking her arm before she
reached the door.

"Oh, you needn't bother." The contact reminded her how
slight was her will when he touched her.

"It's no bother," he countered, leading her through the
inn's front door. "I feel I must see the woman who, how did
you put it? 'Raises flowers with an angel's touch.'"

"Did I say that?" B.J. struggled to prevent a smile.

"That was one of your milder compliments."

"Desperate circumstances call for desperate measures," B.J. claimed and slid into Taylor's Mercedes. "Besides, Miss Jackson does have an extraordinary garden. Her rosebush won a prize last year. Turn left here," she instructed as he came to a fork in the road. "You know, you should be grateful to me instead of making fun. If you'd had your way, we'd be eating up a healthy percentage of the inn's profits in delivery fees."

"My dear Miss Clark," Taylor drawled, "if there's one thing I can't deny, it's that you are a top flight manager. Of course, I'm also aware that a raise is in order."

"When I want a raise, I'll ask for one," B.J. snapped. As she gave her attention to the view out the side window, she missed Taylor's glance of speculation. She had not liked his use of her surname, nor had she liked being reminded again so soon of the status of their positions. He was her employer, and there was no escaping it. Closing her eyes, she chewed on her lower lip. The day had not run smoothly, perhaps that was why she had been so acutely annoyed over such a small thing. *And so rude,* she added to herself. Decidedly, it was her responsibility to offer the olive branch. Turning, she gave Taylor a radiant smile.

"What sort of raise?"

He laughed, and reached over to ruffle her hair. "What an odd one you are, B.J."

"Oh, I know," she agreed, wishing she could understand her own feelings. "I know. There's the house." She gestured as they approached. "Third from the corner."

They alighted from opposite sides of the car, but Taylor

took her arm as they swung through Betty Jackson's gate. This visit, B.J. decided, thinking of the silver blue Mercedes and Taylor's elegantly simple silk shirt, should keep Miss Jackson in news for six months. The doorbell was answered before it had stopped ringing.

"Hello, Miss Jackson," B.J. began and prepared to launch into her first thank you speech. She closed her mouth as she noticed Betty's attention was focused well over her head. "Oh, Miss Jackson, this is Taylor Reynolds, the owner of the inn. Taylor, Betty Jackson." B.J. made introductions as Betty simultaneously pulled her apron from her waist and metal clips from her hair.

"Miss Jackson." Taylor took her free hand as Betty held the apron and clips behind her back. "I've heard so much about your talents, I feel we're old friends." Blushing like a teenager, Betty was, for the first time in her sixty odd years, at a loss for words.

"We came by for the flowers," B.J. reminded her, fascinated by Betty's reaction.

"Flowers? Oh, yes, of course. Do come in." She ushered them into the house and into her living room, all the while keeping her hand behind her back.

"Charming," Taylor stated, gazing around at chintz and doilies. Turning, he gave Betty his easy smile. "I must tell you, Miss Jackson, we're very grateful to you for helping us out this way."

"It's nothing, nothing at all," Betty said, fluttering her hand with the words. "Please sit down. I'll fix us a nice pot of tea. Come along, B.J." She scurried from the room, leaving B.J. no choice but to follow. Safely enclosed in the kitchen, Betty began to move at lightning speed. "Why didn't you tell me you were bringing *him?*" she demanded, flourishing a teapot.

"Well, I didn't know until . . ."

"Goodness, you could have given a person a chance to comb her hair and put her face on." Betty dug out her best china cups and inspected them for chips.

B.J. bit the inside of her lip to keep a grin from forming. "I'm sorry, Betty. I had no idea Mr. Reynolds was coming until I was leaving."

"Never mind, never mind." Betty brushed aside the apology with the back of her hand. "You did bring him after all. I'm positively dying to talk to him. Why don't you run out and get your flowers now before tea?" She produced a pair of scissors. "Just pick whatever you need." She dismissed B.J. with a hasty wave. "Take your time."

After the back door had closed firmly in her face, B.J. stood for a moment, torn between amusement and exasperation before heading toward Betty's early spring blooms.

When she re-entered the kitchen about twenty minutes later, armed with a selection of daffodils and early tulips, she could hear Betty laughing. Carefully placing her bouquet on the kitchen table, she walked into the living room.

Like old friends, Taylor and Betty sat on the sofa, a rose patterned teapot nestled cozily on the low table. "Oh, Taylor," Betty said, still laughing, "you tell such stories! What's a poor woman to believe?"

B.J. looked on in stunned silence. She was certain Betty Jackson had not flirted this outrageously in thirty years. And, she noted with a shake of her head, Taylor was flirting with equal aplomb. As Betty leaned forward to pour more tea, Taylor glanced over her head and shot B.J. a grin so endearingly boyish it took all her willpower not to cross the room and throw herself into his arms. He was, she thought with a curious catch in her heart, impossible. No female under a hundred and two was safe around him. Unable to do otherwise, B.J. answered his grin.

"Miss Jackson," B.J. said, carefully readjusting her features. "Your garden is lovely as always."

"Thanks, B.J. I really do work hard on it. Did you get all that you wanted?"

"Yes, thank you. I don't know how I would have managed without you."

"Well." Betty sighed as she rose. "I'll just get a box for them."

Some fifteen minutes later, after Betty had exacted a promise from Taylor that he drop by again, B.J. was in the Mercedes beside him. In the back seat were the assortment of flowers and half a dozen jars of jelly as a gift to Taylor.

"You," B.J. began in the sternest voice she could manage, "should be ashamed."

"I?" Taylor countered, giving her an innocent look. "Whatever for?"

"You know very well what for," B.J. said severely. "You very near had Betty swooning."

"I can't help it if I'm charming and irresistible."

"Oh, yes, you can," she disagreed. "You were deliberately charming and irresistible. If you'd said the word, she'd have ripped up her prize rosebush and planted it at the inn's front door."

"Nonsense," Taylor claimed. "We were simply having an enjoyable conversation."

"Did you enjoy the camomile tea?" B.J. asked sweetly.

"Very refreshing. You didn't get a cup, did you?"

"No." B.J. sniffed and folded her arms across her chest. "I wasn't invited."

"Ah, now I see." Taylor sighed as he pulled in front of the inn. "You're jealous."

"Jealous?" B.J. gave a quick laugh and brushed the dust from her skirt. "Ridiculous."

"Yes, I see it now," he said smugly, repressing a grin. "Silly girl!" With this, he stopped the car, and turning to B.J. lowered his smiling mouth to hers. Imperceptibly, his lips lost their teasing quality, becoming warm and soft on her skin. B.J.'s playful struggles ceased, and she stiffened in his arms.

"Taylor, let me go." She found it was more difficult now to catch her breath than it had been when she had been laughing. A small moan escaped her as his lips trailed to her jawline. "No," she managed, and putting her fingers to his lips, pushed him away. He studied her, his eyes dark and full of knowledge as she fought to control her breathing. "Taylor, I think it's time we established some rules."

"I don't believe in rules between men and women, and I don't follow any." He said this with such blatant arrogance, B.J. was shocked into silence. "I'll let you go now, because I don't think it's wise to make love with you in broad daylight in the front seat of my car. However, the time will come when the circumstances will be more agreeable."

B.J. narrowed her eyes and found her voice. "You seriously don't think I'll agree to that, do you?"

"When the time comes, B.J.," he said with maddening confidence, "you'll be happy to agree."

"Fat chance," she said as she struggled out of the car. "We're never going to agree about anything." Slamming the door gave her some satisfaction.

As she ran up the front steps and into the inn, B.J. decided she never wanted to hear the word *businesslike* again.

CHAPTER 6

B.J. was standing on the wide lawn enjoying the warmth of the spring sun. She had decided to avoid Taylor Reynolds as much as possible and concentrate on her own myriad responsibilities. Unfortunately, that had not been as easy as she had hoped: she had been forced to deal with him on a daily business basis.

Though the inn was relatively quiet, B.J. knew that in a month's time, when the summer season began, the pace would pick up. Her gaze traveled the length and height of the inn, admiring the mellowed bricks serene against the dark pines, the windows blinking in the bright spring sun. On the back porch, two guests were engaged in an undemanding game of checkers. From where she was standing, B.J. could barely hear the murmur of their conversation without hearing the words.

All too soon, this peace would be shattered by children shouting to each other as they raced across the lawn, by the purr of motorboats as they sped past the inn. Yet, somehow, the inn never lost its informal air of tranquility. Here, she mused, the shade was for relaxing, the grass for bare feet, the drifting snow for sleigh rides and snow men. Elegance had its place, B.J. acknowledged, but the Lakeside Inn had a charm of its own. *And Taylor Reynolds was not going to destroy it.*

You've only got ten days left. He leaves in ten days, she reminded herself. She sighed.

The sigh was as much for herself as for the inn's fate. *I wish he'd never come. I wish I'd never laid eyes on him.* Scowling, she headed back toward the inn.

"That face is liable to turn guests away." Startled, B.J. stared at Taylor as he blocked the doorway. "I think it's best for business if I get you away from here for a while." Stepping forward, he took her hand and pulled her across the lawn.

"I have to go in," she protested. "I . . . I have to phone the linen supplier."

"It'll keep. Your duties as guide come first."

"Guide? Would you please let me go? Where are we going?"

"Yes. No. And we're going to enjoy one of Elsie's famous picnics." Taylor held up the hamper he held in his free hand. "I want to see the lake."

"You don't need me for that. You can't miss it. It's the huge body of water you come to at the end of the path."

"B.J." He stopped, turning directly to face her. "For two days you've avoided me. Now, I'm well aware we have differences in our outlook on the inn."

"I hardly see . . ."

"Be quiet," he said pleasantly. "I am willing to give you my word that no major alterations will be started without your being notified. Whatever changes I decide upon will be brought to your attention before any formal plans are drawn up." His tone was brisk and businesslike even while he ignored her attempts to free her hand. "I respect your dedication and loyalty to the inn." His tone was coolly professional.

"But . . ."

"However," he cut her off easily, "I do own the inn, and you are in my employ. As of now you have a couple hours off. How do you feel about picnics?"

"Well, I . . ."

"Good. I'm fond of them myself." Smiling easily, he began to move down the well-worn path through the woods.

The undergrowth was still soft from winter. Beneath the filtered sunlight wild flowers were a multicolored carpet, bright against their brown background of decaying leaves. Squirrels darted up the trunks of trees where birds had already begun to nest.

"Do you always shanghai your companions?" B.J. demanded, angry and breathless at keeping pace with Taylor's long strides.

"Only when necessary," he replied curtly.

The path widened, then spread into the grassy banks of the lake. Taylor stopped, surveying the wide expanse of lake with the same absorption that B.J. had observed in him earlier.

The lake was unruffled, reflecting a few clouds above it. The mountains on its opposite edge were gently formed. They were not like the awesome, demanding peaks of the

West, but sedate and well-behaved. The silence was broken once by the quick call of a chickadee, then lay again like a calming hand on the air.

"Very nice," Taylor said at length, and B.J. listened for but heard no condescension in his tone. "A very lovely view. Do you ever swim here?"

"Only since I was two," B.J. answered, groping for a friendly lightness. She wished he would not continue to hold her hand as if he had done so a thousand times before, wished hers did not fit into his as if molded for the purpose.

"Of course." He turned his head, switching his study from the lake to her face. "I'd forgotten, you were born here, weren't you?"

"I've always lived in Lakeside." Deciding that setting up the picnic things was the most expedient way to break the hand contact, B.J. took the hamper and began spreading Elsie's neatly folded cloth. "My parents moved to New York when I was nineteen, and I lived there for almost a year. I transferred colleges at mid-term and enrolled back here."

"How did you find New York?" Taylor dropped down beside her, and B.J. glimpsed at the bronzed forearms which his casually rolled up sleeves revealed.

"Noisy and confusing," she replied, frowning at a platter of crisp golden chicken. "I don't like to be confused."

"Don't you?" His swift grin appeared at her frown. With one deft motion, he pulled out the ribbon which held her hair neatly behind her back. "It makes you look like my adolescent niece." He tossed it carelessly out of reach as B.J. grabbed for it.

"You are an abominably rude man." Pushing back her newly liberated hair, she glared into his smiling face.

"Often," he agreed and lifted a bottle of wine from the hamper. He drew the cork with the ease of experience while B.J. fumed in silence. "How did you happen to become manager of the Lakeside Inn?"

The question took her off guard. For a moment she watched him pour the inn's best Chablis into Dixie cups. "I sort of gravitated to it." Accepting the offered cup, she met the directness of his gaze and realized he would not be content with the vagueness of her answer. "I worked summers at the inn when I was in high school, sort of filling in here and there at first. By the time I graduated, I was assistant manager. Anyway," she continued, "when I moved back from New York, I just slid back in. Mr. Blakely, the old manager, recommended me when he retired, and I took over." She shrugged and bit into a drumstick.

"Between your education and your dedication to your career, where did you find the time to learn how to swing a bat like Reggie Jackson?"

"I managed to find a few moments to spare. When I was fourteen," she explained, grinning at the memory, "I was madly in love with this older man. He was seventeen." She gave Taylor a sober nod. "Baseball oozed from his pores, so I enthusiastically took up the game. He'd call me shortstop, and my toes would tingle."

Taylor's burst of laughter startled a slumbering blue jay who streaked across the sky with an indignant chatter. "B.J., I don't know anyone like you. What happened to the toe tingler?"

Overcome by the pleasure his laughter had brought her, she fumbled for the thread of the conversation. "Oh . . . he . . . uh . . . he's got two kids and sells used cars."

"His loss," Taylor commented, cutting a thin wedge of cheese.

B.J. broke a fragrant hunk of Elsie's fresh bread and held it out to Taylor for a slice of cheese. "Do you spend much time at your other hotels?" she asked, uncomfortable at the personal tone the conversation seemed to be taking.

"Depends." His eyes roamed over her as she sat cross-legged on the grass, her soft hair tumbling over her shoulders, her lips slightly parted.

"Depends?" she inquired. He stared a moment at her and she fought not to fidget under his encompassing gaze.

"I make certain my managers are competent." He broke the silence with a smile. "If there's a specific problem, I'll deal with it. First, I like to get the feel of a new acquisition, determine if a policy change is warranted."

"But you work out of New York?" The trend of the conversation was much more to her liking. The tension eased from her shoulders.

"Primarily. I've seen fields in Kansas that looked less like wheat than your hair." He captured a generous handful. B.J. swallowed in surprise. "The fog in London isn't nearly as gray or mysterious as your eyes."

B.J. swallowed and moistened her lips. "Your chicken's getting cold."

His grin flashed at her feeble defense but his hand relinquished its possession of her hair. "It's supposed to be cold." Lifting the wine bottle, Taylor refilled his cup. "Oh, by the way, there was a call for you."

B.J. took a sip of Chablis with apparent calm. "Oh, was it important?"

"Mmm." Taylor moved his shoulders under his cream

colored tailored shirt. "A Howard Beall. He said you had his number."

"Oh." B.J. frowned, recalling it was about time for her duty date with Betty Jackson's nephew. Her sigh was automatic.

"My, you simply reek of enthusiasm."

Taylor's dry comment brought on a smile and a shrug. "He's just a man I know."

Taylor contented himself with a slight raising of his brow.

The sky was now an azure arch, without even a puff of cloud to spoil its perfection. Replete and relaxed, B.J. rolled over on her back to enjoy it. The grass was soft and smelled fresh. Overhead, the maple offered a half-shade. Its black branches were touched with young, tender leaves. Through the spreading cluster of trees, dogwoods bloomed white.

"In the winter," she murmured, half to herself, "it's absolutely still here after a snowfall. Everything's white. Snow hangs and drips from the trees and carpets the earth. The lake's like a mirror. The ice is as clear as rainwater. You almost forget there's any place else in the world, or that spring will come. Do you ski, Taylor?" She rolled over on her stomach, her elbows supporting her head to smile at him, all animosity forgotten.

"I've been known to." He returned her smile, studying the soft, drowsy face, rosy from the sun and the unaccustomed wine.

"The skiing's marvelous here." She tossed back her hair with a quick movement of her shoulders. "Snow skiing's so much more exciting than water skiing, I think. The food at the inn brings the skiing crowd. There's nothing like Elsie's stew after a day on the slopes." Plucking a blade of grass, she twirled it idly.

Taylor moved to lie down beside her. She was too content to be alarmed at his proximity.

"Dumplings?" he inquired, and she grinned down into his face.

"Of course. Hot buttered rum or steaming chocolate."

"I'm beginning to regret I missed the season."

"Well, you're in time for strawberry shortcake," she offered in consolation. "And the fishing's good year round."

"I've always favored more active sports." His finger ran absently up her arm, and B.J. tried hard to ignore the pleasure it gave her.

"Well." Her brow creased as she considered. "There's a good stable about fifteen miles from here, or boats for rent at the marina, or . . ."

"Those aren't the sports I had in mind." With a swift movement, he dislodged her elbows and brought her toppling onto his chest. "Are they the best you can do?" His arms held her firmly against him, but she was already captured by the fascination of his eyes.

"There's hiking," she murmured, unaware of the strange husky texture of her own voice.

"Hiking," Taylor murmured, before altering their positions in one fluid motion.

"Yes, hiking's very popular." She felt her consciousness drifting as she gazed up at him and struggled to retain some hold on lucidity. "And . . . and swimming."

"Mmm." Absently, his fingers traced the delicate line of her cheek.

"And there's . . . uh . . . there's camping. A lot of people like camping. We have a lot of parks." Her voice faltered as his thumb ran over her lips.

"Parks?" he repeated, prompting her.

"Yes, a number of parks, quite a number. The facilities are excellent for camping." She gave a small moan as his mouth lowered to tease the curve of her neck.

"Hunting?" Taylor asked conversationally as his lips traveled over her jawline to brush the corner of her mouth.

"I, yes. I think . . . what did you say?" B.J. closed her eyes on a sigh.

"I wondered about hunting," he murmured, kissing closed lids as his fingers slid under her sweater to trace her waist.

"There's bobcat in the mountains to the north."

"Fascinating." He rubbed his mouth gently over hers as his fingers trailed lightly up her flesh to the curve of her breast. "The chamber of commerce would be proud of you." Lazily, his thumb ran over the satin swell. Pleasure became a need as warmth spread from her stomach to tremble in her veins and cloud her brain.

"Taylor." Unable to bring her voice above a whisper, her hand sought the thick mass of his hair. "Kiss me."

"In a minute," he murmured, obviously enjoying the taste of her neck, until with devastating leisure, he moved his mouth to hers.

Trembling with a new, unfamiliar hunger, B.J. pulled him closer until his mouth was no longer teasing but avid on hers. Warmth exploded into fire. His tongue was searching, demanding all of her sweetness, his body as taut as hers was fluid. He took possession of her curves with authority, molding them with firm, strong hands. His mouth no longer roamed from hers but remained to devour what she offered. The heat grew to an almost unbearable intensity, her soul melting in it to flow into his. For a moment, she was lost in the discovery of merging, feeling it with as much clarity as she felt his hands and mouth. Soaring freedom and the chains of need were interchangeable. As time ceased to flow, she plunged deeper and deeper into the all-enveloping present.

His hands took more, all gentleness abandoned. It flashed across the mists in her brain that beneath the control lay a primitive, volatile force from which she had no defense. She struggled weakly. Her protests were feeble murmurs against the demands of his mouth. Feeling her tense, Taylor lifted his head, and she felt the unsteady rhythm of his breathing on her face.

"Please, let me go." Hating the weak timbre of her own voice, she sank her teeth into the lip still tender from his.

"Why should I do that?" Temper and passion threatened his control. She knew she had neither the strength nor the will to resist him if he chose to take.

"Please."

It seemed an eternity that he studied her, searching the smoky depths of her eyes. She watched the anger fade from his eyes as he took in the fair hair spread across the grass, the vulnerable, soft mouth. Finally, he released her with a brief, muttered oath.

"It appears," he began as she scrambled to sit up, "that pigtails suit you more than I realized." He took out a cigarette and lit it deliberately. "Virginity is a rare commodity in a woman your age."

Color flooded her cheeks as B.J. began to pack up the remains of the picnic. "I hardly see what business that is of yours."

"It doesn't matter," he countered easily and she cursed him

for his ability to retain his composure so effortlessly while her entire body still throbbed with need. "It will simply take a bit more time." At her uncomprehending stare, he smiled and folded the cloth. "I told you I always win, B.J. You'd best get used to it."

"You listen to me." Storming, she sprang to her feet. "I am not about to be added to your list. This was . . . this was . . ." Her hands spread out to sweep away the incident while her brain searched for the proper words.

"Just the beginning," he supplied. Rising with the hamper, he captured her arm in a firm grip. "We haven't nearly finished yet. I wouldn't argue at the moment, B.J.," he warned as she began to sputter. "I might decide to take what you so recently offered here and now, rather than giving you some time."

"You are the most arrogant—" she began. Her voice sounded hopelessly childish even to her own ears.

"That's enough for now, B.J." Taylor interrupted pleasantly. "There's no point saying anything you might regret." He leaned down and kissed her firmly before helping her to her feet. With an easy swing, he reached for the hamper. B.J. was too dazed to do anything but meekly follow him as he led the way toward the homeward wooded path.

CHAPTER 7

Once back at the inn, B.J. wanted nothing more than to disengage her arm from Taylor's grasp and find a dark, quiet hole in which to hide. She knew all too well that she had responded completely to Taylor's demands. Moreover, she knew she had made demands of her own. She was confused by her own reactions. Never before had she had difficulty in avoiding or controlling a romantic interlude, but she was forced to admit that from the moment Taylor had touched her, her mind had ceased to function.

Biology, she concluded, darting Taylor a sidelong glance as they approached the skirting porch. It was simply a matter of basic biology. Any woman would naturally be attracted to a man like Taylor Reynolds. He has a way of looking at you, B.J. mused, that makes your mind go fuzzy, then blank. He has a way of touching you that makes you feel as though you never had been touched before. He's nothing like any other man I've ever known. And *I asked him to kiss me*. Color rose to her cheeks. *I actually asked him to kiss me*. It must have been the wine.

Soothed by this excuse, B.J. turned to Taylor as they entered the side door. "I'll take the basket back to the kitchen. Do you need me for anything else?"

"That's an intriguing question," he drawled.

B.J. shot him a quelling glance. "I have to get back to work now," she said briskly. "Now, if you'll excuse me?"

B.J.'s dignified exit was aborted by a flurry of activity in the lobby. Curiosity outweighing pride, she allowed Taylor to lead her toward the source.

A tall, svelte brunette stood by the desk, surrounded by a clutter of shocking pink luggage. Her pencil-slim form was draped in a teal blue suit of raw silk. The scent of gardenias floated toward B.J.

"If you'll see to my luggage, darling, and tell Mr. Reynolds I'm here, I'd be very grateful." She addressed these requests in a low, husky voice to Eddie who stood gaping beside her.

"Hello, Darla. What are you doing here?"

At Taylor's voice, the dark head turned. B.J. noted the eyes were nearly the same shade as the exquisite suit.

"Taylor." Impossibly graceful on four-inch heels, Darla glided across the lobby to embrace Taylor warmly. "I'm just back from checking on the job in Chicago. I knew you'd want me to look this little place over and give you my ideas."

Disengaging himself, Taylor met Darla's glowing smile with an ironic smile. "How considerate of you. B.J. Clark, Darla Trainor. Darla does the majority of my decorating, B.J. manages the inn."

"How interesting." Darla gave B.J.'s sweater and jeans a brief, despairing glance and patted her own perfectly styled hair. "From what I've seen so far, my work is certainly cut out for me." With a barely perceptible shudder, Darla surveyed the lobby's hand hooked rugs and Tiffany lamps.

"We've had no complaints on our decor." B.J. leaped to the inn's defense.

"Well." She was given a small, pitying smile from deeply colored lips. "It's certainly quaint, isn't it? Rather sweet for Ma and Pa Kettle. You'll have to let me know, Taylor, if you plan to enlarge this room." Transferring her attention, Darla's expression softened and warmed. "But, of course, red's always an eye-catcher. Perhaps red velvet drapes and carpeting."

B.J.'s eyes darkened to flint. "Why don't you take your red velvet drapes and . . ."

"I believe we'll discuss this later," Taylor said diplomatically, tightening his hold on B.J.'s arm. Struggling to prevent herself from crying with the pain, B.J. found argument impossible.

"I'm sure you'd like to get settled in," she forced out between clenched lips.

"Of course." Darla viewed B.J.'s brief outburst with a fluttering of heavy lashes. "Come up for a drink, Taylor. I assume this place has room service."

"Of course. Have a couple of martinis sent up to Miss Trainor's room," Taylor said to Eddie. "What's your room number, Darla?"

"I don't believe I have one yet." Again using her extensive lashes to advantage, Darla turned to a still dazed Eddie. "There seems to be a small communication problem."

"Give Miss Trainor 314, Eddie, and see to her bags." The

sharp command in B.J.'s voice snapped Eddie's daydream, and he scurried to comply. "I hope you find it suitable." B.J. turned her best managerial smile on her new and unwelcome guest. "Please let me know if there's anything you need. I'll see to your drinks."

Taylor's hand held her still another moment. "I'll speak with you later."

"Delighted," B.J. turned, feeling the circulation slowly returning to her arm as he released it. "I'll wait to be summoned at your convenience, Mr. Reynolds. Welcome to the Lakeside Inn, Miss Trainor. Have a nice stay."

*   *   *

It was a simple matter to avoid a private meeting with Taylor as he spent the remainder of the day in Darla Trainor's company. They were closeted in 314 for what seemed to B.J. a lifetime. To boost her ego B.J. decided to phone Howard. They arranged a date for the following evening. *Well, at least Howard doesn't closet himself downing martinis with Miss Glamorpuss,* she thought. Somehow this knowledge was not as comforting as it should have been.

*   *   *

The dress B.J. had chosen for dinner was black and sleek. It molded her subtle curves with a lover's intimacy, falling in a midnight pool around her ankles, with a gentle caress for thighs and calves. Small pearl buttons ran from her throat to her waist. The high, puritanical neckline accentuated her firm, small breasts and emphasized her slender neck. She left her hair loose to float in a pale cloud around her shoulders. She touched her scent behind her ears before leaving her room to descend to the dining room.

The candle-lit, corner table where Taylor sat with Darla was intimate and secluded. Glancing in their direction, B.J. could not suppress a scowl. There was no denying that they were a handsome couple. *Made for each other,* she thought bitterly. Darla's vermilion sheath plunged to reveal the creamy swell of her breasts. Taylor's dark suit was impeccably cut. In spite of herself, B.J.'s eyes were drawn to the breadth of his shoulders. She drew in her breath sharply, recalling the feel of his corded muscles now expertly concealed by the fine tailoring, and shivered involuntarily.

Taylor glanced over, his expression indefinable as he made a slow, exacting survey, his eyes lingering on the gentle curves draped in the simplicity of unrelieved black. Though her skin grew warm, B.J. met his eyes levelly. Examination complete, Taylor lifted one brow, whether in approval or disapproval, she could not determine. With a brief gesture of his hand, he ordered B.J. to his table.

Fuming at the casual insolence of the command, she schooled her features into tranquility. She wove her way through the room, deliberately stopping to speak with diners along the route.

"Good evening." B.J. greeted Taylor and his companion with a professional smile. "I hope you're enjoying your meal."

"As always, the food is excellent." Taylor rose and pulled up a chair expectantly. His eyes narrowed in challenge. It was not the moment to cross him, B.J. decided.

"I trust your room pleases you, Miss Trainor," she said pleasantly, as she sat down.

"It's adequate, Miss Clark. Though I must say, I was rather taken aback by the decorating scheme."

"You'll join us for a drink," Taylor stated, motioning a waitress over without waiting for B.J.'s consent. She glared at him for a moment before she glanced up at Dot.

"My usual," she said, not feeling obliged to explain this was a straight ginger ale. She turned back to Darla, coating her voice with polite interest. "And what is it about the decorating which took you aback, Miss Trainor?"

"Really, Miss Clark," Darla began as though the matter was obvious. "The entire room is *provincial,* don't you agree? There are some rather nice pieces, I admit, if one admires American antiques, but Taylor and I have always preferred a modern approach."

Fighting her annoyance and an all too unwanted spasm of jealousy, B.J. said sarcastically, "I see. Perhaps you'd care to elaborate on the modern approach for this country bumpkin. I so seldom get beyond the local five and dime."

Dot set B.J.'s drink in front of her and scurried away, recognizing storm warnings.

"In the first place," Darla began, immune to her frosty gray eyes, "the lighting is all wrong. Those glass domed lamps with pull chains are archaic. You need wall to wall carpeting. The hand hooked rugs and faded Persians will have to go. And the bathroom . . . Well, needless to say, the bathroom is hopeless." With a sigh, Darla lifted her champagne cocktail and sipped. "Footed tubs belong in period comedies, not in hotels."

B.J. chewed on a piece of ice to keep her temper from boiling over. "Our guests have always found a certain charm in the baths."

"Perhaps," Darla acknowledged with a depreciating shrug. "But with the proper changes and improvements, you'll be catering to a different type of clientele." She drew out a slim cigarette, giving Taylor a brief flutter of lashes as he lit it.

"Do you have any objections to footed tubs and pull chains?" B.J. asked him, voice precise, eyes stormy.

"They suit the present atmosphere of the inn." His voice was equally precise, his eyes cool.

"Maybe I've got a few fresh ideas for you, Miss Trainor, if and when you pull out your little book of samples." Setting down her glass, B.J. watched from the corner of her eye as Taylor flicked his lighter at the end of his cigarette. "Mirrors should be good on the ceiling in particular. Just a light touch of decadence. Lots of chrome and glass to give the rooms that spacious, symmetrical look. And white, plenty of white as well, perhaps with fuchsia accents. The bed, of course," she continued with fresh inspiration. "A large circular bed with fuchsia coverings. Do you like fuchsia, Taylor?"

"I don't believe I asked for your advice on decorating tonight, B.J." Taylor drew casually on his cigarette. The smoke traveled in a thin column toward the exposed beam ceiling.

"I'm afraid, Miss Clark," Darla commented, spurred on by Taylor's mild reproof, "that your taste runs to the vulgar."

"Oh really?" B.J. blinked as if surprised. "I suppose that's what comes from being a country bumpkin."

"I'm sure whatever I ultimately decide will suit you, Taylor." Darla placed a hand with easy familiarity on his as B.J.'s temper rose. "But it will take a bit longer than usual as the alterations will be so drastic."

"Take all the time you need." B.J. gestured with magnanimity as she rose. "In the meantime, keep your hands off my footed tubs."

The dignity of her exit was spoiled by a near collision with Dot who had been discreetly eavesdropping.

"An order of arsenic for table three . . . on the house," B.J. muttered, skirting around the wide-eyed waitress and sweeping from the room.

B.J.'s intention to stalk straight to her room and cool off was undone by a series of small, irritating jobs. It was after ten when the last had been dealt with and she was able to shut the door to her room and give vent to suppressed temper.

"Country bumpkin," she hissed through clenched teeth. Her eyes rested on a William and Mary table. *She'd* probably prefer plastic cubes in black and white checks. Her eyes moved from the dower chest to the schoolmaster's desk and on to the Bostonian rocker and wing chair in softly faded green. Each room of the inn was distinctive, with its own personality, its own treasures. Closing her eyes, B.J. could clearly see the room which Darla now occupied, the delicate pastel of the flowered wallpaper, the fresh gleam of the oak floor, the charm of the narrow, cushioned window seat. The pride of that particular room was an antique highboy in walnut with exquisite teardrop pulls. B.J. could not recall an occasion when a guest who had stayed in that room had done other than praise its comforts, its quiet charm, its timeless grace.

Darla Trainor, B.J. vowed, *is not getting her hands on my inn.* Walking to the mirrored bureau, she stared at her reflection, then let out a long disgusted breath. She's got a face that belongs on a cameo, and mine belongs on a milk commercial, she thought. Picking up her brush, she told herself that these reflections had nothing to do with the problem at hand.

How am I going to convince Taylor that the inn should stay as it is when she's already rattling off changes and giving him intimate smiles? I suppose, B.J. continued, giving her reflection a fierce scowl, *she's not just his decorator.* The kiss she gave him when she arrived wasn't very businesslike. I don't believe for a moment they spent all that time in her room discussing fabrics.

That's no concern of mine, she decided with a strong tug of the brush. But if they think they're going to start steaming off wallpaper without a fight, they're in for a surprise. She put down her brush and turned just as the door swung open to admit Taylor.

Before her astonished eyes, he closed and locked her door before placing the key in his pocket. As he advanced toward her, she could see that he was obviously angry.

"Being the owner doesn't give you the right to use the master key without cause," she snapped, as she backed against the bureau.

"It appears I haven't made myself clear." Taylor's voice was deceptively gentle. "You have, for the time being, a free hand in the day to day managing of this inn. I have not, nor do I desire to infringe upon your routine. However—"

He took a step closer. B.J. discovered her hands were clutching the edge of the bureau in a desperate grip. "All orders, all decisions, all changes in policy come from me, and only me."

"Of all the dictatorial . . ."

"This isn't a debate," he cut her off sharply. "I won't have you issuing orders over my head. Darla is employed by me. I tell her what to do, and when to do it."

"But surely you don't want her to toss out all these lovely old pieces for gooseneck floor lamps and modular shelving. The server in the dining room is Hepplewhite. There're two Chippendale pieces in your room alone, and . . ."

The hand which moved from the back of her neck to circle her throat halted B.J.'s furious rush of words. She became uncomfortably aware of the strength of his fingers. No pressure was applied, but the meaning was all too evident.

"Whatever I want Darla to do is my concern, and my concern only." He tightened his grip, bringing her closer. Now B.J. read the extent of his anger in his eyes. Like two dark suns, they burned into hers. "Keep your opinions to yourself until I ask for them. Don't interfere or you'll pay for it. Is that understood?"

"I understand perfectly. Your relationship with Miss Trainor has overruled any opinion of mine."

"That—" his brow lifted "—is none of your business."

"Whatever concerns the inn is my business," B.J. countered. "I offered you my resignation once, and you refused it. If you want to get rid of me now, you'll have to fire me."

"Don't tempt me." He lowered his hand and rested his fingers on the top button of her bodice. "I have my reasons for wanting you around, but don't push it. I agreed to keep you abreast of any alterations I decide on, but if you persist in being rude to others in my employ, you'll be out on your ear."

"I can't see that Darla Trainor needs protection from me," B.J. remarked resentfully.

"Don't you?" His temper appeared to drift toward amusement as he scanned her face. "A couple of centuries ago, you'd have been burned at the stake for looking as you do at this moment. Hell smoke in your eyes, your mouth soft and defiant, all that pale hair tumbling over a black dress." Deftly, his fingers undid the top button and moved down to the next as his eyes kept hers a prisoner. "That dress is just puritanical enough to be seductive. Was it accident or design that you wore it tonight?"

With casual ease, he unloosed half the range of buttons, continuing his progress as his gaze remained fixed on hers.

"I don't know what you mean." Yet her traitorous feet refused to walk away. B.J. found herself powerless to move. "I want . . . I want you to go."

"Liar," he accused quietly, his hands slipping inside the opened front of her dress. His fingers traced lightly over her skin. "Tell me again you want me to go." His hands rose, his thumbs moving gently under the curve of her breasts. The room began to sway like the deck of a ship.

"I want you to go." Her voice was husky, her lids felt heavy with a tantalizing languor.

"Your body contradicts you, B.J." His hands claimed her breasts briefly before sliding to the smooth skin of her back. He brought her hard against him. "You want me just as much as I want you." His mouth lowered to prove his point.

Surrendering to a force beyond her understanding, B.J. rested in his arms. His demands increased with her submission, his mouth drawing the response she had no strength to withhold. While her mind screamed no, her arms drew him closer. The warnings to run were lost as his lips moved to the vulnerable skin of her throat, teasing the softness with tongue and teeth. She could only cling and fret for more. Mouth returned to mouth. While his hands roamed, arousing fresh pleasure, hers slipped under his jacket.

With a suddenness that gave her no time for defense, no thought of resistance, he fell deep into her heart. He claimed its untouched regions with the deftness of a seasoned explorer. The emotion brought B.J. to a spinning ecstasy which vied with a crushing, hopeless despair. To love him was certain disaster, to need him, undeniable misery, to be in his arms, both the darkness and the light. Trapped in the cage of her own desire, she would never find escape.

Helpless to do other than answer the hunger of his mouth, submit to the caressing journey of his hands, she felt the sting of emptiness behind her closed lids. Her arms pulled him closer to avert the insidious chill of reason.

"Admit it," he demanded, his lips moving again to savage her throat. "Admit you want me. Tell me you want me to stay."

"Yes, I want you." The words trembled on a sob as she buried her face in his shoulder. "Yes, I want you to stay."

She felt him stiffen and burrowed deeper until his hand forced her face to his. Her eyes were luminous, conquering the darkness with the glimmer of unshed tears. Her mouth was soft and tremulous as she fought the need to throw herself into his arms and weep out her newly discovered love. For eternity, he stared, and she watched without comprehension as his features hardened with fresh temper. When he spoke, however, his voice was calm and composed and struck like a fist on the jaw.

"It appears we've gotten away from the purpose of this meeting." Stepping away, his hands retreated to his pockets. "I believe I've made my wishes clear."

She shook her head in confusion. As her hand lifted to her tousled hair, the opening of her dress shifted in innocent suggestion over creamy skin. "Taylor, I . . ."

"Tomorrow—" she shivered as the coolness of his voice sapped the warmth from her skin "—I expect you to give Miss Trainor your complete cooperation, and your courtesy. Regardless of your disagreement, she is a guest of the inn and shall be treated as such."

"Of course." The hated tears began to flow as pain and rejection washed over her. "Miss Trainor shall be given every consideration." She sniffed, brushed at tears and continued with dignity. "You have my word."

"Your word!" Taylor muttered, taking a step toward her. B.J. streaked to the bath and locked the door.

"Go away!" No longer able to control the sobs, one small fist pounded impotently against the panel. "Go away and leave me alone. I gave you my promise, now I'm off duty."

"B.J., open this door."

She recognized both anger and exasperation in his tone and wept more desperately. "No, go away! Go keep Miss Perfect company and let me alone. Your orders will be carried out to the letter. Just go. I don't have to answer to you until morning."

Taylor's swearing and storming around the room were quite audible, though to B.J. his muttered oaths and comments made little sense. Finally, the bedroom door slammed with dangerous force. In an undignified huddle on the tiled floor, B.J. wept until she thought her heart would break.

CHAPTER 8

W ell, you did it again, didn't you?" B.J. stared at her reflection as the morning sun shone in without mercy.
You made a total fool of yourself. With a weary sigh, she
ran a hand through her hair before turning her back on the
accusing face in the mirror. *How could I have known I'd fall
in love with him?* she argued as she buttoned a pale green
cap-sleeved blouse. *I didn't plan it. I didn't want it.*

"Blast," she muttered and pulled on a matching skirt. *How
can I control the way he makes me feel? The minute he puts
his hands on me, my brain dissolves. To think that I would
have let him stay last night knowing all he wanted from me
was a quick affair! How could I be so stupid? And then,* she
added, shame warring with injured pride, *he didn't want me
after all. I suppose he remembered Darla. Why should he
waste his time with me when she's available?*

The next ten minutes were spent in fierce self-flagellation
as B.J. secured her hair in a roll at the base of her neck. These
tasks completed, she squared her shoulders and went out to
meet whatever task the day brought.

A casual question to Eddie informed her Taylor was already closeted in the office, and Darla Trainor had not yet risen. B.J. was determined to avoid them both and succeeded throughout the morning.

The lunch hour found her in the lounge, conducting an inventory on the bar stock. The room was quiet, removed from the luncheon clatter. She found the monotony soothing on her nerves.

"So, this is the lounge."

The intrusion of the silky voice jolted B.J.'s calm absorption. She whirled around, knocking bottles of liquor together.

Darla glided into the room looking elegantly business-like in an oatmeal colored three piece suit, a pad and pencil in perfectly manicured hands. She surveyed the cluster of white clothed tables, the postage stamp dance floor, the vintage upright Steinway. Flicking a finger down the muted glow of knotty pine paneling, she advanced to the ancient oak bar.

"How incredibly drab."

"Thank you," B.J. returned in her most courteous voice before she turned to replace a bottle on the mirrored shelves.

"Fix me a sweet vermouth," Darla ordered, sliding gracefully onto a stool and dropping her pad on the bar's surface.

B.J.'s mouth opened, furious retorts trembling on her tongue. Recalling her promise to Taylor, she clamped it shut and turned to comply.

"You must remember, Miss Clark," Darla's triumphant smile made B.J.'s hand itch to connect with ivory skin, "I'm merely doing my job. There's nothing personal in my observations."

Attempting to overcome her instinctive dislike, B.J. conceded. "Perhaps that's true. But, I have a very personal feeling about the Lakeside Inn. It's more home than a place of business to me." She set the glass of vermouth at Darla's fingertips before turning back to count bottles.

"Yes, Taylor told me you're quite attached to this little place. He found it amusing."

"Did he?" Feeling her hand tremble, B.J. gripped the shelves until her knuckles whitened. "What a strange sense of humor Taylor must have."

"Well, when one knows Taylor as I do, one knows what to expect." Their eyes met in the mirror. Darla smiled and lifted her glass. "He seems to think you're a valuable employee. What did he say . . . rather adept at making people comfortable." She smiled again and sipped. "Taylor demands value from his employees as well as obedience. At times, he uses unorthodox methods to keep them satisfied."

"I'm sure you'd know all about that." B.J. turned slowly, deciding wars should be fought face to face.

"Darling, Taylor and I are much more than business associates. And I, of course, understand his . . . ah . . . distractions with business."

"How magnanimous of you."

"It would never do to allow emotion to rule a relationship with Taylor Reynolds." Drawing a long, enameled nail over the rim of her glass, Darla gave B.J. a knowledgeable look. "He has no patience with emotional scenes or complications."

The memory of her weeping spell and Taylor's angry swearing played back in B.J.'s mind. "Perhaps we've at last reached a point of agreement."

"The first warning is always friendly, Miss Clark." Abruptly, Darla's voice hardened, throwing B.J. momentarily off balance. "Don't get too close. I don't allow anyone to infringe on my territory for long."

"Are we still talking about Taylor?" B.J. inquired. "Or did I lose part of this conversation?"

"Just take my advice." Leaning over the bar, Darla took B.J.'s arm in a surprisingly strong grip. "If you don't, the next place you manage will be a dog kennel."

"Take your hand off me." B.J.'s tone was soft and ominous, as the well-shaped nails dug into her flesh.

"As long as we understand each other." With a pleasant smile, Darla released B.J.'s arm and finished her drink.

"We understand each other very well." Taking the empty glass, B.J. placed it under the bar. "Bar's closed, Miss Trainor." She turned her back to recount already counted bottles.

"Ladies." B.J. stiffened and watched Taylor's reflection enter the room. "I hadn't expected to find you at the bar at this time of day." His voice was light, but the eyes which met B.J.'s in the glass did not smile.

"I've been wandering around making notes," Darla told him. B.J. watched her hand rub lightly over the back of his. "I'm afraid the only thing this lounge has going for it is its size. It's quite roomy, and you could easily fit in double the tables. But then, you'll have to let me know if you want to go moody, or modern. Actually, it might be an idea to add another lounge and do both, along the lines of your place in San Francisco."

His murmur was absent as he watched B.J. move to the next shelf.

"I thought I'd get a good look at the dining room if the luncheon crowd is gone." Darla's smile was coaxing. "Why don't you come with me, Taylor, and you can give me a clearer picture of what you have in mind?"

"Hmm?" His attention shifted, but the imperceptible frown remained. "No, I haven't decided on anything yet. Go ahead and take a look, I'll get back to you."

Well-arched brows rose at the dismissive tone, but Darla remained cool and composed. "Of course. I'll bring my notes to your office later and we can discuss it."

Her heels echoed faintly on the wooden floor. Her heavy perfume scent lingered in the air after she faded from view.

"Do you want a drink?" B.J. questioned, keeping her back to him and her voice remote.

"No, I want to talk to you."

With great care, B.J. avoided meeting his eyes in the mirror. She lifted a bottle, carefully examining the extent of its contents. "Haven't we covered everything?"

"No, we haven't covered everything. Turn around B.J., I'm not going to talk to your back."

"Very well, you're the boss." As she faced him, she caught a flash of anger in his eyes.

"Do you provoke me purposely, B.J., or is it just an accidental talent?"

"I have no idea. Take your choice." Suddenly, she was struck by inspiration. "Taylor," she said urgently, "I *would* like to talk to you. I'd like to talk to you about buying the inn. It can't be as important to you as it is to me. You could build a resort farther south that would suit you better. I could raise the money if you gave me some time."

"Don't be ridiculous." His abrupt words cooled her enthusiasm. "Where would you come up with the kind of money required to buy a property like this?"

"I don't know." She paced back and forth behind the bar. "Somewhere. I could get a loan for part of it, and you could hold a note for the rest. I've some money saved . . ."

"No." Standing, he skirted the bar and closed the distance between them. "I have no intention of selling."

"But, Taylor . . ."

"I said no. Drop it."

"Why are you being so stubborn? You won't even consider changing your mind? I might even be able to come up with a good offer if you gave me time—" Her voice trailed off uncertainly.

"I said I wanted to *talk* to you. At the moment I don't care to discuss the inn or any part of it."

He gripped her arm to spin her around, connecting with the flesh tender from Darla's nails. B.J. gave a cry of pain and jerked away. Taylor loosened his hold immediately, and she fell into the shelves, knocking glasses in a crashing heap on the floor.

"What the devil's got into you?" he demanded as her hand went automatically to nurse her bruised arm. "I barely touched you. Listen, B.J., I'm not tolerating you jumping like a scared rabbit every time I get close. I haven't hurt you. Stop that!" He pulled her hand away, then stared in confusion at the marks on her arm. "Good Lord. I didn't . . . I'd swear I barely touched you." Astonished, his eyes lifted to hers, darkened with emotions she could not understand. For a moment, she merely stared back, fascinated by seeing his habitual assurance rattled.

"No, I did it before." Dropping her eyes, B.J. busied

herself by resecuring the pins in her hair. "It's just a bit sore. You startled me when you grabbed it."

"How did you do that?" He moved to take her arm for a closer examination, but B.J. stepped away quickly.

"I bumped into something. I've got to start looking where I'm going." She began to gather shards of broken glass, fresh resentment causing her head to ache.

"Don't do that," Taylor commanded. "You'll cut yourself."

Like an echo to his words, B.J. jerked as a piece of glass sliced her thumb. Moaning in pain and disgust, she dropped the offending glass back into the heap.

"Let me see." Taylor pulled her to her feet, ignoring her struggles for release. "Ah, B.J." With a sigh of exasperation, he drew a spotless white handkerchief from his pocket, dabbing at the cut. "I'm beginning to think I have to keep you on a very short leash."

"It's nothing," she mumbled, fighting the warmth of his fingers on her wrist. "Let me go, you'll have blood all over you."

"Scourges of war." He brought the wounded thumb briefly to his lips, then wrapped the cloth around it. "You will continue to bind up your hair, won't you?" With his free hand, he dislodged pins, clattering them among broken glass. Studying the flushed face and tumbled hair, his mouth lifted in a smile which brought B.J. new pain. "What is it about you that constantly pulls at my temper? At the moment, you look as harmless as a frazzled kitten."

His fingers combed lightly through her hair, then rested on her shoulders. She felt the sweet, drawing weakness seeping through her limbs. "Do you know how close I came to kicking in that foolish bathroom door last night? You should be careful with tears, B.J., they affect men in strange ways."

"I hate to cry." She lifted her chin, terrified she would do so again. "It was your fault."

"Yes, I suppose it was. I'm sorry."

She stared, stunned by the unexpected apology. In a featherlight caress, he lowered his mouth to brush hers. "It's all right . . . It doesn't matter." She backed away, frightened by her own need to respond, but found herself trapped against the bar. Taylor made no move toward her, but merely said, "Have dinner with me tonight. Up in my room where we can talk privately."

Her head shook before her lips could form a refusal. He closed the space between them before she could calculate an escape.

"B.J., I'm not going to let you run away. We need to talk somewhere where we won't be interrupted. You know that I want you, and . . ."

"You should be satisfied with your other acquisitions," she retorted, battling the creeping warmth.

"I beg your pardon?" At her tone, his face hardened. The hand which had lifted to brush through her hair dropped back to his side.

"I'm sure you'll understand if you give it a bit of thought." She lifted her own hand to the sore flesh of her arm as if to keep the memory fresh. His eyes followed her gesture in puzzlement.

"It would be simpler if you elaborated."

"No, I don't think so. Just don't let your ego get out of

hand, Taylor. I'm not running from you, I simply have a date tonight."

"A date?" He slipped his hands into his pockets as he rocked back on his heels. His voice was hard.

"That's right. I'm entitled to a personal life. I don't think it's included in my job contract that I have to spend twenty-four hours at your beck and call." Adding salt to her own wound, she continued, "I'm sure Miss Trainor will fill your requirements for the evening very well."

"Undoubtedly," he agreed with a slow nod. Stung by the ease of his answer, B.J.'s ice became fire.

"Well then, that's all decided, isn't it? Have a delightful evening, Taylor. I assure you, I intend to. If you'll excuse me, I've work to do." She brushed by him, only to be brought up short by a hand on her hair.

"Since we're both going to be otherwise engaged this evening, perhaps we can get this out of the way now."

His mouth took hers swiftly, and she could taste his smoldering fury. She made a futile attempt to clamp her lips tightly against his. Ruthlessly, his hand jerked her hair. As she gasped in pained surprise he invaded her mouth, conquering her senses one by one. Just as she had abandoned all semblance of resistance, he drew back, his hands moving with slow insistence from her waist to her shoulders.

"Are you through?" Her voice was husky. Despising the longing to feel his mouth again, she forced herself rigid, keeping her eyes level.

"Oh no, B.J." The tone was confident. "I'm a long way from through. But for now," he continued as she braced herself for another assault, "you'd best tend to that cut."

Too unnerved to answer, B.J. rushed from the lounge. She had left dignity to lay with the scattered pieces of glass.

She felt the kitchen would be the quietest sanctuary at that time of day and entered on the pretext of wanting a cup of coffee.

"What did you do to your hand?" Elsie's question was off-handed as she completed the assembly line production of apple cobblers.

"Just a scratch." Frowning down at Taylor's handkerchief, B.J. shrugged and advanced on the coffee pot.

"Better put some iodine on it."

"Iodine stings."

Tongue clucking, Elsie wiped her hands on her full apron before foraging in a small cabinet for medical supplies. "Sit down and don't be a baby."

"It's just a scratch. It's not even bleeding now." Helplessly, B.J. dropped into a chair as Elsie flourished a small bottle and a bandage. "It's nothing at all. Ouch! Blast it, Elsie! I told you that wretched stuff stings."

"There." Elsie secured the bandage with a satisfied smile. "Out of sight, out of mind."

"So you say." B.J. rested her chin on her hand and stared into the depth of her coffee cup.

"Miss Snooty tried to get into my kitchen," Elsie announced with an indignant sniff.

"Who? Oh, Miss Trainor." Throbbing thumb momentarily forgotten, B.J. gave her cook her full attention. "What happened?"

"I tossed her out, of course." Elsie flicked flour from her abundant bosom and looked pleased.

"Oh." Leaning back in her chair, B.J. laughed at the picture of Elsie ordering sophisticated Darla out of her kitchen. "Was she furious?"

"Fit to be tied," Elsie returned pleasantly. B.J.'s grin widened before she could prevent it. "Going out with Howard tonight?"

"Yes." Her answer was automatic, not even vaguely surprised that communications had delivered this information to Elsie's ears. "To the movies, I think."

"Don't know why you're wasting your time going off with him when Mr. Reynolds is around."

"Well, it keeps Betty Jackson happy, and . . ." B.J. stopped and frowned as the complete sentence seeped through. "What does Taylor . . . Mr. Reynolds have to do with it?"

"I don't see why you're going out with Howard Beall when you're in love with Taylor Reynolds." Elsie's statement was matter-of-factly delivered as she poured herself a cup of coffee.

"I am not in love with Taylor Reynolds," B.J. declared, gulping down coffee and scalding both tongue and throat.

"Yes, you are," Elsie corrected, adding cooling cream to her own cup.

"I am not."

"Are too."

"I am not. I am absolutely not! Just what makes you so smart?" she added nastily.

"Fifty years of living, and twenty-four of knowing you." The reply was smug.

"La de da." B.J. attempted to appear sublimely unconcerned.

"Be real nice if you got married and settled down right

here." Ignoring B.J.'s fit of choking, Elsie calmly sipped her coffee. "You could keep right on managing the inn."

"Stick to chicken and dumplings, Elsie," B.J. advised when she had recovered. "As a fortune teller, you're a complete failure. Taylor Reynolds would no more marry me and settle here than he would marry a porcupine and live on the moon. I'm a bit too countrified and inexperienced for his taste."

"Hmph." Elsie sniffed again and shook her head. "Sure does a lot of looking in your direction."

"I'm sure in the vast wisdom you've amassed in your famous fifty years, you know the difference between a physical attraction and the urge to marry and settle down. Even in our sheltered little town, we learn the difference between love and lust."

"My, my, aren't we all grown up and sassy," Elsie observed with the mild tolerance of an adult watching a child's tantrum. "Finish your coffee and scoot, I've got a prime rib that needs tending. And don't worry that bandage off your thumb," she ordered as B.J. swung through the door.

* * *

Obviously, B.J. decided as she prepared for her date that evening, I don't project an imposing enough authority figure. She frowned again as she recalled Elsie dismissing her like a bad-tempered child. A breeze wafted through her opened window, billowing the curtains and wafting in the smell of freshly mowed grass. B.J. shrugged off her black mood. I'll simply change my image a bit.

She rooted through her closet and pulled out her birthday

present from her grandmother. The blouse was pure white silk and plunged deep to cling provocatively to every curve and plane before it tapered to the narrow waist of sleek black pants. The slacks continued a loving embrace over hips and down the length of shapely legs, molding her shape with the accuracy of a second skin.

"I'm not sure I'm ready for a new image," she muttered, turning sideways in front of her mirror. "I'm not sure Howard's ready either." The thought brought an irrepressible giggle as Howard's pleasantly homely face loomed in her mind.

He had the eyes of a faithful puppy, made all the more soulful by the attempt of a moustache which hung apologetically over his top lip. The main problem, B.J. decided, concentrating on his image, is that he lacks a chin. His face seemed to melt into his neck.

But he's a nice man, B.J. reminded herself. A nice, uncomplicated, predictable, undemanding man. Easing her feet into leather slides, she grabbed her bag and scurried from the room.

Her hopes to slip unseen outside to await Howard's arrival were shattered by a panic-stricken Eddie.

"B.J. Hey, B.J.!" He loped across the lobby and cornered her before she could reach the door.

"Eddie, if the place isn't burning down, hold it until tomorrow. I'm just leaving."

"But, B.J.," he continued, grabbing her hand and ignoring her unconscious search of the room for a tall, dark man. "Dot told Maggie that Miss Trainor is going to redecorate the inn, and that Mr. Reynolds plans to make it into a resort

with saunas in every room and an illegal casino in the back."
Horrified, his hand clung to hers for reassurance, his eyes
pleading behind the thickness of his glasses.

"In the first place," B.J. began patiently, "Mr. Reynolds has
no intention of running an illegal casino."

"He has one in Las Vegas," Eddie whispered in confidence.

"Gambling is a prerequisite in Las Vegas, it's not illegal."

"But, B.J., Maggie said the lounge is going to be done in
red and gold plush with nude paintings on the walls."

"Nonsense." She patted his hand in amusement as color
rose to his cheeks. "Mr. Reynolds hasn't decided anything
yet. When he does, I'm sure it won't run to red and gold plush,
and nudes!"

"Thank you," Taylor said at her back. B.J. jumped. "Eddie, I believe the Bodwin sisters are looking for you," he
added.

"Oh, yes, sir." Face flaming, Eddie shot off, leaving B.J.
in the very position she had sought to avoid.

"Well, well." Taylor surveyed her, an encompassing, thoroughly male examination, lingering on the point where her
blouse joined above her breasts. "I trust your date has a high
boiling point."

She started to snap that Howard had no boiling point at
all, but changed her mind. "Do you really like it?" Tossing
clouds of hair over her shoulder, B.J. gave Taylor the benefit
of a melting, sultry smile.

"Let's say I might find it appealing under different circumstances," he said dryly.

Pleased to observe he was annoyed, B.J. recklessly gave
his cheek a brief pat and glided to the door. "Good night,

Taylor. Don't wait up now." Triumphant, she stepped out into the pink-clouded evening.

Howard's reaction to her appearance caused her ego to soar yet higher. He swallowed, eyes blinking rapidly, and stammered in small, incoherent sentences the entire distance to town. Finding this a pleasant change from self-assured amusement, B.J. basked in his admiration as she watched the hazy sun sink beyond the hills through the car window.

In town, the streets were already quiet with the mid-week, mid-evening hush which isolates small towns from the outside world. A few windows glowed like cats' eyes in the dark, but most of the houses had bedded down for the night like so many contented domestic pets.

At the far end of town where the theater was, there were more signs of activity. Howard pulled into the parking lot with his usual, plodding precision. The neon sign glowed somewhat ludicrously against the quiet sky. The *L* in PLAZA had been retired for the past six months.

"I wonder," B.J. mused as she alighted from Howard's sensible Buick, "if Mr. Jarvis will ever get that sign fixed or if each of the letters will die a quiet death." Howard's answer was muffled by the car door slam. She was faintly surprised as he took her arm with a possessive air and led her into the theater.

An hour through the feature, B.J decided Howard was not at all himself. He did not consume his popcorn with his usual voracity, nor did he shift throughout the film on the undeniably uncomfortable seats the Plaza offered. Rather, he sat in a glazed-eyed state that seemed almost catatonic.

"Howard." Keeping her voice low, B.J. placed her hand on his. To her surprise he jumped as though she had pinched him. "Howard, are you all right?"

Her astonishment changed to stunned disbelief when he grabbed her, scattering popcorn, and pressed a passionate if fumbling kiss to her mouth. At first, B.J. sat stunned. All other advances by Howard had consisted of a brotherly embrace at the door of the inn. Then, hearing a few snickers from the back of the theater, she wiggled from his arms and pushed against his stocky chest.

"Howard, behave yourself!" She gave an exasperated sigh and straightened in her seat.

Abruptly, Howard gripped her arm and pulled her to her feet, dragging her up the aisle and out of the theater.

"Howard, have you lost your mind?"

"I couldn't sit in there any more," he muttered, bundling her into his car. "It's too crowded."

"Crowded?" She blew an errant curl from her eyes. "Howard, there couldn't have been more than twenty people in there. I think you should see a doctor." She patted his shoulder then tested his brow for signs of fever. "You're a bit warm and not at all yourself. I can get a ride back, you'd better just go home."

"No!" There was no mistaking the vehemence of his tone.

B.J. gave Howard a long, searching stare before settling back uneasily into her seat. Though it was too dark to tell much, he appeared to be concentrating on his driving. He drove rapidly over the winding country road. Soon B.J. was able to distinguish the blinking lights of the hotel.

Suddenly, Howard pulled off the road and seized her. In

the beginning, B.J. was more surprised than angry. "Stop it! Stop this, Howard! What in the world has gotten into you?"

"B.J." His mouth searched for hers, and this time his kiss was neither fumbling nor brotherly. "You're so beautiful." His groping hand reached for her blouse.

"Howard Beall, I'm ashamed of you!" B.J. remonstrated, pushing Howard firmly away and sliding toward the car door. "You get home right now and take a cold shower and go to bed!"

"But, B.J.—"

"I mean it." She wrenched open the car door and jumped out. Standing by the road, she tossed back her hair and adjusted her clothes. "I'm walking right back to the inn before you grow fangs again. Consider yourself lucky if I don't say something to your aunt about your temporary bout of insanity." Turning, she began the half-mile hike to the hotel.

*   *   *

Ten minutes later, shoes in hand and muttering disjointed imprecations toward the entire male sex, B.J. panted up the steep hill. The shadowy trees sighed softly in the moonlight. A lone owl hooted above her. But B.J. was in no mood for the beauties of the evening. "You be quiet," she commanded, glaring up at the bundle of feathers.

"I haven't said anything yet," a deep voice answered.

On the verge of screaming, B.J. found a hand over her mouth. Struggling to escape, she found a hard arm gripping her around the waist. "What the—?"

"Out for a stroll?" Taylor inquired mildly, releasing her. "It does seem an odd place to take a walk," he commented.

"Very funny." She managed two outraged steps before he caught her wrist.

"What's the matter? Your friend run out of gas?"

"Listen, I don't need this right now." Realizing she had dropped her shoes in her fright, B.J. searched the ground. "I've just walked a hundred miles after wrestling with a crazy man."

"Did he hurt you?" The grip on her wrist increased, as Taylor examined her more closely.

"Of course not." Tossing back her hair, B.J. let out a sigh of exasperation. "Howard wouldn't hurt a fly. I don't know what came over him. He's never acted like that before."

"Are you really that artless, or am I watching the second feature?" At her baffled expression, Taylor took her shoulders and administered a brief shake. "Grow up, B.J.! Look at yourself, the poor guy didn't have a chance."

"Don't be ridiculous." She shrugged out of his hold. "Howard's known me forever. He's never behaved like this before. He's just been reading too many romances or something. Good grief, I used to go skinny dipping with him when I was ten years old."

"Has anyone bothered to point out that you're no longer ten years old?"

Something in his voice made her raise her eyes to his.

"Stand still, B.J." He spoke in quiet command, and she felt her knees tremble. "I feel like a mountain lion stalking a house kitten."

For a moment, they stood apart, the stars glimmering above their heads, the moon a pale white guardian. Somewhere, a nightbird called to its mate, a plaintive sound. It echoed into silence as she melted in his arms.

She rose on her toes to offer him the gift of her mouth, her sigh of surrender merging with the wind's murmur. Her breasts crushed against his chest as his hands molded her hips closer. For this moment, she was his. Her heart sought no past or future but only the warmth and knowledge of now—the eternity of the present. She moaned with pleasure as his mouth sought the curve of her neck. Her fingers tangled with his dark hair as his mouth met hers again and she opened her lips to his kiss.

Locked together, they were oblivious to the sounds of night; the sigh of wind, the mellow call of an owl and the chirp of crickets. With a harsh suddenness, the inn door opened, pooling them in artificial light.

"Oh, Taylor, I've been waiting for you."

B.J. pulled away in humiliation as Darla leaned against the doorway, draped in a flowing black negligee. Her ivory skin gleamed against the lace. Her smooth, raven hair fell loose and full down her back.

"What for?" Taylor's question was abrupt.

Darla pouted and moved lace clad shoulders. "Taylor, darling, don't be a bear."

Devastated that he should have used her so blatantly while he had another woman waiting, B.J. stooped to retrieve her shoes.

"Where do you think you're going?" Taylor captured her wrist and aborted her quick escape.

"To my room," B.J. informed him with her last vestige of calm. "It appears you have a previous engagement."

"Just a minute."

"Please, let me go. I've done my quota of wrestling for one evening."

His fingers tightened on her flesh. "I'm tempted to wring your neck." Taylor tossed her wrist away as though the small contact was abhorrent.

Turning on bare heels, B.J. rushed up the steps and past a sweetly smiling Darla.

CHAPTER 9

B.J. moved her files to her room. There, she determined, she could work in peace without Taylor's disturbing presence. She immersed herself in paperwork and tried to block all else from her mind. The gray, drizzling rain which hissed at her windows set the stage for her mood. Thick, low hanging clouds allowed no breath of sun. Still, her eyes were drawn to the misty curtain, her mind floating with the clear rivulets which ran down the glass. Shaking her head to bring herself to order, B.J. concentrated on her linen supply.

Her door swung open, and she turned from the slant top desk. With sinking heart, she watched Taylor enter.

"Hiding out?"

It was apparent from the set of his mouth that his mood had not mellowed since her departure the previous evening.

"No." The lifting of her chin was instinctive. "It's simply more convenient for me to work out of my room while you need the office."

"I see." He towered menacingly over her desk, making her

feel small and insignificant. "Darla tells me you two had quite a session yesterday in the lounge."

B.J.'s mouth opened in surprise. She could not believe Darla would have disclosed her own behavior so readily.

"I warned you, B.J., that as long as Darla is a guest at the inn, you're to treat her with the same courtesy you show all other guests."

B.J. was astonished. "I'm sorry, Taylor, perhaps I'm dim. Would you mind explaining that?"

"She told me you were inexcusably rude, that you made some comments on her relationship with me, refused to serve her a drink, made yourself generally unpleasant, and told the staff not to cooperate with her."

"She said that, did she?" B.J.'s eyes darkened with rage. She set her pen down carefully and rose despite Taylor's proximity. "Isn't it odd how two people can view the same scene from entirely different perspectives! Well." She stuck her hands in her pockets and planted her feet firmly. "I have news for you—"

"If you've another version," Taylor returned evenly, "I'd like to hear it."

"Oh!" Unable to prevent herself, she lifted her fist to give his chest a small, inadequate punch. His eyes dropped to it in amused indulgence. "How generous of you. The condemned man is given a fair trial." Whirling, she paced the room in a swirl of agitation, debating whether to give him a verbatim account of her meeting with Darla. Finally, her pride won over her desire to clear herself in Taylor's eyes. "No thanks, your honor. I'll just take the fifth."

"B.J." Taylor took her shoulders and spun her to face him. "Must you constantly provoke me?"

"Must you constantly pick on me?" she countered.

"I wouldn't have said I was doing that." His tone had changed from anger to consideration.

"That's your opinion. I'm the one who's constantly in the position of justifying myself. I'm tired of having to explain my every move, of trying to cope with your moods. I never know from one minute to the next if you're going to kiss me or sit me in the corner with a dunce hat. I'm tired of feeling inadequate, naive and stupid. I never felt like any of those things before, and I don't like it."

Her words tumbled out in a furious rush while Taylor merely looked on, politely attentive.

"And I'm sick of your precious Darla altogether. Sick of her criticizing every aspect of the inn, sick of her looking at me as though I were some straw-chewing hick from Dog-patch. And, I resent her running to you with fabricated stories, and, I detest your using me to boost your over-inflated ego while she's floating around half naked waiting to warm your bed. And . . . Oh, blast!"

Her torrent of complaints was interrupted by the shrill ringing of the phone. Ripping the receiver from its cradle, B.J. snapped into it.

"What is it? No, nothing's wrong. What is it, Eddie?" Pausing, she listened, her hand lifting to soothe the back of her neck where tension lodged. "Yes, he's here." She turned back to Taylor and held out the phone. "It's for you, a Mr. Paul Bailey."

He took the receiver in silence, his eyes still on her face. As she turned to leave the room, his hand caught her wrist. "Stay here." Waiting for her nod of agreement, he released her. B.J. moved to the far side of the room and stared out at the insistent rain.

Taylor's conversation consisted of monosyllabic replies which B.J. blocked from her mind. Frustrated by the inability to complete her outburst, she now felt the impetus fading. Just as well, she admitted with a sigh of weary resignation. I've already said enough to insure the job at that dog kennel Darla mentioned. Blast! She rested her forehead on the cool glass. Why did I have to fall in love with an impossible man?

"B.J." She started at the sound of her name, then twisted her head to watch Taylor cradle the phone. "Pack," he said simply and moved to the door.

Closing her eyes, she tried to tell herself it was better that she leave, better not to be connected with him even as an employee. Nodding mutely, she turned back to the window.

"Enough for three days," he added in afterthought as his hand closed over the knob.

"What?" Thrown into confusion, she turned, staring with a mixture of grief and bewilderment.

"We'll be gone for three days. Be ready in fifteen minutes." Halting, Taylor's features softened suddenly at her clouded expression. "B.J., I'm not firing you. Give me credit for a bit more class than that."

She shook her head, washed with relief and the knowledge of the inevitable. He started to cross the room, then paused and merely leaned against the closed door.

"That was a call from the manager of one of my resorts. There's a bit of a problem, and I've got to see to it. You're coming with me."

"Coming with you?" Her fingers lifted to her temple as if she could smooth in understanding. "What on earth for?"

"In the first place, because I say so." He folded his arms across his chest and became the complete employer. "And secondly, because I like my managers well-rounded. No pun intended," he added, smiling as her color rose. "This is a good opportunity for you to see how my other hotels are run."

"But I can't just leave at a moment's notice," she objected, as her mind struggled to cope with the new development. "Who'll take care of things here?"

"Eddie will. It's about time he had a bit more responsibility. You let him lean on you too much. You let all of them lean on you too much."

"But we have five new reservations over the weekend, and . . ."

"You're down to ten minutes, B.J.," he informed her with a glance at his watch. "If you don't stop arguing, you'll only have the clothes on your back to take with you."

Seeing all of her objections would be overruled, she tried not to think of what going away with Taylor would do to her nervous system. *Business,* she reminded herself. *Just business.*

Somewhat annoyed that he was already walking through the door, having taken it for granted that she was going with him, she called after him, "I can't simply pack because you say to."

He turned back, his temper fraying. "B.J."

"You never said where," she reminded him. "I don't know if I need mukluks or bikinis."

A ghost of a smile played on his lips before he answered. "Bikinis. We're going to Palm Beach."

* * *

B.J. was to find her surprises were not yet over for the morning. First, her last-minute flurry of instructions was cut off by Taylor's order as she was bundled out of the dripping rain and into his car. On the drive to the airport, she mentally reviewed every possible disaster which could occur during her absence. She opened her mouth to enlighten Taylor only to be given a quelling look which had her suffering in silence.

At the airport, she found herself confronted not with a commercial jet, but with Taylor's private one, already primed for take-off. B.J. stood motionless, staring at the small trim plane as he retrieved their luggage.

"B.J., don't stand in the rain. Go on up."

"Taylor." Unmindful of the rain which pelted her, B.J. turned to him. "I think there's something you should know. I'm not very good at flying."

"That's all right." He secured cases under his arm and grabbed her hand. "The plane does most of the work."

"Taylor, I'm serious," she objected, as he dragged her inside the plane.

"Do you get air sick? You can take a pill."

"No." She swallowed and lifted her shoulders. "I get paralyzed. Stewardesses have been known to stow me in the baggage compartment so I don't panic the other passengers."

He rubbed his hands briskly through her hair, scattering

rain drops. "So, I've found your weakness. What are you afraid of?"

"Mostly of crashing."

"It's all in your head," he said easily as he helped her off with her jacket. "There's a term for it."

"Dying," she supplied, causing him to laugh again. Miffed by his amusement, she turned away to examine the plush luxury of the cabin. "This looks more like an apartment than a plane." She ran a hand over the soft maroon of a chair. "Everyone's entitled to a phobia," she muttered.

"You're absolutely right." His voice trembled on the edge of laughter. B.J. turned to snap at him but found his smile too appealing.

"You won't think it's so funny when I'm lying in a moaning heap on your shag carpet."

"Possibly not." He moved toward her and she stiffened in defense. Brooding down at her a moment, he searched her wary gray eyes. "B.J.," he began, "shall we call a moratorium on our disagreements? At least for the duration of the trip?"

"Well, I . . ." His voice was soft and persuasive, and she lowered her eyes to study the buttons of his shirt.

"An armed truce?" he suggested, capturing her chin between his thumb and forefinger and lifting her face. "With negotiations to follow?" He was smiling, his charming, utterly disarming smile. She knew resistance was hopeless.

"All right, Taylor." Unable to prevent her own smile from blossoming, she remained still as his finger lifted to trace it.

"Sit down and fasten your seat belt." He kissed her brow with an easy friendliness which left her weak.

B.J. found that the easy flow of his conversation from the

moment of take off eased her tension. Incredibly, she felt no fear as the plane soared into the air.

* * *

It's so flat and so warm!" B.J. exclaimed as she stepped off the plane steps and looked around her.

Taylor chuckled as he led the way to a sleek black Porsche. He exchanged a few words with a waiting attendant, accepted the keys, unlocked the door, and motioned B.J. inside.

"Where is your hotel?" she asked.

"In Palm Beach. This is West Palm Beach. We have to cross Lake Worth to get to the island."

"Oh!" Enchanted by roadside palms, she lapsed into silence.

The white, sandy soil and splashes of brilliant blossoms were so far removed from the scenery of her native New England, she felt as though she had entered another world. The waters of Lake Worth, separating Palm Beach from the mainland, sparkled blue and white under the afternoon sun. The oceanside was lined with resort hotels. B.J. recognized the elaborate initials *T.R.* atop a sleek white building which rose twelve stories over the Atlantic. Hundreds of windows winked back at her. Taylor pulled into the semi-circular macadam drive and stopped the car. B.J. narrowed her eyes against the streaming rays of the sun. The archway which formed the entrance was guarded by palms and semi-tropical plants, their tangle of color obviously well planned and scrupulously tended. The lawn spread, perfectly level and unbelievably green.

"Come," said Taylor, coming around to open the door for her. He helped her out of the car and led her inside.

To B.J. the lobby was a tropical paradise. The floor was flagstoned, the walls a half-circle of windows at the front. A center fountain played over a rocky garden, dotted with lush plants and ferns. B.J. saw that the interior was round, an open circle spiraling to the ceiling where a mural emulating the sky had been painted. The effect was one of limitless space. *How different from the cozy familiarity of the Lakeside Inn!* she thought.

"Ah, Mr. Reynolds." Her meditation was interrupted by the appearance of a slender, well-dressed man with a shock of steel gray hair and a lean, bronzed face. "So good to see you."

"Paul." Taylor accepted the proffered hand and returned the smile of greeting. "B.J., this is Paul Bailey, the manager. Paul, B.J. Clark."

"A pleasure, Miss Clark." B.J.'s hand was engulfed by a smooth, warm grasp. His eyes surveyed her fresh, slender beauty with approval. She found herself smiling back.

"See to our bags and I'll take Miss Clark up. After we've settled in a bit, I'll get back to you."

"Of course. Everything's quite ready." With another flash of teeth, he led the way to the registration desk and secured a key. "Your bags will be right up, Mr. Reynolds. Is there anything else you'd like?"

"Not at the moment. B.J.?"

"What?" B.J. was still admiring the luxurious lobby.

"Would you like anything?" Taylor smiled at her and brushed a curl from her cheek.

"Oh . . . no, nothing. Thank you."

With a final nod for Bailey, Taylor secured her hand in his and led her to one of the three elevators. They glided up in a cage of octagon glass high above the cluster of greenery.

When they reached the top floor, Taylor moved along the thick carpeting to unlock the door. B.J. entered and crossing the silent plush of ivory carpet, stared down from the dizzying height at the white beach which jutted out into an azure span of sea. In the distance, she could see the churning whitecaps and the flowing grace of gulls as they circled and dove.

"What an incredible view. I'm tempted to dive straight off the balcony." Turning, she caught Taylor watching her from the center of the room. She could not decipher the expression in his eyes. "This is lovely," she said to break the long silence.

She ran a finger over the smooth surface of an ebony bar and wondered if Darla had decorated the room. Grudgingly, she admitted to herself if this were the case, Darla had done a good job.

"Would you like a drink?" Taylor pushed a button cunningly concealed in the mirror tiles on the wall behind the bar. A panel slid open to reveal a fully stocked bar.

"Very clever," B.J. smiled. "Some club soda would be nice," she said, leaning elbows on the bar.

"Nothing stronger?" he asked as he poured the soda over crackling ice. "Come in," he responded to the quiet knock on the door.

"Your luggage, Mr. Reynolds." A red-and-black-uniformed bellboy carried in the cases. B.J. was conscious of his curious gaze and blushed self-consciously.

"Fine, just leave them there." He accepted the tip from Taylor and vanished, closing the door with quiet respect.

B.J. eyed the cases. Taylor's elegant gray sat neatly beside her practical brown. "Why did he bring it all in here?" Setting down her glass, she lifted her eyes. "Shouldn't he have just taken mine to my room?"

"He did." Taylor secured another bottle and poured himself a portion of Scotch.

"But, I thought this was your suite." B.J. glanced around the luxurious room again.

"It is."

"But you just said . . ." She faltered, as her color rose. "Surely you don't think I'm going to—to . . ."

"What did you have in mind?" Taylor inquired with infuriating amusement.

"You said you wanted me to see how one of your other hotels was run, you never said anything about . . . about . . ."

"You really must learn to complete a sentence, B.J."

"I'm not sleeping with you," she stated very positively, her eyes like two summer storm clouds.

"I don't believe I asked you to," he said lazily before he took an easy sip of Scotch. "There are two very adequate bedrooms in this suite. I'm sure you'll find yours comfortable."

Embarrassment flooded her cheeks. "I'm not staying in here with you. Everyone will think that I'm . . . that we're . . ."

"I've never known you to be quite so coherent." His mockery increased her wrath, and her eyes narrowed to dangerous slits. "In any case," he continued unperturbed, "the purity of your reputation is already in question. As you're traveling with me, it will naturally be assumed that we're lovers.

As we know differently," he went on as her mouth dropped open, "that hardly matters. Of course, if you'd like to make rumor fact, I might be persuaded."

"Oh, you insufferable, egotistical, conceited . . ."

"Name calling can hardly be considered persuasion," Taylor admonished, patting her head in an infuriating manner. "I assume, therefore, you'll want your own bedroom?"

"As this is off season," B.J. began, gaining a tenuous grip on her temper, "I'm sure there are a surplus of available rooms."

Smiling, he ran a finger down her arm. "Afraid you won't be able to resist temptation, B.J.?"

"Of course not," she said though her senses tingled at his touch.

"Then that's settled," he said, finishing off his drink. "If you're harboring the notion that I'll be overcome by lust, there's a perfectly sturdy lock on your bedroom door. I'm going down to see Bailey; why don't you change and grab some time at the beach? Your room's the second door on your left down the hall." He pointed as he moved to the door and slipped through before she had time to frame a response.

* * *

Before lifting her case and beginning to unpack, B.J. thought of at least a half a dozen withering remarks she should have made. However, she soon regained her sense of proportion.

After all, it wasn't every day that she had the opportunity to indulge in such luxury. She might as well enjoy it. Besides, the suite was certainly large enough for both of them.

Slipping into brief tan shorts and a lime green halter, B.J. decided to finish her unpacking later and head for the beach.

* * *

Taylor had certainly made the most of nature's gift, offering a luxury playground with an ocean and sky backdrop. B.J. had seen the huge mosaic tiled pool for those who preferred its filtered water to the sea. On her way to the beach, she glimpsed at the expanse of tennis courts with palms and flowering shrubs skirting about the entrance gate. She had seen enough of the hotel's interior to be certain that Taylor left his guests wanting for nothing.

From the beach B.J. shaded her eyes and studied again the perfection of the imposing resort. It was, she admitted with a sigh, elegantly appealing. As far out of her realm as its owner. *Egg noodles and caviar,* she thought ruefully, reflecting both on the comparison between inn and resort and Taylor and herself. They simply don't belong on the same plate.

"Hello."

Startled, B.J. turned, blinked against the brilliant sun and stared at an even white smile in a bronzed face.

"Hello." Returning the smile with a bit more caution, B.J. studied the attractive face surrounded by thick masses of light, sun-bleached hair.

"Aren't you going to give the ocean a try?"

"Not today."

"That's very unusual." He fell into step beside her as she began to cross the sand. "Usually everyone spends their first day roasting and splashing."

"How did you know it was my first day?" B.J. asked.

"Because I haven't noticed you here before, and I would have." He gave her an encompassing and intensely male survey. "And because you're still peaches and cream instead of parboiled."

"Hardly the time of year," B.J. commented, admiring the deep, even tan as he shrugged on his shirt. "I'd say you've been here for some time."

"Two years," he returned, with an appealing grin. "I'm the tennis pro, Chad Hardy."

"B.J. Clark." She paused on the tiled walkway which led to the hotel's beach entrance. "How come you're on the beach instead of the courts?"

"My day off," he explained and surprised her by winding the tips of her hair around his finger. "But if you'd like a private lesson, it could be arranged."

"No, thanks," she declined lightly and turned again toward the door.

"How about dinner?" Chad captured her hand, gently but insistently bringing her back to face him.

"I don't think so."

"A drink?"

She smiled at his persistence. "No, sorry, it's a bit early."

"I'll wait."

Laughing, she shook her head and disengaged her hand. "No, but I appreciate the offer. Goodbye, Mr. Hardy."

"Chad." He moved with her through the archway into the hotel's coolness. "What about tomorrow? Breakfast, lunch, a weekend in Vegas?"

B.J. laughed; such ingenuous charm was hard to resist. "I don't think you'll have any trouble finding a companion."

"I'm having a great deal of trouble securing the one I want," he countered. "If you had any compassion, you'd take pity on me."

With a rueful smile, B.J. surrendered. "All right, I wouldn't mind an orange juice."

In short order, B.J. found herself seated at an umbrella table beside the pool.

"It's not really that early," Chad objected when she adhered to her choice of fruit juice. "Most of the crowd is straggling in to wash off the sand and change for dinner."

"This hits the spot." She sipped from the frosted glass. Then, gesturing with one slender hand, she glanced around at green fan palms and scarlet blooms. "You must find it easy to work here."

"It suits me," Chad agreed, swirling his own drink. "I like the work, the sun." He lifted his glass and smiled with the half toast. "And the benefits." His smile widened. Before she had the opportunity to draw them away, his hand captured her fingers. "How long will you be here?"

"A couple of days." She let her hand lie limp, feeling a struggle would make her appear foolish. "This was actually a spur-of-the-moment trip rather than a vacation."

"Then I'll drink to spur-of-the-moment trip," said Chad.

The friendly, polished charm was potent, and B.J. could not resist beaming him a smile. "Is that your best serve?"

"Just a warm-up." Returning the smile, his grip on her hand tightened slightly. "Watch out for my ace."

"*B.J.*"

Twisting her head, she stared up at Taylor, frowning above her. "Hello, Taylor. Are you finished with Mr. Bailey?"

"For the moment." His glance shifted to Chad, drifted over

their joined hands and returned to her face. "I've been look-ing for you."

"Oh?" Feeling unaccountably guilty, B.J. nibbled her lip in a tell-tale sign of agitation. "I'm sorry, this is Chad Hardy," she began.

"Yes, I know. Hello, Hardy."

"Mr. Reynolds," Chad returned with a polite nod. "I didn't know you were in the hotel."

"For a day or two. When you've finished," he continued, giving B.J. the full benefit of a cold disapproving stare, "I suggest you come up and change for dinner. I don't think that outfit's suitable for the dining room." With a curt nod, he turned on his heel and stalked away.

"Well, well." Releasing her hand, Chad leaned back in his chair and studied B.J. with new interest. "You might have told me you were the big man's lady. I'm rather fond of my job here."

Her mouth opened and closed twice. "I am not Taylor's lady," B.J. spurted on her third try.

Chad's lips twisted in a wry grin. "You'd better tell him that. A pity." He sighed with exaggerated regret. "I was work-ing on some interesting fantasies, but I steer clear of tread-ing on dangerous ground."

Standing, he lifted her chin and gave her a rather wistful smile. "If you find yourself down here again without com-plications, look me up."

CHAPTER 10

The emphatic slamming of the suite's door gave B.J. small satisfaction. Advancing with purpose on Taylor's bedroom, she pounded on his door.

"Looking for me?" The voice was dry.

She whirled around. For a moment, she could only gape at the sight of Taylor leaning against the bathroom door, clad only in a dark green towel tied low over lean hips. His hair fell in tendrils over the lean planes of his face.

"Yes, I . . ." She faltered and swallowed. "Yes," she repeated with more firmness as she recalled Chad's comments. "That was an uncalled for exhibition out there. You deliberately left Chad with the impression that I was your . . ." She hesitated, eyes darkening with outraged impotence, as she searched for the right word.

"Mistress?" Taylor suggested amiably.

B.J.'s pupils dilated with fury. "He at least used the term lady." Forgetting the corded arms and dark mat of hair covering his chest, she stalked forward until she stood toe to toe. "You did it on purpose, and I won't tolerate it."

"Oh, really?" Had she not been so involved venting her own anger, B.J. might have recognized the dangerous pitch of his voice. "It appears by the speed with which Hardy lured you into his corner, you're remarkably easy prey. I feel it's my obligation to look out for you."

"Find someone else to protect," she retorted. "I'm not putting up with it."

"Just what do you intend to do about it?" The simple arrogance of the question was accompanied by a like smile which robbed B.J. of all coherency. "If giving Hardy and others of his type the impression that you're my property keeps you from making a fool of yourself, that's precisely what I'll do. Actually," he continued, "you should be grateful."

"Grateful?" B.J. repeated, her voice rising. "Your property? *A fool of myself?* Of all the arrogant, unspeakable gall!"

Her arm pulled back with the intention of connecting her fist with his midsection, but she found it twisted behind her back with astonishing speed. Her body was crushed against the hard undraped lines of his.

"I wouldn't try that again." The warning was soft. "You wouldn't like the consequences." His free hand lowered to her hip, bringing her closer as she tried to back away. "Don't do that," he ordered, holding her still and trapped against him. "You'll just hurt yourself. It seems we've broken our truce." His words were light, though she saw the signs of lingering temper in his eyes.

"You started it." Her declaration was half-defiant, half-defensive. She kept her eyes level with sheer determination.

"Did I?" he murmured before he took her mouth.

She was washed by the familiar flood of need. Offering no struggle, she went willingly into the uncharted world where

only the senses ruled. His hand released her arm in order
to roam over the bareness of her back, and she circled his
neck, wanting only to remain in the drifting heat and velvet
darkness.

Abruptly, he set her free. She stumbled back against the
wall, thrown off balance by the swiftness of her liberation.

"Go change." He turned and gripped the knob of his door.

B.J. reached out to touch his arm.

"Taylor . . ."

"Go change!" he shouted. She stumbled back again, eyes
round and wide at the swift flare of violence. He slammed
the door behind him.

B.J. retreated to her room to sort out her feelings. Was it
injured pride? Or was it rage? She could not for the life of
her tell.

* * *

The early sky lightened slowly from black to misty blue.
The stars faded, then died as the sun still lay hidden beneath the horizon. B.J. rose, grateful the restless night was
behind her.

She had shared an uncomfortably polite dinner with Taylor, the elegance of the dining room only adding to the sensation that she had stood aside and watched two strangers go
through the motions of dining. Taylor's solicitous and unfamiliar formality had disturbed her more than his sudden
seething fury. Her own responses had been stilted and cool.
Immediately after dinner she pleaded fatigue and crept off
unescorted to pass the evening hours alone and miserably
awake in her room.

It had been late when she had heard Taylor's key in the lock, his footsteps striding down the hall to pause outside her room. She had held her breath as if he might sense her wakefulness through the panel. Not until she had heard the muffled sound of his door closing had she let it out again.

* * *

B.J. felt no better the next morning. The events of the day before had left her with a lingering sense of loss and sorrow. Though she knew that there was little hope, she had finally acknowledged to herself that she was in love with Taylor. But there was no point thinking about it.

She slipped on her bikini, grabbed a terry robe, and tiptoed from her room.

The view from the wide window in the living room drew her. With a sigh of pleasure, she moved closer to watch the birth of day. The sun had tinted the edge of sea and sky with rose-gold streaks. Pinks and mauves shot through the dawning sky.

"Quite a view."

With a gasp, B.J. spun around, nearly colliding with Taylor whose footsteps had been hidden by the thickness of carpet. "Yes," she returned as their hands lifted simultaneously to brush back the fall of her hair which tumbled to her cheek. "There's nothing so beautiful as a sunrise." Disturbed by his closeness, she found her own words silly.

He was clad only in short denim cut-offs, frayed at the cuffs.

"How did you sleep?" His voice was politely concerned.

She shrugged off his question, evading a direct lie. "I thought I'd take an early swim before the beach gets crowded."

Deliberately, he turned her to face him, while he searched her face with habitual thoroughness. "Your eyes are shadowed." His finger traced the mauve smudges as a frown deepened the angles of his face. "I don't believe I've ever seen you look tired before. You seem to have some inner vitality that continually feeds itself. You look pale and fragile, quite unlike the pigtailed brat I watched sliding into home plate."

His touch was radiating the weakness through her so she stepped back in defense. "I . . . It's just the first night in a strange bed."

"Is it?" His brow lifted. "You're a generous creature, B.J. You don't even expect an apology, do you?"

Charmed by his smile, her weariness evaporated. "Taylor, I want . . . I'd like it if we could be friends." She finished in an impulsive rush.

"Friends?" he repeated as the sudden boyish grin split his face. "Oh, B.J., you're sweet, if a bit slow." Taking both hands in his, he lifted them to his lips before speaking again. "All right, friend, let's go for a swim."

* * *

But for gulls, the beach was deserted, a stretch of white pure and welcoming. The air already glowed with the promise of heat and light. B.J. stopped and gazed around, pleased with the quiet and the solitude.

"It's like everyone went away."

"You're not much for crowds, are you, B.J.?"

"No, I suppose not." She turned to him with a lift of bare

shoulders. "I enjoy people, but more on a one to one level. When I'm around people, I like to know who they are, what they need. I'm good with small problems. I can shore up a brick here, hammer a nail there. I don't think I'm equipped to construct an entire building the way you are."

"One can't keep a building standing without someone shoring up bricks and hammering nails."

She smiled, so obviously pleased and surprised by his observation that he laughed and tousled her hair. "I'll race you to the water."

Giving him a considering look, B.J. shook her head in reluctance. "You're a lot taller than I am. You have an advantage."

"You forget, I've seen you run. And—" His eyes dropped to the length of shapely legs. "For a small woman, you have amazingly long legs."

"Well." She drew the word out, lips pursed. "O.K." Without waiting for his assent, she streaked across the sand and plunged into the sea, striking out with long strokes.

She was brought up short by hands on her waist. Laughing, she struggled away, only to be caught and submerged in the ensuing tussle.

"Taylor, you're going to drown me," she protested as her legs tangled with his.

"That is not my intention," he informed her as he drew her closer. "Hold still a minute or you'll take yourself under again."

Relaxing in his hold, B.J. allowed him to keep them both afloat. She permitted herself a few moments of ecstasy cradled in his arms as the water pooled around them like a cool satin blanket. The change began like a gradual drizzle as she became more aware of his shoulder beneath her cheek, the possessive hold of the arm which banded her bare waist. Powerless to resist, she floated with him as his lips descended to the sleek cap of her hair, then wandered to tease the lobe of her ear with tongue and teeth before moving to the curve of her neck. His fingers traced the low line of the bikini snug at her hips as his mouth roamed her cheek in its journey to hers.

Her lips parted before he requested it, but his kiss remained gentle, the passion simmering just below the surface. His hand touched and fondled, slipping easily under the barrier of her brief top to trail over the curve of her breast. The water sighed gently as flesh met flesh.

What with gentle caresses, the drifting buoyancy of the sea, and the growing heat of the ascending sun B.J. fell into a trancelike state. Perhaps, she thought, mind and limbs lethargic, she was meant to float forever in his arms. She shivered with pleasure.

"You're getting cold," Taylor murmured, drawing her away to study her face. "Come on." He released her, leaving her without support in the sighing sea. The magic shattered. "We'll sit in the sun."

B.J. started for the shore with Taylor swimming easily beside her.

On the beach, she fanned her hair in the sun while Taylor stretched negligently beside her. She tried not to look at the strong planes of his face, his bronzed, glistening skin.

He told me how it would be, she reminded herself. Right from the beginning. I don't seem to be able to do anything about it and if I don't, I'll end up being just another Darla in his life. Bringing her knees to her chest, she rested her chin on them and stared at the distant horizon. He's attracted to me for some reason, perhaps because I'm different from other women in his life. I haven't their sophistication or experience and I suppose he finds that appealing and amusing. I don't know how to fight both loving him and wanting him. If it were just physical, I could avoid being hurt. If it were only an attraction, I could resist him.

She recalled suddenly his quick violence of the previous day and realized he was a man capable of employing whatever means necessary to gain an objective. At the moment, she knew he was playing her like a patient fisherman casting his line into calm waters. But ultimately, they both knew she would be captured in his net. Though it might be silk, it would still lead to eventual disaster.

"You're very far away." Sitting up, Taylor tangled his fingers in her damp hair and turned her to face him.

Silently, she studied every plane and angle of his face, engraving them on both heart and mind. *There is too much strength there,* she thought, rocked by a surge of love. Too much virility, too much knowledge. She scrambled to her feet, needing to postpone the inevitable.

"I'm starving," she claimed. "Are you going to spring for breakfast? After all, I did win the race."

"Did you?" He rose as she pulled the short robe over the briefness of her bikini.

"Yes," she said, "positively." Picking up Taylor's light blue pullover, she held it out. "I was the undisputed winner." She watched as he dragged the snug, crew necked shirt over his head then bent to retrieve the towels.

"Then you should buy my breakfast." Smiling, he held out his hand. After a brief hesitation, she accepted.

"How do you feel about corn flakes?"

"Unenthusiastic."

"Well." Her shoulders moved in regret. "I'm afraid my funds are rather limited as I was hauled to Florida without ceremony."

"Your credit's good." He released her hand and swung a friendly arm around her shoulders. They moved away from the sea.

* * *

By mid afternoon, B.J. felt euphoric. There was a new, charming friendliness about Taylor that made her realize she liked him every bit as much as she loved him.

She was given a thorough if belated tour of the hotel, allowed to wander through the silver and cobalt lounge, linger in the two elegantly stocked boutiques and examine the enormous expanse of the steel and white kitchen. In the game room, she was provided with an endless supply of change as Taylor watched her reckless enthusiasm with tolerance.

Leaning against a machine, he looked on as she steered her computer car to another horrendous wreck. "You know," he commented as she held her hand for another quarter, "by the time you've finished, you'll have spent every bit as much as that dress in the boutique cost. Why is it, you'll take the money for these noisy machines, but you refuse to let me buy you that very appealing dress?"

"This is different," she said vaguely, maneuvering the car around obstructions.

"How?" He grimaced as she narrowly missed an unwary pedestrian and skidded around a corner.

"You never said if you worked out the problem," B.J. murmured as she twisted the wheel to avoid a slow moving vehicle.

"Problem?"

"Yes, the one you came down here to see to."

"Oh, yes." He smiled and brushed an insistent wisp from her cheek. "It's working out nicely."

"Oh, blast!" B.J. frowned as her car careened into a telephone pole, flipped through the air and landed with an impressive show of computer color and sound.

"Come on." Taylor grabbed her hand as she looked up hopefully. "Let's have some lunch before I go bankrupt."

On the sundeck above the pool, they enjoyed quiche Lorraine and Chablis. A handful of people splashed and romped in the pale blue water. Toying with the remains of her meal, B.J. stared down at the swimmers and sun bathers. Her gaze swept to include the curve of beach before returning to Taylor. He was watching her, a small secret smile on his lips and in his eyes. She blinked in confused embarrassment.

"Is something wrong?" Battling the urge to wipe her cheek to see if it was smudged, she lifted her glass and sipped the cool wine.

"No, I just enjoy looking at you. Your eyes are constantly changing hues. One minute they're like peat smoke, and the next clear as a lake. You'll never be able to keep secrets; they say too much." His smile spread as her color rose. Her eyes shifted to the golden lights in her glass. "You're an incredibly beautiful creature, B.J."

She lifted her head, her eyes wide in surprise.

With a light chuckle, he captured her hand and brought it to his lips. "I don't suppose I should tell you that too often.

You'll begin to see how true it is and lose that appealing air
of innocence."

Rising, he maintained possession of her hand, pulling her
to her feet. "I'm going to take you to the Health Club. You
can get a firsthand impression of how this place works."

"All right, but . . ."

"I'm leaving instructions that you're to have the complete
routine," he interrupted. "And when I meet you at seven for
dinner, I don't want to see any shadows under your eyes."

*   *   *

Transferred from Taylor's authority to a perfectly shaped
brunette, B.J. was whirlpooled, saunaed, pummeled
and massaged. For three hours, she was alternately steamed
and sprayed, plied with iced fruit juice and submerged in
churning water. Her first instinct was to retrieve her clothes
and quietly slip out. After finding they had been conveniently cached out of sight, she submitted, and soon found
tensions she had been unaware of possessing seeping out
of her.

Stomach down on a high table, she sighed under the magic
hands of the masseuse and allowed her mind to float in the
twilight world of half sleep. Dimly, the conversation of two
women enjoying the same wonder drifted across to her.

"I happened to be staying here two years ago . . . so incredibly handsome . . . what a marvelous catch . . . All that
lovely money as well . . . The Reynolds empire."

At Taylor's name, B.J.'s eyes opened and her inadvertent
eavesdropping became deliberate.

"It's a wonder some smart woman hasn't snagged him yet."

An auburn haired woman tucked a bright strand behind her ear and folded her arms under her chin.

"Darling, you can be sure scores have tried." Her brunette companion stifled a yawn and smiled with wry humor. "I don't imagine he's averse to the chase. A man like that thrives on feminine adulation."

"He's got mine."

"Did you see his companion? I caught a glimpse last night and again today by the pool."

"Mmm, I saw them when they arrived, but I was too busy looking at him to take much notice. A blonde, wasn't she?"

"Um-hum, though I don't think that pale wheat shade was a gift of nature."

B.J.'s first surge of outrage was almost immediately replaced by amusement. So, she decided, if I'm to be Taylor's temporary, if fictional mistress, I might as well hear the opinion of the masses.

"Do you think this one will get her hooks in? Who is she, anyway?"

"That's precisely what I attempted to find out." The brunette grimaced and mirrored her companion's position of chin on arms. "It cost me twenty dollars to learn her name is B.J. Clark of all things. Beyond that, not even dear Paul Bailey knows anything. She just popped up out of the blue. She's never been here before. As for getting her hooks in." Elegantly tanned shoulders shrugged. "I wouldn't bet either way. His eyes simply devour her; it's enough to make you drool with envy."

B.J. raised a skeptical eyebrow.

"I suppose," the brunette went on, "huge gray eyes and

masses of blond hair are appealing. And she is rather attractive in a wholesome, peaches and cream sort of way."

B.J. rose on her elbows and smiled across the room. "Thank you," she said simply, then lowered her head and grinned into the ensuing silence.

CHAPTER 11

Refreshed and pleased with herself, B.J. entered Taylor's suite, carrying a dress box under her arm. Though she had lost the minor tussle with the sales clerk in the boutique, she remained in high spirits. After her session in the spa, she had returned to the shop. Pointing to the gown of silver silk which Taylor had admired, she was prepared to surrender a large hunk of her bank account only to be told Mr. Reynolds had left instructions that any purchases she made were to be billed to him.

Annoyed by his arrogance, however generous, B.J. had argued with the implacable salesgirl. Ultimately, she had left the shop with the dress in hand, vowing to see to the monetary details later.

If, she decided, pouring a substantial stream of bath salts under the rushing water of the tub, she was to portray the image of the mysterious lady from nowhere she was going to dress the part. She lowered herself into hot, frothy water and had just begun to relax when the door swung open.

"So, you're back," Taylor said easily, leaning against the door, "Did you enjoy yourself?"

"Taylor!" B.J. slid down in the tub, attempting to cover herself with the blanket of bubbles. "I'm having a bath!"

"Yes. I can see that, and little else. There's no need to drown yourself. Would you like a drink?" The question was pleasant and impersonal.

Recalling the overheard conversation in the spa, B.J.'s pride rallied. It's time, she decided, to give him back a bit of his own.

"That would be lovely." Fluttering her lashes, she hoped her expression was unconcerned. "Some sherry would be nice, if it's no bother."

Watching his brow lift in surprise, B.J. felt decidedly smug. "It's no trouble," he said as he retreated, leaving the door ajar. She prayed fervently the bubbles would not burst until she had a chance to leave the tub and slip into her robe.

"Here you are." Reentering, Taylor handed her a small glass shimmering with golden liquid.

B.J. gave him a smile and sipped. "Thanks. I'll be finished soon if you want the bath."

"Don't rush," he returned, delighted to see her coolness had somewhat rattled him, "I'll use the other."

"Suit yourself," she said agreeably, making sure her shrug was mild and did little to disturb her peaceful waters. Relieved that the door closed behind him, B.J. expelled a long breath and set the remains of her drink on the edge of the tub.

* * *

For a full five minutes, B.J. stared at her reflection in the full-length mirror. Silver silk draped crossways over the curve of each breast, narrowing to thin straps over her shoulders before continuing down her sides to leave her back bare to the waist. The skirt fell straight over her slender hips and legs, one side slit to mid-thigh. She had piled her hair in a loose knot on top of her head, allowing a few curling tendrils to escape and frame her face.

B.J. found the stranger in the mirror intimidating. With a flash of intuition, she knew B.J. Clark could not live up to the promises hinted at by the woman in the glass.

"Almost ready?" Taylor's knock and question jolted her out of her reverie.

"Yes, just coming." Shaking her head, she gave the reflection a reassuring smile. "It's just a dress," she reminded both B.J. Clarks and turned from the mirror.

Taylor's hand paused midway in the action of pouring pre-dinner drinks. He lifted his cigarette to his lips, inhaling slowly as he surveyed B.J.'s entrance. "Well," he said as she hesitated, "I see you bought it after all."

"Yes." With a surge of confidence, she crossed the room to join him. "As a woman of ill fame I felt my wardrobe inadequate."

"Care to elaborate?" He handed B.J. a delicate glass.

She accepted automatically. "Just a conversation I overheard in the spa." Her eyes lit with amusement, she set her glass on the bar. "Oh, Taylor, it was funny. I'm sure you have no idea how ardently your . . . ah . . . affairs are monitored." Describing her afternoon at the spa, she was unable to suppress her giggles.

"I can't tell you how it boosts the ego to be envied and

touted as a woman of mystery! I certainly hope it's not dis-covered that I'm a hotel manager from Lakeside, Vermont. It would spoil it."

"No one would believe it anyway." He did not appear to be amused by her story as, frowning, he sipped at his drink.

Confused by his expression, B.J. asked, "Don't you like the dress after all?"

"I like it." He took her hand, the smile at last taking com-mand of his mouth. "Obviously, we'll have to have cham-pagne. You look much too elegant for anything else."

* * *

They began their meal with oysters Rockefeller and cham-pagne. Their table sat high in the double level dining room, in front of a wide wall aquarium. As the London broil was served, B.J. sipped her wine and glanced around the room.

"This is a lovely place, Taylor." She gestured with a fine-boned hand to encompass the entire resort.

"It does the job." He spoke with the smooth confidence of one who knew the worth of his possessions.

"Yes, it certainly does. It runs beautifully. The staff is ef-ficient and discreet, almost to the point of being invisible. You hardly know they're there, yet everything's perfect. I sup-pose it's elbow to elbow in here during the winter."

With a movement of his shoulders, he followed her gaze. "I try to avoid hitting the resorts during the heavy season."

"Our summer season will begin in a few weeks," she

began, only to find her hand captured and her glass replenished with champagne.

"I've managed to keep you from bringing up the inn all day; let's see if we can finish the evening without it. When we get back tomorrow, we can talk about vacancies and cancellations. I don't discuss business when I'm having dinner with a beautiful woman."

B.J. smiled and surrendered. If only one evening remained of the interlude, she wanted to savor each moment.

"What do you discuss over dinner with a beautiful woman?" she countered, buoyed by the wine.

"More personal matters." His finger traced the back of her hand. "The way her voice flows like an easy river, the way her smile touches her eyes before it moves her mouth, the way her skin warms under my hand." With a low laugh, he lifted her hand, lips brushing the inside of her wrist.

Glancing up warily, B.J. asked, "Taylor, are you making fun of me?"

"No." His voice was gentle. "I have no intention of making fun of you, B.J."

Satisfied with his answer, she smiled and allowed him to lead the conversation into a lighter vein.

Flickering candles, the muted chink of crystal and silver, the low murmur of voices, Taylor's eyes meeting hers—it was an evening B.J. knew she would always remember.

"Let's go for a walk." Taylor rose and pulled back her chair. "Before you fall asleep in your champagne." Hand in hand they walked to the beach.

They walked in silence, enjoying each other and the night. Merging with the aroma of the sea and the night was the tenuous scent of orange blossoms. B.J. knew the fragrance would be forever melded with her memory of the man whose hand lay warm and firm over hers. Would she ever look at the moon again without thinking of him? Ever walk beneath the stars without remembering? Ever draw a breath without longing for him?

Tomorrow, she reflected, it would be business as usual, and a handful of days after, he would be gone. Only a name on a letterhead. Still, she would have the inn, she reminded herself. He'd said no more about changes. She'd have her home and her work and her memories, and that was much more than some ever had.

"Cold?" Taylor asked, and she shivered, afraid he had read her mind. "You're trembling." His arm slipped around her shoulders, bringing aching warmth. "We'd better go back."

Mutely, she nodded and forced tomorrows out of her mind. Relaxing, she felt the remnants of champagne mist pleasurably in her head.

"Oh, Taylor," she whispered as they crossed the lobby. "That's one of the women from the spa this afternoon." She inclined her head toward the brunette watching them with avid interest.

"Hmm." Taylor pushed the button for the glass enclosed elevator.

"Do you think I should wave?" B.J. asked before Taylor pulled her inside.

"No, I've a better idea."

Before she realized his intent, he had her gathered into his arms, silencing her protest with a mind-spinning kiss.

Releasing her, he grinned down at the openly staring brunette.

* * *

B.J. turned to Taylor as the door of the suite shut behind him. "Really, Taylor, it's a crime I haven't a lurid past she could dig up."

"It's perfectly all right, she'll invent one for you. Want a brandy?" He moved to the bar and released the concealing panel.

"No, my nose is already numb."

"I see; is that a congenital condition?"

"It is," she stated, sliding onto a bar stool, "my gauge for the cautious consumption of liquor. When my nose gets numb, I've already had one more than my limit."

"I see." Turning, he poured amber liquid into a solitary snifter. "Obviously, my plan to ply you with liquor is doomed to fail."

"I'm afraid so."

"What's your weakness, B.J.?" The question was so unexpected she was caught unaware. *You,* she almost answered but caught herself in time. "I'm a pushover for soft lights and quiet music."

"Is that so?"

Magically, the lights lowered and music whispered through the room.

"How did you do that?"

He rounded the bar and stood in front of her. "There's a panel in back of the bar."

"The wonders of technology." Nerves prickling, she tensed like a cornered cat when his hand took her arm.

"I want to dance with you." He drew her to her feet. "Take the pins out of your hair. It smells like wildflowers; I want to feel it in my hands."

"Taylor, I . . ."

"Ssh." Slowly, he took out the pins until her hair tumbled free over her shoulders. Then, his fingers combed through the length of it before he gathered her close in his arms.

He moved gently to the music, keeping her molded against him. Her tension flowed away, replaced by a sleepy excitement. Her cheek rested naturally in the curve of his shoulder, as if they had danced countless times before, would dance countless times again.

"Are you going to tell me what B.J. stands for?" he murmured against her ear.

"No one knows," she responded hazily as his fingers followed the tingling delight along her bare skin. "Even the F.B.I. is baffled."

"I suppose I'll have to get it from your mother."

"She doesn't remember." She sighed and snuggled closer.

"How do you sign official papers?" His hand caressed the small of her back.

"Just B.J., I always use B.J."

"On a passport?"

She shrugged, her lips unconsciously brushing his neck, her cheek nuzzling the masculine roughness of his chin. "I haven't got one. I've never needed one."

"You need one to fly to Rome."

"Yes, I'll make sure I have one the next time I do. But I'd sign it Bea Jay." She grinned, knowing he would not realize she had just answered his question. She lifted her face to smile at him and found her lips captured in a gentle, teasing kiss.

"B.J.," he murmured and drew her away before her lips were satisfied. "I want . . ."

"Kiss me again, Taylor." Sweet and heavy, love lay on her. "Really kiss me," she whispered, shutting out the voice of reason. Her eyes fluttered closed as she urged his mouth back to hers.

He said her name again, the words soft on the lips which clung to his in silent request. With a low groan, he crushed her against him.

He swept her feet off the floor as his mouth took hers with unbridled hunger. In dizzying circles, the room whirled as she felt herself lowered to the thick plush of carpet. Unrestrained, his mouth savaged the yielding softness of hers, tongue claiming the sweet moistness. His hand pushed aside the thin silk of her bodice, seeking and finding the smooth promise for more, his mouth and hands roaming over her, finding heat beneath the cool silk, fingers trailing up the slit of her skirt until they captured the firm flesh of her thigh.

Tossed on the turbulent waves of love and need, B.J. responded with a burst of fire. His possession of her mouth and flesh was desperate. She answered by instinct, moving with a woman's hidden knowledge as he took with insatiable appetite the fruits she offered. Her own hands, no longer shy, found their way under his jacket to explore the hard ripple of muscles of his back and shoulders, half-terrified, half-delighting in their strength. From the swell and valley of her breasts, his mouth traveled, burning, tantalizing, to burrow against her neck. Her own lips sought to discover his taste and texture, to assuage her new and throbbing hunger.

His loving had lost all gentleness, his mouth and hands now bringing painful excitement. Her fragile innocence began to dissolve with the ancient cravings of womanhood. B.J. began to tremble with fear and anticipation.

Taylor's mouth lifted from the curve of her neck, and he stared into the eyes cloudy with desire and uncertainty. Abruptly he rose and pulled her to her feet. "Go to bed," he commanded shortly. Turning to the bar, he poured himself another brandy.

Dazed by the abruptness of the rejection, B.J. stood frozen.

"Didn't you hear me? I said go to bed." Downing half his brandy, Taylor pulled out a cigarette.

"Taylor, I don't understand. I thought . . ." A hand lifted to push at her hair, her eyes liquid and pleading. "I thought you wanted me."

"I do." He drew deep on his cigarette. "Now, go to bed."

"Taylor." The fury in his eyes caused her to flinch.

"Just get out of here before I forget all the rules."

B.J. straightened her shoulders and swallowed her tears. "You're the boss." She ignored the swift flame of temper in his eyes and plunged on. "But I want you to know, what I offered you tonight was a one-time deal. I'll never willingly go into your arms again. From now on, the only thing between you and me is the Lakeside Inn."

"We'll leave it at that for now," he said in curt agreement as he turned away and poured another drink. "Just go to bed."

B.J. ran from the room and turned the lock on her door with an audible click.

CHAPTER 12

B.J. threw herself into the inn's routine like a bruised child returning to a mother's arms. She and Taylor had flown from Florida to Vermont in almost total silence, he working on his papers while she had buried herself in a magazine. Avoiding Taylor for the next two days was easy. He made no effort to see her. Annoyance made hurt more tolerable. B.J. worked with dedication to construct a wall of resentment to shield the emptiness she would experience when he left both the inn and her.

Furthering her resentment was the stubborn presence of Darla Trainor. Although B.J. observed Taylor was not often in her company, her mere existence rubbed the sore of wounded pride. Seeing Darla was a constant reminder of B.J.'s uncomfortable and confusing relationship with Taylor.

B.J. knew she could not have mistaken the desire he had felt for her the last night in Florida. She concluded, watching Darla's sensuous elegance, that he had ultimately been

disappointed in her lack of experience in the physical demands of love.

Wanting to avoid any unnecessary contact with Taylor,
B.J. established her office in her room for the duration of his
stay. Buried to her elbows in paperwork one afternoon, she
jumped and scattered receipts as the quiet afternoon was
shattered by screams and scrambling feet above her head.
Racing to the third floor, B.J. followed the sounds into 314.
For a moment she could only stand in the doorway and gape
at the tableau. In the center of the braid rug, Darla Trainor
was engaged in a major battle with one of the housemaids. A
helpless Eddie was caught in the middle, his pleas for peace
ignored.

"Ladies, ladies, please." Taking her life in her hands, B.J.
plunged into the thick of battle and attempted to restore order.
Hands and mixed accusations flew. "Louise, Miss Trainor is
a guest! What's gotten into you?" She tugged, without success, on the housemaid's arm, then switched her attention to
Darla. "Please, stop shouting, I can't understand." Frustrated
because she was shouting herself, B.J. lowered her voice and
tried to pull Darla away. "Please, Miss Trainor, she's half
your size and twice your age. You'll hurt her."

"Take your hands off me!" Darla flung out an arm, and by
accident or design, her fist connected, sending B.J. sprawling
against the bedpost. The light shattered into fragments, then
smothered with darkness as she slid gently to the floor.

"B.J." A voice called from down a long tunnel. B.J. responded with a moan and allowed her eyes to open into
slits. "Lie still," Taylor ordered. Gingerly, she permitted her
eyes to open farther and focused on his lean features. He

was leaning over her, his face lined with concern while he
stroked the hair away from her forehead.

"What happened?" She ignored his command and attempted to sit up. Taylor pushed her back against the pillow.

"That's precisely what I want to know." As he glanced
around, B.J. followed his gaze. Eddie sat on a small settee
with his arm around a sniffling Louise. Darla stood by the
window, her profile etched in indignation.

"Oh." Memory clearing, B.J. let out a long breath and
shut her eyes. Unconsciousness, she decided, had its advantages. "The three of them were wrestling in the middle of
the room. I'm afraid I got in the path of Miss Trainor's left
hook."

The hand stroking her cheek stopped as Taylor's fingers
tensed against her skin. "She hit you?"

"It was an accident, Taylor." Darla interrupted B.J.'s
response, her eyes shining with regret and persecution. "I
was simply trying to take these tacky curtains down when
this . . . this maid—" she gestured regally toward Louise "—
this maid comes in and begins shouting and pulling on me.
Then he's shouting—" She fluttered a hand toward Eddie before passing it across her eyes. "Then Miss Clark appears
from nowhere, and she begins pulling and shouting. It was
a dreadful experience." With a long, shuddering sigh, Darla
appeared to collect herself. "I only tried to push her away.
She had no business coming into my room in the first place.
None of these people belong in my room."

"She had no business trying to take down those curtains,"
Louise chimed in, wringing Eddie's handkerchief. She
waved the soggy linen until all eyes shifted to the window

in question. The white chintz hung drunkenly against the frame. "She said they were out-of-date and impractical like everything else in this place. I washed those curtains myself two weeks ago." Louise placed a hand on her trembling bosom. "I was not going to have her soiling them. I asked her very nicely to stop."

"Nicely?" Darla exploded. "You attacked me."

"I only attacked her," Louise countered with dignity, "when she wouldn't come down. B.J., she was standing on the Bentwood chair. Standing on it!" Louise buried her face in Eddie's shoulder, unable to go on.

"Taylor." Tucking an errant lock behind her ear, Darla moved toward him, blinking moist eyes. "You aren't going to allow her to speak to me that way, are you? I want her fired. She might have injured me. She's unstable." Darla placed a hand on his arm as the first tear trembled on her lashes.

Infuriated by the display of helpless femininity, B.J. rose. She ignored both Taylor's restraining hand and the throbbing in her head. "Mr. Reynolds, am I still manager of this inn?"

"Yes, Miss Clark."

B.J. heard the annoyance in his voice and added it to her list of things to ignore. "Very well. Miss Trainor, it falls under my jurisdiction as manager of the inn to oversee all hirings and firings. If you wish to lodge a formal complaint, please do so in writing to my attention. In the meantime, I should warn you that you will be held responsible for any damages done to the furnishings of your room. You should know, as well, that the inn will stand behind Louise in this matter."

"Taylor." Nearly sputtering with anger, Darla turned back to him. "You're not going to allow this?"

"Mr. Reynolds," B.J. interrupted, wishing for a bottle of aspirin and oblivion. "Perhaps you'll take Miss Trainor to the lounge for a drink, and we can discuss this matter later."

After a brief study, Taylor nodded. "All right, we'll talk later. Rest in your room for the remainder of the day. I'll see you're not disturbed."

B.J. accepted the display of gratitude and sympathy by both Eddie and Louise before trudging down to her room. Stepping over scattered papers, she secured much-needed aspirin then curled up on the quilt of her bed. Dimly, she heard the door open and felt a hand brush through her hair. The grip of sleep was too strong, and she could not tell if the elusive kiss on her mouth was dream or reality.

When she woke up the throbbing had decreased to a negligible ache. Sitting up, B.J. stared at the neat stack of papers on her desk. Maybe it was a dream, she mused, confused by the lack of disorder on her floor. She touched the back of her head and winced as her fingers contacted with a small lump. Maybe I picked them up and don't remember. It's always the mediator who gets clobbered, she thought in disgust, and prepared to go downstairs to confront Taylor. In the lobby, she came upon Eddie, Maggie and Louise in a heated, low-voiced debate. With a sigh, she moved toward them to restore order.

"Oh, B.J." Maggie started with comical guilt. "Mr. Reynolds said you weren't to be disturbed. How are you feeling? Louise said that Miss Trainor gave you a nasty lump."

"It's nothing." She glanced from one solemn face to the

next. She moved her shoulders in resignation. "All right, what's the problem?"

The question produced a jumble of words from three different tongues. Pampering her still aching head, B.J. held up a hand for silence. "Eddie," she decided, choosing at random.

"It's about the architect," he began, and she raised her brows in puzzlement.

"What architect?"

"The one who was here when you were in Florida. Only we didn't know he was an architect. Dot thought he was an artist because he was always walking around with a pad and pencil and making drawings."

Resigning herself to a partially coherent story, B.J. prompted, "Drawings of what?"

"Of the inn," Eddie announced with a flourish. "But he wasn't an artist."

"He was an architect," Maggie interrupted, unable to maintain her silence. Eddie shot her a narrow-eyed frown.

"And how do you know he was an architect?" After asking, B.J. wondered why it mattered. Her wandering attention was soon drawn back with a jolt.

"Because Louise heard Mr. Reynolds talking to him on the phone."

B.J.'s gaze shifted to the housemaid as a hollow feeling grew in the pit of her stomach. "How did you hear, Louise?"

"I wasn't eavesdropping," she claimed with dignity, then amended as B.J. raised her brows. "Well, not really, until I heard him talking about the inn. I was going to dust the office, and since Mr. Reynolds was on the phone, I waited outside. When I heard him say something about a new building, and he said the man's name, Fletcher, I remembered Dot talking about this man named Fletcher making sketches of the inn." She gave the group a small smile in self-reward for her memory. "Anyway, they talked awhile, technical sort of things about dimensions and timber. Then Mr. Reynolds said how he appreciated the Fletcher person not letting on he was an architect until he had everything settled."

"B.J.," Eddie began urgently, grabbing her arm. "Do you think he's going to remodel the inn after all? Do you think he's going to let us all go?"

"No." Feeling her head increase its throbbing, B.J. repeated more emphatically, "No, it's just some mix-up, I'll see about it. Now, you all go back to work and don't spread this around anymore."

"It's no mix up." Darla glided over to the group.

"I told you three to go back to work," B.J. ordered in a voice which they recognized as indisputable. They dispersed, waiting until a safe distance before murmuring among themselves. "If you'll pardon me, Miss Trainor, I'm busy."

"Yes, Taylor's quite anxious to see you."

Cursing herself, B.J. nibbled at the bait. "Is he?"

"Oh, yes. He's ready to tell you about his plans for this little place. It's quite a challenge." She surveyed the lobby with the air of one planning a siege.

"What exactly do you know of his plans?" B.J. demanded.

"You didn't really think he intended to leave this place in this condition simply because you want him to?" With a light laugh, Darla brushed away a fictional speck of dust from her vivid blue blouse. "Taylor is much too practical for grand gestures. Though, he might keep you on in some minor capacity once the alterations are complete. You're hardly qualified to manage one of his resorts, but he does seem to think you have some ability. Of course, if I were you, I'd pack up and bow out now to spare myself the humiliation."

"Are you saying," B.J. began, spacing words with great care, "that Taylor has made definite plans to convert the inn into a resort?"

"Well, of course." Darla smiled indulgently. "He'd hardly need me and an architect otherwise, would he? I wouldn't worry. I'm sure he'll keep the bulk of your staff on, at least temporarily."

With a final smile, Darla turned and left B.J. staring at her retreating back.

After the first flow of despair, fury bubbled. She took the steps two at a time and slammed into her room. Minutes later, she sped out again, taking stairs in a headlong flight and stomping into the office unannounced.

"B.J." Rising from the desk, Taylor studied her furious face. "What are you doing out of bed?"

For an answer, she slammed the paper on his desk. He lifted it, scanning her resignation. "It seems we've been through this before."

"You gave me your word." Her voice trembled at the breach of trust but she lifted her chin. "You can tear that one up too, but it won't change anything. Find yourself a new patsy, Mr. Reynolds. I quit!"

Streaking from the room, she collided bodily with Eddie, brushed him aside and rushed up the stairs. In her room, she pulled out her cases and began to toss articles in them at random. Clothing, cosmetics, knickknacks, whatever was close at hand was dumped, until the first case overflowed.

She stopped her frantic activities to whirl around at the metallic click of the lock. The door opened to admit Taylor.

"Get out!" she commanded, wishing fleetingly she was big enough to toss him out. "This is my room until I leave."

"You're making one beautiful mess," he observed calmly. "You might as well stop that, you're not going anywhere."

"Yes, I am." She caught herself before she tossed her asparagus fern among her lingerie. "I'm leaving just as fast as I can pack. Not only is working for you intolerable, but being under the same roof is more than I can stand. You promised!" She spun to face him, cursing the mist which clouded her eyes. "I believed you. I trusted you. How could I have been so stupid! There's no way I could have prevented you once you'd made your decision, and I would have adjusted somehow. You could have been honest with me."

Tears were spilling over with more speed than she could blink them away, and impatiently she brushed at them with the back of her hand. "Oh!" She spun away to pull pictures from the wall. "I wish I were a man!"

"If you were a man, we'd have had no problem to begin with. If you don't stop tearing up the room, I'll have to stop you. I think you've been battered enough for one day."

She heard it in his voice, the calm control, the half-amused exasperation. Despair for her abiding love merged with fury at his betrayal.

"Just leave me alone!"

"Lie down, B.J., and we'll talk later."

"No, don't you touch me," she ordered as he made to take her arm. "I mean it, Taylor, don't touch me!"

At the desperation in her voice, he dropped his hand to

his side. "All right then." The first warning signals of anger touched his face. In the cool precision of his voice, she could hear the danger. "Suppose you tell me what exactly it is I've done?"

"You know very well."

"Spell it out for me," he interrupted, moving away and lighting a cigarette.

"That architect you brought here while we were in Florida."

"Fletcher?" Taylor cut her off again, but this time he gave her his full attention. "What about him?"

"What about him?" B.J. repeated incredulously. "You brought him here behind my back, making all his little drawings and plans. You probably took me to Florida just to get me out of the way while he was here."

"That was a consideration."

His easy admission left her speechless. A wave of pain washed over her, reflecting in her eyes.

"B.J." Taylor's expression became more curious than angry. "Suppose you tell me precisely what you know."

"Darla was only too happy to enlighten me." Turning away, she assuaged the hurt with more furious packing. "Go talk to her."

"She's gone by now. I told her to leave, B.J., did you think I'd let her stay after she hit you?" The soft texture of his voice caused her hands to falter a moment. Quickly, she forced them to move again. "What did she say to you?"

"She told me everything. How you'd brought in the architect to draw up plans for turning the inn into a resort. That you're going to bring in someone to manage it, how . . ." Her voice broke. "It's bad enough you've been lying to me, Taylor, bad enough you broke your word, but that's personal. What is more important is that you're going to change the whole structure of this community, alter dozens of lives for a few more dollars you don't even need. Your resort in Palm Beach is beautiful and perfect for where and what it is, but the inn . . ."

"Be quiet, B.J." He crushed out his cigarette then thrust his hands in his pockets. "I told you before, I make my own decisions. I called Fletcher in for two reasons." A swift gesture of his hand halted her furious retort. "One, to design a house for a piece of property my agent picked up for me last week. It's about ten miles outside of town, five acres on a hill overlooking the lake. You probably know it."

"Why do you need . . ."

"The second purpose," he continued, ignoring her, "was to design an addition to the inn, adhering to its present architecture. The office space is just too limited. Since I plan to move my base from New York to the inn after we're married, I require larger accommodations."

"I don't see . . ." Her words stumbled to a halt, as she stared into calm brown eyes. A medley of emotions played through her, eradicating the ache in her head. "I never agreed to marry you," she managed at length.

"But you will," he countered and leaned against her desk. "In the meantime, you can ease the various minds downstairs that the inn will remain as is, and you'll remain in the position of manager with some adjustments."

"Adjustments?" She could only parrot his last word and sink into a chair.

"I have no problem basing my business in Vermont, but I won't base my marriage in a hotel. Therefore, we'll live in the house when it's completed, and Eddie can take over some of your duties. You'll also have to be free to travel from time to time. We leave for Rome in three weeks."

"Rome?" she echoed him again, dimly remembering his speaking of Rome and passports.

"Yes, your mother's sending your birth certificate so you can see to getting a passport."

"My mother?" Unable to sit, B.J. rose and paced to the window, trying to clear the fog which covered her brain. "You seem to have everything worked out very neatly." She struggled for control. "I don't suppose it occurred to you to ask my feelings on the matter?"

"I know your feelings." His hands descended to her shoulders, and she stiffened. "I told you once, you can't keep secrets with those eyes."

"I guess it's very convenient for you that I happen to be in love with you." She swallowed, focusing on the gleam of the sun as it filtered through the pines on the hillside.

"It makes things less complicated." His fingers worked at the tension in her shoulders but she held herself rigid.

"Why do you want to marry me, Taylor?"

"Why do you think?" She felt his lips in her hair and squeezed her eyes shut.

"You don't have to marry me for that, and we both know it." Taking a deep breath, she gripped the windowsill tighter. "That first night you came to my room, you'd already won."

"It wasn't enough." His arms circled her waist and brought her back against him. She struggled to keep her mind clear.

"The minute you swaggered into the office with invisible six guns at your hips, I made up my mind to marry you. I knew I could make you want me, I'd felt that the first time I held you, but the night in your room, you looked up at me, and I knew making you want me wasn't enough. I wanted you to love me."

"So—" she moved her shoulders as if it was of little consequence "—you comforted yourself with Darla in the meantime."

She was spun around so quickly, her hair flew out to fall over her face, obscuring vision. "I never touched Darla or anyone from the first minute I saw you. That little charade in the nightgown was strictly for your benefit, and you were stupid enough to fall for it. Do you think I could touch another woman when I had you on my mind?"

Without giving her time to answer, his mouth closed over hers, commanding and possessive. His arms banded her waist, dragging her against him. "You've been driving me crazy for nearly two weeks." Allowing her time to draw a quick breath, his mouth crushed hers again. Slowly, the kiss altered in texture, softening, sweetening, his hand moving with a tender lightness which drugged her reason.

"B.J.," he murmured, resting his chin on her hair. "It would be less intimidating if you owned a few more pounds and inches. I've had a devil of a time fighting my natural instincts. I don't want to hurt you, and you're too small and much too innocent." Lifting her chin, he framed her face with his hands. "Have I told you yet that I love you?"

Her eyes grew wide, her mouth opening, but powerless to form sound. She shook her head briskly and swallowed the obstruction in her throat.

"I didn't think I had. Actually, I think I was hit the minute you stood up from home plate, turned those eyes on me and claimed you were absolutely safe." He bent down and brushed her lips.

She threw her arms around his neck as though he might vanish in a puff of smoke. "Taylor, why have you waited so long?"

Drawing her away, he lifted a brow in amusement, reminding her of the brevity of their relationship.

"It's been years," she claimed, burying her face in his shoulder as joy washed over her. "Decades, centuries."

"And during the millennium," he replied, stroking fingers through her hair, "you've been more exasperating than receptive. The day I came into the lounge and found you ticking off bourbon bottles, I had hoped to start things along a smooth road, but you turned on the ice very effectively. The next day in your room, when you switched to fire, it was very illuminating. The things you said made a great deal of sense, so I decided a change of setting and attitude were in order. Providentially, Bailey called from Florida."

"You said you had to go to Palm Beach to help him with a problem."

"I lied," he said simply, then laughed with great enjoyment at her astonishment. "I had planned," he began, dropping into a chair and pulling her into his lap, "to get you away from the inn for a couple of days. More important to have you to myself. I wanted you relaxed and perhaps a bit off-guard." He laughed again and nuzzled her ear. "Of course, then I had to see you sitting with Hardy and looking like a fresh peach ripe for picking."

"You were jealous." Indescribably pleased, she sighed and burrowed closer.

"That's a mild word for it."

They spent the next few minutes in mutually agreeable silence. Taylor lingered over the taste of her mouth, his hand sliding beneath the barrier of her shirt. "I was quite determined to do things properly, hence the dinner and wine and soft music. I had fully intended to tell you I loved you and ask you to marry me that last night in Florida."

"Why didn't you?"

"You distracted me." His lips trailed along her cheek, reminding her of the power of their last night together. "I had no intention of allowing things to progress the way they did, but you have a habit of stretching my willpower. That night it snapped. Then, I felt you trembling, and your eyes were so young." He sighed and rested his cheek on her hair. "I was furious with myself for losing control of the situation."

"I thought you were furious with me."

"It was better that you did. If I had told you then how I felt about you, nothing would have stopped me from taking you. I was in no frame of mind to introduce you gently to the ways of love. I've never needed anyone so much in my life as I needed you that night."

Round and liquid with love, her eyes lifted to his. "Do you need me, Taylor?"

His hand lifted to brush back her hair. The arm cradling her shifted her closer. "You look like a child," he murmured, tracing her lips with his finger. "A child's mouth, and I can't seem to do without the taste of it. Yes, B.J., I need you."

His mouth lowered, featherlight, but her arm circled his

neck and demanded more. The pressure increased, and the door opened to the world of heat and passion. She felt his hand on her breast, never aware that the buttons of her shirt had been loosened. Her fingers tightened in his hair, willing him to prolong the ecstasy.

His mouth moved to her brow, then rested on her hair, his fingers tracing lightly over her bare skin. "You can see why I've been keeping away from you the last day or so."

With a soft sound of agreement, she buried her face against his shoulder.

"I wanted to get everything set up before I got near you again. I could have done with one more day; we still need a marriage license."

"I'll talk to Judge Walker," she murmured, "if you want one quickly. He's Eddie's uncle."

"Small towns are the backbone of America," Taylor decided. He pulled her close to cover her mouth again when a frantic knock sounded on the door.

"B.J." Eddie's voice drifted through the panel. "Mrs. Frank wants to feed Julius, and I can't find his dinner. And the Bodwin sisters are out of sunflower seeds for Horatio."

"Who's Horatio?" Taylor demanded.

"The Bodwins' parakeet."

"Tell him to feed Horatio to Julius," he suggested, giving the door a scowl.

"It's a thought." Lingering on it briefly, B.J. cast it aside. "Julius's dinner is on the third shelf right hand side of the fridge," she called out. "Send someone into town for a package of sunflower seeds. Now, go away, Eddie, I'm very busy. Mr. Reynolds and I are in conference." With a smile, she circled Taylor's neck again. "Now, Mr. Reynolds, perhaps you'd like my views on the construction of this house you're planning as well as my educated opinion on the structure of your office space."

"Be quiet, B.J."

"You're the boss," she agreed the moment before their lips met.

Storm Warning

CHAPTER 1

The Pine View Inn was nestled comfortably in the Blue Ridge Mountains. After leaving the main road, the meandering driveway crossed a narrow ford just wide enough for one car. The inn was situated a short distance beyond the ford.

It was a lovely place, full of character, the lines so clean they disguised the building's rambling structure. It was three stories high, built of brick that had been weathered to a soft rose, the facade interspersed with narrow, white-shuttered windows. The hipped roof had faded long ago to a quiet green, and three straight chimneys rose from it. A wide wooden porch made a white skirt around the entire house and doors opened out to it from all four sides.

The surrounding lawn was smooth and well-tended. There was less than an acre, house included, before the trees and outcroppings of rock staked their claim on the land. It was as if nature had decided that the house could have this much and no more. The effect was magnificent. The house and mountains stood in peaceful coexistence, neither detracting from the other's beauty.

As she pulled her car to the informal parking area at the side of the house, Autumn counted five cars, including her aunt's vintage Chevy. Though the season was still weeks off, it appeared that the inn already had several guests.

There was a light April chill in the air. The daffodils had yet to open, and the crocuses were just beginning to fade. A few azalea buds showed a trace of color. The day was poised and waiting for spring. The higher, surrounding mountains clung to their winter brown, but touches of green were creeping up them. It wouldn't be gloomy brown and gray for long.

Autumn swung her camera case over one shoulder and her purse over the other—the purse was of secondary importance. Two large suitcases also had to be dragged from the trunk. After a moment's struggle, she managed to arrange everything so that she could take it all in one load, then mounted the steps. The door, as always, was unlocked.

There was no one about. The sprawling living room which served as a lounge was empty, though a fire crackled in the grate. Setting down her cases, Autumn entered the room. Nothing had changed.

Rag rugs dotted the floor; hand-crocheted afghans were draped on the two patchworked sofas. At the windows were chintz priscillas and the Hummel collection was still on the mantel. Characteristically, the room was neat, but far from orderly. There were magazines here and there, an overflowing sewing basket, a group of pillows piled for comfort rather than style on the windowseat. The ambience was friendly with a faintly distracted charm. Autumn thought with a smile that the room suited her aunt perfectly.

She felt an odd pleasure. It was always reassuring to find that something loved hasn't changed. Taking a last quick glance around the room, she ran a hand through her hair. It hung past her waist and was tousled from the long drive with open windows. She gave idle consideration to digging out a brush, but promptly forgot when she heard footsteps down the hall.

"Oh, Autumn, there you are." Typically, her aunt greeted her as though Autumn had just spent an hour at the local supermarket rather than a year in New York. "I'm glad you got in before dinner. We're having pot roast, your favorite."

Not having the heart to remind her aunt that pot roast was her brother Paul's favorite, Autumn smiled. "Aunt Tabby, it's so good to see you!" Quickly she walked over and kissed her aunt's cheek. The familiar scent of lavender surrounded her.

Aunt Tabby in no way resembled the cat her name brought to mind. Cats are prone to snobbishness, disdainfully tolerating the rest of the world. They are known for speed, agility and cunning. Aunt Tabby was known for her vague meanderings, disjointed conversations and confused thinking. She had no guile. Autumn adored her.

Drawing her aunt away, Autumn studied her closely. "You look wonderful." It was invariably true. Aunt Tabby's hair was the same deep chestnut as her niece's, but it was liberally dashed with gray. It suited her. She wore it short, curling haphazardly around her small round face. Her features were all small-scaled—mouth, nose, ears, even her hands and feet.

Her eyes were a mistily faded blue. Though she was halfway through her fifties, her skin refused to wrinkle; it was smooth as a girl's. She stood a half-foot shorter than Autumn and was pleasantly round and soft. Beside her, Autumn felt like a gangly toothpick. Autumn hugged her again, then kissed her other cheek. "Absolutely wonderful."

Aunt Tabby smiled up at her. "What a pretty girl you are. I always knew you would be. But so awfully thin." She patted Autumn's cheek and wondered how many calories were in pot roast.

With a shrug, Autumn thought of the ten pounds she had gained when she'd stopped smoking. She had lost them again almost as quickly.

"Nelson always was thin," Aunt Tabby added, thinking of her brother, Autumn's father.

"Still is," Autumn told her. She set her camera case on a table and grinned at her aunt. "Mom's always threatening to sue for divorce."

"Oh well." Aunt Tabby clucked her tongue and looked thoughtful. "I don't think that's wise after all the years they've been married." Knowing the jest had been lost, Autumn merely nodded in agreement. "I gave you the room you always liked, dear. You can still see the lake from the window. The leaves will be full soon though, but . . . Remember when you fell in when you were a little girl? Nelson had to fish you out."

"That was Will," Autumn reminded her, thinking back on the day her younger brother had toppled into the lake.

"Oh?" Aunt Tabby looked faintly confused a moment, then smiled disarmingly. "He learned to swim quite well, didn't he? Such an enormous young man now. It always surprised me. There aren't any children with us at the moment," she added, flowing from sentence to sentence with her own brand of logic.

"I saw several cars. Are there many people here?" Autumn stretched her cramped muscles as she wandered the room. It smelled of sandalwood and lemon oil.

"One double and five singles," she told her. "One of the singles is French and quite fond of my apple pie. I must go check on my blueberry cobbler," she announced suddenly. "Nancy is a marvel with a pot roast, but helpless with baking. George is down with a virus."

She was already making for the door as Autumn tried to puzzle out the last snatch of information.

"I'm sorry to hear that," she replied with what she hoped was appropriate sympathy.

"I'm a bit shorthanded at the moment, dear, so perhaps you can manage your suitcases yourself. Or you can wait for one of the gentlemen to come in."

George, Autumn remembered. Gardener, bellboy and bartender.

"Don't worry, Aunt Tabby. I can manage."

"Oh, by the way, Autumn." She turned back, but Autumn knew her aunt's thoughts were centered on the fate of her cobbler. "I have a little surprise for you—oh, I see Miss Bond is coming in." Typically, she interrupted herself, then smiled. "She'll keep you company. Dinner's at the usual time. Don't be late."

Obviously relieved that both her cobbler and her niece were about to be taken care of, she bustled off, her heels tapping cheerfully on the hardwood floor.

Autumn turned to watch her designated companion enter through the side door. She found herself gaping.

Julia Bond. Of course, Autumn recognized her instantly. There could be no other woman who possessed such shimmering, golden beauty. How many times had she sat in a crowded theater and watched Julia's charm and talent transcend the movie screen? In person, in the flesh, her beauty didn't diminish. It sparkled, all the more alive in three dimensions.

Small, with exquisite curves just bordering on lush, Julia Bond was a magnificent example of womanhood at its best. Her cream-colored linen slacks and vivid blue cashmere sweater set off her coloring to perfection. Pale golden hair framed her face like sunlight. Her eyes were a deep summer blue. The full, shapely mouth lifted into a smile even as the famous brows arched. For a moment, Julia stood, fingering her silk scarf. Then she spoke, her voice smoky, exactly as Autumn had known it would be. "What fabulous hair."

It took Autumn a moment to register the comment. Her mind was blank at seeing Julia Bond step into her aunt's lounge as casually as she would have strolled into the New York Hilton. The smile, however, was full of charm and so completely unaffected that Autumn was able to form one in return.

"Thank you. I'm sure you're used to being stared at, Miss Bond, but I apologize anyway."

Julia sat, with a grace that was at once insolent and admirable, in a wingback chair. Drawing out a long, thin cigarette, she gave Autumn a full-power smile. "Actors adore being stared at. Sit down." She gestured. "I have a feeling I've at last found someone to talk to in this place."

Autumn's obedience was automatic, a tribute to the actress's charm.

"Of course," Julia continued, still studying Autumn's face, "you're entirely too young and too attractive." Settling back, she crossed her legs. Somehow, she managed to transform the wingback chair, with the small darning marks in the left arm, into a throne. "Then your coloring and mine offset each other nicely. How old are you, darling?"

"Twenty-five." Captivated, Autumn answered without thinking.

Julia laughed, a low bubbling sound that flowed and ebbed like a wave. "Oh, so am I. Perennially." She tossed her head in amusement, then left it cocked to the side. Autumn's fingers itched for her camera. "What's your name, darling, and what brings you to solitude and pine trees?"

"Autumn," she responded as she pushed her hair off her shoulders. "Autumn Gallegher. My aunt owns the inn."

"Your aunt?" Julia's face registered surprise and more amusement. "That dear fuzzy little lady is your aunt?"

"Yes." A grin escaped at the accuracy of the description. "My father's sister." Relaxed, Autumn leaned back. She was doing her own studying, thinking in angles and shadings.

"Incredible," Julia decided with a shake of her head. "You don't look like her. Oh, the hair," she corrected with an envious glance. "I imagine hers was once your color. Magnificent. I know women who would kill for that shade, and you seem to have about three feet of it." With a sigh, she drew delicately on her cigarette. "So, you've come to pay your aunt a visit."

There was nothing condescending in her attitude. Her eyes were interested and Autumn began to find her not only charming but likable. "For a few weeks. I haven't seen her in nearly a year. She wrote and asked me to come down, so I'm taking my vacation all at one time."

"What do you do?" Julia pursed her lips. "Model?"

"No." Autumn's laughter came quickly at the thought of it. "I'm a photographer."

"Photographer!" Julia exclaimed. She glowed with pleasure. "I'm very fond of photographers. Vanity, I suppose."

"I imagine photographers are fond of you for the same reason."

"Oh, my dear." When Julia smiled, Autumn recognized both pleasure and amusement. "How sweet."

"Are you alone, Miss Bond?" Her sense of curiosity was ingrained. Autumn had already forgotten to be overwhelmed.

"Julia, please, or you'll remind me of the half-decade that separates our ages. The color of that sweater suits you," she commented, eyeing Autumn's crewneck. "I never could wear gray. Sorry, darling," she apologized with a lightning-quick smile. "Clothes are a weakness of mine. Am I alone?" The smile deepened. "Actually, this little hiatus is a mixture of business and pleasure. I'm in between husbands at the moment—a glorious interlude." Julia tossed her head. "Men are delightful, but husbands can be dreadfully inhibiting. Have you ever had one?"

"No." The grin was irrepressible. From the tone, Julia might have asked if Autumn had ever owned a cocker spaniel.

"I've had three." Julia's eyes grew wicked and delighted. "In this case, the third was *not* the charm. Six months with an English baron was quite enough."

Autumn remembered the photos she had seen of Julia with

a tall, aristocratic Englishman. She had worn tweed brilliantly.

"I've taken a vow of abstinence," Julia continued. "Not against men—against marriage."

"Until the next time?" Autumn ventured.

"Until the next time," Julia agreed with a laugh. "At the moment, I'm here for platonic purposes with Jacques Le-Farre."

"The producer?"

"Of course." Again, Autumn felt the close scrutiny. "He'll take one look at you and decide he has a new star on the horizon. Still, that might be an interesting diversion." She frowned a moment, then shrugged it away. "The other residents of your aunt's cozy inn have offered little in the way of diversions thus far."

"Oh?" Automatically, Autumn shook her head as Julia offered her a cigarette.

"We have Dr. and Mrs. Spicer," Julia began. One perfectly shaped nail tapped against the arm of her chair. There was something different in her attitude now. Autumn was sensitive to moods, but this was too subtle a change for her to identify. "The doctor himself might be interesting," Julia continued. "He's very tall and nicely built, smoothly handsome with just the right amount of gray at the temples."

She smiled. Just then Autumn thought Julia resembled a very pretty, well-fed cat.

"The wife is short and unfortunately rather dumpy. She spoils whatever attractiveness she might have with a continually morose expression." Julia demonstrated it with terrifying skill. Autumn's laughter burst out before she could stop it.

"How unkind," Autumn chided, smiling still.

"Oh, I know." A graceful hand waved in dismissal. "I have no patience for women who let themselves go, then look daggers at those who don't. He's fond of fresh air and walking in the woods, and she grumbles and mopes along after him." Julia paused, giving Autumn a wary glance. "How do you feel about walking?"

"I like it." Hearing the apology in her voice, Autumn grinned.

"Oh well." Julia shrugged at eccentricities. "It takes all kinds. Next, we have Helen Easterman." The oval, tinted nails began to tap again. Her eyes drifted from Autumn's to the view out the window. Somehow, Autumn didn't think she was seeing mountains and pine trees. "She says she's an art teacher, taking time off to sketch nature. She's rather attractive, though a bit overripe, with sharp little eyes and an unpleasant smile. Then, there's Steve Anderson." Julia gave her slow, cat smile again. Describing men, Autumn mused, was more to her taste. "He's rather delicious. Wide shoulders, California blond hair. Nice blue eyes. And he's embarrassingly rich. His father owns, ah . . ."

"Anderson Manufacturing?" Autumn prompted and was rewarded with a beam of approval.

"How clever of you."

"I heard something about Steve Anderson aiming for a political career."

"Mmm, yes. It would suit him." Julia nodded. "He's very well-mannered and has a disarmingly boyish smile—that's always a political asset."

"It's a sobering thought that government officials are elected on their smiles."

"Oh, politics." Julia wrinkled her nose and shrugged away the entire profession. "I had an affair with a senator once. Nasty business, politics." She laughed at some private joke.

Not certain whether her comment had been a romantic observation or a general one, Autumn didn't pursue it. "So far," Autumn said, "it seems an unlikely menagerie for Julia Bond and Jacques LeFarre to join."

"Show business." With a smile, she lit another cigarette, then waved it at Autumn. "Stick with photography, Autumn, no matter what promises Jacques makes you. We're here due to a whim of the last and most interesting character in our little play. He's a genius of a writer. I did one of his screenplays a few years back. Jacques wants to produce another, and he wants me for the lead." She dragged deep on the cigarette. "I'm willing—really good scripts aren't that easy to come by—but our writer is in the middle of a novel. Jacques thinks the novel could be turned into a screenplay, but our genius resists. He told Jacques he was coming here to write in peace for a few weeks, and that he'd think it over. The charming LeFarre talked him into allowing us to join him for a few days."

Autumn was both fascinated and confused. Her question was characteristically blunt. "Do you usually chase writers around this way? I'd think it would be more the other way around."

"And you'd be right," Julia said flatly. With only the movement of her eyebrows, her expression turned haughty. "But Jacques is dead set on producing this man's work, and he caught me at a weak moment. I had just finished reading one of the most appalling scripts. Actually," she amended with a grimace, "three of the most appalling scripts. My work feeds me, but I won't do trash. So . . ." Julia smiled and moved her hands. "Here I am."

"Chasing a reluctant writer."

"It has its compensations."

I'd like to shoot her with the sun at her back. Low sun, just going down. The contrasts would be perfect. Autumn pulled herself back from her thoughts and caught up with Julia's conversation. "Compensations?" she repeated.

"The writer happens to be incredibly attractive, in that carelessly rugged sort of way that no one can pull off unless he's born with it. A marvelous change of pace," she added with a wicked gleam, "from English barons. He's tall and bronzed with black hair that's just a bit too long and always disheveled. It makes a woman itch to get her fingers into it. Best, he has those dark eyes that say 'go to hell' so eloquently. He's an arrogant devil." Her sigh was pure feminine approval. "Arrogant men are irresistible, don't you think?"

Autumn murmured something while she tried to block out the suspicions Julia's words were forming. It had to be someone else, she thought frantically. Anyone else.

"And, of course, Lucas McLean's talent deserves a bit of arrogance."

The color drained from Autumn's face and left it stiff. Waves of almost forgotten pain washed over her. *How could it hurt so much after all this time?* She had built the wall so carefully, so laboriously—how could it crumble into dust at the sound of a name? She wondered, dully, what sadistic quirk of fate had brought Lucas McLean back to torment her.

"Why, darling, what's the matter?"

Julia's voice, mixed with concern and curiosity, penetrated. As if coming up for air, Autumn shook her head. "Nothing." She shook her head again and swallowed. "It was just a surprise to hear that Lucas McLean is here." Drawing a deep breath, she met Julia's eyes. "I knew him . . . a long time ago."

"Oh, I see."

And she did see, Autumn noted, very well. Sympathy warred with speculation in both her face and voice. Autumn shrugged, determined to treat it lightly.

"I doubt he remembers me." Part of her prayed with fervor it was true, while another prayed at cross-purposes. Would he forget? she wondered. Could he?

"Autumn, darling, yours is a face no man is likely to forget." Through a mist of smoke, Julia studied her. "You were very young when you fell in love with him?"

"Yes." Autumn was trying, painfully, to rebuild her protective wall and wasn't surprised by the question. "Too young, too naive." She managed a brittle smile and for the first time in six months accepted a cigarette. "But I learn quickly."

"It seems the next few days might prove interesting, after all."

"Yes." Autumn's agreement lacked enthusiasm. "So it does." She needed time to be alone, to steady herself. "I have to take my bags up," she said as she rose.

While Autumn stretched her slender arms toward the ceiling, Julia smiled. "I'll see you at dinner."

Nodding, Autumn gathered up her camera case and purse and left the room.

In the hall, she struggled with her suitcases, camera and purse before beginning the task of transporting them up the stairs. Throughout the slow trek up the stairs, Autumn relieved tension by muttering and swearing. *Lucas McLean,* she thought and banged a suitcase against her shin. She nearly convinced herself that her ill humor was a result of the bruise she'd just given herself. Out of breath and patience, she reached the hallway outside her room and dumped everything on the floor with an angry thud.

"Hello, Cat. No bellboy?"

The voice—and the ridiculous nickname—knocked a few of her freshly mortared bricks loose. After a brief hesitation, Autumn turned to him. The pain wouldn't show on her face. She'd learned that much. But the pain was there, surprisingly real and physical. It reminded her of the day her brother had swung a baseball bat into her stomach when she had been twelve. *I'm not twelve now,* she reminded herself. She met Lucas's arrogant smile with one of her own.

"Hello, Lucas. I heard you were here. The Pine View Inn is bursting with celebrities."

He was the same, she noted. Dark and lean and male. There was a ruggedness about him, accented by rough black brows and craggy, demanding features that couldn't be called handsome. Oh, no, that was much too tame a word for Lucas McLean. Arousing, irresistible. Fatal. Those words suited him better.

His eyes were nearly as black as his hair. They kept secrets easily. He carried himself well, with a negligent grace that was natural rather than studied. His not-so-subtle masculine power drifted with him as he ambled closer and studied her.

It was then that Autumn noticed how hellishly tired he looked. There were shadows under his eyes. He needed a shave. The creases in his cheeks were deeper than she remembered—and she remembered very well.

"You look like yesterday." He grabbed a handful of her hair as he fastened his eyes on hers. She wondered how she could have ever thought herself over him. No woman ever got over Lucas. Sheer determination kept her eyes level.

"You," she countered as she opened her door, "look like hell. You need some sleep."

Lucas leaned on the doorjamb before she could drag her cases inside and slam the door. "Having trouble with one of my characters," he said smoothly. "She's a tall, willowy creature with chestnut hair that ripples down her back. Narrow hipped, with legs that go right up to her waist."

Bracing herself, Autumn turned back and stared at him. Carefully, she erased any expression from her face.

"She has a child's mouth," he continued, dropping his glance to hers a moment. "And a small nose, somewhat at odds with high, elegant cheekbones. Her skin is ivory with touches of warmth just under the surface. Her eyes are long lidded and ridiculously lashed—green that melts into amber, like a cat's."

Without comment, she listened to his description of herself. She gave him a bored, disinterested look he would never have seen on her face three years before. "Is she the murderer or the corpse?" It pleased Autumn to see his brows lift in surprise before they drew together in a frown.

"I'll send you a copy when it's done." He searched her face, then a shutter came down, leaving his expression unreadable. That, too, she noted, hadn't changed.

"You do that." After giving her cases a superhuman tug, jettisoning them into her room, Autumn rested against the door. Her smile had no feeling. "You'll have to excuse me, Lucas, I've had a long drive and want a bath."

She closed the door firmly and with finality, in his face.

Autumn's movements then became brisk. There was unpacking to do and a bath to draw and a dress to choose for dinner. Those things would give her time to recover before she allowed herself to think, to feel. When she slipped into lingerie and stockings, her nerves were steadier. The worst of it had been weathered. Surely, she mused, the first meeting, the first exchange of words were the most difficult. She had seen him. She had spoken to him. She had survived. Success made her bold. For the first time in nearly two years, Autumn allowed herself to remember.

She had been so much in love. Her assignment had been an ordinary one—a picture layout of mystery novelist Lucas McLean. The result had been six months of incredible joy followed by unspeakable hurt.

He had overwhelmed her. She'd never met anyone like him. She knew now that there was no one else like him. He was a law unto himself. He had been brilliant, compelling, selfish and moody. After the first shock of learning he was interested in her, Autumn had floated along on a cloud of wonder and admiration. And love.

His arrogance, as Julia had said, was irresistible. His phone calls at three in the morning had been treasured. The last time she had been held in his arms, experiencing the wild demands of his mouth, had been as exciting as the first. She had tumbled into his bed like a ripe peach, giving up her innocence with the freedom that comes with blind, trusting love.

She remembered he'd never said the words she wanted to hear. She'd told herself she had no need for them—words weren't important. There were unexpected boxes of roses, surprise picnics on the beach with wine in paper cups and lovemaking that was both intense and all-consuming. What did she need with words? When the end had come it had been swift—but far from painless.

Autumn put his distraction, his moodiness down to trouble with the novel he was working on. It didn't occur to her that he'd been bored. It was her habit to fix dinner on Wednesdays at his home. It was a small, private evening, one she prized above all others. Her arrival was so natural to her, so routine, that when she entered his living room and found him dressed in dinner clothes, she only thought he had decided to add a more formal atmosphere to their quiet dinner.

"Why, Cat, what are you doing here?" The unexpected words were spoken so easily, she merely stared. "Ah, it's Wednesday, isn't it?" There was a slight annoyance in his tone, as though he had forgotten a dentist appointment. "I completely forgot. I'm afraid I've made other plans."

"Other plans?" she echoed. Comprehension was still a long way off.

"I should have phoned you and saved you the trip. Sorry, Cat, I'm just leaving."

"Leaving?"

"I'm going out." He moved across the room and stared at her. She shivered. No one's eyes could be as warm—or as cold—as Lucas McLean's. "Don't be difficult, Autumn, I don't want to hurt you any more than is necessary."

Feeling the tears of realization rush out, she shook her head and fought against acceptance. The tears sent him into a fury.

"Stop it! I haven't the time to deal with weeping. Just pack it in. Chalk it up to experience. God knows you need it."

Swearing, he stomped away to light a cigarette. She had stood there, weeping without sound.

"Don't make a fool of yourself, Autumn." The calm, rigid voice was more frightening to her than his anger. At least anger was an emotion. "When something's over, you forget it and move on." He turned back with a shrug. "That's life."

"You don't want me anymore?" She stood meekly, like a dog who waits to feel the lash again. Her vision was too clouded with tears to see his expression. For a moment, he was silent.

"Don't worry, Cat," he answered in a careless, brutal voice. "Others will."

She turned and fled. It had taken over a year before he had stopped being the first thing in her mind every morning.

But she had survived, she reminded herself. She slipped into a vivid green dress. And I'll keep right on surviving. She knew she was basically the same person who had fallen in love with Lucas, but now she had a more polished veneer. Innocence was gone, and it would take more than Lucas McLean to make a fool of her again. She tossed her head, satisfied with the memory of her reception to him. That had given him a bit of a surprise. No, Autumn Gallegher was no one's fool any longer.

Her thoughts drifted to her aunt's odd assortment of guests.

She wondered briefly why the rich and famous were gathering here instead of at some exclusive resort. Dismissing the thought with a shrug, she reminded herself it was dinnertime. Aunt Tabby had told her not to be late.

CHAPTER 2

It was a strange assortment to find clustered in the lounge of a remote Virginia inn: an award-winning writer, an actress, a producer, a wealthy California businessman, a successful cardiovascular surgeon and his wife, an art teacher who wore St. Laurent. Before Autumn's bearings were complete, she found herself enveloped in them. Julia pounced on her possessively and began introductions. Obviously, Julia enjoyed her prior claim and the center-stage position it gave her. Whatever embarrassment Autumn might have felt at being thrust into the limelight was overridden by amusement at the accuracy of Julia's earlier descriptions.

Dr. Robert Spicer was indeed smoothly handsome. He was drifting toward fifty and bursting with health. He wore a casually expensive green cardigan with brown leather patches at the elbows. His wife, Jane, was also as Julia had described: unfortunately dumpy. The small smile she gave Autumn lasted about two seconds before her face slipped back into the dissatisfied grooves that were habitual. She cast dark, bad-tempered glances at her husband while he gave Julia the bulk of his attention.

Watching them, Autumn could find little sympathy for Jane and no disapproval for Julia—no one disapproves of a flower for drawing bees. Julia's attraction was just as natural, and just as potent.

Helen Easterman was attractive in a slick, practiced fashion. The scarlet of her dress suited her, but struck a jarring note in the simply furnished lounge. Her face was perfectly made-up and reminded Autumn of a mask. As a photographer, she knew the tricks and secrets of cosmetics. Instinctively, Autumn avoided her.

In contrast, Steve Anderson was all charm. Good looks, California style, as Julia had said. Autumn liked the crinkles at the corners of his eyes and his careless chic. He wore chinos easily. From his bearing, she knew he would wear black tie with equal aplomb. If he chose a political career, she mused, he should make his way very well.

Julia had offered no description of Jacques LeFarre. What Autumn knew of him came primarily from either the gossip magazines or his films. He was smaller than she had imagined, barely as tall as she, but with a wiry build. His features were strong and he wore his brown hair brushed back from his forehead where three worry lines had been etched. She liked the trim moustache over his mouth, and the way he lifted her hand to kiss it when they were introduced.

"Well, Autumn," Steve began with a smile. "I'm playing bartender in George's absence. What can I fix you?"

"Vodka Collins, easy on the vodka," Lucas answered. Autumn gave up the idea of ignoring him.

"Your memory's improved," she said coolly.

"So's your wardrobe." He ran a finger down the collar of her dress. "I remember when it ran to jeans and old sweaters."

"I grew up." Her eyes were as steady and as measuring as his.

"So I see."

"Ah, you have met before," Jacques put in. "But this is fascinating. You are old friends?"

"Old friends?" Lucas repeated before Autumn could speak. He studied her with infuriating amusement. "Would you say that was an accurate description, Cat?"

"Cat?" Jacques frowned a moment. "Ah, the eyes, *oui*." Pleased, he brushed his index finger over his moustache. "It suits. What do you think, *chérie*?" He turned to Julia, who seemed to be enjoying herself watching the unfolding scene. "She's enchanting, and her voice is quite good."

"I've already warned Autumn about you," Julia drawled, then gave Robert Spicer a glorious smile.

"Ah, Julia," Jacques said mildly, "how wicked of you."

"Autumn works the other side of the camera," Lucas stated. Knowing his eyes had been on her the entire time, Autumn was grateful when Steve returned with her drink. "She's a photographer."

"Again, I'm fascinated." Autumn's free hand was captured in Jacques's. "Tell me why you are behind the camera instead of in front of it? Your hair alone would cause poets to run for their pens."

No woman was immune to flattery with a French accent,

and Autumn smiled fully into his eyes. "I doubt I could stand still long enough to begin with."

"Photographers can be quite useful," Helen Easterman stated suddenly. Lifting a hand, she patted her dark, sleek cap of hair. "A good, clear photograph is an invaluable tool . . . to an artist."

An awkward pause followed the statement. Tension entered the room, so out of place in the comfortable lounge with its chintz curtains that Autumn thought it must be her imagination. Helen smiled into the silence and sipped her drink. Her eyes swept over the others, inclusively, never centering on one.

Autumn knew there was something here which isolated Helen and set her apart from the rest. Messages were being passed without words, though there was no way for Autumn to tell who was communicating what to whom. The mood changed swiftly as Julia engaged Robert Spicer in bright conversation. Jane Spicer's habitual frown became more pronounced.

The easy climate continued as they went in to dinner. Sitting between Jacques and Steve, Autumn was able to add to her education as she observed Julia flirting simultaneously with Lucas and Robert. She was, in Autumn's opinion, magnificent. Even through the discomfort of seeing Lucas casually return the flirtation, she had to admire Julia's talent. Her charm and beauty were insatiable. Jane ate in sullen silence.

Dreary woman, Autumn mused, then wondered what her own reaction would be if it were her husband so enchanted. Action, she decided, not silence. I'd simply claw her eyes out. The image of dumpy Jane wrestling with the elegant Julia made her smile. Even as she enjoyed the notion, she looked up to find Lucas's eyes on her.

His brows were lifted at an angle she knew meant amusement. Autumn turned her attention to Jacques.

"Do you find many differences in the movie industry here in America, Mr. LeFarre?"

"You must call me Jacques." His smile caused the tips of his moustache to rise. "There are differences, yes. I would say that Americans are more . . . adventurous than Europeans."

Autumn lifted her shoulders and smiled. "Maybe because we're a mixture of nationalities. Not watered down. Just Americanized."

"Americanized." Jacques tried out the word and approved it. His grin was younger than his smile, less urbane. "Yes, I would say I feel Americanized in California."

"Still, California's only one aspect of the country," Steve put in. "And I wouldn't call L.A. or southern California particularly typical." Autumn watched his eyes flick over her hair. His interest brought on a small flutter of response that pleased her. It proved that she was still a woman, open to a man—not just one man. "Have you ever been to California, Autumn?"

"I lived there . . . once." Her response to Steve, and the need to prove something to herself, urged her to turn her eyes to Lucas. Their gazes locked and held for one brief instant. "I relocated to New York three years ago."

"There was a family here from New York," Steve went on. If he'd noticed the look that had passed, he gave no sign. Yes, a good politician, Autumn thought again. "They just checked out this morning. The woman was one of those robust types with energy pouring out of every cell. She needed it," he added with a smile that was for Autumn alone. "She had three boys. Triplets. I think she said they were eleven."

"Oh, those beastly children!" Julia switched her attention from Robert and looked across the table. She rolled her summer blue eyes. "Running around like a pack of monkeys. Worse, you could never tell which one of them it was zooming by or leaping down. They did everything in triplicate." She shuddered and lifted her water glass. "They ate like elephants."

"Running and eating are part of childhood," Jacques commented with a shake of his head. "Julia," he told Autumn with a conspirator's wink, "was born twenty-one and beautiful."

"Anyone with manners is born twenty-one," Julia countered. "Being beautiful was simply a bonus." Her eyes were laughing now. "Jacques is crazy about kids," she informed Autumn. "He has three specimens of his own."

Interested, Autumn turned to him. She'd never thought of Jacques LeFarre in terms other than his work. "I'm crazy about them, too," she confessed and shot Julia a grin. "What sort of specimens do you have?"

"Boys," he answered. Autumn found the fondness in his eyes curiously touching. "They are like a ladder." With his hand, he formed imaginary steps. "Seven, eight and nine years. They live in France with my wife—my ex-wife." He frowned, then smoothed it away. Autumn realized how the worry lines in his brow had been formed.

"Jacques actually wants custody of the little monsters."

Julia's look was more tolerant than her words. Here, Autumn saw, affection transcended flirtation. "Even though I hold your sanity suspect, Jacques, I'm forced to admit you make a better father than Claudette makes a mother."

"Custody suits are sensitive matters," Helen announced from the end of the table. She drank from her water glass, peering over the rim with small, sharp eyes. The look that she sent Jacques seemed to brush everyone else out of her line of vision. "It's so important that any . . . unsuitable information doesn't come to light."

Tension sprang back. Autumn felt the Frenchman stiffen beside her. But there was more. Undercurrents flowed up and down the long pine table. It was impossible not to feel them, though there was nothing tangible, nothing solid. Instinctively, Autumn's eyes sought Lucas's. There was nothing there but the hard, unfathomable mask she had seen too often in the past.

"Your aunt serves such marvelous meals, Miss Gallegher." With a puzzling, satisfied smirk, Helen shifted her attention to Autumn.

"Yes." She blundered into the awful silence. "Aunt Tabby gives food a high rating of importance."

"Aunt Tabby?" Julia's rich laugh warred with the tension, and won. The air was instantly lighter. "What a wonderful name. Did you know Autumn has an Aunt Tabby when you christened her Cat, Lucas?" She stared up at him, her eyes wide and guileless. Autumn was reminded of a movie Julia had been in, in which she played the innocent ingenue to perfection.

"Lucas and I didn't know each other well enough to

discuss relatives." Autumn's voice was easy and careless and pleased her very much. So did Lucas's barely perceptible frown.

"Actually," he replied, recovering quickly, "we were too occupied to discuss family trees." He sent her a smile which sneaked through her defenses. Autumn's pulse hammered. "What did we talk about in those days, Cat?"

"I've forgotten," she murmured, knowing she had lost the edge before she'd really held it. "It was a long time ago."

Aunt Tabby bustled in with her prize cobbler.

There was music on the stereo and a muted fire in the hearth when they returned to the lounge. The scene, if Autumn could have captured it on film, was one of relaxed camaraderie. Steve and Robert huddled over a chessboard while Jane made her discontented way through a magazine. Even without a photographer's eye for color, Autumn knew the woman should never wear brown. She felt quite certain that Jane invariably would.

Lucas sprawled on the sofa. Somehow, he always managed to relax in a negligent fashion without seeming sloppy; there was always an alertness about him, energy simmering right under the surface. Autumn knew he watched people without being obvious—not because he cared if he made them uncomfortable, he didn't in the least—it was simply something he was able to do. And in watching them, he was able to learn their secrets. An obsessive writer, he drew his characters from flesh and blood. With no mercy, Autumn recalled.

At the moment, he seemed content with his conversation with Julia and Jacques. They flanked him on the sofa and spoke with the ease that came from familiarity; they shared the same world.

But it's not my world, Autumn reminded herself. I only pretended it was for a little while. I only pretended he was mine for a little while. She had been right when she told Lucas she had grown up. Pretend games were for children.

Yet, Autumn thought as she sat back and observed, there was a game of some sort going on here. There was a faint glistening of unease superimposed over the homey picture. Always attuned to contrasts, she could sense it, feel it. They're not letting me in on the rules, she mused, and found herself grateful. She didn't want to play. Making her excuses to no one in particular, Autumn slipped from the room to find her aunt.

Whatever tension she had felt evaporated the moment Autumn stepped into her aunt's room.

"Oh, Autumn." Aunt Tabby lifted her glasses from her nose and let them dangle from a chain around her neck. "I was just reading a letter from your mother. I'd forgotten it was here until this minute. She says by the time I read this, you'll be here. And here you are." Smiling, she patted Autumn's hand. "Debbie always was so clever. Did you enjoy your pot roast, dear?"

"It was lovely, Aunt Tabby, thank you."

"We'll have to have it once a week while you're with us." Autumn smiled and thought of how she liked spaghetti. Paul probably gets spaghetti on his visits, she mused. "I'll just make a note of that, else it'll slip right through my mind." Autumn recalled that Aunt Tabby's notes were famous for their ability to slip into another dimension, and felt more hopeful. "Where are my glasses?" Aunt Tabby murmured, puckering her impossibly smooth brow. Standing, she rummaged through her desk, lifting papers and peering under books. "They're never where you leave them."

Autumn lifted the dangling glasses from her aunt's bosom, then perched them on her nose. After blinking a moment, Aunt Tabby smiled in her vague fashion.

"Isn't that strange?" she commented. "They were here all along. You're just as clever as your mother."

Autumn couldn't resist giving her a bone-crushing hug. "Aunt Tabby, I adore you!"

"You always were such a sweet child." She patted Autumn's cheek, then moved away, leaving the scent of lavender and talc hanging in the air. "I hope you like your surprise."

"I'm sure I will."

"You haven't seen it yet?" Her small mouth pouted in thought. "No, I'm quite sure I haven't shown you yet, so you can't know if you like it. Did you and Miss Bond have a nice chat? Such a lovely lady. I believe she's in show business."

Autumn's smile was wry. There was no one, she thought, absolutely no one like Aunt Tabby. "Yes, I believe she is. I've always admired her."

"Oh, have you met before?" Aunt Tabby asked absently as she shuffled the papers on her desk back into her own particular order. "I suppose I'd better show you now while I have it on my mind."

Autumn tried to keep up with her aunt's thought processes, but it had been a year since her last visit and she was rusty. "Show me what, Aunt Tabby?"

"Oh now, it wouldn't be a surprise if I told you, would it?"

Playfully, she shook her finger under Autumn's nose. "You'll just have to be patient and come along with me." With this, she bustled from the room.

Autumn followed, deducing they were again discussing the surprise. She had to shorten her gait to match her aunt's. Autumn usually moved in a loose-limbed stride, a result of leanness and lengthy legs, while her aunt scuttled unrhythmically. Like a rabbit, Autumn thought, that dashes out in the road then can't make up its mind which way to run. As they walked, Aunt Tabby muttered about bed linen. Autumn's thoughts drifted irresistibly to Lucas.

"Now, here we are." Aunt Tabby stopped. She gave the door an expectant smile. The door itself, Autumn recalled, led to a sitting room long since abandoned and converted into a storage room. It was a convenient place for cleaning supplies, as it adjoined the kitchen. "Well," Aunt Tabby said, beaming, "what do you think?"

Searching for the right comment, Autumn realized the surprise must be inside. "Is my surprise in there, Aunt Tabby?"

"Yes, of course, how silly." She clucked her tongue. "You won't know what it is until I open the door."

With this indisputable logic, she did.

When the lights were switched on, Autumn stood stunned. Where she had expected to see mops, brooms and buckets was a fully equipped darkroom. Every detail, every piece of apparatus stood neat and orderly in front of her. Her voice had been left outside the door.

"Well, what do you think?" Aunt Tabby repeated. She moved around the room, stopping now and again to peer at bottles of developing fluid, tongs and trays. "It all looks so technical and scientific to me." The enlarger caused her to frown and tilt her head. "I'm sure I don't understand a thing about it."

"Oh, Aunt Tabby." Autumn's voice finally joined her body. "You shouldn't have."

"Oh dear, is something wrong with it? Nelson told me you developed your own film, and the company that brought in all these things assured me everything was proper. Of course . . ." Her voice wavered in doubt. "I really don't know a thing about it."

Her aunt looked so distressed, Autumn nearly wept with love. "No, Aunt Tabby, it's perfect. It's wonderful." She enveloped the small, soft body in her arms. "I meant that you shouldn't have done this for me. All the trouble and the expense."

"Oh, is that all?" Aunt Tabby interrupted. Her distress dissolved as she beamed around the room again. "Well, it was no trouble at all. These nice young men came in and did all the work. As for the expense, well . . ." She shrugged her rounded shoulders. "I'd rather see you enjoy my money now than after I'm dead."

Sometimes, Autumn thought, the fuzzy little brain shot straight through to sterling sense. "Aunt Tabby." She framed her aunt's face with her hands. "I've never had a more wonderful surprise. Thank you."

"You just have a good time with it." Aunt Tabby's cheeks grew rosy with pleasure when Autumn kissed them, and she eyed the chemicals and trays again. "I don't suppose you'll blow anything up."

Knowing this wasn't a pun, and that her aunt was concerned about explosions in her vague way, Autumn assured her she would not. Satisfied, Aunt Tabby then bustled off, leaving Autumn to explore on her own.

For more than an hour, Autumn lost herself in what she knew best. Photography, started as a hobby when she had been a child, had become both craft and profession. The chemicals and complicated equipment were no strangers to her. Here, in a darkroom, or with a camera in her hands, she knew exactly who she was and what she wanted. This was where she had learned control—the same control she knew she had to employ over her thoughts of Lucas. She was no longer a dewy-eyed girl, ready to follow the crook of a finger. She was a professional woman with a growing reputation in her field. She had to hang on to that now, as she had for three years. There was no going back to yesterday.

Pleasantly weary after rearranging the darkroom to her own preference, Autumn wandered into the kitchen to fix herself a solitary cup of tea. The moon was round and white with a thin cloud drifting over it. Unexpectedly, a shudder ran through her, quick and chilling. The odd feeling she had sensed several times that evening came back. She frowned. Imagination? Autumn knew herself well enough to admit she had her share. It was part of her art. But this was different.

Discovering Lucas at the inn had jolted her system, and her emotions had been strained. That, she decided, was all that was wrong. The tension she had felt earlier was her own tension; the strain, her own strain. Dumping the remaining tea into the sink, she decided that what she needed was a good night's sleep. No dreams, she ordered herself firmly. She'd had her fill of dreams three years before.

The house was quiet now. Moonlight filtered in, leaving the corners shadowed. The lounge was dark, but as she passed, Autumn heard muted voices. She hesitated a moment, thinking to stop and say good-night, then she detected the subtle signs that told her this wasn't a conversation, but an argument. There was anger in the hushed, sexless voices. The undistinguishable words were quick, staccato and passionate. She walked by quickly, not wanting to overhear a private battle. A brief oath shot out, steeped in temper, elegant in French.

Climbing the stairs, Autumn smothered a grin. Jacques, she concluded, was probably losing patience with Lucas's artistic stubbornness. For entirely malicious reasons, she hoped the Frenchman gave him an earful.

It wasn't until she was halfway down the hall to her room that Autumn saw that she'd been wrong. Even Lucas McLean couldn't be two places at once. And he was definitely in this one. In the doorway of another room, Lucas was locked in a very involved embrace with Julia Bond.

Autumn knew how his arms would feel, how his mouth would taste. She remembered it all, completely, as if no years had come between to dull the sensations. She knew how his hand would trail up the back until he cupped around the neck. And that his fingers wouldn't be gentle. No, there were no gentle caresses from Lucas.

There was no need for her to worry about being seen. Both Lucas and Julia were totally focused on each other. Autumn was certain that the roof could have toppled over their heads, and they would have remained unmoving and entwined. The pain came back, hatefully, in full force.

Hurrying by, she gave vent to hideous and unwelcome jealousy by slamming her door.

CHAPTER 3

The forest was morning fresh. It held a tranquility that was full of tangy scents and bird song. To the east, the sky was filled with scuttling rags of white clouds. An optimist, Autumn put her hopes in them and ignored the dark, threatening sky in the west. Streaks of red still crowned the peaks of the mountains. Gently, the color faded to pink before it surrendered to blue.

The light was good, filtering through the white clouds and illuminating the forest. The leaves weren't full enough to interfere with the sun, only touching the limbs of trees with dots of green. Sometimes strong, the breeze bent branches and tugged at Autumn's hair. She could smell spring.

Wood violets popped out unexpectedly, the purple dramatic against the moss. She saw her first robin marching importantly on the ground, listening for worms. Squirrels scampered up trees, down trees and over the mulch of last year's leaves.

Autumn had intended to walk to the lake, hoping to catch a deer at early watering, but when her camera insisted on planting itself in front of her face again and again, she didn't resist. She ambled along, happy in the solitude and in tune with nature.

In New York, she never truly felt alone—lonely sometimes, but not solitary. The city intruded. Now, cocooned by mountains and trees, she realized how much she'd needed to feel alone. To recharge. Since leaving California and Lucas, Autumn hadn't permitted herself time alone. There had been a void that had to be filled, and she'd filled it with people, with work, with noise—anything that would keep her mind busy. She'd used the pace of the city. It had been necessary. Now, she wanted the pace of the mountains.

In the distance, the lake shimmered. Reflections of the surrounding mountains and trees were mirrored in the water, reversed and shadowy. There were no deer, but as she drew closer, Autumn noticed two figures circling the far side. The ridge where she stood was some fifty feet above the small valley which held the lake. The view was spectacular.

The lake itself stretched in a wide finger, about a hundred feet in length, forty in width. The breeze that caught at Autumn's hair where she strode didn't reach down to the water; its surface was clear and still. The opaque water gradually darkened toward the center, warning of dangerous depths.

Autumn forgot the people walking around the lake, her mind fully occupied with angles and depths of field and shutter speeds. The distance was too great for her to make them out even if she had been interested.

The sun continued its rise, and Autumn was content. She stopped only to change film. As she replaced the roll, she noted that the lake was now deserted. The light was wrong for the mood she wanted and, turning, she began her leisurely journey back to the inn.

This time, the stillness of the forest seemed different. The sun was brighter, but she felt an odd disquiet she hadn't experienced in the paler light of dawn. Foolishly, she looked back over her shoulder, then told herself she was an idiot. Who would be following her? And why? Yet the feeling persisted.

The serenity had vanished. Autumn forced herself to put aside an impulsive desire to run back to the inn where there would be people and coffee brewing. She wasn't a child to take flight at the thought of ogres or gnomes. To prove to herself that her fantasies hadn't affected her, she forced herself to stop and take the time to perfect a shot of a cooperative squirrel. A faint rustle of dead leaves came from behind her and terror brought her scrambling to her feet.

"Well, Cat, still attached to a camera?"

Blood pounding in her head, Autumn stared at Lucas. His hands were tucked comfortably into the pockets of his jeans as he stood directly in front of her. For a moment, she couldn't speak. The fear had been sharp and real.

"What do you mean by sneaking up behind me that way?" When it returned, her voice was furious. She was annoyed that she'd been foolish enough to be frightened, and angry that he'd been the one to frighten her. She pushed her hair back and glared at him.

"I see you've finally developed the temper to match your hair," he observed in a lazy voice. He crossed the slight distance between them and stood close. Autumn had also developed pride and refused to back away.

"It gets particularly nasty when someone spoils a shot."

It was a simple matter to blame her reaction on his interference with her work. Not for a moment would she amuse him
by confessing fear.

"You're a bit jumpy, Cat." The devil himself could take
lessons on smiling from Lucas McLean, she thought bitterly.
"Do I make you nervous?"

His dark hair curled in a confused tangle around his lean
face, and his eyes were dark and confident. It was the confidence, she told herself, that she cursed him for. "Don't flat-
ter yourself," she tossed back. "I don't recall you ever being
one for morning hikes, Lucas. Have you developed a love of
nature?"

"I've always had a fondness for nature." He was studying
her with deep, powerful eyes while his mouth curved into a
smile. "I've always had a penchant for picnics."

The pain started, a dull ache in her stomach. She could
remember the gritty feel of sand under her legs, the tart taste
of wine on her tongue and the scent of the ocean everywhere. She forced her gaze to stay level with his. "I lost my
taste for them." She turned in dismissal, but he fell into step
beside her. "I'm not going straight back," she informed him.
The chill in her voice would have discouraged anyone else.
Stopping, she took an off-center picture of a blue jay.

"I'm in no hurry," he returned easily. "I've always enjoyed
watching you work. It's fascinating how absorbed you become." He watched her back, and let his eyes run down the
length of her hair. "I believe you could be snapping a charg-
ing rhino and not give an inch until you'd perfected the shot."
There was a slight pause as she remained turned away from
him. "I saw that photo you took of a burned-out tenement in
New York. It was remarkable. Hard, clean and desperate."

Wary of the compliment, Autumn faced him. She knew
Lucas wasn't generous with praise. Hard, clean and desperate,
she thought. He had chosen the words perfectly. She didn't
like discovering that his opinion still mattered. "Thank you."
She turned back to focus on a grouping of trees. "Still having trouble with your book?"

"More than I'd anticipated," he muttered. Suddenly, he
swooped her hair up into his hands. "I never could resist it,
could I?" She continued to give her attention to the trees.
Her answer was an absent shrug, but she squeezed her eyes
tightly shut a moment. "I've never seen another woman with
hair like yours. I've looked, God knows, but the shade is always wrong, or the texture or the length." There was a seductive quality in his voice. Autumn stiffened against it. "It's
unique. A fiery waterfall in the sun, deep and vibrant spilling over a pillowcase."

"You always had a gift for description." She adjusted her
lens without the vaguest idea of what she was doing. Her voice
was detached, faintly bored, while she prayed for him to go.
Instead, his grip tightened on her hair. In a swift move, he
whirled her around and tore the camera from her hands.

"Damn it, don't use that tone with me. Don't turn your
back on me. Don't ever turn your back on me."

She remembered the dark expression and uncertain temper well. There'd been a time when she would have dissolved
when faced with them. But not anymore, she thought fleetingly. Not this time.

"I don't cringe at being sworn at these days, Lucas." She
tossed her head, lifting her chin. "Why don't you save your
attention for Julia? I don't want it."

"So." His smile was light and amused in a rapid-fire

change. "It was you. No need to be jealous, Cat. The lady made the move, not I."

"Yes, I noticed your mad struggle for release." Even as she spoke, she regretted the words. Annoyed, Autumn pushed away, but was only caught closer. His scent teased her senses and reminded her of things she'd rather forget. "Listen, Lucas," she ground out slowly as both anger and longing rose inside her. "It took me six months to realize what a bastard you are, and I've had three years to cement that realization. I'm a big girl now, and not susceptible to your abundant charms. Now, take your hands off me and get lost."

"Learned to sink your teeth in, have you, Cat?" To her mounting fury, his expression was more amused than insulted. His eyes lowered to her mouth for a moment, lingered then lifted. "Not malleable anymore, but just as fascinating."

Because his words hurt more than she had thought possible, she hurled a stream of abuse at him.

His laughter cut off her torrent like a slap. Abandoning verbal protest, Autumn began to struggle with a wild, furious rage. Abruptly, he molded her against him. Tasting of punishment and possession, his mouth found hers. The heat was blinding.

The old, churning need fought its way to the surface. For three years she had starved, and now all that hunger spilled out in response. There was no hesitation as her arms found their way around his neck. Eager for more, her lips parted. His mouth was urgent and bruising. The pain was like heaven, and she begged for more. Her blood was flowing again. Lucas let his mouth roam over her face, then come back to hers with new demands. Autumn met them and fretted for more. Time flew backward, then forward again before he lifted his face.

His eyes were incredibly dark, opaque with a passion she recognized. For the first time she felt the faint throbbing where his hands gripped her and his hold eased to a caress. The taste of him lingered on her lips.

"It's still there, Cat," Lucas murmured. With easy familiarity, he combed his fingers through her hair. "Still there."

All at once, pain and humiliation coursed through her. She pulled away fiercely and swung out a hand. He caught her wrist and, frustrated, she drew back with her other hand. His reflexes were too sharp, and she was denied any satisfaction. With both wrists captured, she could only stand struggling, her breath ragged. Tears burned at her throat, but she refused to acknowledge them. He won't make me cry, she vowed fiercely. He won't see me cry again.

In silence, Lucas watched her battle for control. There was no sound in the forest but Autumn's own jerking breaths. When she could speak, her voice was hard and cold. "There's a difference between love and lust, Lucas. Even you should know one from the other. What's there now may be the same for you, but not for me. I loved you. I *loved* you." The words were an accusation in their repetition. His brows drew together as his gaze grew intense. "You took it all once—my love, my innocence, my pride—then you tossed them back in my face. You can't have them back. The first is dead, the second's gone and the third belongs to me."

For a moment, they both were still. Slowly, without taking his eyes from hers, Lucas released her wrists. He didn't speak, and his expression told her nothing. Refusing to run from him a second time, Autumn turned and walked away. Only when she was certain he wasn't following did she allow her tears their freedom. Her statements about pride and innocence had been true. But her love was far from dead. It was alive, and it hurt.

As the red bricks of the inn came into view, Autumn dashed the drops away. There would be no wallowing in what was over. Loving Lucas changed nothing, any more than it had changed anything three years before. But she'd changed. He wouldn't find her weeping, helpless and—as he had said himself—malleable.

Disillusionment had given her strength. He could still hurt her. She'd learned that quickly. But he could no longer manipulate her as he had once. Still, the encounter with him had left her shaken, and she wasn't pleased when Helen approached from a path to the right.

It was impossible, without being pointedly rude, for Autumn to veer off and avoid her. Instead, she fixed a smile on her face. When Helen turned her head, the livid bruise under her eye became noticeable. Autumn's smile faded into quick concern.

"What happened?" The bruise looked painful and aroused Autumn's sympathy.

"I walked into a branch." Helen gave a careless shrug as she lifted her fingers to stroke the mark. "I'll have to be more careful in the future."

Perhaps it was her turmoil over Lucas that made Autumn detect some hidden shade of meaning in those words, but Helen seemed to mean more than she said. Certainly the eyes which met Autumn's were as hot and angry as the bruise. And the mark itself, Autumn mused, looked more like the result of contact with a violent hand than with any stray branch. She pushed the thought aside. Who would have struck Helen? she asked herself. And why would she cover up the abuse? Her own carelessness made more sense.

"It looks nasty," Autumn commented as they began to walk toward the inn. "You'll have to do something about it. Aunt Tabby should have something to ease the soreness."

"Oh, I intend to do something about it," Helen muttered, then gave Autumn her sharp-eyed smile. "I know just the thing. Out early taking pictures?" she asked while Autumn tried to ignore the unease her words brought. "I've always found people more interesting subjects than trees. I'm especially fond of candid shots." She began to laugh at some private joke. It was the first time Autumn had heard her laugh, and she thought how suited the sound was to Helen's smile. They were both unpleasant.

"Were you down at the lake earlier?" Autumn recalled the two figures she had spotted. To her surprise, Helen's laughter stopped abruptly. Her eyes grew sharper.

"Did you see someone?"

"No," she began, confused by the harshness of the question. "Not exactly. I saw two people by the lake, but I was too far away to see who they were. I was taking pictures from the ridge."

"Taking pictures," Helen repeated. Her mouth pursed as if she were considering something carefully. She began to laugh again with a harsh burst of sound.

"Well, well, such good humor for such early risers." Julia drifted down the porch steps. Her brow lifted as she studied

Helen's cheek. Autumn wondered if the actress's shudder was real or affected. "Good heavens, what have you done to yourself?"

Helen's amusement seemed to have passed. She gave Julia a quick scowl, then fingered the bruise again. "Walked into a branch," she muttered before she stalked up the steps and disappeared inside.

"A fist more likely," Julia commented, and smiled. With a shrug, she dismissed Helen and turned to Autumn. "The call of the wild beckoned to you, too? It seems everyone but me was tramping through forests and over mountains at the cold light of dawn. It's so difficult being sane when one is surrounded by insanity."

Autumn had to smile. Julia looked like a sunbeam. In direct contrast to her own rough jeans and jacket, Julia wore delicate pink slacks and a thin silk blouse flocked with roses. The white sandals she wore wouldn't last fifty yards in the woods. Whatever resentment Autumn had felt for the actress attracting Lucas vanished under her open warmth.

"There are some," Autumn remarked mildly, "who might accuse you of laziness."

"Absolutely," Julia agreed with a nod and a smile. "When I'm not working, I wallow in sloth. If I don't get going again soon, my blood will stop flowing." She gave Autumn a shrewd glance. "Looks like you walked into a rather large branch yourself."

Bewilderment crossed Autumn's face briefly. Julia's eyes, she discovered, were very discerning. The traces of tears hadn't evaporated as completely as Autumn would have liked. Helplessly she moved her shoulders. "I heal quickly."

"Brave child. Come, tell mama all about it." Julia's eyes

were sympathetic, balancing the stinging lightness of the words. Linking her arm through Autumn's, she began to walk across the lawn.

"Julia . . ." Autumn shook her head. Inner feelings were private. She'd broken the rule for Lucas, and wasn't certain she could do so again.

"Autumn." The refusal was firmly interrupted. "You do need to talk. You might not think that you look stricken, but you do." Julia sighed with perfect finesse. "I really don't know why I've become so fond of you; it's totally against my policy. Beautiful women tend to avoid or dislike other beautiful women, especially younger ones."

The statement completely robbed Autumn of speech. The idea of the exquisite, incomparable Julia Bond placing herself on a physical plane anywhere near Autumn's own seemed ludicrous to her. It was one matter to hear the actress speak casually of her own beauty, and quite another for her to speak of Autumn's. Julia's voice flowed over the gaping silence.

"Maybe it's the exposure to those two other females—one so dull and the other so nasty—but I've developed an affection for you." The breeze tugged at her hair, lifting it up so that the sunlight streamed through it. Absently, Julia tucked a strand behind her ear. On the lobe a diamond sparkled. Autumn thought it incongruous that they were walking arm in arm among her aunt's struggling daffodils.

"You're also a kind person," Julia went on. "I don't know a great many kind people." She turned to Autumn so that her exquisite profile became her exquisite full face. "Autumn, darling, I always pry, but I also know how to keep a confidence."

"I'm still in love with him," Autumn blurted out, then followed that rash statement with a deep sigh. Before she knew it, words were tumbling out. She left out nothing, from the beginning to the end, to the new beginning when he had come back into her life the day before. She told Julia everything. Once she'd begun, no effort was needed. She didn't have to think, only feel, and Julia listened. The quality of her listening was so perfect, Autumn all but forgot she was there.

"The monster," Julia said, but with no malice. "You'll find all men, those marvelous creatures, are basically monsters."

Who was Autumn to argue with an expert? As they walked on in silence, she realized that she did feel better. The rawness was gone.

"The main trouble is, of course, that you're still mad about him. Not that I blame you," Julia added when Autumn made a small sound of distress. "Lucas is quite a man. I had a tiny sample last night, and I was impressed." Julia spoke so casually of the passion Autumn had witnessed, it was impossible to be angry. "Lucas is a talented man," Julia went on. By her smile, Autumn knew that Julia was very much aware of the struggle that was going on within Autumn. "He's also arrogant, selfish and used to being obeyed. It's easy for me to see that, because I am, too. We're alike. I doubt very much if we could even enjoy a pleasant affair. We'd be clawing at each other before the bed was turned down."

Autumn found no response to make to the image this produced, and merely walked on.

"Jacques is more my type," Julia mused. "But his attentions are committed elsewhere." She frowned, and Autumn sensed that her thoughts had drifted to something quite different. "Anyway." Julia made an impatient gesture. "You just have to make up your mind what you want. Obviously, Lucas wants you back, at least for as long as it suits him."

Autumn tried to ignore the sting of honesty and just listened.

"Knowing that, you could enjoy a stimulating relationship with him, with your eyes open."

"I can't do that, Julia. The knowing won't stop the hurting. I'm not sure I can survive another . . . relationship with Lucas. And he'd know I was still in love with him." A flash frame of their parting scene three years before jumped into her mind. "I won't be humiliated again. Pride's the only thing I have left that isn't his already."

"Love and pride don't belong together." Julia patted Autumn's hand. "Well then, you'll have to barricade yourself against the assault. I'll run interference for you."

"How will you do that?"

"Darling!" She lifted her brow as the slow, cat smile drifted to her lips.

Autumn had to laugh. It all seemed so absurd. She lifted her face to the sky. The black clouds were winning after all. For a moment, they blotted out the sun and warmth. "Looks like rain."

Her gaze shifted back to the inn. The windows were black and empty. The struggling light fell gloomily over the bricks and turned the white porch and shutters gray. Behind the building, the sky was like slate. The mountains were colorless and oppressive. She felt a tickle at the back of her neck. To her puzzlement, Autumn found she didn't want to go back inside.

Just as quickly, the clouds shifted, letting the sun pour

out through the opening. The windows blinked with light. The shadows vanished. Chiding herself for another flight of fancy, Autumn walked back to the inn with Julia.

Only Jacques joined them for breakfast. Helen was nowhere in sight, and Steve and the Spicers were apparently still hiking. Autumn trained her thoughts away from Lucas. Her appetite, as usual, was unimpaired and outrageous. She put away a healthy portion of bacon, eggs, coffee and muffins while Julia nibbled on a single piece of thin toast and sent her envious scowls.

Jacques seemed preoccupied. His charm was costing him visible effort. Memory of the muffled argument in the lounge came to Autumn's mind. Idly, she began to speculate on who he had been annoyed with. Thinking it over, the entire matter struck her as odd. Jacques LeFarre didn't seem to be the sort of man who would argue with a veritable stranger, yet, as Autumn knew, both Lucas and Julia had been preoccupied elsewhere.

Appearing totally at ease, Julia rambled on about a mutual friend in the industry. But she's an actress, Autumn reminded herself. A good one. She could easily know the cause of last night's animosity and never show a sign. Jacques, however, wasn't an actor. The distress was there; anger lay just beneath the polished charm. Autumn wondered at it throughout the meal, then dismissed it from her mind as she left to find her aunt. After all, she reflected, it wasn't any of her business.

Aunt Tabby was, as Autumn had known she would be, fussing with Nancy the cook over the day's menu. Keeping silent, Autumn let the story unfold. It seemed that Nancy had planned on chicken while Aunt Tabby was certain they had decided on pork. While the argument raged, Autumn helped herself to another cup of coffee. Through the window, she could see the thick, roiling clouds continue their roll from the west.

"Oh, Autumn, did you have a nice walk?" When she turned, Autumn found her aunt smiling at her. "Such a nice morning, a shame it's going to rain. But that's good for the flowers, isn't it? Sweet little things. Did you sleep well?"

After a moment, Autumn decided to answer only the final question. There was no use confusing her aunt. "Wonderfully, Aunt Tabby. I always sleep well when I visit you."

"It's the air," the woman replied. Her round little face lit with pleasure. "I think I'll make my special chocolate cake for tonight. That should make up for the rain."

"Any hot coffee, Aunt Tabby?" Lucas swept into the kitchen as if he enjoyed the privilege daily. As always, when he came into a room, the air charged. This phenomenon Autumn could accept. The casual use of her aunt's nickname was more perplexing.

"Of course, dear, just help yourself." Aunt Tabby gestured vaguely toward the stove, her mind on chocolate cake. Autumn's confusion grew as Lucas strode directly to the proper cupboard, retrieved a cup and proceeded to fix himself a very homey cup of coffee.

He drank, leaning against the counter. The eyes that met Autumn's were very cool. All traces of anger and passion were gone, as if they had never existed. His rough black brows lifted as she continued to stare. The damnable devil smile tugged at his mouth.

"Oh, is that your camera, dear?" Aunt Tabby's voice broke into her thoughts. Autumn lowered her eyes.

The camera still hung around her neck, so much a part of her that she'd forgotten it was there.

"My, my, so many numbers. It looks complicated." Aunt Tabby peered at it through narrowed eyes, forgetting the glasses that dangled from her chain. "I have a very nice one, Autumn. You're welcome to use it whenever you like." After giving the Nikon another dubious glance, she beamed up with her misty smile. "You just push a little red button, and the picture pops right out. You can see if you've cut off some-one's head or have your thumb in the corner right away, so you can take another picture. And you don't have to grope around in that darkroom either. I don't know how you see what you're doing in there." Her brows drew close, and she tapped a finger against her cheek. "I'm almost certain I can find it."

Autumn grinned. She was compelled to subject her aunt to yet another bear hug. Over the gray-streaked head, Autumn saw that Lucas was grinning as well. It was the warm, natu-ral grin which came to his face so rarely. For a moment, she found she could smile back at him without pain.

CHAPTER 4

When the rain came, it didn't begin with the slow drip-drop of an April shower. As the sky grew hazy, the light in the lounge became dim. Everyone was back and the inn was again filled with its odd assortment of guests.

Steve, expanding on his role of bartender, had wandered to the kitchen to get coffee. Robert Spicer had trapped Jacques in what seemed to be a technical explanation of open-heart surgery. During the discussion, Julia sat beside him, hanging on every word—or seeming to. Autumn knew better. Occasionally, Julia sent messages across to her with her extraordinary eyes. She was enjoying herself immensely.

Jane sat sullen over a novel Autumn was certain was riddled with explicit sex. She wore dull brown again, slacks and a sweater. Helen, her bruise livid, smoked quietly in long, deep drags. She reminded Autumn eerily of Alice in Wonderland's caterpillar. Once or twice, Autumn found Helen's sharp eyes on her. The speculative smile left her confused and uncomfortable.

Lucas wasn't there. He was upstairs, Autumn knew, hammering away at his typewriter. She hoped it would keep him busy for hours. Perhaps he'd even take his meals in his room.

Abruptly, the dim light outdoors was snuffed out, and the room plunged into gloom. The warmth fled with it. Autumn shuddered with a sharp premonition of dread. The feeling surprised her, as storms had always held a primitive appeal for her. For a heartbeat, there was no sound, then the rain began with a gushing explosion. With instant force, instant fury, it battered against the windows, punctuated by wicked flashes of lightning.

"A spring shower in the mountains," Steve observed. He paused a moment in the doorway with a large tray balanced in his hands. The friendly scent of coffee entered with him.

"More like special effects," Julia returned. With a flutter of her lashes, she cuddled toward Robert. "Storms are so terrifying and moving. I find myself longing to be frightened."

It was straight out of *A Long Summer's Evening,* Autumn noted, amused. But the doctor seemed too overcome with Julia's ingenuous eyes to recognize the line. Autumn wanted to laugh badly. When Julia cuddled even closer and sent her a wink, Autumn's eyes retreated to the ceiling.

Jane wasn't amused. Autumn noticed she was no longer sullen but smoldering. Perhaps she had claws after all, Autumn thought, and felt she would like her better for it. It might be wise, she mused as Steve passed her a cup of coffee, if Julia concentrated on him rather than the doctor.

"Cream, no sugar, right?" Steve smiled down at her with his California blue eyes. Autumn's lips curved in response.

He was a man with the rare ability to make a woman feel pampered without being patronizing. She admired him for it.

"Right. You've got a better memory than George." Her eyes smiled at him over the rim of her cup. "You serve with such style, too. Have you been in this line of work long?"

"I'm only here on a trial basis," he told her with a grin. "Please pass your comments on to the management."

Lightning speared through the gloom again. Jacques shifted in his seat as thunder rumbled and echoed through the room. "With such a storm, is it not possible to lose power?" he addressed Autumn.

"We often lose power." Her answer, accompanied by an absent shrug, brought on varying reactions.

Julia found the idea marvelous—candlelight was so wonderfully romantic. At the moment, Robert couldn't have agreed more. Jacques appeared not to care one way or the other. He lifted his hands in a Gallic gesture, indicating his acceptance of fate.

Steve and Helen seemed inordinately put out, though his comments were milder than hers. He mumbled once about inconveniences, then stalked over to the window to stare out at the torrent of wind and rain. Helen was livid.

"I didn't pay good money to grope around in the dark and eat cold meals." Lighting another cigarette with a swift, furious gesture, she glared at Autumn. "It's intolerable that we should have to put up with such inefficiency. Your aunt will certainly have to make the proper adjustments. I for one won't pay these ridiculous prices, then live like a pioneer." She waved her cigarette, preparing to continue, but Autumn cut her off. She aimed the cold, hard stare she had recently developed.

"I'm sure my aunt will give your complaints all the consideration they warrant." Turning pointedly away, she allowed Helen's sharp little darts to bounce off her. "Actually," she told Jacques, noting his smile of approval, "we have a generator. My uncle was as practical as Aunt Tabby is . . ."

"Charming," Steve supplied, and instantly became her friend.

After she'd finished beaming at him, Autumn continued. "If we lose main power, we switch over to the generator. With that, we can maintain essential power with little inconvenience."

"I believe I'll have candles in my room anyway," Julia decided. She gave Robert an under-the-lashes smile as he lit her cigarette.

"Julia should have been French," Jacques commented. His moustache tilted at the corner. "She's an incurable romantic."

"Too much . . . romance," Helen murmured, "can be unwise." Her eyes swept the room, then focused on Julia.

Before Autumn's astonished gaze, Julia transformed from mischievous angel to tough lady. "I've always found that only idiots think they're wise." Statement made, she melted back into a celestial being so quickly, Autumn blinked.

Seeing her perform on the screen was nothing compared to a live show. It occurred to Autumn that she had no inkling which woman was the real Julia Bond—if indeed she was either. The notion germinated that she really didn't know any of the people in that room. They were all strangers.

The air was still vibrating with the uncomfortable silence when Lucas entered. He seemed impervious to the swirling tension. Helplessly, Autumn's eyes locked on his. He came to her, ignoring the others in his cavalier fashion. The devil smile was on his face.

She felt a tremor when she couldn't stop the room from receding, leaving only him in her vision. Something of that fear must have been reflected in her face.

"I'm not going to eat you, Cat," Lucas murmured. Against the violent sounds of the storm, his voice was low, only for her. "Do you still like to walk in the rain?" The question was offhand, and didn't require an answer as he searched her face. "I remember when you did." He paused when she said nothing. "Your aunt sent you this." Lucas held out his hand, and Autumn's gaze dropped to it. Tension dissolved into laughter. "I haven't heard that in a long time," Lucas said softly.

She lifted her eyes to his again. He was studying her with a complete, singleminded intensity. "No?" As she accepted Aunt Tabby's famous red-button camera, her shoulders moved in a careless shrug. "Laughing's quite a habit of mine."

"Aunt Tabby says for you to have a good time with it." Dismissively, he turned his back on her and walked to the coffeepot.

"What have you got there, Autumn?" Julia demanded, her eyes following Lucas's progress.

Flourishing the camera, Autumn used a sober, didactic tone. "This, ladies and gentlemen, is the latest technological achievement in photography. At the mere touch of a button, friends and loved ones are beamed inside and spewed out onto a picture which develops before your astonished eyes. No focusing, no need to consult your light meter. The button is faster than the brain. Why, a child of five can operate it while riding his tricycle."

"It should be known," Lucas inserted in a dry voice, "that Autumn is a photographic snob." He stood by the window, carelessly drinking coffee while he spoke to the others. His eyes were on Autumn. "If it doesn't have interchangeable lenses and filters, multispeed shutters and impossibly complicated operations, it isn't a camera, but a toy."

"I've noticed her obsession," Julia agreed. She sent him a delicious look before she turned to Autumn. "She wears that black box like other women wear diamonds. She was actually tramping through the forest at the break of dawn, snapping pictures of chipmunks and bunnies."

With a good-natured grin, Autumn lifted the camera and snapped Julia's lovely face.

"Really, darling," Julia said with a professional toss of the head. "You might have given me the chance to turn my best side."

"You haven't got a best side," Autumn countered.

Julia smiled, obviously torn between amusement and insult while Jacques exploded with laughter. "And I thought she was such a sweet child," she murmured.

"In my profession, Miss Bond," Autumn returned gravely, "I've had occasion to photograph a fair number of women. This one you shoot from the left profile, that one from the right, another straight on. Still another from an upward angle, and so on." Pausing a moment, she gave Julia's matchless face a quick, critical survey. "I could shoot you from any position, any angle, any light, and the result would be equally wonderful."

"Jacques." Julia placed a hand on his arm. "We really must adopt this girl. She's invaluable for my ego."

"Professional integrity," Autumn claimed before placing the quickly developing snapshot on the table. She aimed Aunt Tabby's prize at Steve.

"You should be warned that with a camera of any sort in her hands, Autumn becomes a dangerous weapon." Lucas moved closer. He lifted the snap of Julia and studied it.

Autumn frowned as she remembered the innumerable photographs she had taken of him. Under the pretext that they were art, she'd never disposed of them. She'd snapped and focused and crouched around him until, exasperated, he'd dislodged the camera from her hands and effectively driven photography from her mind.

Lucas saw the frown. With his eyes dark and unreadable, he reached down to tangle his fingers in her hair. "You never could teach me how to take a proper picture, could you, Cat?"

"No." The battle with the growing ache made her voice brittle. "I never taught you anything, Lucas. But I learned quite a bit."

"I've never been able to master anything but a one-button job myself." Steve ambled over. Autumn's camera sat on the table beside her. Picking it up, he examined it as if it were a strange contraption from the outer reaches of space. "How can you remember what all these numbers are for?"

When he perched on the arm of her chair, Autumn grasped at the diversion. She began a lesson in basic photography. Lucas wandered back to the coffeepot, obviously bored. From the corner of her eye, Autumn noticed Julia gliding to join him. Within moments, her hand was tucked into his arm, and he no longer appeared bored. Gritting her teeth, Autumn began to give Steve a more involved lesson.

Lucas and Julia left, arm in arm, ostensibly for Julia to nap and Lucas to work. Autumn's eyes betrayed her by following them.

When she dragged her attention back to Steve, she caught his sympathetic smile. That he understood her feelings was too obvious. Cursing herself, she resumed her explanations of f-stops, grateful that Steve picked up the conversation as if there had been no lull.

The afternoon wore on. It was a long, dreary day with rain beating against windows. Lightning and thunder came and went, but the wind built in force until it was one continuous moan. Robert tended the fire until flames crackled and spit. The cheery note this might have brought to the room was negated by Jane's sullenness and Helen's pacing. The air was tight.

Evading Steve's suggestion of cards, Autumn sought the peace and activity of her darkroom. As she closed and locked the door behind her, the headache which had started to build behind her temples eased.

This room was without tensions. Her senses picked up no nagging, intangible disturbances here, but were clear and ready to work. Step by step, she took her film through the first stages of development, preparing chemicals, checking temperatures, setting timers. Growing absorbed, she forgot the battering storm.

While it was necessary, Autumn worked in a total absence of light. Her fingers were her eyes at this stage and she worked quickly. Over the muffled sound of the storm, she heard a faint rattle. She ignored it, busy setting the timer for the next stage of developing. When the sound came again, it annoyed her.

Was it the doorknob? she wondered. Had she remembered to lock the door? All she needed at that point was for some layman to blunder in and bring damaging light with him.

"Leave the door alone," she called out just as the radio she had switched on for company went dead. There went the power, she concluded. Standing in the absolute darkness, Autumn sighed as the rattle came again.

Was it someone at the door, or just someone in the kitchen? Curious and annoyed, she walked in the direction of the door to make sure it was locked. Her steps were confident. She knew every inch of the room now. Suddenly, to her astonishment, pain exploded inside her head. Lights flashed and fractured before the darkness again became complete.

Autumn, Autumn, open your eyes." Though the sound was far off and muffled, she heard the command in the tone. She resisted it. The nearer she came to consciousness, the more hideous grew the throbbing in her head. Oblivion was painless.

"Open your eyes." The voice was clearer now and more insistent. Autumn moaned.

Reluctantly, she opened her eyes as hands brushed the hair from her face. For a moment, she felt them linger against her cheek. Lucas came into focus gradually, dimming and receding until she forced him back, clear and sharp.

"Lucas?" Disoriented, Autumn could not think beyond his name. It seemed to satisfy him.

"That's better," he said with approval. Before any protest could be made, he kissed her hard, with a briefness that spoke of past intimacy. "You had me worried there a minute. What the hell did you do to yourself?"

The accusation was typical of him. She barely noticed it. "Do?" Autumn lifted a hand to touch the spot on her head where the pain was concentrated. "What happened?"

"That's my question, Cat. No, don't touch the lump." He caught her hand in his and held it. "It'll only hurt more if you do. I'm curious as to how you came by it, and why you were lying in a heap on the floor."

It was difficult to keep clear of the mists in her brain. Autumn tried to center in on the last thing she remembered. "How did you get in?" she demanded, remembering the rattling knob. "Hadn't I locked the door?" It came to her slowly that he was cradling her in his arms, holding her close against his chest. She struggled to sit up. "Were you rattling at the door?"

"Take it easy," he ordered as she groaned with the movement.

Autumn squeezed her eyes shut against the pounding in her head. "I must have walked into the door," she murmured, wondering at the quality of her clumsiness.

"You walked into the door and knocked yourself unconscious?" She couldn't tell if Lucas was angry or amused. The ache in her head kept her from caring one way or the other. "Strange, I don't recall you possessing that degree of uncoordination."

"It was dark," she grumbled, coherent enough to feel embarrassed. "If you hadn't been rattling around at the door . . ."

"I wasn't rattling around at your door," he began, but she cut him off with a startled gasp.

"The lights!" For a second time, she tried to struggle away from him. "You turned on the lights!"

"It was a mad impulse when I saw you crumpled on the floor," he returned dryly. Without any visible effort, he held her still. "I wanted to see the extent of the damage."

"My film!" Her glare was as accusing as her voice, but he responded with laughter.

"The woman's a maniac."

"Let go of me, will you?" Her anger made her less than gracious. Pushing away, she scrambled to her feet. At her movement, the pain grew to a crashing roar. She staggered under it.

"For God's sake, Autumn." Lucas rose and gripped her shoulders, steadying her. "Stop behaving like an imbecile over a few silly pictures."

This statement, under normal conditions, would have been unwise. In her present state of mind, it was a declaration of war. Pain was eclipsed by a pure silver streak of fury. She whirled on him.

"You never could see my work as anything but silly pictures, could you? You never saw me as anything but a silly child, diverting for a while, but eventually boring. You always hated being bored, didn't you, Lucas?" She made a violent swipe at the hair that fell over her eyes. "You sit with your novels and bask in the adulation you get and look down your nose at the rest of us. You're not the only person in the world with talent, Lucas. My abilities are just as creative as yours, and my pictures give me as much fulfillment as your silly little books."

For a moment, he stood in silence, studying her with a frown. When he did speak, his voice was oddly weary. "All right, Autumn, now that you've gotten that out, you'd better get yourself some aspirin."

"Just leave me alone!" She shook off the hand he put on her arm. Turning, she started to take her camera from the shelf she had placed it on before beginning her work. Glancing down at the table, she flared again. "What do you mean by messing around with my equipment? You've exposed an entire roll of film!" Seething with fury, she whirled on him. "It isn't enough to interrupt my work by fooling around at the door, then turn on the lights and ruin what I've started. You have to put your hands into something you know nothing about."

"I told you before, I wasn't fooling around at your door." His eyes were darkening dangerously. "I came back after the power went out and the generator switched on. The door was open, and you were lying in a heap in the middle of the floor. I never touched your damned film."

There was ice in his voice now to go with the heat in his eyes but Autumn was too infuriated to be touched by either. "Foolish as it may seem," he continued, "my concern and attention were on you." Moving toward her, he glanced down at the confusion on her work table. "I don't suppose it occurred to you that in the dark you disturbed the film yourself?"

"Don't be absurd." Her professional ability was again insulted, but he cut off her retort in a voice filled with strained patience. Autumn pondered on it. As she remembered, Lucas had no patience at all.

"Autumn, I don't know what happened to your film. I didn't get any farther into the room than the spot where you were lying. I won't apologize for switching on the lights; I'd do precisely the same thing again." He circled her neck with his fingers and his words took on the old caressing note she remembered. "I happen to think your welfare is more important than your pictures."

Suddenly, her interest in the film waned. She wanted only to escape from him, and the feelings he aroused in her so effortlessly. Programmed response, she told herself. The soft voice and gentle hands tripped the release, and she went under.

"You're pale," Lucas muttered, abruptly dropping his hands and stuffing them into his pockets. "Dr. Spicer can take a look at you."

"No, I don't need—" She got no further. He grabbed her arms with quicksilver fury.

"Damn it, Cat, must you argue with everything I say? Is there no getting past the hate you've built up for me?" He gave a quick shake. The pain rolled and spun in her head. For an instant, his face went out of focus as dizziness blurred her vision. Swearing with short, precise expertise, he pulled her close against him until the faintness passed. In a swift move, he lifted her into his arms. "You're pale as a ghost," he muttered. "Like it or not, you're going to see the doctor. You can vent your venom on him for a while."

By the time Autumn realized he was carrying her to her room, her temper had ebbed. There was only a dull, wicked ache and the weariness. Flagging, she rested her head against his shoulder and surrendered. This wasn't the time to think about the darkroom door or how it had come to be opened. It wasn't the time to think of how she had managed to walk into it like a perfect fool. This wasn't the time to think at all.

Accepting the fact that she had no choice, Autumn closed her eyes and allowed Lucas to take over. She kept them closed when she felt him lower her to the bed, but she knew he stood looking down at her a moment. She knew too that he was frowning.

The sound of his footsteps told her that he had walked into the adjoining bathroom. The faint splash of water in the sink sounded like a waterfall to her throbbing head. In a moment, there was a cool cloth over the ache in her forehead. Opening her eyes, Autumn looked into his.

"Lie still," he ordered curtly. Lucas brooded down at her with an odd, enigmatic expression. "I'll get Spicer," he muttered abruptly. Turning on his heel, he strode to the door.

"Lucas." Autumn stopped him because the cool cloth had brought back memories of all the gentle things he had ever done. He'd had his gentle moments, though she'd tried hard to pretend he hadn't. It had seemed easier.

When he turned back, impatience was evident in the very air around him. What a man of contradictions he was, she mused. Intemperate, with barely any middle ground at all.

"Thank you," she said, ignoring his obvious desire to be gone. "I'm sorry I shouted at you. You're being very kind."

Lucas leaned against the door and stared back at her. "I've never been kind." His voice was weary again.

Autumn found it necessary to force back the urge to go to him, wipe away his lines of fatigue. He sensed her thoughts, and his eyes softened briefly. On his mouth moved one of his rare, disarming smiles.

"My God, Cat, you always were so incredibly sweet. So terrifyingly warm."

With that, he left her.

CHAPTER 5

Autumn was staring at the ceiling when Robert entered. Shifting her eyes, she looked at his black bag dubiously. She'd never cared for what doctors carried inside those innocent-looking satchels.

"A house call," she said and managed a smile. "The eighth wonder of the world. I didn't think you'd have your bag with you on vacation."

He was quick enough to note her uneasy glance. "Do you travel without your camera?"

"Touché." She told herself to relax and not to be a baby.

"I don't think we'll need to operate." He sat on the bed and removed the cloth Lucas had placed there. "Mmm, that's going to be colorful. Is your vision blurred?"

"No."

His hands were surprisingly soft and gentle, reminding Autumn of her father's. She relaxed further and answered his questions on dizziness, nausea and so forth while watching his face. He was different, she noted. The competence was still there, but his dapper self-presentation had been replaced by a quiet compassion. His voice was kind, she thought, and so were his eyes. He was well-suited to his profession.

"How'd you come by this, Autumn?" As he asked he reached in his bag and her attention switched to his hands. He removed cotton and a bottle, not the needle she'd worried about.

She wrinkled her nose ruefully. "I walked into a door."

He shook his head with a laugh and began to bathe the bruise. "A likely story."

"And embarrassingly true. In the darkroom," she added. "I must have misjudged the distance."

His eyes shifted and studied hers a moment before they returned to her forehead. "You struck me as a woman who kept her eyes open," he said a bit grimly, Autumn thought, before he smiled again. "It's just a bump," he told her and held her hand. "Though my diagnosis won't make it hurt any less."

"It's only an agonizing ache now," Autumn returned, trying for lightness. "The cannons have stopped going off."

With a chuckle, he reached into his bag again. "We can do something about smaller artillery."

"Oh." She eyed the bottle of pills he held and frowned. "I was going to take some aspirin."

"You don't put a forest fire out with a water pistol." He smiled at her again and shook out two pills. "They're very mild, Autumn. Take these and rest for an hour or two. You can trust me," he added with exaggerated gravity as her brows stayed lowered. "Even though I am a surgeon."

"Okay." His eyes convinced her and she smiled back, accepting the glass of water and pills. "You're not going to take out my appendix or anything, are you?"

"Not on vacation." He waited until she had swallowed the

medication, then pulled a light blanket over her. "Rest," he ordered and left her.

The next time Autumn opened her eyes, the room was in shadows. Rest? she thought and shifted under the blanket. I've been unconscious. How long? She listened. The storm was still raging, whipping against her windows with a fury she'd been oblivious to. Carefully, she pushed herself into a sitting position. Her head didn't pound, but a touch of her fingers assured her she hadn't dreamed up the entire incident. Her next thought was entirely physical—she discovered she was starving.

Rising, she took a quick glance in the mirror, decided she didn't like what she saw and went in search of food and company. She found them both in the dining room. Her timing was perfect.

"Autumn." It was Robert who spotted her first. "Feeling better?"

She hesitated a moment, embarrassed. Hunger was stronger, however, and the scent of Nancy's chicken was too tempting. "Much," she told him. She glanced at Lucas, but he said nothing, only watched her. The gentleness she had glimpsed so briefly before might have been an illusion. His eyes were dark and hard. "I'm starving," she confessed as she took her seat.

"Good sign. Any more pain?"

"Only in my pride." Forging ahead, she began to fill her plate. "Clumsiness isn't a talent I like to brag about, and walking into a door is such a tired cliché. I wish I'd come up with something more original."

"It's odd." Jacques twirled his fork by the stem as he studied her. "It doesn't seem to me that you would have the power enough to knock yourself unconscious."

"An amazon," Autumn explained and let the chicken rest for a delicious moment on her tongue.

"She eats like one," Julia commented. Autumn glanced over in time to catch the speculative look on her face before it vanished into a smile. "I gain weight watching her."

"Metabolism," Autumn claimed and took another forkful of chicken. "The real tragedy is that I lost the two rolls of film I shot on the trip from New York."

"Perhaps we're in for a series of accidents." Helen's voice was as hard as her eyes as they swept the table. "Things come in threes, don't they?" No one answered and she went on, fingering her own bruise. "It's hard to say what might happen next."

Autumn had come to detest the odd little silences that followed Helen's remarks, the fingers of tension that poked holes in the normalcy of the situation. On impulse, she broke her rule and started a conversation with Lucas.

"What would you do with this setting, Lucas?" She turned to him, but found no change in his expression. He's watching all of us, she thought. Just watching. Shaking off her unease, Autumn continued. "Nine people—ten really, counting the cook—isolated in a remote country inn, a storm raging. The main power's already snuffed out. The phone's likely to be next."

"The phone's already out," Steve told her. Autumn drew out a dramatic "Ah."

"And the ford, of course, is probably impassable." Robert winked at her, falling in with the theme.

"What more could you ask for?" Autumn demanded of Lucas. Lightning flashed, as if on cue.

"Murder." Lucas uttered the six-letter word casually, but it hung in the air as all eyes turned to him. Autumn shuddered involuntarily. It was the response she'd expected, yet she felt a chill on hearing it. "But, of course," he continued as the word still whispered in the air, "it's a rather overly obvious setting for my sort of work."

"Life is sometimes obvious, is it not?" Jacques stated. A small smile played on his mouth as he lifted his glass of golden-hued wine.

"I could be very effective," Julia mused. "Gliding down dark passageways in flowing white." She placed her elbows on the table, folded her hands and rested her chin on them. "The flame of my candle flickering into the shadows while the murderer waits with a silk scarf to cut off my life."

"You'd make a lovely corpse," Autumn told her.

"Thank you, darling." She turned to Lucas. "I'd much rather remain among the living, at least until the final scene."

"You die so well." Steve grinned across the table at her. "I was impressed by your Lisa in *Hope Springs*."

"What sort of murder do you see, Lucas?" Steve was eating little, Autumn noted; he preferred the wine. "A crime of passion or revenge? The impulsive act of a discarded lover or the evil workings of a cool, calculating mind?"

"Aunt Tabby could sprinkle an exotic poison over the food and eliminate us one by one," Autumn suggested as she dipped into the mashed potatoes.

"Once someone's dead, they're no more use." Helen brought the group's attention back to her. "Murder is a waste. You gain more by keeping someone alive. Alive and vulnerable." She shot Lucas a look. "Don't you agree, Mr. McLean?"

Autumn didn't like the way she smiled at him. *Cool and calculating.* Jacques's words repeated in her mind. Yes, she mused, this was a cool and calculating woman. In the silence, Autumn shifted her gaze to Lucas.

His face held the faintly bored go-to-hell look she knew so well. "I don't think murder is always a waste." Again, his voice was casual, but Autumn, in tune with him, saw the change in his eyes. They weren't bored, but cold as ice. "The world would gain much by the elimination of some." He smiled, and it was deadly.

They no longer seemed to be speaking hypothetically. Shifting her gaze to Helen, Autumn saw the quick fear. *But it's just a game,* she told herself frantically and looked at Julia. The actress was smiling, but there was none of her summer warmth in it. She was enjoying watching Helen flutter like a moth on a pin. Noting Autumn's expression of dismayed shock, Julia changed the subject without a ripple.

After dinner, the group loitered in the lounge, but the storm, which continued unabated, was wearing on the nerves. Only Julia and Lucas seemed unaffected. Autumn noted how they huddled together in a corner, apparently enthralled with each other's company. Julia's laughter was low and rich over the sound of rain. Once, she watched Lucas pinch a strand of the pale hair between his fingers. Autumn turned away. Julia ran interference expertly, and the knowledge depressed her.

The Spicers, without Julia as a distraction, sat together on the sofa nearest the fire. Though their voices were low, Autumn sensed the strain of a domestic quarrel. She moved farther out of earshot. A bad time, she decided, for Jane to confront Robert on his fascination with Julia when the actress was giving another man the benefit of her attentions. When they left, Jane's face was no longer sullen, but simply miserable. Julia never glanced in their direction, but leaned closer to Lucas and murmured something in his ear that made him laugh. Autumn found she, too, wanted out of the room.

It has nothing to do with Lucas, she told herself as she moved down the hall. I just want to say good-night to Aunt Tabby. Julia's doing precisely what I want her to—keeping Lucas entertained. He never even looked at me once Julia stepped in between. Shaking off the hurt, Autumn opened the door to her aunt's room.

"Autumn, dear! Lucas told me you bumped your head." Aunt Tabby stopped clucking over her laundry list and rose to peer at the bruise. "Oh, poor thing. Do you want some aspirin? I have some somewhere."

Though she appreciated Lucas's consideration in giving her aunt a watered-down version, Autumn wondered at the ease of their relationship. It didn't seem quite in character for Lucas McLean to bother overmuch with a vague old woman whose claim to fame was a small inn and a way with chocolate cake.

"No, Aunt Tabby, I'm fine. I've already taken something."

"That's good." She patted Autumn's hand and frowned briefly at the bruise. "You'll have to be more careful, dear."

"I will. Aunt Tabby . . ." Autumn poked idly at the papers on her aunt's desk. "How well do you know Lucas? I don't recall you ever calling a roomer by his first name." She knew there was no use in beating around the bush with her aunt. It would produce the same results as reading *War and Peace* in dim light—a headache and confusion.

"Oh, now that depends, Autumn. Yes, that really does depend." Aunt Tabby gently removed her papers from Autumn's reach before she focused on a spot in the ceiling. Autumn knew this meant she was thinking. "There's Mrs. Nollington. She has a corner room every September. I call her Frances and she calls me Tabitha. Such a nice woman. A widow from North Carolina."

"Lucas calls you Aunt Tabby," Autumn pointed out before her aunt could get going on Frances Nollington.

"Yes, dear, quite a number of people do. You do."

"Yes, but—"

"And Paul and Will," Aunt Tabby continued blithely. "And the little boy who brings the eggs. And . . . oh, several people. Yes, indeed, several people. Did you enjoy your dinner?"

"Yes, very much. Aunt Tabby," Autumn continued, determined that tenacity would prevail. "Lucas seems very much at home here."

"Oh, I am glad!" She beamed at her niece as she took Autumn's hand and patted it. "I do try so hard to make everyone feel at home. It always seems a shame to have to make them pay, but . . ." She glanced down at her laundry bills and began to mutter.

Give up, Autumn told herself. She kissed her aunt's cheek and left her to her towels and pillowcases.

It was growing late when Autumn finished putting her darkroom back in order. She left the door open this time and kept all the lights on. The echo of rain followed her inside as it beat on the kitchen windows. Other than its angry murmur, the house was silent.

No, Autumn thought, old houses are never silent. They creak and whisper, but the groaning boards and settling didn't disturb her. She liked the humming quality of the silence. Absorbed and content, she emptied trays and replaced bottles. She threw her ruined film into the wastecan with a sigh.

That hurts a bit, she thought, but there's nothing to be done about it. Tomorrow, she decided, she'd develop the film she'd taken that morning—the lake, the early sun, the mirrored trees. It would put her in a better frame of mind. Stretching her back, she lifted her hair from her neck, feeling pleasantly tired.

"I remember you doing that in the mornings."

Autumn whirled, her hair flying out from her shoulders as quick fear brought her heart to her throat. Pushing strands from her face, she stared at Lucas.

He leaned against the open doorway, a cup of coffee in his hand. His eyes locked on hers without effort.

"You'd pull up your hair, then let it fall, tumbling down your back until I ached to get my hands on it." His voice was deep and strangely raw. Autumn couldn't speak at all. "I often wondered if you did it on purpose, just to drive me mad." As he studied her face, he frowned, then lifted the coffee to his lips. "But, of course you didn't. I've never known anyone else who could arouse with such innocence."

"What are you doing here?" The trembling in her voice took some of the power out of the demand.

"Remembering."

Turning, she began to juggle bottles, jumbling them out of their carefully organized state. "You always were clever with words, Lucas." Cooler now that she wasn't facing him, she meticulously studied a bottle of bath soap. "I suppose you have to be in your profession."

"I'm not writing at the moment."

It was easier to deliberately misunderstand him. "Your book still giving you trouble?" Turning, Autumn again noticed the signs of strain and fatigue on his face. Sympathy and love flared up, and she struggled to bank them down. His eyes were much too keen. "You might have more success if you'd get a good night's sleep." She gestured toward the cup in his hands. "Coffee's not going to help."

"Perhaps not." He drained the cup. "But it's wiser than bourbon."

"Sleep's better than both." She shrugged her shoulders carelessly. Lucas's habits were no longer her concern. "I'm going up." Autumn walked toward him, but he stayed where he was, barring the door. She pulled up sharply. They were alone. The ground floor was empty but for them and the sound of rain.

"Lucas." She sighed sharply, wanting him to think her impatient rather than vulnerable. "I'm tired. Don't be troublesome."

His eyes smoldered at her tone. Though Autumn remained calm, she could feel her knees turning to water. The dull, throbbing ache was back in her head. When he moved aside, she switched off the lights, then brushed past him. Swiftly, he took her arm, preventing what she had thought was going to be an easy exit.

"There'll come a time, Cat," he murmured, "when you won't walk away so easily."

"Don't threaten me with your overactive masculinity." Her temper rose and she forgot caution. "I'm immune now."

She was jerked against him. All she could see was his fury. "I've had enough of this."

His mouth took hers roughly; she could taste the infuriated desire. When she struggled, he pinned her back against the wall, holding her arms to her sides and battering at her will with his mouth alone. She could feel herself going under and hating herself for it as much, she told herself, as she hated him. His lips didn't soften, even when her struggles ceased. He took and took as the anger vibrated between them.

Her heart was thudding wildly, and she could feel the mad pace of his as they pressed together. Passion was all-encompassing, and her back was to the wall. There's no escape, she thought dimly. There's never been any escape from him. No place to run. No place to hide. She began to tremble with fear and desire.

Abruptly he pulled away. His eyes were so dark, she saw nothing but her own reflection. I'm lost in him, she thought. I've always been lost in him. Then he was shaking her, shocking a gasp out of her.

"Watch how far you push," he told her roughly. "Damn it, you'd better remember I haven't any scruples. I know how to deal with people who pick fights with me." He stopped, but his fingers still dug into her skin. "I'll take you, Cat, take you kicking and screaming if you push me much further."

Too frightened by the rage she saw in his face to think of pride, she twisted away. She flew down the hall and up the stairs.

CHAPTER 6

Autumn reached her door, out of breath and fighting tears. He shouldn't be allowed to do this to her. She couldn't allow it. Why had he barged back into her life this way? Just when she was beginning to get over him. *Liar.* The voice was clear as crystal inside her head. You've never gotten over him. Never. But I will. She balled her hands into fists as she stood outside her door and caught her breath. I will get over him.

Hearing the sound of his footsteps on the stairs, she fumbled with the doorknob. She didn't want to deal with him again tonight. Tomorrow was soon enough.

Something was wrong. Autumn knew it the moment she opened her door and stumbled into the dark. The scent of perfume was so strong, her head whirled with it. She groped for the light and when it flashed on, she gave a small sound of despair.

The drawers and closet had been turned out and her clothes were tossed and scattered across the room. Some were ripped and torn, others merely lay in heaps. Her jewelry had been dumped from its box and tossed indiscriminately over the mounds of clothes. Bottles of cologne and powder had been emptied out and flung everywhere. Everything—every small object or personal possession—had been abused or destroyed.

She stood frozen in shock and disbelief. The wrong room, she told herself dumbly. This had to be the wrong room. But the lawn print blouse with its sleeve torn at the shoulder had been a Christmas gift from Will. The sandals, flung into a corner and slashed, she had bought herself in a small shop off Fifth Avenue the summer before.

"No." She shook her head as if that would make it all go away. "It's not possible."

"Good God!" Lucas's voice came from behind her. Autumn turned to see him staring into her room.

"I don't understand." The words were foolish, but they were all she had. Slowly, Lucas shifted his attention to her face. She made a helpless gesture. "Why?"

He came to her, and with his thumb brushed a tear from her cheek. "I don't know, Cat. First we have to find out who."

"But it's—it's so spiteful." She wandered through the rubble of her things, still thinking she must be dreaming. "No one here would have any reason to do this to me. You'd have to hate someone to do this, wouldn't you? No one here has any reason to hate me. No one even knew me before last night."

"Except me."

"This isn't your style." She pressed her fingers to her temple and struggled to understand. "You'd find a more direct way of hurting me."

"Thanks."

Autumn looked over at him and frowned, hardly aware of what was being said. His expression was brooding as he studied her face. She turned away. She wasn't up to discussing Lucas McLean. Then she saw it.

"Oh, *no!*"

Scrambling on all fours, Autumn worked her way over the mangled clothes and began pushing at the tangled sheets of her bed. Her hands shook as she reached for her camera. The lens was shattered, with spiderweb cracks spreading over the surface. The back was broken, hanging drunkenly on one hinge. The film streamed out like the tail of a kite. Exposed. Ruined. The mirror was crushed. With a moan, she cradled it in her hands and began to weep.

Her clothes and trinkets meant nothing, but the Nikon was more to her than a single-reflex camera. It was as much a part of her as her hands. With it, she had taken her first professional picture. Its mutilation was rape.

Her face was suddenly buried against a hard chest. She made no protest as Lucas's arms came around her, but wept bitterly. He said nothing, offered no comforting words, but his hands were unexpectedly gentle, his arms strong.

"Oh, Lucas." She drew away from him with a sigh. "It's so senseless."

"There's sense to it somewhere, Cat. There always is."

She looked back up at him. "Is there?" His eyes were keeping their secrets so she dropped her own back to her mangled camera. "Well, if someone wanted to hurt me, this was the right way."

Her fingers clenched on the camera. She was suddenly, fiercely angry; it pushed despair and tears out of her mind. Her body flooded with it. She wasn't going to sit and weep any longer. She was going to do something. Pushing her camera into Lucas's hands, Autumn scrambled to her feet.

"Wait a minute." He grabbed her hand before she could rush from the room. "Where are you going?"

"To drag everyone out of bed," she snapped at him, jerking her hand. "And then I'm going to break someone's neck."

He didn't have an easy time subduing her. Ultimately, he pinned her by wrapping his arms around her and holding her against him. "You probably could." There was a touch of surprised admiration in his tone, but it brought her no pleasure.

"Watch me," she challenged.

"Calm down first." He tightened his grip as she squirmed against him.

"I want—"

"I know what you want, Cat, and I don't blame you. But you have to think before you rush in."

"I don't have anything to think about," she tossed back. "Someone's going to pay for this."

"All right, fair enough. Who?"

His logic annoyed her, but succeeded in taking her temper from boil to simmer. "I don't know yet." With an effort, she managed to take a deep breath.

"That's better." He smiled and kissed her lightly. "Though your eyes are still lethal enough." He loosened his grip, but kept a hold on her arm. "Just keep your claws sheathed, Cat, until we find out what's going on. Let's go knock on a few doors."

Julia's room adjoined hers, so Autumn steered there first. Her rage was now packed in ice. Systematic, she told herself, aware of Lucas's grip. All right, we'll be systematic until we find out who did it. And then . . .

She knocked sharply on Julia's door. After the second knock, Julia answered with a soft, husky slur.

"Get up, Julia," Autumn demanded. "I want to talk to you."

"Autumn, darling." Her voice evoked a picture of Julia snuggling into her pillows. "Even I require beauty sleep. Go away like a good girl."

"Up, Julia," Autumn repeated, barely restraining herself from shouting. "Now."

"Goodness, aren't we grumpy. I'm the one who's being dragged from my bed."

She opened the door, a vision in a white lace negligee, her hair a tousled halo around her face, her eyes dark and heavy with sleep.

"Well, I'm up." Julia gave Lucas a slow, sensual smile and ran a hand through her hair. "Are we going to have a party?"

"Someone tore my room apart," Autumn stated bluntly. She watched Julia's attention switch from the silent flirtation with Lucas to her.

"What?" The catlike expression had melted into a frown of concentration. An actress, Autumn reminded herself. She's an actress and don't forget it.

"My clothes were pulled out and ripped, tossed around the room. My camera's broken." She swallowed on this. It was the most difficult to accept.

"That's crazy." Julia was no longer leaning provocatively against the door, but standing straight. "Let me see." She brushed past them and hurried down the hall. Stopping in the doorway of Autumn's room, she stared. Her eyes, when they turned back, were wide with shock. "Autumn, how awful!" She came back and slipped an arm around Autumn's waist. "How perfectly awful. I'm so sorry."

Sincerity, sympathy, shock. They were all there. Autumn wanted badly to believe them.

"Who would have done that?" she demanded of Lucas. Autumn saw that Julia's eyes were angry now. She was again the tough lady Autumn had glimpsed briefly that afternoon.

"We intend to find out. We're going to wake the others." Something passed between them. Autumn saw it flash briefly, then it was gone.

"All right," Julia said. "Then let's do it." She pushed her hair impatiently behind her ears. "I'll get the Spicers, you get Jacques and Steve. You," she continued to Autumn, "wake up Helen."

Her tone carried enough authority that Autumn found herself turning down the hall to Helen's room. She could hear the pounding, the answering stirs and murmurs from behind her. Reaching Helen's door, Autumn banged against it. This, at least, she thought, was progress. Lucas was right. We need a trial before we can hang someone.

Her knock went unanswered. Annoyed, Autumn rapped again. She wasn't in the mood to be ignored. Now there was more activity behind her as people came out of their rooms to stare at the disaster in hers.

"Helen!" She knocked again with fraying patience. "Come out here." She pushed the door open. It would give her some satisfaction to drag at least one person from bed. Ruthlessly, she switched on the light. "Helen, I—"

Helen wasn't in bed. Autumn stared at her, too shocked to feel horror. She was on the floor, but she wasn't sleeping. She was done with sleeping. Was that blood? Autumn thought in dumb fascination. She took a step forward before the reality struck her.

Horror gripped her throat, denying her the release of screaming. Slowly, she backed away. It was a nightmare. Starting with her room, it was all a nightmare. None of it was real. Lucas's careless voice played back in her head. *Murder.* Autumn shook her head as she backed into a wall. No, that was only a game. She heard a voice shouting in terror for Lucas, not even aware it was her own. Then blessedly, her hands came up to cover her eyes.

"Get her out of here." Lucas's rough command floated through Autumn's brain. She was trapped in a fog of dizziness. Arms came round her and led her from the room.

"Oh my God." Steve's voice was unsteady. When Autumn found the strength to look up at him, his face was ashen. She struggled against the faintness and buried her face in his chest. When was she going to wake up?

Confusion reigned around her. She heard disembodied voices as she drifted from horror to shock. There were Julia's smoky tones, Jane's gravelly voice and Jacques's rapid French-English mixture. Then Lucas's voice joined in— calm, cool, like a splash of cold water.

"She's dead. Stabbed. The phone's out so I'm going into the village to get the police."

"Murdered? She was murdered? Oh God!" Jane's voice rose, then became muffled. Raising her head, Autumn saw Jane being held tightly against her husband.

"I think, as a precaution, Lucas, no one should leave the inn alone." Robert took a deep breath as he cradled his wife. "We have to face the implications."

"I'll go with him." Steve's voice was strained and uneven. "I could use the fresh air."

With a curt nod, Lucas focused on Autumn. His eyes never left hers as he spoke to Robert. "Have you got something to put her out? She can double up with Julia tonight."

"I'm fine." Autumn managed to speak as she drew back from Steve's chest. "I don't want anything." It wasn't a dream, but real, and she had to face it. "Don't worry about me, it's not me. I'm all right." Hysteria was bubbling, and she bit down on her lip to cut it off.

"Come on, darling." Julia's arm replaced Steve's. "We'll go downstairs and sit down for a while. She'll be all right."

"I want—"

"I said she'll be all right," Julia cut off Lucas's protest sharply. "I'll see to her. Do what you have to do." Before he could speak again, she led Autumn down the staircase.

"Sit down," she ordered, nudging Autumn onto the sofa. "You could use a drink."

Looking up, Autumn saw Julia's face hovering over hers. "You're pale," she said stupidly before the brandy burned her throat and brought the world into focus with a jolt.

"I'm not surprised," Julia murmured and sank down on the low table in front of Autumn. "Better?" she asked when Autumn lifted the snifter again.

"Yes, I think so." She took a deep breath and focused on Julia's eyes. "It's really happening, isn't it? She's really lying up there."

"It's happening." Julia drained her own brandy. Color seeped gradually into her cheeks. "The bitch finally pushed someone too far."

Stunned by the hardness of Julia's voice, Autumn could only stare. Calmly, Julia set down her glass.

"Listen." Her tone softened, but her eyes were still cold. "You're a strong lady, Autumn. You've had a shock, a bad one, but you won't fall apart."

"No." Autumn tried to believe it, then said with more strength, "No, I won't fall apart."

"This is a mess, and you have to face it." Julia paused, then leaned closer. "One of us killed her."

Part of her had known it, but the rest had fought against the knowledge, blocking it out. Now that it had been said in cool, simple terms, there was no escape from it. Autumn nodded again and swallowed the remaining brandy in one gulp.

"She got what she deserved."

"Julia!" Jacques strode into the room. His face was covered with horror and disapproval.

"Oh, Jacques, thank God. Give me one of those horrible French cigarettes. Give one to Autumn, too. She could use it."

"Julia." He obeyed her automatically. "You musn't speak so now."

"I'm not a hypocrite." Julia drew deeply on the cigarette, shuddered, then drew again. "I detested her. The police will find out soon enough why we all detested her."

"*Nom de Dieu!* How can you speak so calmly of it?" Jacques exploded in a quick, passionate rage Autumn hadn't thought him capable of. "The woman is dead, murdered. You didn't see the cruelty of it. I wish to God I had not."

Autumn drew hard on her cigarette, trying to block out the picture that flashed back into her mind. She gasped and choked on the power of the smoke.

"Autumn, forgive me." Jacques's anger vanished as he sat

down beside her and draped an arm over her shoulders. "I shouldn't have reminded you."

"No." She shook her head, then crushed out the cigarette. It wasn't going to help. "Julia's right. It has to be faced."

Robert entered, but his normally swinging stride was slow and dragging. "I gave Jane a sedative." With a sigh, he too made for the brandy. "It's going to be a long night."

The room grew silent. The rain, so much a part of the night, was no longer noticeable. Jacques paced the room, smoking continually while Robert kindled a fresh fire. The blaze, bright and crackling, brought no warmth. Autumn's skin remained chilled. In defense, she poured herself another brandy but found she couldn't drink it.

Julia remained seated. She smoked in long, slow puffs. The only outward sign of her agitation was the continual tapping of a pink-tipped nail against the arm of her chair. The tapping, the crackling, the hiss of rain, did nothing to diminish the overwhelming power of the silence.

When the front door opened with a click and a thud, all eyes flew toward the sound. Strings of tension tightened and threatened to snap. Autumn waited to see Lucas's face. It would be all right, somehow, as long as she could see his face.

"Couldn't get through the ford," he stated shortly as he came into the room. He peeled off a sopping jacket, then made for the community brandy.

"How bad is it?" Robert looked from Lucas to Steve, then back to Lucas. Already, the line of command had been formed.

"Bad enough to keep us here for a day or two," Lucas informed him. He swallowed a good dose of the brandy, then

stared out the window. There was nothing to see but the reflection of the room behind him. "That's if the rain lets up by
morning." Turning, he locked onto Autumn, making a long,
thorough study. Again he had, in his way, pushed everyone
from the room but the two of them.

"The phones," she blurted out, needing to say something,
anything. "We could have phone service by tomorrow."

"Don't count on it." Lucas ran a hand through his dripping hair, showering the room with water. "According to the
car radio, this little spring shower is the backlash of a tor-
nado. The power's out all over this part of the state." He lit
a cigarette with a shrug. "We'll just have to wait and see."

"Days." Steve flopped down beside Autumn, his face still
gray. She gave him her unwanted brandy. "It could be days."

"Lovely." Rising, Julia went to Lucas. She plucked the cigarette from his fingers and drew on it. "Well." She stared at
him. "What the hell do we do now?"

"First we lock and seal off Helen's room." Lucas lit another cigarette. His eyes stayed on Julia's. "Then we get some
sleep."

CHAPTER 7

Sometime during the first murky light of dawn, Autumn did sleep. She'd passed the night lying wide-eyed, listening to the sound of Julia's gentle breathing beside her. Though she'd envied her ability to sleep, Autumn had fought off the drowsiness. If she closed her eyes, she might see what she'd seen when she opened Helen's door. When her eyes did close, however, the sleep was dreamless—the total oblivion of exhaustion.

It might have been the silence that woke her. Suddenly, she found herself awake and sitting straight up in bed. Confused, she stared around her.

Julia's disorder greeted her. Silk scarves and gold chains were draped here and there. Elegant bottles cluttered the bureau. Small, incredibly high Italian heels littered the floor. Memory returned.

With a sigh, Autumn rose, feeling a bit ridiculous in Julia's black silk nightgown; it neither suited nor fit. After seeing herself in the mirror, Autumn was glad Julia had already awakened and gone. She didn't want to wear any of the clothes that might have survived the attack on her room, and prepared to change back into yesterday's shirt and jeans.

A note lay on them. The elegant, sloping print could only have been Julia's:

Darling, help yourself to some undies and a blouse or sweater. I'm afraid my slacks won't fit you. You're built like a pencil. You don't wear a bra, and in any case, the idea of you filling one of mine is ridiculous.

J.

Autumn laughed, as Julia had intended. It felt so good, so normal, that she laughed again. Julia had known exactly how I'd feel, Autumn realized, and a wave of gratitude swept through her for the simple gesture. She showered, letting the water beat hot against her.

Coming back to the bedroom, Autumn pulled out a pair of cobwebby panties. There was a stack of them in misted pastels that she estimated would cost as much as a wide-angle lens. She tugged on one of Julia's sweaters, then pushed it up to her elbows—it was almost there in any case. Leaving the room, she kept her eyes firmly away from Helen's door.

"Autumn, I was hoping you'd sleep longer."

She paused at the foot of the stairs and waited for Steve to reach her. His face was sleep shadowed and older than it had been the day before. A fragment of his boyish smile touched his lips for her, but his eyes didn't join in.

"You don't look as if you got much," he commented and lifted a finger to her cheek.

"I doubt any of us did."

He draped an arm over her shoulder. "At least the rain's slowed down."

"Oh." Realization slowly seeped in and Autumn gave a weak laugh. "I knew there was something different. The quiet woke me. Where is . . ." She hesitated as Lucas's name trembled on her tongue. "Everyone?" she amended.

"In the lounge," he told her, but steered her toward the dining room. "Breakfast first. I haven't eaten myself, and you can't afford to drop any weight."

"How charming of you to remind me." She managed a friendly grimace. If he could make the effort to be normal, so could she. "Let's eat in the kitchen, though."

Aunt Tabby was there, as usual, giving instructions to a much subdued Nancy. She turned as they entered, then enfolded Autumn in her soft, lavender-scented arms.

"Oh, Autumn, what a dreadful tragedy. I don't know what to make of it." Autumn squeezed her. Here was something solid to hold on to. "Lucas said someone killed the poor thing, but that doesn't seem possible, does it?" Drawing back, Aunt Tabby searched Autumn's face. "You didn't sleep well, dear. Only natural. Sit down and have your breakfast. It's the best thing to do."

Aunt Tabby could, Autumn mused, so surprisingly cut through to the quick when she needed to. She began to bustle around the room, murmuring to Nancy as Autumn and Steve sat at the small kitchen table.

There were simple, normal sounds and scents. Bacon, coffee, the quick sizzle of eggs. It was, Autumn had to agree, the best thing to do. The food, the routine, would bring some sense of order. And with the order, she'd be able to think clearly again.

Steve sat across from her, sipping coffee while she toyed with her eggs. She simply couldn't summon her usual appetite, and turned to conversation instead. The questions she asked Steve about himself were general and inane, but he picked up the effort and went with it. She realized, as she nibbled without interest on a piece of toast, that they were supporting each other.

Autumn discovered he was quite well-traveled. He'd crisscrossed all over the country performing various tasks in his role as troubleshooter for his father's conglomerate. He treated wealth with the casual indifference of one who has always had it, but she sensed a knowledge and a dedication toward the company which had provided him with it. He spoke of his father with respect and admiration.

"He's sort of a symbol of success and ingenuity," Steve said, pushing his own half-eaten breakfast around his plate. "He worked his way up the proverbial ladder. He's tough." He grinned and shrugged. "He's earned it."

"How does he feel about you going into politics?"

"He's all for it." Steve glanced down at her plate and sent her a meaningful look. Autumn only smiled and shook her head. "Anyway, he's always encouraged me to 'go for what I want and I better be good at it.'" He grinned again. "He's tough, but since I am good at it and intend to keep it that way, we'll both be satisfied. I like paperwork." He gestured with both hands. "Organizing. Refining the system from within the system."

"That can't be as easy as it sounds," Autumn commented, encouraging his enthusiasm.

"No, but—" He shook his head. "Don't get me started. I'll make a speech." He finished off his second cup of coffee.

"I'll be making enough of those when I get back to California and my campaign officially starts."

"It just occurs to me that you, Lucas, Julia and Jacques are all from California." Autumn pushed her hair behind her back and considered the oddity. "It's strange that so many people from the coast would be here at one time."

"The Spicers, too," Aunt Tabby added from across the room, deeply involved in positioning pies in the oven. "Yes, I'm almost sure Dr. Spicer told me they were from California. So warm and sunny there. Well—" she patted the range as if to give it the confidence it needed to handle her pies "—I must see to the rooms now. I moved you next door to Lucas, Autumn. Such a terrible thing about your clothes. I'll have them cleaned for you."

"I'll help you, Aunt Tabby." Pushing away her plate, Autumn rose.

"Oh no, dear, the cleaners will do it."

Smiling wasn't as difficult as Autumn had thought. "I meant with the rooms."

"Oh . . ." Aunt Tabby trailed off and clucked her tongue. "I do appreciate it, Autumn, I really do, but . . ." She looked up with a touch of distress in her eyes. "I have my own system, you see. You'd just confuse me. It's all done with numbers."

Leaving Autumn to digest this, she gave her an apologetic touch on the cheek and bustled out.

There seemed nothing to do but join the others in the lounge.

The rain, though it was little more than a mist now, seemed to Autumn like prison bars. Standing at the window in the lounge, she wished desperately for sun. Conversation did not sparkle. When anyone spoke, it was around or over or under Helen Easterman. Perhaps it would have been better if they'd closeted themselves in their rooms, but human nature had them bound together.

Julia and Lucas sat on the sofa, speaking occasionally in undertones. Autumn found his eyes on her too often. Her defenses were too low to deal with what one of his probing looks could do to her, so she kept her back to him and watched the rain.

"I really think it's time we talked about this," Julia announced suddenly.

"Julia." Jacques's voice was both strained and weary.

"We can't go on like this," Julia stated practically. "We'll all go crazy. Steve's wearing out the floor, Robert's running out of wood to fetch and if you smoke another cigarette, you'll keel over." Contrarily, she lit another herself. "Unless we want to pretend that Helen stabbed herself, we've got to deal with the fact that one of us killed her."

Into the penetrating silence, Lucas's voice flowed, calm and detached. "I think we can rule out suicide." He watched as Autumn pressed her forehead to the glass. "And conveniently, we all had the opportunity to do it. Ruling out Autumn and her aunt, that leaves the six of us."

Autumn turned from the window and found every eye in the room on her. "Why should I be ruled out?" She shuddered and lifted her arms to hug herself. "You said we all had the opportunity."

"Motive, Cat," he said simply. "You're the only one in the room without a motive."

"Motive?" It was becoming too much like one of his screenplays. She needed to cling to reality. "What possible motive could any of us have had?"

"Blackmail." Lucas lit a cigarette as she gaped at him. "Helen was a professional leech. She thought she had quite a little goldmine in the six of us." He glanced up and caught Autumn with one of his looks. "She miscalculated."

"Blackmail." Autumn could only mumble the word as she stared at him. "You're—you're making this up. This is just one of your scenarios."

He waited a beat, his eyes locked on hers. "No."

"How do you know so much?" Steve demanded. Slowly, Lucas's eyes swerved from Autumn. "If she were blackmailing you, it doesn't necessarily follow that she was blackmailing all of us."

"How clever of you, Lucas," Julia interjected, running a hand down his arm, then letting it rest on his. "I had no idea she was sticking her fangs in anyone other than the three of us." Glancing at Jacques, she gave him a careless shrug. "It seems we're in good company."

Autumn made a small sound, and Julia's attention drifted over to her. Her expression was both sympathetic and amused. "Don't look so shocked, darling. Most of us have things we don't particularly want made public. I might have paid her off if she'd threatened me with something more interesting." Leaning back, she pouted effectively. "An affair with a married senator . . ." She sent a lightning smile to Autumn. "I believe I mentioned him before. That hardly had me quaking in my shoes at the thought of exposure. I'm not squeamish about my indiscretions. I told her to go to hell. Of course," she added, smiling slowly, "there's only my word for that, isn't there?"

"Julia, don't make jokes." Jacques lifted a hand to rub his eyes.

"I'm sorry." Julia rose to perch on the arm of his chair. Her hand slipped to his shoulder.

"This is crazy." Unable to comprehend what was happening, Autumn searched the faces that surrounded her. They were strangers again, holding secrets. "What are you all doing here? Why did you come?"

"It's very simple." Lucas rose and crossed over to her, but unlike Julia, he didn't touch to comfort. "I made plans to come here for my own reasons. Helen found out. She was very good at finding things out—too good. She learned that Julia and Jacques were to join me." He turned, half blocking Autumn from the rest with his body. Was it protection, she wondered, or defense? "She must have contacted the rest of you, and made arrangements to have all her . . . clients here at once."

"You seem to know quite a bit," Robert muttered. He poked unnecessarily at the fire.

"It isn't difficult to figure out," Lucas returned. "I knew she was holding nasty little threats over three of us; we'd discussed it. When I noticed her attention to Anderson, and you and your wife, I knew she was sucking elsewhere, too."

Jane began to cry in dry, harsh sobs that racked her body. Instinctively, Autumn moved past Lucas to offer comfort. Before she was halfway across the room, Jane stopped her with a look that was like a fist to the jaw.

"You could have done it just as easily as anyone else. You've been spying on us, taking that camera everywhere." Jane's voice rose dramatically as Autumn froze. "You were working for her, you could have done it. You can't prove you didn't. I was with Robert." There was nothing bland or dull about her now. Her eyes were wild. "I was with Robert. He'll tell you."

Robert's arm came around her. His voice was quiet and soothing as she sobbed against his chest. Autumn didn't move. There seemed no place to go.

"She was going to tell you I was gambling again, tell you about all the money I'd lost." She clung to him, a sad sight in a dirt-brown dress. Robert continued to murmur and stroke her hair. "But I told you last night, I told you myself. I couldn't pay her anymore, and I told you. I didn't kill her, Robert. Tell them I didn't kill her."

"Of course you didn't, Jane. Everyone knows that. Come with me now, you're tired. We'll go upstairs."

He was leading her across the room as he spoke. His eyes met Autumn's half in apology, half in a plea for understanding. She saw, quite suddenly, that he loved his wife very much.

Autumn turned away, humiliated for Jane, sorry for Robert. The faint trembling in her hands indicated she'd been dealt one more shock. When Steve's arm came around her, she turned into it and drew the comfort offered.

"I think we could all use a drink," Julia announced. Moving to the bar, she poured a hefty glass of sherry, then took it to Autumn. "You first," she ordered, pressing the glass into her hand. "Autumn seems to be getting the worst of this. Hardly seems fair, does it, Lucas?" Her eyes lifted to his and held briefly before she turned back to the bar. He made no answer. "She's probably the only one of us here who's even remotely sorry that Helen's dead."

Autumn drank, wishing the liquor would soften the words.

"She was a vulture," Jacques murmured. Autumn saw the message pass between him and Julia. "But even a vulture doesn't deserve to be murdered." Leaning back, he accepted the glass Julia brought him. He clasped her hand as she once again sat on the arm of his chair.

"Perhaps my motive is the strongest," Jacques said and drank once, deeply. "When the police come, all will be opened and studied. Like something under a microscope." He looked at Autumn, as if to direct his explanation to her. "She threatened the happiness of the two things most important to me—the woman I love and my children." Autumn's eyes skipped quickly to Julia's. "The information she had on my relationship with this woman could have damaged my suit for custody. The beauty of that love meant nothing to Helen. She would turn it into something sordid and ugly."

Autumn cradled her drink in both hands. She wanted to tell Jacques to stop, that she didn't want to hear, didn't want to be involved. But it was too late. She was already involved.

"I was furious when she arrived here with her smug smile and evil eyes." He looked down into his glass. "There were times, many times, I wanted my hands around her throat, wanted to bruise her face as someone else had done."

"Yes, I wonder who." Julia caught her bottom lip between her teeth in thought. "Whoever did that was angry, perhaps angry enough to kill." Her eyes swept up, across Steve and Autumn and Lucas.

"You were at the inn that morning," Autumn stated. Her voice sounded odd, thready, and she swallowed.

"So I was." Julia smiled at her. "Or so I said. Being alone in bed is hardly an airtight alibi. No . . ." She leaned back on the wing of the chair. "I think the police will want to know who socked Helen. You came in with her, Autumn. Did you see anyone?"

"No." Her eyes flew instantly to Lucas. His were dark, already locked on her face. There were warning signals of anger and impatience she could read too easily. She dropped her gaze to her drink. "No, I . . ." How could she say it? How could she think it?

"Autumn's had enough for a while." Steve tightened his arm protectively around her. "Our problems don't concern her. She doesn't deserve to be in the middle."

"Poor child." Jacques studied her pale, strained face. "You've walked into a viper's nest, *oui*? Go sleep, forget us for a while."

"Come on, Autumn, I'll take you up." Steve slipped the glass from her hand and set it on the table. With one final glance at Lucas, Autumn went with him.

CHAPTER 8

They didn't speak as they mounted the steps. Autumn was too busy trying to force the numbness from her brain. She hadn't been able to fully absorb everything she'd been told. Steve hurried her by Helen's door before stopping at the one beside Lucas's.

"Is this the room your aunt meant?"

"Yes." She lifted both hands to her hair, pushing its weight away from her face. "Steve." She searched his face and found herself faltering. "Is all this true? Everything Lucas said? Was Helen really blackmailing all of you?" She noted the discomfort in his eyes and shook her head. "I don't mean to pry, but—"

"No," he cut her off, then let out a long breath. "No, it's hardly prying at this point. You're not involved, but you're caught, aren't you?"

The word was so apt, so close to her own thinking, that she nearly laughed. Caught. Yes, that was it exactly.

"It seems McLean is right on target. Helen had information concerning a deal I made for the company—perfectly within the circle of the law, but . . ." He gave a rueful smile and lifted his shoulders. "Maybe not quite as perfectly as it should have been. There was an ethical question, and it wouldn't look so good on paper. The technicalities are too complicated to explain, but the gist of it is I didn't want any shadows on my career. These days, when you're heading into politics, you have to cover all the angles."

"Angles," Autumn repeated and pressed her fingers to her temple. "Yes, I suppose you do."

"She threatened me, Autumn, and I didn't care for it—but it wasn't enough to provoke murder." He drew a quick breath and shook his head. "But that doesn't help much, does it? None of us are likely to admit it."

"I appreciate you telling me anyway," Autumn said. Steve's eyes were gentle on her face, but the lines and strain of tension still showed. "It can't be pleasant for you to have to explain."

"I'll have to explain to the police before long," he said grimly, then noted her expression. "I don't mind telling you, Autumn, if you feel better knowing. Julia's right." His fingers strayed absently to her hair. "It's much healthier to get it out in the open. But you've had enough for now." He smiled at her, then realized his hands were in her hair. "I suppose you're used to this. Your hair's not easy to resist. I've wanted to touch it since the first time I saw it. Do you mind?"

"No." She wasn't surprised to find herself in his arms, his mouth on hers. It was an easy kiss, one that comforted rather than stirred. Autumn relaxed with it, and gave back what she could.

"You'll get some rest?" Steve murmured, holding her to his chest a moment.

"Yes. Yes, I will. Thank you." She pulled back to look up at him, but her eyes were drawn past him. Lucas stood at the doorway of his room, watching them both. Without speaking, he disappeared inside.

When she was alone, Autumn lay down on the white heirloom bedspread, but sleep wouldn't come. Her mind ached with fatigue. Her body was numb from it, but sleep, like a spiteful lover, stayed away. Time drifted as her thoughts ran over each member of the group.

She could feel nothing but sympathy for Jacques and the Spicers. She remembered the Frenchman's eyes when he spoke of his children and could still see Robert protecting his wife as she sobbed. Julia, on the other hand, needed no sympathy. Autumn felt certain the actress could take care of herself; she'd need no supporting arm or soothing words. Steve had also seemed more annoyed than upset by Helen's threats. He, too, could handle himself, she felt. There was a streak of street sense under the California gloss; he didn't need Autumn to worry for him.

Lucas was a different matter. Though he had nudged admissions from the rest of them, whatever threat Helen had held over him was still his secret. He had seemed very cool, very composed when he'd spoken of blackmail—but Autumn knew him. He was fully capable of concealing his emotions when there was a purpose to it. He was a hard man. Who knew better than she?

Cruel? Yes, she mused. Lucas could be cruel. She still had the scars attesting to it. But murder? No. Autumn couldn't picture Lucas plunging something sharp into Helen Easterman. Scissors, she remembered, though she tried hard not to.

The scissors that had lain on the floor beside Helen. No, she couldn't believe him capable of that. She wouldn't believe him capable of it.

Neither could she rationally believe it of any of the others. Could they all conceal such hate, such ugliness behind their shocked faces and shadowed eyes?

But, of course, one of them was the killer.

Autumn blanked it from her mind. She couldn't think of it anymore. Not just then. Steve's prescription was valid—she needed to rest. Yet she rose and walked to the window to stare out at the slow, hateful rain.

The knock at her door vibrated like an explosion. Whirling, she wrapped her arms protectively around her body. Her heart pounded while her throat dried up with fear. Stop it! she ordered herself. No one has any cause to hurt you.

"Yes, come in." The calmness of her own voice brought her relief. She was hanging on.

Robert entered. He looked so horribly weary and stricken, Autumn automatically reached out to him. She thought no more of fear. He clasped her hands and squeezed once, hard.

"You need food," he stated as he searched her face. "It shows in the face first."

"Yes, I know. My delicate hollows become craters very quickly." She made her own search. "You could use some yourself."

He sighed. "I believe you're one of those rare creatures who is inherently kind. I apologize for my wife."

"No, don't." His sigh had been long and broken. "She didn't mean it. We're all upset. This is a nightmare."

"She's been under a lot of strain. Before . . ." He broke off and shook his head. "She's sleeping now. Your head—" he brushed the hair from her forehead to examine the colorful bruise "—is it giving you any trouble?"

"No, none. I'm fine." The mishap seemed like some ridiculous comic relief in the midst of a melodrama now. "Can I help you, Robert?"

His eyes met hers, once, desperately, then moved away. "That woman put Jane through hell. If I'd just known, I would have put a stop to it long ago." Anger overpowered his weariness and he turned to prowl the room. "She tormented her, drained every drop of money Jane could raise. She played on a sickness, encouraging Jane to gamble to meet the payments. I knew nothing about it! I should have. Yesterday, Jane told me herself and I was going to enjoy dealing with the Easterman woman this morning." Autumn saw the soft, gentle hands clench into fists. "God help me, that's the only reason I'm sorry she's dead."

"Robert . . ." She wasn't certain what to say, how to deal with this side of his character. "Anyone would feel the same way," she said carefully. "She was an evil woman. She hurt someone you love." Autumn watched the fingers in his left hand relax, one at a time. "It isn't kind, but none of us will mourn her. Perhaps no one will. I think that's very sad."

He turned back and focused on her again. After a moment, he seemed to pull himself back under control. "I'm sorry you're caught up in this." With the anger gone from his eyes, they were vulnerable. "I'm going to go check on Jane. Will you be all right?"

"Yes."

She watched him go, then sank down into a chair. Each different crisis drained her. If possible, she was wearier now than before. When did the madness start? Only a few days ago she'd been safe in her apartment in Manhattan. She'd never met any of these people who were tugging at her now. Except one.

Even as she thought of him, Lucas strode in through the door. He stalked over to her, stared down and frowned.

"You need to eat," he said abruptly. Autumn thought of how tired she was of hearing that diagnosis. "I've been watching the pounds drop off you all day. You're already too thin."

"I adore flattery." His arrogant entrance and words boosted her flagging energy. She didn't have to take abuse from Lucas McLean anymore. "Don't you know how to knock?"

"I've always appreciated the understatedness of your body, Cat. You remember." He pulled her to her feet, then molded her against him. Her eyes flashed with quick temper. "Anderson seems to have discovered the charm as well. Did it occur to you that you might have been kissing a murderer?"

He spoke softly while his hand caressed her back. His eyes were mocking her. Her temper snapped at the strain of fighting her need for him.

"One might be holding me now."

He tightened his fingers on her hair so that she cried out in surprise. The mockery was replaced by a burning, terrifying rage. "You'd like to believe that, wouldn't you? You'd like to see me languishing in prison or, better yet, dangling from the end of a rope." She would have shaken her head, but his grip on her hair made movement impossible. "Would that be suitable punishment for my rejecting you, Cat? How deep is the hate? Deep enough to pull the lever yourself?"

"No, Lucas. Please, I didn't mean—"

"The hell you didn't." He cut off her protest. "The thought of me with blood on my hands comes easily to you. You can cast me in the role of murderer, can't you? Standing over Helen with the scissors in my hand."

"No!" In defense, she closed her eyes. "Stop it! Please stop it." He was hurting her now, but not with his hands. The words cut deeper.

He lowered his voice in a swift change of mood. Ice ran down Autumn's back. "I could have used my hands and been more tidy." A strong, lean-fingered hand closed around her throat. Her eyes flew open.

"Lucas—"

"Very simple and no mess," he went on, watching her eyes widen. "Quick enough, too, if you know what to do. More my style. More—as you put it—direct. Isn't that right?"

"You're only doing this to frighten me." Her breath was trembling in and out of her lungs. It was as if he were forcing her to think the worst of him, wanting her to think him capable of something monstrous. She'd never seen him like this. His eyes were black with fury while his voice was cold, so cold. She shivered. "I want you to leave, Lucas. Leave right now."

"Leave?" He slid his hand from her throat to the back of her neck. "I don't think so, Cat." His face inched closer. "If I'm going to hang for murder, I'd best take what consolation I can while I have the chance."

His mouth closed fast over hers. She struggled against him, more frightened than she'd been when she'd turned on the light in Helen's room. She could only moan; movement was impossible when he held her this close. He slipped a

hand under her sweater to claim her breast with the swift expertise of experience. Heart thudded madly against heart.

"How can anyone so skinny be so soft?" he murmured
against her mouth. The words he'd spoken so often in the past
brought more agony than she could bear. The hunger from
him was thunderous; he was like a man who had finally
broken free of his tether. "My God, how I want you." The
words were torn from him as he ravaged her neck. "I'll be
damned if I'll wait any longer."

They sank onto the bed. With all the strength that remained, she flailed out against him. Pinning her arms to
her sides, Lucas stared down at her with a wild kind of
fury. "Bite and scratch all you want, Cat. I've reached my
limit."

"I'll scream, Lucas." The words shuddered out of her. "If
you touch me again, I'll scream."

"No, you won't."

His mouth was on hers, proving him right and her wrong.
His body molded to hers with bittersweet accuracy. She arched
once in defense, in desperation, but his hands were roaming,
finding all the secret places he'd discovered over three years
before. There was no resisting him. The wild, reckless demand that had always flavored his lovemaking left her weak.
He knew too much of her. Autumn knew, before his fingers
reached the snap of her jeans, that she couldn't prevent her
struggles from becoming demands. When his mouth left hers
to roam her neck, she didn't scream, but moaned with the
need he had always incited in her.

He was going to win again, and she would do nothing to
stop him. Tears welled, then spilled from her eyes as she

knew he'd soon discover her pitiful, abiding love. Even her pride, it seemed, again belonged to him.

Lucas stopped abruptly. All movement ceased when he drew back his head to stare down at her. She thought, through her blurred vision, that she saw some flash of pain cross his face before it became still and emotionless. Lifting a hand, he caught a teardrop on his fingertip. With a swift oath, he lifted his weight from her.

"No, I won't be responsible for this again." Turning, he stalked to the window and stared out.

Sitting up, Autumn lowered her face to her knees and fought against the tears. She'd promised herself he'd never see her cry again. Not over him. Never over him. The silence stretched on for what seemed an eternity.

"I won't touch you like this again," he said quietly. "You have my word, for what it's worth."

Autumn thought she heard him sigh, long and deep, before his footsteps crossed to her. She didn't look up, but only squeezed her eyes closed.

"Autumn, I . . . oh, sweet God." He touched her arm, but she only curled herself tighter into a ball in defense.

The room fell silent again. The dripping rain seemed to echo into it. When Lucas spoke again, his voice was harsh and strained. "When you've rested, get something to eat. I'll have your aunt send up a tray if you're not down for dinner. I'll see that no one disturbs you."

She heard him leave, heard the quiet click of her door. Alone, she kept curled in her ball as she lay down. Ultimately, the storm of tears induced sleep.

CHAPTER 9

It was dark when Autumn awoke, but she was not refreshed. The sleep had been only a temporary relief. Nothing had changed while she had slept. But no, she thought as she glanced around the room. She was wrong. Something had changed. It was quiet. Really quiet. Rising, she walked to the window. She could see the moon and a light scattering of stars. The rain had stopped.

In the dim light, she moved to the bathroom and washed her face. She wasn't certain she had the courage to look in the mirror. She let the cold cloth rest against her eyes for a long time, hoping the swelling wasn't as bad as it felt. She felt something else as well. Hunger. It was a healthy sign, she decided. A normal sign. The rain had stopped and the nightmare was going to end. And now she was going to eat.

Her bare feet didn't disturb the silence that hung over the inn. She was glad of it. She wanted food now, not company. But when she passed the lounge, she heard the murmur of voices. She wasn't alone after all. Julia and Jacques were silhouetted by the window. Their conversation was low and urgent. Before she could melt back into the shadows, Julia turned and spotted her. The conversation ceased abruptly.

"Oh, Autumn, you've surfaced. We thought we'd seen the last of you until morning." She glided to her, then slipped a friendly arm around her waist. "Lucas wanted to send up a tray, but Robert outranked him. Doctor's orders were to let you sleep until you woke up. You must be famished. Let's see what your Aunt Tabby left for you."

Julia was doing all the talking, and quite purposefully leading Autumn away. A glance showed her that Jacques was still standing by the window, unmoving. Autumn let it go, too hungry to object.

"Sit down, darling," Julia ordered as she steered Autumn into the kitchen. "I'm going to fix you a feast."

"Julia, you don't have to fix me anything. I appreciate it, but—"

"Now let me play mother," Julia interrupted, pressing down on Autumn's shoulder until she sat. "You're past the sticky-finger stage, so I really quite enjoy it."

Sitting back, Autumn managed a smile. "You're not going to tell me you can cook."

Julia aimed an arched glance. "I don't suppose you should eat anything too heavy at this time of night," she said mildly. "There's some marvelous soup left from dinner, and I'll fix you my specialty. A cheese omelette."

Autumn decided that watching Julia Bond bustle around a kitchen was worth the market price of an ounce of gold. She seemed competent enough and kept up a bouncy conversation that took no brainpower to follow. With a flourish, she plopped a glass of milk in front of Autumn.

"I'm not really very fond of milk," Autumn began and glanced toward the coffeepot.

"Now, drink up," Julia instructed. "You need roses in your cheeks. You look terrible."

"Thanks."

Steaming chicken soup joined the milk, and Autumn attacked it with singleminded intensity. Some of the weakness drained from her limbs.

"Good girl," Julia approved as she dished up the omelette. "You look nearly human again."

Glancing over, Autumn smiled. "Julia, you're marvelous."

"Yes, I know. I was born that way." She sipped coffee and watched Autumn start on the eggs. "I'm glad you were able to rest. This day has been a century."

For the first time, Autumn noticed the mauve shadows under the blue eyes and felt a tug of guilt. "I'm sorry. You should be in bed, not waiting on me."

"Lord, but you're sweet." Julia pulled out a cigarette. "I haven't any desire to go up to my room until exhaustion takes over. I'm quite selfishly prepared to keep you with me until it does. Actually, Autumn," she added, watching through a mist of smoke, "I wonder if it's very wise for you to be wandering about on your own."

"What?" Autumn looked up again and frowned. "What do you mean?"

"It was your room that was broken into," Julia pointed out.

"Yes, but . . ." She was surprised to realize she'd almost overlooked the ransacking of her room with everything else that had happened. "It must have been Helen," she ventured.

"Oh, I doubt that," Julia returned and continued to sip contemplatively. "I very much doubt that. If Helen had broken

into your room, it would have been to look for something
she could use on you. She'd have been tidy. We've given this
some thought."

"We?"

"Well, I've given it some thought," Julia amended smoothly.
"I think whoever tore up your things was looking for something, then covered the search with overdone destruction."

"Looking for what?" Autumn demanded. "I don't have
anything anyone here could be interested in."

"Don't you?" Julia ran the tip of her tongue over her teeth.
"I've been thinking about what happened in your darkroom."

"You mean when the power went off?" Autumn shook her
head and touched the bruise on her forehead. "I walked into
the door."

"Did you?" Julia sat back and studied the harsh ceiling
light. "I wonder. Lucas told me that you said you heard someone rattling at the knob and walked over. What if . . ." She
brought her eyes back to Autumn's. "What if someone swung
the door open and hit you with it?"

"It was locked," Autumn insisted, then remembered that
it had been open when Lucas found her.

"There are keys, darling." She watched Autumn's face
closely. "What are you thinking?"

"The door was open when Lucas—" She cut herself off
and shook her head. "No, Julia, it's ridiculous. Why would
anyone want to do that to me?"

Julia lifted a brow. "Interesting question. What about your
ruined film?"

"The film?" Autumn felt herself being pulled in deeper.
"It must have been an accident."

"You didn't spoil it, Autumn, you're too competent." She

waited while Autumn spread her hands on the table and looked down at them. "I've watched you. Your movements are very fluid, very assured. And you're a professional. You wouldn't botch up a roll of film without being aware of it."

"No," Autumn agreed and looked back up. Her eyes were steady again. "What are you trying to tell me?"

"What if someone's worried that you took a picture they don't want developed? The film in your room was ruined, too."

"I can follow your logic that far, Julia." Autumn pushed aside the remaining omelette. "But then it's a dead end. I haven't taken any pictures anyone could worry about. I was shooting scenery. Trees, animals, the lake."

"Maybe someone isn't certain about that." She crushed out her cigarette in a quick motion and leaned forward. "Whoever is worried enough about a picture to risk destroying your room and knocking you unconscious is dangerous. Dangerous enough to murder. Dangerous enough to hurt you again if necessary."

Staring back, Autumn controlled a tremor. "Jane? Jane accused me of spying, but she couldn't—"

"Oh yes, she could." Julia's voice was hard again, and definite. "Face it, Autumn, anyone pushed hard enough is capable of murder. Anyone."

Autumn's thoughts flicked back to Lucas and the look on his face when he had slipped his hand around her throat.

"Jane was desperate," Julia continued. "She claims to have made a full confession to Robert, but what proof is there? Or Robert, furious at what Helen had put his wife through, could have done it himself. He loves Jane quite a lot."

"Yes, I know." The sudden, sweeping anger in Robert's eyes flashed through her mind.

"Or there's Steve." Julia's finger began to tap on the table. "He tells me that Helen found out about some unwise deal he put through, something potentially damaging to his political career. He's very ambitious."

"But, Julia—"

"Then there's Lucas." Julia went on as if Autumn hadn't spoken. "There's a matter of a delicate divorce suit. Helen held information she claimed would interest a certain estranged husband." She lit another cigarette and let the smile float up and away. "Lucas is known for his temper. He's a very physical man."

Autumn met the look steadily. "Lucas is a lot of things, not all of them admirable, but he wouldn't kill."

Julia smiled and said nothing as she brought the cigarette to her lips. "Then there's me." The smile widened. "Of course, I claim I didn't care about Helen's threats, but I'm an actress. A good one. I've got an Oscar to prove it. Like Lucas, my temper is no secret. I could give you a list of directors who would tell you I'm capable of anything." Idly she tapped her cigarette in the ashtray. "But then, if I had killed her, I would have set the scene differently. I would have discovered the body myself, screamed, then fainted magnificently. As it was, you stole the show."

"That's not funny, Julia."

"No," she agreed and rubbed her temple. "It's not. But the fact remains that I could have killed Helen, and you're far too trusting."

"If you'd killed her," Autumn countered, "why would you warn me?"

"Bluff and double bluff," Julia answered with a new smile that made Autumn's skin crawl. "Don't trust anyone, not even me."

Autumn wasn't going to let Julia frighten her, though she seemed determined to do so. She kept her eyes level. "You haven't included Jacques."

To Autumn's surprise, Julia's eyes flickered, then dropped. The smooth, tapering fingers crushed out her cigarette with enough force to break the filter. "No, I haven't. I suppose he must be viewed through your eyes like the rest of us, but I know . . ." She looked up again, and Autumn saw the vulnerability. "I know he isn't capable of hurting anyone."

"You're in love with him."

Julia smiled, quite beautifully. "I love Jacques very much, but not the way you mean." She rose then and, getting another cup, poured them both coffee. "I've known Jacques for ten years. He's the only person in the world I care about more than myself. We're friends, real friends, probably because we've never been lovers."

Autumn drank the coffee black. She wanted the kick of it. *She'd protect him,* she thought. *She'd protect him any way she could.*

"I have a weakness for men," Julia continued, "and I indulge it. With Jacques, the time or place was never right. Ultimately, the friendship was too important to risk messing it up in the bedroom. He's a good, gentle man. The biggest mistake he ever made was in marrying Claudette."

Julia's voice hardened. Her nails began to tap on the table again, quicker than before. "She did her best to eat him alive. For a long time, he tried to keep the marriage together for the children. It simply wasn't possible. I won't go into details;

they'd shock you." Tilting her head, Julia gave Autumn a
smile that put her squarely into adolescence. "And, in any
case, it's Jacques's miserable secret. He didn't divorce her,
on the numerous grounds he could have, but allowed her to
file."

"And Claudette got the children."

"That's right. It nearly killed him when she was awarded
custody. He adores them. And, I must admit, they are rather
sweet little monsters." The nails stopped tapping as she
reached for her coffee. "Anyway, skipping over this and that,
Jacques filed a custody suit about a year ago. He met someone shortly after. I can't tell you her name—you'd recognize
it, and I have Jacques's confidence. But I can tell you she's
perfect for him. Then Helen crawled her slimy way in."

Autumn shook her head. "Why don't they just get married?"

Julia leaned back with an amused sigh. "If life were only
so simple. Jacques is free, but his lady won't be for another
few months. They want nothing more than to marry, bring
Jacques's little monsters to America and raise as many more
as possible. They're crazy about each other."

Julia sipped her cooling coffee. "They can't live together
openly until the custody thing is resolved so they rented
this little place in the country. Helen found out. You can
figure out the rest. Jacques paid her, for his children and
because his lady's divorce isn't as cut-and-dried as it might
be, but when Helen turned up here, he'd reached his limit.
They argued about it one night in the lounge. He told her
she wouldn't get another cent. I'm sure, no matter how much
Jacques had already paid her, Helen would still have turned
her information over to Claudette—for a price."

Autumn stared at her, unable to speak. She had never seen Julia look so cold. She saw the ruthlessness cover the exquisite face. Julia looked over, then laughed with genuine amusement.

"Oh, Autumn, you're like an open book!" The hard mask had melted away, leaving her warm and lovely again. "Now you're thinking I could have murdered Helen after all. Not for myself, but for Jacques."

Autumn fell into a fitful sleep sometime after dawn. This was no deep, empty sleep brought on by medication or exhaustion, but was confused and dream riddled.

At first, there were only vague shadows and murmured voices floating through her mind, taunting her to try to see and hear more clearly. She fought to focus on them. Shadows moved, shapes began to sharpen, then became fuzzy and disordered again. She pitted all her determination against them, wanting more than hints and whispers. Abruptly, the shadows evaporated. The voices grew to a roar in her ears.

Wild-eyed, Jane crushed Autumn's camera underfoot. She screamed, pointing a pair of scissors to keep Autumn at bay. "Spy!" she shouted as the cracking of the camera's glass echoed like gunfire. "Spy!"

Wanting to escape the madness and accusations, Autumn turned. Colors whirled around her, then there was Robert.

"She tormented my wife." His arm held Autumn firmly, then slowly tightened, cutting off her breath. "You need some food," he said softly. "It shows in the face first." He was smiling, but the smile was a travesty. Breaking away, Autumn found herself in the corridor.

Jacques came toward her. There was blood on his hands. His eyes were sad and terrifying as he held them out to her. "My children." There was a tremor in his voice as he gestured to her. Turning, she fell into Steve.

"Politics," he said with a bright, boyish smile. "Nothing personal, just politics." Taking her hair, he wrapped it around her throat. "You got caught in the middle, Autumn." The smile turned into a leer as he tightened the noose. "Too bad."

Pushing away, she fell through a door. Julia's back was to her. She wore the lovely, white lace negligee. "Julia!" In the dream, the urgency in Autumn's voice came at a snail's pace. "Julia, help me."

When Julia turned, the slow, cat smile was on her face and the lace was splattered with scarlet. "Bluff and double bluff, darling." Throwing back her head, she laughed her smoky laugh. With the sound still spinning in her head, Autumn pressed her hands to her ears and ran.

"Come back to mother!" Julia called, still laughing as Autumn stumbled into the corridor.

There was a door blocking her path. Throwing it open, Autumn dashed inside. She knew only a desperate need for escape. But it was Helen's room. Terrified, Autumn turned, only to find the door closed behind her. She battered on it, but the sound was dull and flat. Fear was raw now, a primitive fear of the dead. She couldn't stay there. Wouldn't stay. She turned, thinking to escape through the window.

It wasn't Helen's room, but her own. There were bars at the windows, gray liquid bars of rain, but when she ran to them, they solidified, holding her in. She pulled and tugged, but they were cold and unyielding in her hands. Suddenly,

Lucas was behind her, drawing her away. He laughed as he turned her into his arms.

"Bite and scratch all you want, Cat."

"Lucas, please!" There was hysteria in her voice that even the dream couldn't muffle. "I love you. I love you. Help me get out. Help me get away!"

"Too late, Cat." His eyes were dark and fierce and amused. "I warned you not to push me too far."

"No, Lucas, not you." She clung to him. He was kissing her hard, passionately. "I love you. I've always loved you." She surrendered to his arms, to his mouth. Here was her escape, her safety.

Then she saw the scissors in his hand.

CHAPTER 10

Autumn sat straight up in bed. The film of cold sweat had her shivering. During the nightmare, she had kicked off the sheets and blankets and lay now with only a damp nightgown for cover. Needing the warmth, she pulled the tangled blanket around her and huddled into it.

Only a dream, she told herself, waiting for the clarity of it to fade. It was only a dream. It was natural enough after the late-night conversation with Julia. Dreams couldn't hurt you. Autumn wanted to hang on to that.

It was morning. She trembled still as she watched the sunlight pour into her window. No bars. That was over now, just as the night was over. The phones would soon be repaired. The water in the ford would go down. The police would come. Autumn sat, cocooned by the blanket, and waited for her breathing to even.

By the end of the day, or tomorrow at the latest, everything would be organized and official. Questions would be answered, notes would be taken, the wheels of investigation would start to turn, settling everything into facts and reality. Slowly her muscles began to relax and she loosened her desperate grip on the blanket.

Julia's imagination had gotten out of hand, Autumn decided. She was so used to the drama of her profession that she had built up the scenario. Helen's death was a hard, cold fact. None of them could avoid that. But Autumn was certain her two misfortunes had been unconnected. If I'm going to stay sane until the police come, she amended, I *have* to believe it.

Calmer now, she allowed herself to think. Yes, there had been a murder. There was no glossing over that. Murder was a violent act, and in this case, it had been a personal one. She had no involvement in it. There wasn't any correlation. What had happened in the darkroom had been simple clumsiness. That was the cleanest and the most reasonable explanation. As for the invasion of her room . . . Autumn shrugged. It had been Helen. She'd been a vicious, evil woman. The destruction of Autumn's clothes and personal belongings had been a vicious, evil act. For some reason of her own, Helen had taken a dislike to her. There was no one else at the inn who would have any reason to feel hostility toward her.

Except Lucas. Autumn shook her head firmly, but the thought remained. Except Lucas. She huddled the blanket closer, cold again.

No, even that made no sense. Lucas had rejected her, not the other way around. She had loved him. And he, very simply, hadn't loved her. *Would that matter to him?* The voice in her brain argued with the voice from her heart. Ignoring the queaziness in her stomach, Autumn forced herself to consider, dispassionately, Lucas in the role of murderer.

It had been obvious from the beginning that he was under strain. He hadn't been sleeping well and he'd been tense. Autumn had known him to struggle over a stage of a book for a week on little sleep and coffee, but he'd never shown the effects. All that stored energy he had was just waiting to take over whenever he needed it. No, in all her memory, she had never seen Lucas McLean tired. Until now.

Helen's blackmail must have disturbed him deeply. Autumn couldn't imagine Lucas concerning himself over publicity, adverse or otherwise. The woman involved in divorce must mean a great deal to him. She shut her eyes on a flash of pain and forced herself to continue.

Why had he come to the Pine View Inn? Why would he choose a remote place nearly a continent away from his home? To work? Autumn shook her head. It just didn't follow. She knew Lucas never traveled when he was writing. He'd do his research first, extensively if necessary, before he began. Once he had a plot between his teeth, he'd dig into his beachside home for the duration. Come to Virginia to write in peace? No. Lucas McLean could write on the 5:15 subway if he chose to. She knew no one else with a greater ability to block people out.

So, his reason for coming to the inn was quite different. Autumn began to wonder if Helen had been a pawn as well as a manipulator. Had Lucas lured her to this remote spot and surrounded her with people with reasons to hate her? He was clever enough to have done it, and calculating enough. How difficult was it going to be to prove which one of the six had killed her? Motive and opportunity he'd said—six people had both. Why should one be examined any closer than the others?

The setting would appeal to him, she thought as she looked out at mountains and pines. Obvious, Lucas had called it. An obvious setting for murder. But then, as Jacques had pointed out, life was often obvious.

She wouldn't dwell on it. It brought the nightmare too close again. Pushing herself from the bed, Autumn began to dress in her very tired jeans and a sweater Julia had given her the night before. She wasn't going to spend another day picking at her doubts and fears. It would be better to hang on to the knowledge that the police would be there soon. It wasn't up to her to decide who had killed Helen.

When she started down the stairs, she felt better. She'd take a long, solitary walk after breakfast and clear the cobwebs from her mind. The thought of getting out of the inn lifted her spirits.

But her confidence dropped away when she saw Lucas at the foot of the stairs. He was watching her closely, silently. Their eyes met for one brief, devastating moment before he turned to walk away.

"Lucas." She heard herself call out before she could stop herself. Stopping, he turned to face her again. Autumn gathered all her courage and hurried down the rest of the stairs. She had questions, and she had to ask them. He still mattered much too much to her. She stood on the bottom step so that their eyes would be level. His told her nothing. They seemed to look through her, bored and impatient.

"Why did you come here?" Autumn asked him quickly.

"Here, to the Pine View Inn?" She wanted him to give her any reason. She wanted to accept it.

Lucas focused on her intensely for a moment. There was something in his face for her to read, but it was gone before she could decipher it. "Let's just say I came to write, Autumn. Any other reason has been eliminated."

There was no expression in his voice, but the words chilled her. *Eliminated.* Would he choose such a clean word for murder? Something of her horror showed in her face. She watched his brows draw together in a frown.

"Cat—"

"No." Before he could speak again, she darted away from him. He'd given her an answer, but it wasn't one she wanted to accept.

The others were already at the table. The sun had superficially lightened the mood, and by unspoken agreement, the conversation was general, with no mention of Helen. They all needed an island of normalcy before the police came.

Julia, looking fresh and lovely, chattered away. Her attitude was so easy, even cheerful, that Autumn wondered if their conversation in the kitchen was as insubstantial as her nightmare. She was flirting again, with every man at the table. Two days of horror hadn't dulled her style.

"Your aunt," Jacques told Autumn, "has an amazing cuisine." He speared a fluffy, light pancake. "It surprises me at times because she has such a charming, drifting way about her. Yet, she remembers small details. This morning, she tells me she has saved me a piece of her apple pie to enjoy with my lunch. She doesn't forget I have a fondness for it. Then when I kiss her hand because I find her so enchanting, she smiled and wandered away, and I heard her say something about towels and chocolate pudding."

The laughter that followed was so normal, Autumn wanted to hug it to her. "She has a better memory about the guests' appetites than her family's," Autumn countered, smiling at him. "She's decided that pot roast is my favorite and has promised to provide it weekly, but it's actually my brother Paul's favorite. I haven't figured out how to move her toward spaghetti."

She gripped her fork tightly at a sudden flash of pain. Very clearly, Autumn could see herself stirring spaghetti sauce in Lucas's kitchen while he did his best to distract her. Would she never pry herself loose from the memories? Quickly, she plunged into conversation again.

"Aunt Tabby sort of floats around the rest of the world," she continued. "I remember once, when we were kids, Paul smuggled some formaldehyde frog legs out of his biology class. He brought them with him when we came on vacation and gave them to Aunt Tabby, hoping for a few screams. She took them, smiled and told him she'd eat them later."

"Oh God." Julia lifted her hand to her throat. "She didn't actually eat them, did she?"

"No." Autumn grinned. "I distracted her, which of course is the easiest thing in the world to do, and Paul disposed of his biology project. She never missed them."

"I must remember to thank my parents for making me an only child," Julia murmured.

"I can't imagine growing up without Paul and Will."

Autumn shook her head as old memories ran through her mind. "The three of us were always very close, even when we tormented each other."

Jacques chuckled, obviously thinking of his own children. "Does your family spend much time here?"

"Not as much as we used to." Autumn lifted her shoulders. "When I was a girl, we'd all come for a month during the summer."

"To tramp through the woods?" Julia asked with a wicked gleam in her eyes.

"That," Autumn returned mildly, and imitated the actress's arched-brow look, "and some camping." She went on, amused by Julia's rolling eyes. "Boating and swimming in the lake."

"Boating," Robert spoke up, cutting off a small, nagging memory. Autumn looked over at him, unable to hang on to it. "That's my one true vice. Nothing I like better than sailing. Right, Jane?" He patted her hand. "Jane's quite a sailor herself. Best first mate I've ever had." He glanced over at Steve. "I suppose you've done your share of sailing."

Steve answered with a rueful shake of his head. "I'm afraid I'm a miserable sailor. I can't even swim."

"You're joking!" This came from Julia. She stared at him in disbelief. Her eyes skimmed approvingly over his shoulders. "You look like you could handle the English Channel."

"I can't even handle a wading pool," he confessed, more amused than embarrassed. He grinned and gestured with his fork. "I make up for it in land sports. If we had a tennis court here, I'd redeem myself."

"Ah well." Jacques gave his French shrug. "You'll have to content yourself with hiking. The mountains here are beautiful. I hope to bring my children one day." He frowned, then stared into his coffee.

"Nature lovers!" Julia's smiling taunt kept the room from sliding into gloom. "Give me smog-filled L.A. anytime. I'll look at your mountains and squirrels in Autumn's photographs."

"You'll have to wait until I add to my supply." She kept her voice light, trying not to be depressed over the loss of her film. She couldn't yet bring herself to think of the loss of her camera. "Losing that film is like losing a limb, but I'm trying to be brave about it." Taking a bite of pancake, she shrugged. "And I could have lost all four rolls instead of three. The shots I took of the lake were the best, so I can comfort myself with that. The light was perfect that morning, and the shadows . . ."

She trailed off as the memory seeped through. She could see herself, standing on the ridge looking down at the glistening water, the mirrored trees. And the two figures that walked the far side. That was the morning she had met Lucas in the woods, then Helen. Helen with an angry bruise under her eye.

"Autumn?"

Hearing Jacques's voice, she snapped herself back. "I'm sorry, what?"

"Is something wrong?"

"No, I . . ." She met his curious eyes. "No."

"I would think light and shadow are the very essence of photography," Julia commented, flowing over the awkward silence. "But I've always concerned myself with looking into the lens rather than through. Remember that horrible little man, Jacques, who used to pop up at the most extraordinary times and stick a camera in my face. What was his name? I really became quite fond of him."

Julia had centered the attention on herself so smoothly that Autumn doubted anyone had noticed her own confusion. She stared down at the pancakes and syrup on her plate as if the solution to the mysteries of the universe were written there. But she could feel Lucas's eyes boring into her averted head. She could feel them, but she couldn't look at him.

She wanted to be alone, to think, to reason out what was whirling in her head. She forced down the rest of her breakfast and let the conversation buzz around her.

"I have to see Aunt Tabby," Autumn murmured, at last thinking she could leave without causing curiosity. "Excuse me." She had reached the kitchen door before Julia waylaid her.

"Autumn, I want to talk to you." The grip of the slender fingers was quite firm. "Come up to my room."

From the expression on the enviable face, Autumn could see arguing was useless. "All right, right after I see Aunt Tabby. She'll be worried because I didn't say good-night to her yesterday. I'll be up in a few minutes." She kept her voice reasonable and friendly, and managed a smile. Autumn decided she was becoming quite an actress herself.

For a small stretch of silence, Julia studied Autumn's face, then loosened her grip. "All right, come up as soon as you've finished."

"Yes, I will." Autumn slipped into the kitchen with the promise still on her lips. It wasn't difficult to go through the kitchen to the mud room without being noticed. Aunt Tabby and Nancy were deep in their morning argument. Taking down her jacket from the hook where she had placed it the morning of the storm, Autumn checked the pocket. Her fingers closed over the roll of film. For a moment, she simply held it in the palm of her hand.

Moving quickly, she changed from shoes to boots, transferred the film to the pocket of Julia's sweater, grabbed her jacket and went out the back door.

CHAPTER 11

The air was sharp. The rain had washed it clean. Budded leaves Autumn had photographed only days before were fuller, thicker, but still tenderly green. Her mind was no longer on the freedom she had longed for all the previous day. Now, Autumn was only intent on reaching the cover of the forest without being seen. She ran for the trees, not stopping until she was surrounded. Silence was deep and it cradled her.

The ground sucked and skidded under her feet, spongy with rain. There was some wind damage here and there that she noticed when she forced herself to move more carefully. Broken limbs littered the ground. The sun was warm, and she shed her jacket, tossing it over a branch. She made herself concentrate on the sights and sounds of the forest until her thoughts could calm.

The mountain laurel hinted at blooms. A bird circled overhead, then darted deeper into the trees with a sharp cry. A squirrel scurried up a tree trunk and peered down at her. Autumn reached in her pocket and closed her hand over the roll of film. The conversation in the kitchen with Julia now made horrible sense.

Helen must have been at the lake that morning. From the evidence of the bruise, she had argued violently with someone. And that someone had seen Autumn on the ridge. That someone wanted the pictures destroyed badly enough to risk breaking into both her darkroom and her bedroom. The film had to be potentially damaging for anyone to risk knocking her unconscious and ransacking her room. Who else but the killer would care enough to take such dangerous actions? Who else? At every turn, logic pointed its finger toward Lucas.

It had been his plans that brought the group together in the first place. Lucas was the person Autumn had met just before coming across Helen. Lucas had bent over her as she lay on the darkroom floor. Lucas had been up, fully dressed, the night of Helen's murder. Autumn shook her head, wanting to shatter the logic. But the film was solid in her hand.

He must have seen her as she stood on the ridge. She would have been in clear view. When he intercepted her, he had tried to rekindle their relationship. He would have known better than to have attempted to remove the film from her camera. She would have caused a commotion that would have been heard in two counties. Yes, he knew her well enough to use subtler means. But he wouldn't have known she had already switched to a fresh roll.

He had played on her old weakness for him. If she had submitted, he would have found ample time and opportunity to destroy the film. Autumn admitted, painfully, that she would have been too involved with him to have noticed the loss. But she hadn't submitted. This time, she had rejected him. He would have been forced to employ more extreme measures.

He only pretended to want me, she realized. That, more than anything else, hurt. He had held her, kissed her, while his mind had been busy calculating how best to protect himself. Autumn forced herself to face facts. Lucas had stopped wanting her a long time ago, and his needs had never been the same as hers. Two facts were very clear. She had never stopped loving him, and he had never begun to love her.

Still, she balked at the idea of Lucas as a cold-blooded killer. She could remember his sudden spurts of gentleness, his humor, the careless bouts of generosity. That was part of him, too—part of the reason she had been able to love him so easily. Part of the reason she had never stopped.

A hand gripped her shoulder. With a quick cry of alarm, she whirled and found herself face-to-face with Lucas. When she shrank from him, he dropped his hands and stuffed them into his pockets. His eyes were dark and his voice was icy.

"Where's the film, Autumn?"

Whatever color was left in her face drained. She hadn't wanted to believe it. Part of her had refused to believe it. Now, her heart shattered. He was leaving her no choice.

"Film?" She shook her head as she took another step back. "What film?"

"You know very well what film." Impatience pulled at the words. He narrowed his eyes, watching her retreat. "I want the fourth roll. Don't back away from me!"

Autumn stopped at the curt command. "Why?"

"Don't play stupid." His impatience was quickly becoming

fury. She recognized all the signs. "I want the film. What I do with it is my business."

She ran, thinking only to escape from his words. It had been easier to live with the doubt than the certainty. He caught her arm before she had dashed three yards. Spinning her around, he studied her face.

"You're terrified." He looked stunned, then angry. "You're terrified of me." With his hands gripping hard on her arms he brought her closer. "We've run the gamut, haven't we, Cat? Yesterday's gone." There was a finality in his voice that brought more pain than his hands or his temper.

"Lucas." Autumn was trembling, emotionally spent. "Please don't hurt me anymore." The pain she spoke of had nothing to do with the physical, but he released her with a violent jerk. The struggle for control was visible on his face.

"I won't lay a hand on you now, or ever again. Just tell me where that film is. I'll get out of your life as quickly as possible."

She had to reach him. She had to try one last time. "Lucas, please, it's senseless. You must see that. Can't you—"

"Don't push me!" The words exploded at her, rocking her back on her heels. "You stupid fool, do you have any idea how dangerous that film is? Do you think for one minute I'm going to let you keep it?" He took a step toward her. "Tell me where it is. Tell me now, or by God, I'll throttle it out of you."

"In the darkroom." The lie came quickly and without calculation. Perhaps that was why he accepted it so readily.

"All right. Where?" She watched his features relax slightly. His voice was calmer.

"On the bottom shelf. On the wet side."

"That's hardly illuminating to a layman, Cat." There was a touch of his old mockery as he reached for her arm. "Let's go get it."

"No!" She jerked away wildly. "I won't go with you. There's only one roll; you'll find it. You found the others. Leave me alone, Lucas. For God's sake, leave me alone!"

She ran again, skidding on the mud. This time he didn't stop her.

Autumn had no idea how far she ran or even the direction she took. Ultimately, her feet slowed to a walk. She stopped to stare up at a sky that had no clouds. What was she going to do?

She could go back. She could go back and try to get to the darkroom first, lock herself in. She could develop the film, blow up the two figures beside the lake and see the truth for herself. Her hand reached for the hated film again. She didn't want to see the truth. With absolute certainty, she knew she could never hand the film over to the police. No matter what Lucas had done or would do, she couldn't betray him. He'd been wrong, she thought. She could never pull the lever.

Withdrawing the film from her pocket, she stared down at it. It looked so innocent. She had felt so innocent that day, up on the ridge with the sun coming up. But when she had done what she had to do, she would never feel innocent again. She would expose the film herself.

Lucas, she thought and nearly laughed. Lucas McLean was the only man on earth who could make her turn her back on her own conscience. And when it was done, only the two of them would know. She would be as guilty as he.

Do it quickly, she told herself. Do it fast and think about it later. Her palm was damp where the film was cradled in it. You're going to have a whole lifetime to think about it. Taking a deep breath, Autumn started to uncap the plastic capsule she used to protect her undeveloped film. A movement on the path behind her had her stuffing the roll back into her pocket and whirling around.

Could Lucas have searched the darkroom so quickly? What would he do now that he knew she had lied to him? Foolishly, Autumn wanted to run again. Instead, she straightened and waited. The final encounter would have to come sooner or later.

Autumn's relief when she saw Steve approaching quickly became irritation. She wanted to be alone, not to make small talk and useless conversation while the film burned in her pocket.

"Hi!" Steve's lightning smile did nothing to decrease her annoyance, but Autumn pasted on one of her own. If she were going to be playing a game for the rest of her life, she might as well start now.

"Hello. Taking Jacques up on the hiking?" God, how normal and shallow her voice sounded! Was she going to be able to live like this?

"Yeah. I see you needed to get away from the inn, too." Taking a deep breath of the freshened air, he flexed his shoulders. "Lord, it feels good to be outside again."

"I know what you mean." Autumn eased the tension from her own shoulders. This was a reprieve, she told herself. Accept it. When it's over, nothing's ever going to be the same again.

"And Jacques is right," Steve went on, staring out through the thin leaves. "The mountains are beautiful. It reminds you that life goes on."

"I suppose we all need to remember that now." Unconsciously, Autumn dipped her hand in her pocket.

"Your hair glows in the sunlight." Steve caught at the ends and moved them between his fingertips. Autumn saw, with some alarm, that warmth had crept into his eyes. A romantic interlude was more than she could handle.

"People often seem to think more about my hair than me." She smiled and kept her voice light. "Sometimes I'm tempted to hack it off."

"Oh no." He took a more generous handful. "It's very special, very unique." His eyes lifted to hers. "And I've been thinking quite a lot about you the last few days. You're very special, too."

"Steve . . ." Autumn turned and would have walked on, but his hand was still in her hair.

"I want you, Autumn."

The words, so gentle, almost humble, nearly broke her heart. She turned back with apology in her eyes. "I'm sorry, Steve. I really am."

"Don't be sorry." He lowered his head to brush her lips. "If you let me, I could make you happy."

"Steve, please." Autumn lifted her hands to his chest. If only he were Lucas, she thought as she stared up at him. If only it were Lucas looking at me like this. "I can't."

He let out a long breath, but didn't release her. "McLean? Autumn, he only makes you unhappy. Why won't you let go?"

"I can't tell you how many times I've asked myself the same question." She sighed, and he watched the sun shoot into her eyes. "I don't have the answer—except that I love him."

"Yes, it shows." Frowning, he brushed a strand of hair from her cheek. "I'd hoped you'd be able to get over him, but I don't suppose you will."

"No, I don't suppose I will. I've given up trying."

"Now I'm sorry, Autumn. It makes things difficult."

Autumn dropped her eyes to stare at the ground. She didn't want pity. "Steve, I appreciate it, but I really need to be alone."

"I want the film, Autumn."

Astonished, she jerked her head up. Without consciously making the step, she aligned herself with Lucas. "Film? I don't know what you mean."

"Oh yes, I'm afraid you do." He was still speaking gently, one hand stroking her hair. "The pictures you took of the lake the morning Helen and I were down there. I have to have them."

"You?" For a moment, the implication eluded her. "You and Helen?" Confusion turned into shock. She could only stare at him.

"We were having quite a row that morning. You see, she had decided she wanted a lump-sum payment from me. Her other sources were drying up fast. Julia wouldn't give her a penny, just laughed at her. Helen was furious about that." His face changed with a grim smile. "Jacques had finished with her, too. She never had anything worthwhile on Lucas in the first place. She counted on intimidating him. Instead, he told her to go to hell and threatened to press charges. That threw her off balance for a while. She must have realized Jane was on the edge. So . . . she concentrated on me."

He had been staring off into the distance as he spoke. Now,

his attention came back to Autumn. The first hint of anger swept into his eyes. "She wanted two hundred and fifty thousand dollars in two weeks. A quarter of a million, or she'd hand over the information she had on me to my father."

"But you said what she knew wasn't important." Autumn let her eyes dart past his for a moment. The path behind them was empty. She was alone.

"She knew a bit more than I told you." Steve gave her an apologetic smile. "I could hardly tell you everything then. I've covered my tracks well enough now so that I don't think the police will ever know. It was actually a matter of extortion."

"Extortion?" The hand on her hair was becoming more terrifying with each passing moment. Keep him talking, she told herself frantically. Keep him talking and someone will come.

"Borrowing, really. The money will be mine sooner or later." He shrugged it off. "I just took some a little early. Unfortunately, my father wouldn't see it that way. I told you, remember? He's a tough man. He wouldn't think twice about booting me out the door and cutting off my income. I can't have that, Autumn." He flashed her a smile. "I have very expensive tastes."

"So you killed her." Autumn said it flatly. She was finished with horror.

"I didn't have a choice. I couldn't possibly get my hands on that much cash in two weeks." He said it so calmly, Autumn could almost see the rationale behind it. "I nearly killed her that morning down by the lake. She just wouldn't listen to me. I lost my temper and hit her. Knocked her cold. When I saw her lying there on the ground, I realized how much I wanted her dead."

Autumn didn't interrupt. She could see he was far from finished. Let him talk it out, she ordered herself, controlling the urge to break from him and run. Someone's going to come.

"I bent over her," he continued. "My hands were almost around her throat when I saw you standing up on the ridge. I knew it was you because the sun was shining on your hair. I didn't think you could recognize me from that distance, but I had to be sure. Of course, I found out later that you weren't paying attention to us at all."

"No, I barely noticed." Her knees were starting to shake. He was telling her too much. Far too much.

"I left Helen and circled around, thinking to intercept you. Lucas got to you first. Quite a touching little scene."

"You watched us?" She felt a stir of anger edge through the fear.

"You were too involved in each other to notice." He smiled again. "In any case, that's when I learned you'd been taking pictures. I had to get rid of that film; it was too chancy. I hated to hurt you, Autumn. I found you very attractive right from the first."

A rabbit darted down the path, veering off and bounding into the woods. She heard the call of a quail, faint with distance. The simple, natural texture of her surroundings gave his words a sense of unreality. "The darkroom."

"Yes. I was glad the blow with the door knocked you out. I didn't want to have to hit you with the flashlight. I didn't see your camera, but found a roll of film. I was so certain I had things taken care of. You can imagine how I felt when you said you'd lost two rolls, and that they were shots of your trip down from New York. I didn't know how the other roll had been ruined."

"Lucas. Lucas turned on the lights when he found me." Suddenly, through the horror came a bright flash of realization. *It hadn't been Lucas.* He'd done nothing but simply be who he was. She felt overwhelming relief at his innocence, then guilt at ever having believed what she had of him. "Lucas," she said again, almost giddy with the onslaught of sensations.

"Well, it hardly matters now," Steve said practically. Autumn snapped back. She had to keep alert, had to keep a step ahead of him. "I knew if I just took the film from your camera, you'd begin to wonder. You might start thinking too closely about the pictures you'd taken. I hated doing that to your things, breaking your camera. I know it was important to you."

"I have another at home." It was a weak attempt to sound unconcerned. Steve only smiled.

"I went to Helen's room right after I'd finished with yours. I knew I was going to have to kill her. She stood there pointing to the bruise and telling me it was going to cost me another hundred thousand. I didn't know what I was going to do . . . I thought I was going to strangle her. Then I saw the scissors. That was better—anyone could have used scissors. Even little Jane. I stopped thinking when I picked them up until it was over."

He shuddered, and Autumn thought, *Run! Run now!* But his hand tightened on her hair. "I've never been through anything like that. It was terrible. I almost folded. I knew I had to think, had to be careful, or I'd lose everything. Staying in that room was the hardest thing I've ever done. I wiped the handles of the scissors clean and tore up my shirt. Her blood was on it. I flushed the pieces down the toilet. When I got back to my room, I showered and went to bed. I remember being surprised that the whole thing took less than twenty minutes. It seemed like years."

"It must have been dreadful for you," Autumn murmured, but he was oblivious to the edge in her voice.

"Yes, but it was all working out. No one could prove where they were when Helen was killed. The storm—the phones, the power—that was all a bonus. Every one of us had a reason to want Helen out of the way. I really think Julia and I will be the least likely suspects when the time comes. The police should look to Jacques because he had more cause, and Lucas because he has the temper."

"Lucas couldn't kill anyone," Autumn said evenly. "The police will know that."

"I wouldn't bank on it." He gave her a crooked smile. "You haven't been so sure of that yourself."

She could say nothing when struck with the truth. *Why wasn't someone coming?*

"This morning, you started talking about four rolls of film, and the pictures you took of the lake. I could tell the moment when you remembered."

So much for my talent at acting, she thought grimly. "I only remembered there'd been people down by the lake that morning."

"You were putting it all together quickly." He traced a finger down her cheek and Autumn forced herself not to jerk away. "I had hoped to distract you, gain your affection. It was obvious you were hurting over McLean. If I could have moved in, I might have gotten my hands on that film without having to hurt you."

Autumn kept her eyes and voice steady. He'd finished talking now; she could sense it. "What are you going to do?"

"Damn it, Autumn. I'm going to have to kill you."

He said it in much the same way her father had said, *"Damn it, Autumn, I'm going to have to spank you."* She nearly broke into hysterical giggles.

"They'll know this time, Steve." Her body was beginning to shake, but she spoke calmly. If she could reason with him . . .

"No, I don't think so." He spoke practically, as if he considered she might have a viable point. "I was careful to get out without being seen. Everyone's spread out again. I doubt anyone even knows you went outside. I wouldn't have known myself if I hadn't found your jacket and boots missing. Then again, if I hadn't found the jacket hanging on a branch and been able to follow your tracks from there, I wouldn't have found you so easily."

He shrugged, as if showing her why his reasoning was better than hers. "When you're found missing, I'll make certain I come this way when we look for you. I can do a lot of damage to the tracks and no one will know any better. Now, Autumn, I need the film. Tell me where you've put it."

"I'm not going to tell you." She tossed back her head. As long as she had the film, he had to keep her alive. "They'll find it. When they do, they'll know it was you."

He made a quick sound of impatience. "You'll tell me Autumn, eventually. It would be easier for you if you told me now. I don't want to hurt you any more than I have to. I can make it quick, or I can make it painful."

His hand shot out so swiftly, Autumn had no time to dodge the blow. The force of it knocked her back into a tree. The pain welled inside her head and rolled through, leaving dizziness. She clutched at the rough bark to keep her balance as she saw him coming toward her.

Oh no, she wasn't going to stand and be hit again. He'd gotten away with it twice, and twice was enough. With as much force as she could muster, she kicked, aiming well below the waist. He went down on his knees like a shot. Autumn turned and fled.

CHAPTER 12

She ran blindly. *Escape!* It was the only coherent thought in her brain. It wasn't until the first wave of panic had ebbed that Autumn realized she had run not only away from Steve, but away from the inn. It was too late to double back. She could only concentrate as much effort as possible into putting distance between them. She veered off the path and into thicker undergrowth.

When she heard him coming after her, Autumn didn't look back, but increased her pace. His breathing was labored, but close. Too close. She swerved again and plunged on. The ground sucked and pulled at her boots, but she told herself she wouldn't slip. If she slipped, he would be on top of her in a moment. His hands would be at her throat. *She would not slip.*

Her heart was pounding and her lungs were screaming in agony for more air. A branch whipped back, stinging her cheek. But she told herself she wouldn't stop. She would run and run and run until she no longer heard him coming after her.

A tree had fallen and lay drunkenly in her path. Without breaking stride, Autumn vaulted it, sliding for a moment when her boots hit the mud, then pounding on. He slipped. She heard the slick sound of his boots as they lost traction, then his muffled curse. She kept up her wild pace, nearly giddy at the few seconds his fall had given her.

Time and direction ceased to exist. For her, the pursuit had no beginning, no end. It was only the race. Her thoughts were no longer rational. She knew only that she had to keep running though she'd almost forgotten why. Her breath was coming in harsh gasps, her legs were like rubber. She knew only the mindless flight of the hunted—the naked fear of the hunter.

Suddenly, she saw the lake. It glistened as the sun hit its surface. With some last vestige of lucidity, Autumn remembered Steve's admission that morning. He couldn't swim. The race had a goal now, and she dashed for it.

Her crazed approach through the woods had taken her away from the ridge where the incline graduated for easy descent. Instead, she came to the edge of a cliff that fell forty feet in a sheer drop. Without hesitation, Autumn plunged down at full speed. She scrambled and slid, her fingers clawing to keep herself from overbalancing. Like a lizard, she clung to the mountain. Her body scraped on jagged rocks and slid on mud. Julia's designer sweater shredded. Autumn realized, as the pain grew hot, that her skin suffered equally. Fear pushed her beyond the pain. The lake beckoned below. Safety. Victory.

Still, he came after her. She could hear his boots clatter on the rocks above her head, jarring pebbles that rained down on her. Autumn leaped the last ten feet. The force of the fall shot up her legs, folding them under her until she rolled into a heap. Then she was scrambling and streaking for the lake.

She heard him cry out for her. With a final mad impetus, she flung herself into the water, slicing through its surface. Its sharp frigidity shocked her system and gave her strength. Clawing through it, she headed for depth. She was going to win.

Like a light switched off, the momentum which had driven her so wildly, sapped. The weight of her boots pulled her down. The water closed over her head. Thrashing and choking, Autumn fought for the surface. Her lungs burned as she tried to pull in air. Her arms were heavy, and her feeble strokes had her bobbing up and down. Mists gathered in front of her eyes. Still, she resisted, fighting as the water sucked at her. It was now as deadly an enemy as the one she had sought to escape.

She heard someone sobbing, and realized dimly it was her own voice calling for help. But she knew there would be none. The fight was gone out of her. Was it music she heard? She thought it came from below her, deep, beckoning. Slowly, surrendering, she let the water take her like a lover.

Someone was hurting her. Autumn didn't protest. Darkness blanketed her mind and numbed the pain. The pushing and prodding were no more irritating to her than a faint itch. Air forced its way into her lungs, and she moaned gently in annoyance.

Lucas's voice touched the edges of her mind. He was

calling her back in a strange, unnatural voice. Panic? Yes, even through the darkness she could detect a note of panic. What an odd thing to hear in Lucas's voice. Her eyelids were heavy, and the darkness was so tempting. The need to tell him was stronger. Autumn forced her eyes open. Blackness receded to a verge of mist.

His face loomed over her, water streaming from it and his hair. It splattered cold on her cheeks. Yet her mouth felt warm, as if his had just left it. Autumn stared at him, groping for the power of speech.

"Oh God, Autumn." Lucas brushed the water from her cheeks even as it fell on them again from his own hair. "Oh God. Listen to me. It's all right, you're going to be all right, do you hear? You're going to be all right. I'm going to take you back to the inn. Can you understand me?"

His voice was desperate, as were his eyes. She'd never heard that tone or seen that expression. Not from Lucas. Autumn wanted to say something that would comfort him, but lacked the strength. The mists were closing in again, and she welcomed them. For a moment, she held them off and dug deep for her voice.

"I thought you killed her, Lucas. I'm sorry."

"Oh, Cat." His voice was intolerably weary. She felt his mouth touch hers. Then she felt nothing.

Voices, vague and without texture, floated down a long tunnel. Autumn didn't welcome them. She wanted her peace. She tried to plunge deeper into the darkness again, but Lucas had no respect for what anyone else wanted. His voice broke into her solitude, suddenly clear and, as always, demanding.

"I'm staying with her until she wakes up. I'm not leaving her."

"Lucas, you're dead on your feet." Robert's voice was low and soothing, in direct contrast to Lucas's. "I'll stay with Autumn. It's part of my job. She's probably going to be floating in and out all night. You wouldn't know what to do for her."

"Then you'll tell me what to do. I'm staying with her."

"Of course you are, dear." Aunt Tabby's voice surprised Autumn even in the dim, drifting darkness. It was so firm and strong. "Lucas will stay, Dr. Spicer. You've already said it's mainly a matter of rest, and waiting until she wakes naturally. Lucas can take care of her."

"I'll sit with you, Lucas, if you'd like . . . all right, but you've only to call me." Julia's voice rolled over Autumn, as smoky as the mists.

Suddenly, she wanted to ask them what was happening. What they were doing in her own private world. She struggled for words and formed a moan. A cool hand fell on her brow.

"Is she in pain?" Was that Lucas's voice? Autumn thought. Trembling? "Damn it, give her something for the pain!"

The darkness was whirling again, jumbling the sounds. Autumn let it swallow her.

She dreamed. The deep black curtain took on a velvet, moonlight texture. Lucas stared down at her. His face seemed oddly vivid for a dream. His hand felt real and cool on her cheek. "Cat, can you hear me?"

Autumn stared at him, then drew together all her scraps

and rags of concentration. "Yes." She closed her eyes and let the darkness swirl.

When her eyes reopened, he was still there. Autumn swallowed. Her throat was burning dry. "Am I dead?"

"No. No, Cat, you're not dead." Lucas poured something cool down her throat. Her eyes drooped again as she tried to patch together her memory. It was too hard, and she let it go.

Pain shot through her. Unexpected and sharp, it rocketed down her arms and legs. Autumn heard someone moan pitifully. Lucas loomed over her again, his face pale in a shaft of moonlight. "It hurts," she complained.

"I know." He sat beside her and brought a cup to her lips. "Try to drink."

Floating, like a bright red balloon, Autumn felt herself drift through space. The pain had eased as she stumbled back into consciousness. "Julia's sweater," she murmured as she opened her eyes again. "It's torn. I think I tore it. I'll have to buy her another."

"Don't worry about it, Cat. Rest." Lucas's hand was on her hair and she turned her face to it, seeking reassurance. She floated again.

"I'm sure it was valuable," she murmured, nearly an hour later. "But I don't really need that new tripod. Julia lent me that sweater. I should have been more careful."

"Julia has dozens of sweaters, Cat. Don't worry."

Autumn closed her eyes, comforted. But she knew her tripod would have to wait.

"Lucas." She pulled herself back, but now the moonlight was the gray light of dawn.

"Yes, I'm here."

"Why?"

"Why what, Cat?"

"Why are you here?"

But he moved out of focus again. She never heard his answer.

CHAPTER 13

The sunlight was strong. Used to darkness, Autumn blinked in protest.

"Ah, are you with us to stay this time, Autumn, or is this another quick visit?" Julia bent over her and patted her cheek. "There's a bit of color coming back, and you're cool. How do you feel?"

Autumn lay still for a moment and tried to find out. "Hollow," she decided, and Julia laughed.

"Trust you to think of your stomach."

"Hollow all over," Autumn countered. "Especially my head." She glanced confusedly around the room. "Have I been sick?"

"You gave us quite a scare." Julia eased down on the bed and studied her. "Don't you remember?"

"I was . . . dreaming?" Autumn's search for her memory found only bits and pieces. "Lucas was here. I was talking to him."

"Yes, he said you were drifting in and out through the night. Managed to say a word or two now and again. Did you really think I'd let you sacrifice your new tripod?" She kissed Autumn's cheek, then held her a moment. "God, when Lucas carried you in, we thought . . ." Shaking her head briskly, she sat up. Autumn saw that her eyes were damp.

"Julia." Autumn squeezed her eyes a moment, but nothing came clear. "I was supposed to come to your room, but I didn't."

"No, you didn't. I should have dragged you with me then and there. None of this would have happened." She stood up again. "It appears Lucas and I were both taken in by those big green eyes. I don't know how much time we wasted searching for that damn film before he went back to find you."

"I don't understand. Why . . ." As she reached up to brush at her hair, Autumn noticed the bandages on her hands. "What are these for? Did I hurt myself?"

"It's all right now." Julia brushed away the question. "I'd better let Lucas explain. He'll be furious that I chased him downstairs for some coffee, and you woke up."

"Julia—"

"No more questions now." She cut Autumn off as she plucked a robe from a chair. "Why don't you slip this on. You'll feel better." She eased the silk over Autumn's arms and covered more bandages. The sight of them brought added confusion, more juggled memories. "Just lie still and relax," Julia ordered. "Aunt Tabby already has some soup simmering, just waiting for you. I'll tell her to pour it into an enormous bowl."

She kissed Autumn again, then glided to the door. "Listen, Autumn." Julia turned back with a slow, cat smile. "He's been through hell these past twenty-four hours, but don't make it too easy for him."

Autumn frowned at the door when Julia had gone and wondered what the devil she was talking about.

Deciding she wouldn't find any answers lying in bed, Autumn dragged herself out. Every joint, every muscle revolted. She nearly succumbed to the desire to crawl back in, but curiosity was stronger. Her legs wobbled as she went to the mirror.

"Good God!" She looked, Autumn decided, even worse than she felt. The bruise on her temple had company. There was a light discoloration along her cheekbone and a few odd scratches. There was a sudden, clear memory of rough bark scraping against her hands. Lifting them, Autumn stared at the bandages. "What have I done to myself?" she asked aloud, then belted the robe to disguise the worst of the damage.

The door opened, and in the reflection she watched Lucas enter the room. He looked as though he hadn't slept in days. The lines of strain were deeper now and his chin was shadowed and unshaven. Only his eyes were the same. Dark and intense.

"You look like hell," she told him without turning. "You need some sleep."

He laughed. In a gesture of weariness she had never seen in him, he lifted his hands to run them down his face. "I might have expected it," he murmured. He sighed, then gave her a smile from the past. "You shouldn't be out of bed, Cat. You're liable to topple over any minute."

"I'm all right. At least I was before I looked in the mirror." Turning, she faced him directly. "I nearly fainted from shock."

"You are," he began in quiet, serious tones, "the most beautiful thing I've ever seen."

"Kindness to the invalid," she said, looking away. That had hurt, and she wasn't certain she could deal with any more pain. "I could use some explanations. My mind's a little fuddled."

"Robert said that was to be expected after . . ." He trailed off and jammed clenched fists into his pockets. "After everything that's happened."

Autumn looked again at her bandaged hands. "What did happen? I can't quite remember. I was running . . ." She lifted her eyes to his and searched. "In the woods, down the cliff. I . . ." She shook her head. There were only bits and pieces. "I tore Julia's sweater."

"God! You would latch on to a damn sweater!" His explosion had Autumn's eyes widening. "You almost drowned, and all you think about is Julia's sweater."

Her mouth trembled open. "The lake." Memory flooded back in a tidal wave. She leaned back against the dresser. "Steve. It was Steve. He killed Helen. He was chasing me. The film, I wouldn't give it to him." She swallowed, trying to keep calm. "I lied to you. I had it in my pocket. I kept running, but he was right behind me."

"Cat." She backed away, but he wrapped his arms around her. "Don't. Don't think about it. Damn it, I shouldn't have told you that way." He pressed his cheek against her hair. "I can't seem to do anything properly with you."

"No. No, let me think it through." Autumn pushed away. She wanted the details. Once she had them all, the fear would ease. "He found me in the woods after you'd gone in. He'd been with Helen down by the lake the morning I was taking pictures. He told me he had killed her. He told me everything."

"We know all of it," Lucas cut her off sharply. "He let out with everything once we got him back here. We got through to the police this morning." He whipped out a cigarette and lit it swiftly. "He's already in custody. They've got your film, too, for whatever it's worth. Jacques found it on the path."

"It must have fallen out of my pocket. Lucas, it was so strange." Her brow knitted as she remembered the timeless incident with Steve. "He apologized for having to kill me. Then when I told him I wouldn't give him the film, he slugged me so hard I saw stars."

Face thunderous, Lucas spun around and stalked to the window. He stared out without speaking.

"When he came at me again, I kicked him, hard, where I knew it would do the most damage."

She heard Lucas mutter something so uncharacteristically vulgar she thought she misunderstood. For a time she rambled about her flight through the woods, talking more to herself than to him.

"I saw you when you started your suicidal plunge down the cliff." His back was still to her, his voice still rough. "How in God's name you managed to get to the bottom without cracking your skull . . ." Lucas turned when Autumn remained silent. "I'd been tracking you through the woods. When I saw you were making for the lake, I veered off and started for the ridge. I hoped to cut Anderson off." He pulled on his cigarette, then took a long, shuddering breath. "I saw you flying down those rocks. You never should have made it down alive. I called you, but you just kept tearing for the lake. I was on him before you hit the water."

"I heard someone call. I thought it was Steve." She pushed a bandaged hand against her temple. "All I could think about was getting into the water before he caught me. I remembered he couldn't swim. Then when I had trouble keeping myself up, I panicked and forgot all those nifty rules you learn in lifeguard class."

Very slowly, very deliberately, Lucas crushed out his cigarette. "By the time I finished kicking his head in, you were already floundering. How you got out so far after the run you'd had, and with boots that must weigh twenty pounds, I'll never know. I was a good ten yards from you when you went under the last time. You sank like a stone."

He turned away again to stare out the window. "I thought . . ." He shook his head a moment, then continued. "I thought you were dead when I dragged you out. You were dead white and you weren't breathing. At least not enough that I could tell." He took out another cigarette and this time had to fight with his lighter to get flame. He cursed and drew deeply.

"I remember you dripping on me," Autumn murmured into the silence. "Then I thought I died."

"You damn near did." The smoke came out of his lungs in a violent stream. "I must have pumped two gallons of water out of you. You came around just long enough to apologize for thinking I killed Helen."

"I'm sorry, Lucas."

"Don't!" His tone was curt as he swung around again.

"But I should never have—"

"No?" He cut her off with one angry word. "Why? It's easy enough to see how you reached your conclusions, culminating with my last attack about the film."

After a moment, Autumn trusted herself to speak. "There were so many things you said that made me think . . . and you were so angry. When you asked me for the film, I wanted you to tell me anything."

"But instead of explanations, I bullied you. Typical of me, though, isn't it?" He drew a breath, but his body remained tense. "That's another apology I owe you. I seem to have chalked up quite a few. Would you like them in a group, Cat, or one at a time?"

Autumn turned away from that. It wasn't an apology she wanted, but an explanation. "Why did you want it, Lucas? How did you know?"

"It might be difficult for you to believe at this point, but I'm not completely inhuman. I wanted the film because I hoped, if I had it and made it known that I did, that you'd be safe. And . . ." She turned back as a shadow crossed his face. "I thought you knew, or had remembered what was on the film, and that you were protecting Anderson."

"Protecting him?" Astonishment reflected in her voice. "Why would I do that?"

He moved his shoulders in a shrug. "You seemed fond of him."

"I thought he was nice," Autumn said slowly. "I imagine we all did. But I hardly knew him. As it turns out, I didn't know him at all."

"I misinterpreted your natural friendliness for something else. Then compounded the mistake by overreacting. I was furious that you gave him what you wouldn't give me. Trust, companionship. Affection."

"Dog in the manger, Lucas?" The words shot out icily.

A muscle twitched at the corner of his mouth in contrast to another negligent shrug. "If you like."

"I'm sorry." With a sigh, Autumn pushed wearily at her hair. "That was uncalled for."

"Was it?" he countered and crushed out his cigarette. "I doubt that. You're entitled to launch a few shafts, Cat. You've taken enough of them from me."

"We're getting off the point." She moved away. Julia's silk robe whispered around her. "You thought I was protecting Steve. I'll accept that. But how did you know he needed protecting?"

"Julia and I had already pieced together a number of things. We were almost certain he was the one who had killed Helen."

"You and Julia." Now she turned to him, curious. Autumn gestured with her hands, then stopped as the pain throbbed in them. "You're going to have to clear things up, Lucas. I might still be a little dim."

"Julia and I had discussed Helen's blackmail thoroughly. Until her murder, we centered on Jacques's problem. Neither Julia nor I were concerned with the petty threats Helen held over us. After she was killed and your room broken into, we tossed around the idea that they were connected. Autumn, why don't you get back in bed. You're so pale."

"No." She shook her head, warding off the creeping warmth the concern in his voice brought her. "I'm fine. Please, don't stop now."

He seemed about to argue, then changed his mind. "I'd never believed you'd ruin your own film, or knock yourself senseless. So, Julia and I began a process of elimination. I hadn't killed Helen, and I knew that Julia hadn't. I'd been in her room that night receiving a heated lecture on my technique with women until I came down to see you. And I'd passed Helen in the hall right before I'd gone into Julia's room, so even if Julia'd had the inclination to kill Helen, it's doubtful that she would have had two identical white negligees. There'd have been blood." He shrugged again. "In any case, if Julia had killed her, she probably would have admitted it."

"Yes." Autumn gave a murmured agreement and wondered what Julia's lace-clad lecture had included.

"I've known Jacques for years," Lucas continued. "He's simply not capable of killing. Julia and I all but eliminated the Spicers. Robert is entirely too dedicated to life to take one, and Jane would dissolve into tears."

Lucas began to pace. "Anderson fit the bill. And, for reasons of my own, I wanted it to be him. Our intrepid Julia copped the spare key from Aunt Tabby and searched his room for the shirt he had worn the night of the murder. I nearly strangled her when she told me she'd done it. She's quite a woman."

"Yes." Jealousy warred with affection. Affection won. "She's wonderful."

"The shirt wasn't there. Julia claims to have an unerring eye for wardrobe, and I wanted to believe her. We decided you should be put on guard without going into specifics. I thought it best if you were wary of everyone. We decided that Julia would talk to you because you'd trust her more quickly than you'd trust me. I hadn't done anything to warrant your trust."

"She frightened me pretty successfully," Autumn recalled. "I had nightmares."

"I'm sorry. It seemed the best way at the time. We thought the film had been destroyed, but we didn't want to take any chances."

"She was telling Jacques that night, wasn't she?"

"Yeah." Lucas noted the faint annoyance in her tone. "That way there would have been three of us to look out for you."

"I might have looked out for myself if I'd been told."

"No, I don't think so. Your face is a dead giveaway. That morning at breakfast when you started rambling about a fourth roll and remembered, everything showed in your eyes."

"If I'd been prepared—"

"If you hadn't been a damn fool and had gone with Julia, we could have kept you safe."

"I wanted to think," she began, angry at being kept in the dark.

"It was my fault." Lucas held up a hand to stop her. "The whole thing's been my doing. I should have handled things differently. You'd never have been hurt if I had."

"No, Lucas." Guilt swamped her when she remembered the look on his face after he had dragged her from the lake. "I'd be dead if it weren't for you."

"Good God, Cat, don't look at me like that. I can't cope with it." He turned away. "I'm doing my best to keep my word. I'll get Robert; he'll want to examine you."

"Lucas." She wasn't going to let him walk out that door until he told her everything. "Why did you come here? And don't tell me you came to Virginia to write. I know—I remember your habits."

Lucas turned, but kept his hand on the knob. "I told you before, the other reason no longer exists. Leave it."

He had retreated behind the cool, detached manner he

used so well, but Autumn wasn't going to be shoved aside. "This is my aunt's inn, Lucas. Your coming here, however indirectly, started this chain of events. I have a right to know why you came."

For several seconds, he stared at her, then his hands sought his pockets again. "All right," he agreed. "I don't suppose I have any right to pride after this, and you deserve to get in a few licks after the way I've treated you." He came no closer, but his eyes locked hard on hers. "I came here because of you. Because I had to get you back or go crazy."

"Me?" The pain was so sharp, Autumn laughed. She would not cry again. "Oh Lucas, please, do better." She saw him flinch before he walked again to the window. "You tossed me out, remember? You didn't want me then. You don't want me now."

"Didn't want you!" He whirled, knocking over a vase and sending it crashing. The anger surrounding him was fierce and vivid. "You can't even comprehend how much I wanted you, have wanted you all these years. I thought I'd lose my mind from wanting you."

"No, I won't listen to this." Autumn turned away to lean against the bedpost. "I won't listen."

"You asked for it. Now you'll listen."

"You told me you didn't want me," she flung at him. "I never meant anything to you. You told me it was finished and shrugged your shoulders like it had been nothing all along. Nothing, *nothing's* ever hurt me like the way you brushed me aside."

"I know what I did." The anger was gone from his voice to be replaced by strain. "I know the things I said to you while you stood there staring at me. I hated myself. I wanted you to scream, to rage, to make it easy for me to push you out. But you just stood there with tears falling down your face. I've never forgotten how you looked."

Autumn pulled herself together and faced him again. "You said you didn't want me. Why would you have said it if it weren't true?"

"Because you terrified me."

He said it so simply, she slumped down on the bed to stare at him. "Terrified you? *I* terrified *you*?"

"You don't know what you did to me—all that sweetness, all that generosity. You never asked anything of me, and yet you asked everything." He began to pace again. Autumn watched him in bewilderment. "You were an obsession, that's what I told myself. If I sent you away, hurt you badly enough to make you go, I'd be cured. The more I had of you, the more I needed. I'd wake up in the middle of the night and curse you for not being there. Then I'd curse myself for needing you there. I had to get away from you. I couldn't admit, not even to myself, that I loved you."

"Loved me?" Autumn repeated the words dumbly. "You loved me?"

"Loved then, love now and for the rest of my life." Lucas drew in a deep breath as if the words had left him shaken. "I wasn't able to tell you. I wasn't able to believe it." He stopped pacing and looked at her. "I've kept close tabs on you these past three years. I found all sorts of excuses to do so. When I found out about the inn, and your connection with it, I began to fly out here off and on. Finally, I admitted to myself that I wasn't going to make it without you. I mapped out a plan. I had it all worked out." He gave her an ironic smile.

"Plan?" Autumn repeated. Her mind was still whirling.

"It was easy to plant the idea in Aunt Tabby's head to write you and ask you to visit. Knowing you, I was sure you'd come without question. That was all I needed. I was so sure of myself. I thought all I'd have to do would be to issue the invitation, and you'd fall right back into my arms. Just like old times. I'd have you back, marry you before you sorted things out and pat myself on the back for being so damn clever."

"Marry me?" Autumn's brows flew up in astonishment.

"Once we were married," Lucas went on as if she hadn't interrupted, "I'd never have to worry about losing you again. I'd simply never give you a divorce no matter how you struggled. I deserved a good kick in the teeth, Cat, and you gave it to me. Instead of falling into my arms, you turned up your nose and told me to get lost. But that didn't throw me off for long. No, you'd loved me once, and I'd make you love me again. I could deal with the anger, but the ice . . .

"I didn't know I could be hurt that way. It was quite a shock. Seeing you again . . ." He paused and seemed to struggle for words. "It was torture, pure and simple, to be so close and not be able to have you. I wanted to tell you what you meant to me, then every time I got near you I'd behave like a maniac. The way you cringed from me yesterday, telling me not to hurt you again, I can't tell you what that did to me."

"Lucas—"

"You'd better let me finish," he told her. "I'll never be able to manage this again." He reached for a cigarette, changed his mind, then continued. "Julia roasted me, but I couldn't seem to stop myself. The more you resisted, the worse I treated you. Every time I approached you, I ended up doing the wrong thing. That day, up in your room . . ." He stopped and Autumn watched the struggle on his face. "I nearly raped you. I was crazy with jealousy after seeing you and Anderson. When I saw you cry—I swore I'd never be responsible for putting that look on your face again.

"I'd come up that day, ready to beg, crawl, plead, whatever it took. When I saw you kissing him, something snapped. I started thinking about the men you'd been with these past three years. The men who'd have you again when I couldn't."

"I've never been with any man but you," Autumn interrupted quietly.

Lucas's expression changed from barely suppressed fury to confusion before he studied her face with his familiar intensity. "Why?"

"Because every time I started to, I remembered he wasn't you."

As if in pain, Lucas shut his eyes, then turned from her. "Cat, I've never done anything in my life to deserve you."

"No, you probably haven't." She rose from the bed to stand behind him. "Lucas, if you want me, tell me so, and tell me why. Ask me, Lucas. I want it spelled out."

"All right." He moved his shoulders as he turned back, but his eyes weren't casual. "Cat . . ." He reached up to touch her cheek, then thrust the hand in his pocket. "I want you, desperately, because life isn't even tolerable without you. I need you because you are, and always were, the best part of my life. I love you for reasons it would take hours to tell you. Take me back, please. Marry me."

She wanted to throw herself into his arms, but held back. *Don't make it too easy on him.* Julia's words played back in her head. No, Lucas had had too much come too easily to him. Autumn smiled at him, but didn't reach out.

"All right," she said simply.

"All right?" He frowned, uncertain. "All right what?"

"I'll marry you. That's what you want, isn't it?"

"Yes, damn it, but—"

"The least you could do is kiss me, Lucas. It's traditional."

Lightly, he rested his hands on her shoulders. "Cat, I want you to be sure, because I'll never be able to let go. If it's gratitude, I'm desperate enough to take it. But I want you to think about what you're doing."

She tilted her head. "You did know I thought it was you with Helen on that film?"

"Cat, for God's sake—"

"I went into the woods," she continued mildly. "I was just about to expose that film when Steve found me. Lucas." She inched closer. "Do you know how I feel about the sanctity of film?"

His breath came out in a small huff of relief as he lifted a hand to either side of her face. He grinned. "Yes. Yes, I do. Something about the eleventh commandment."

"Thou shalt not expose unprocessed film. Now—" she slid her arms up his back "—are you going to kiss me, or do I have to make you?"

THE BRAND NEW NOVEL
from the *New York Times* bestselling author

NORA ROBERTS

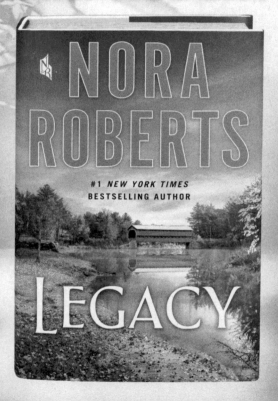

A tale of family tragedy, healing love,
and unnerving suspense.

AVAILABLE WHEREVER BOOKS ARE SOLD